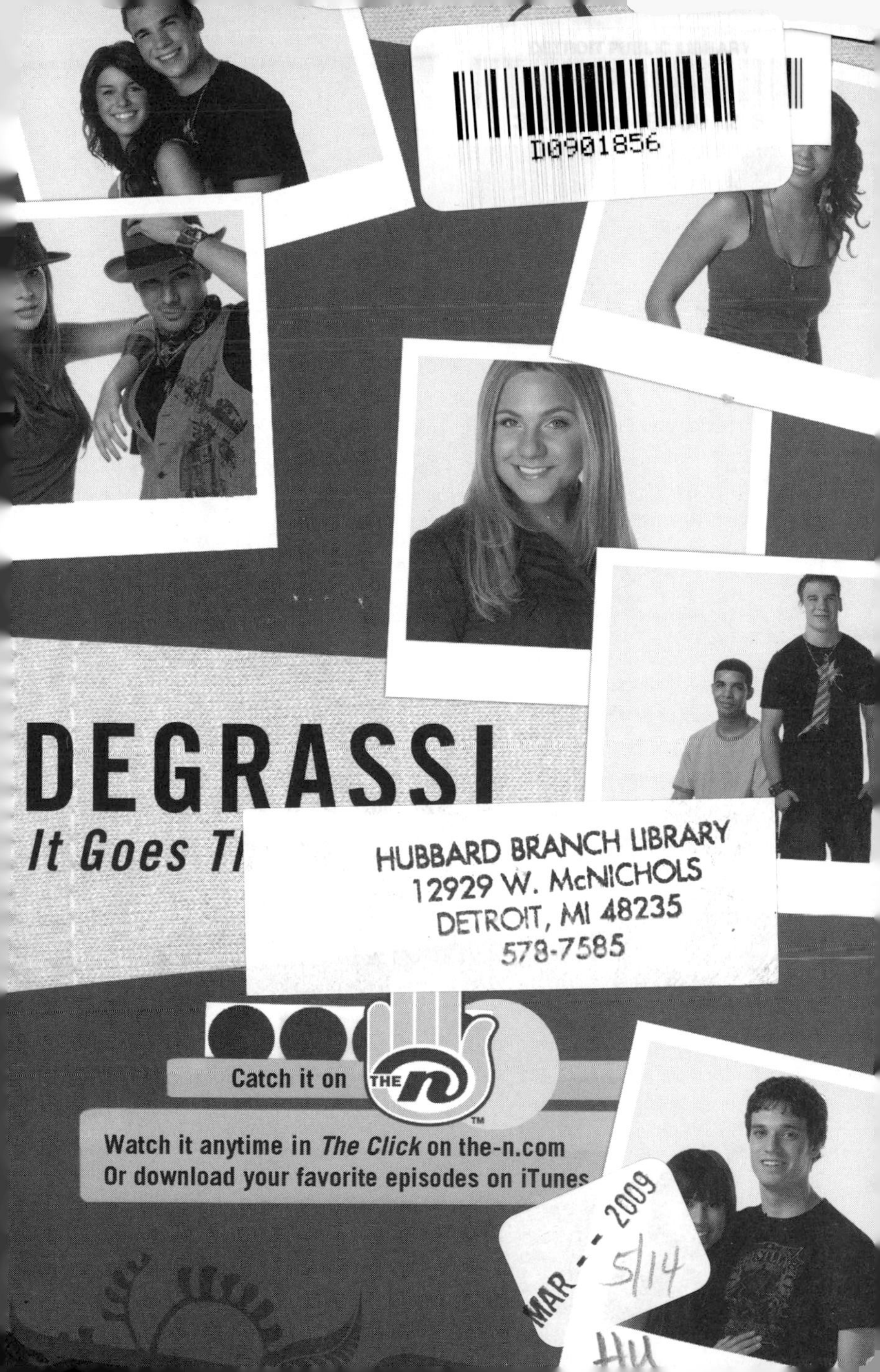
DEGRASSI
It Goes Th
Catch it on THE n
Watch it anytime in The Click on the-n.com
Or download your favorite episodes on iTunes

POCKET BOOKS, a division of Simon & Schuster, Inc.
1230 Avenue of the Americas, New York, NY 10020

Library of Congress Cataloging-in-Publication Data is available.

ISBN-13: 978-1-4165-3077-0
ISBN-10: 1-4165-3077-0

First Pocket Books trade paperback edition January 2007

10 9 8 7 6 5 4 3 2 1

Manufactured in Canada
by Friesens

For information regarding special discounts for bulk purchases, please contact
Simon & Schuster Special Sales at 1-800-456-6798 or
business@simonandschuster.com

Produced by
Madison Press Books
1000 Yonge Street, Suite 200
Toronto, Ontario, Canada M4W 2K2
www.madisonpressbooks.com

Degrassi THE NEXT GENERATION
EXTRA CREDIT

SUDDENLY LAST SUMMER

2

Story by J. Torres

Art by Ramón Pérez

New York | London | Toronto | Sydney

A Pocket Books / Madison Press Book

PREVIOUSLY ON DEGRASSI...

Emma Nelson caught her step-father cheating on her mother with the principal of her school. Meanwhile, she was secretly dating Peter Stone who is not only the principal's son but the sworn enemy of her best friend, Manny Santos. All of these secrets and lies took a terrible toll on Emma, and she developed an eating disorder that eventually landed her in the hospital. Now, Emma is in recovery trying to eat healthier as well as nurture a healthier relationship with Peter.

Jimmy Brooks was shot in the back during the tragic school shooting at Degrassi two years ago and is now confined to a wheelchair. A former basketball star, Jimmy was encouraged by his father to pursue wheelchair basketball, but at the time he seemed more interested in going to art school. These days, he does more coaching than playing basketball, has reunited with ex-girlfriend Ashley Kerwin, and is starting to make new plans for the future.

ACT 1

"Well, I'll eat it, and if it makes me grow larger,
I can reach the key; and if it makes me grow smaller,
I can creep under the door: so either way I'll get into
the garden, and I don't care which happens!"

— *Alice in Wonderland*

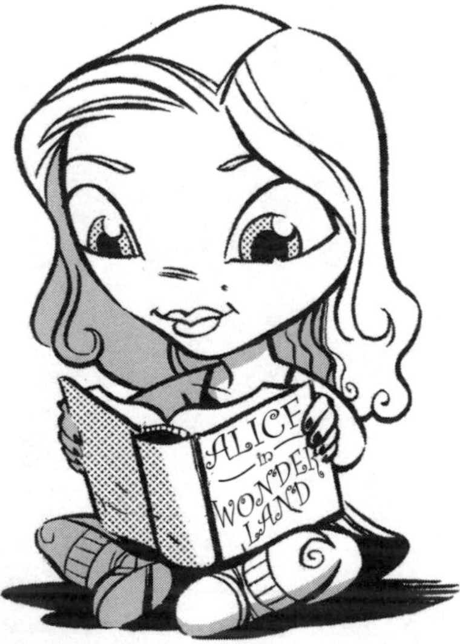
ALICE
in
WONDERLAND

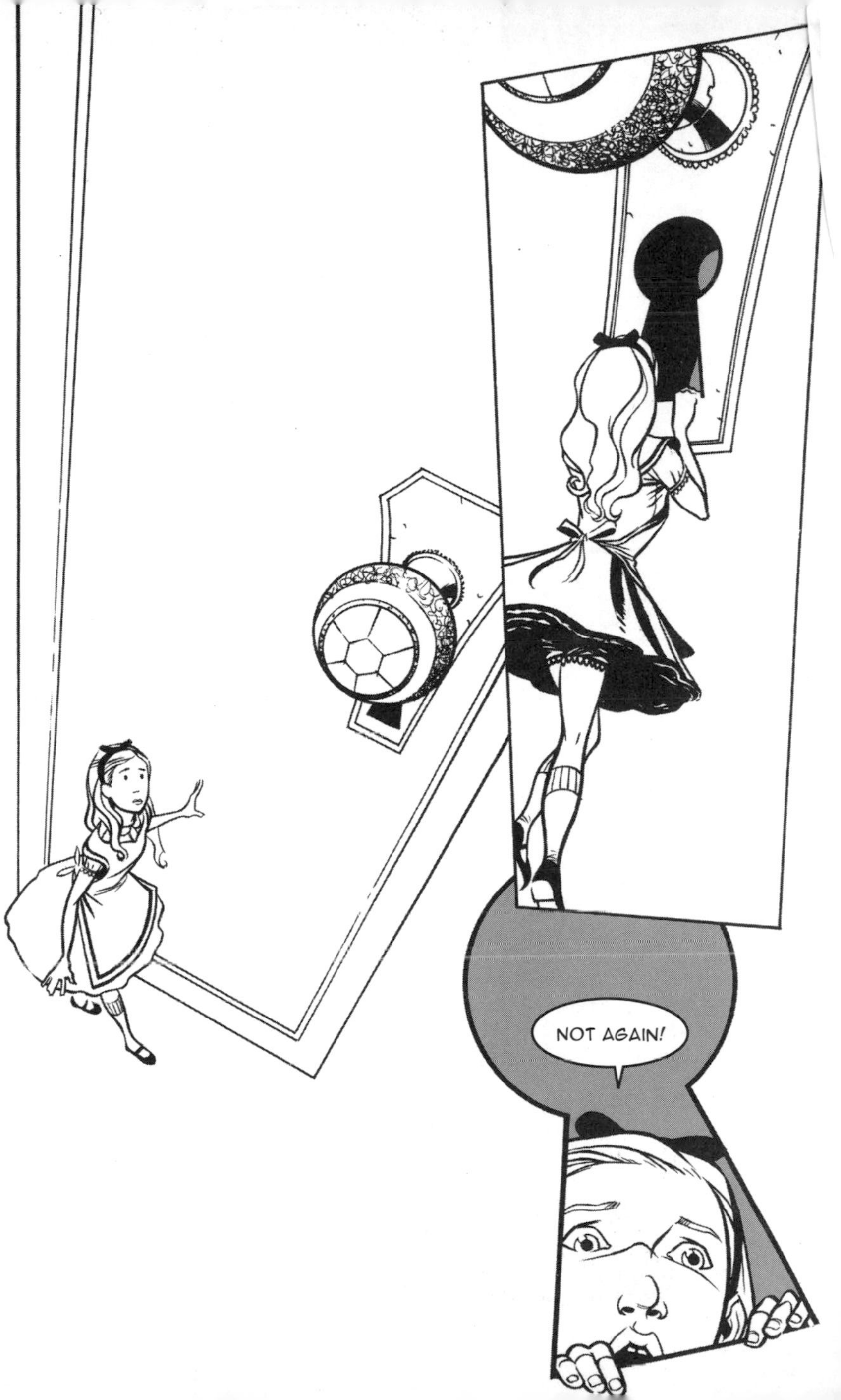
NOT AGAIN!

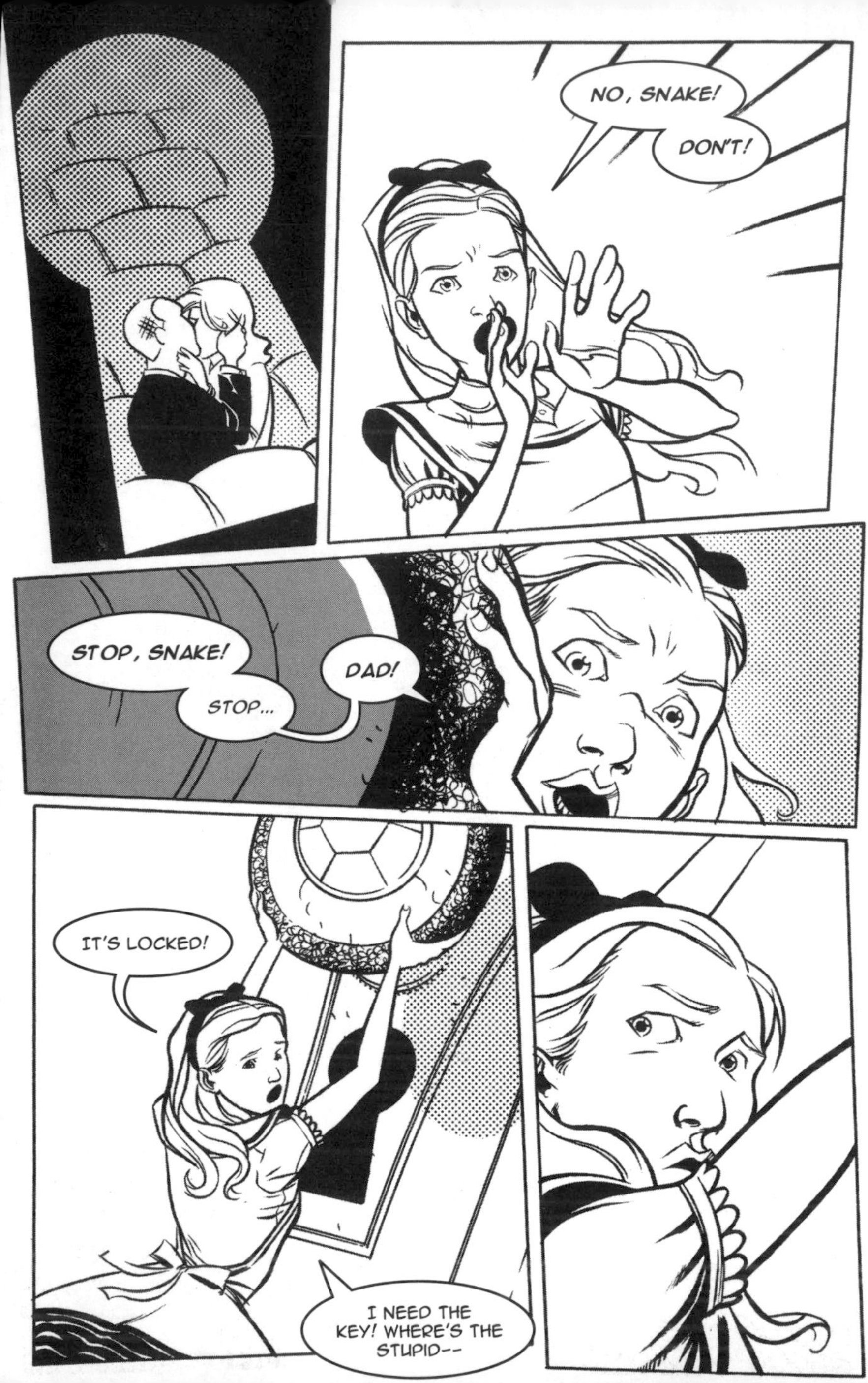
NO, SNAKE!
DON'T!
STOP, SNAKE!
STOP...
DAD!
IT'S LOCKED!
I NEED THE KEY! WHERE'S THE STUPID--

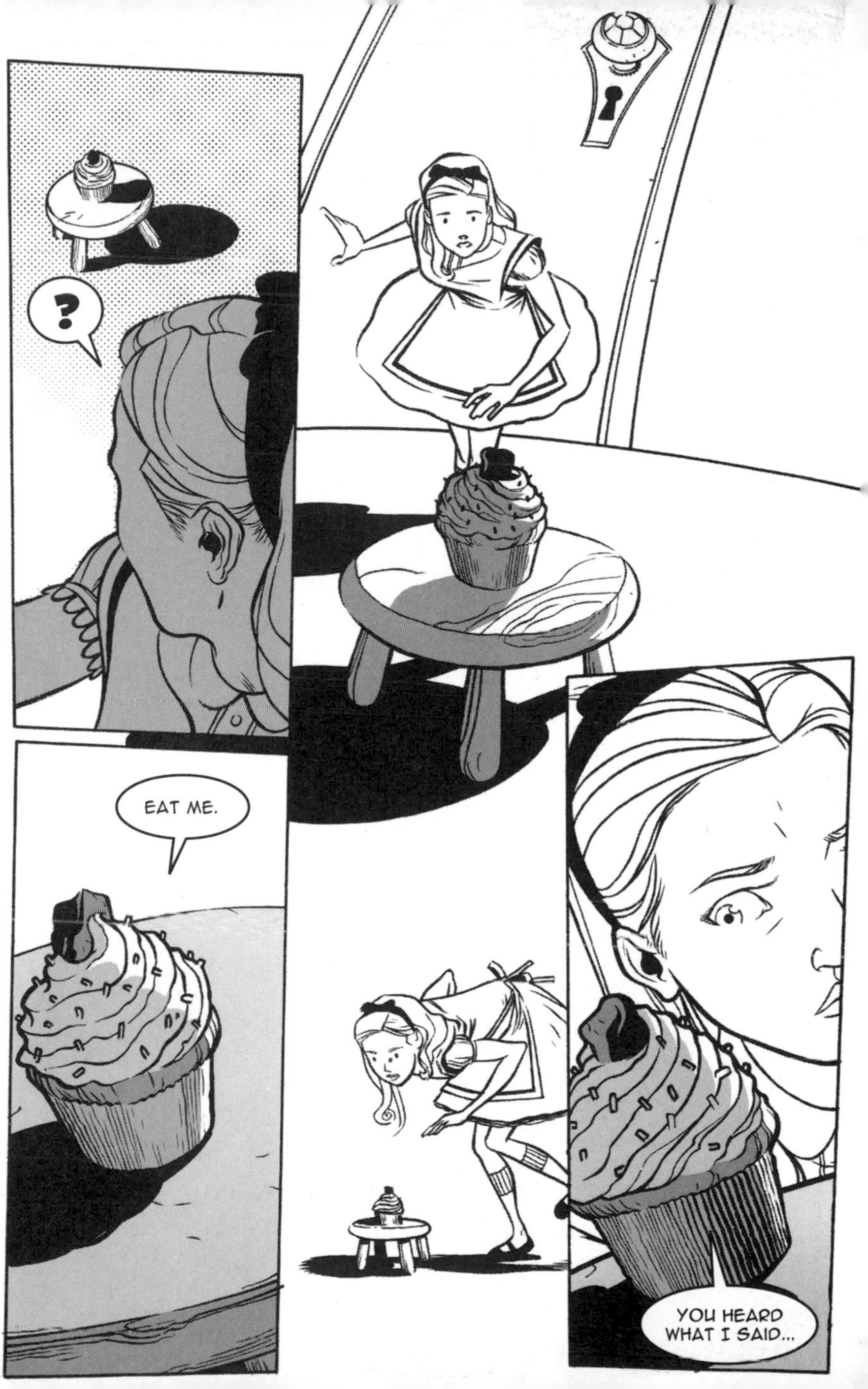
?
EAT ME.
YOU HEARD WHAT I SAID...

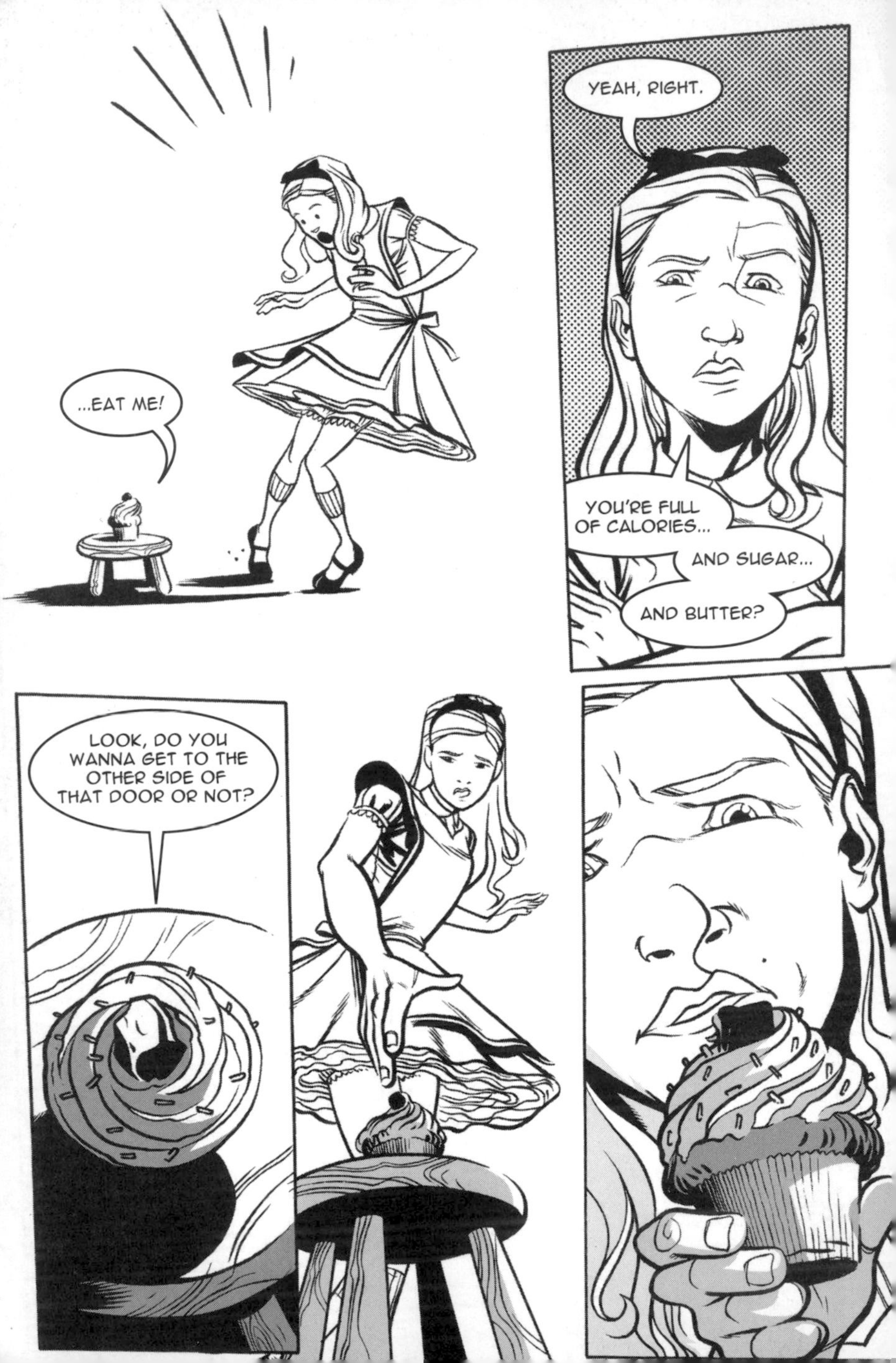
...EAT ME!
YEAH, RIGHT.
YOU'RE FULL OF CALORIES...
AND SUGAR...
AND BUTTER?
LOOK, DO YOU WANNA GET TO THE OTHER SIDE OF THAT DOOR OR NOT?

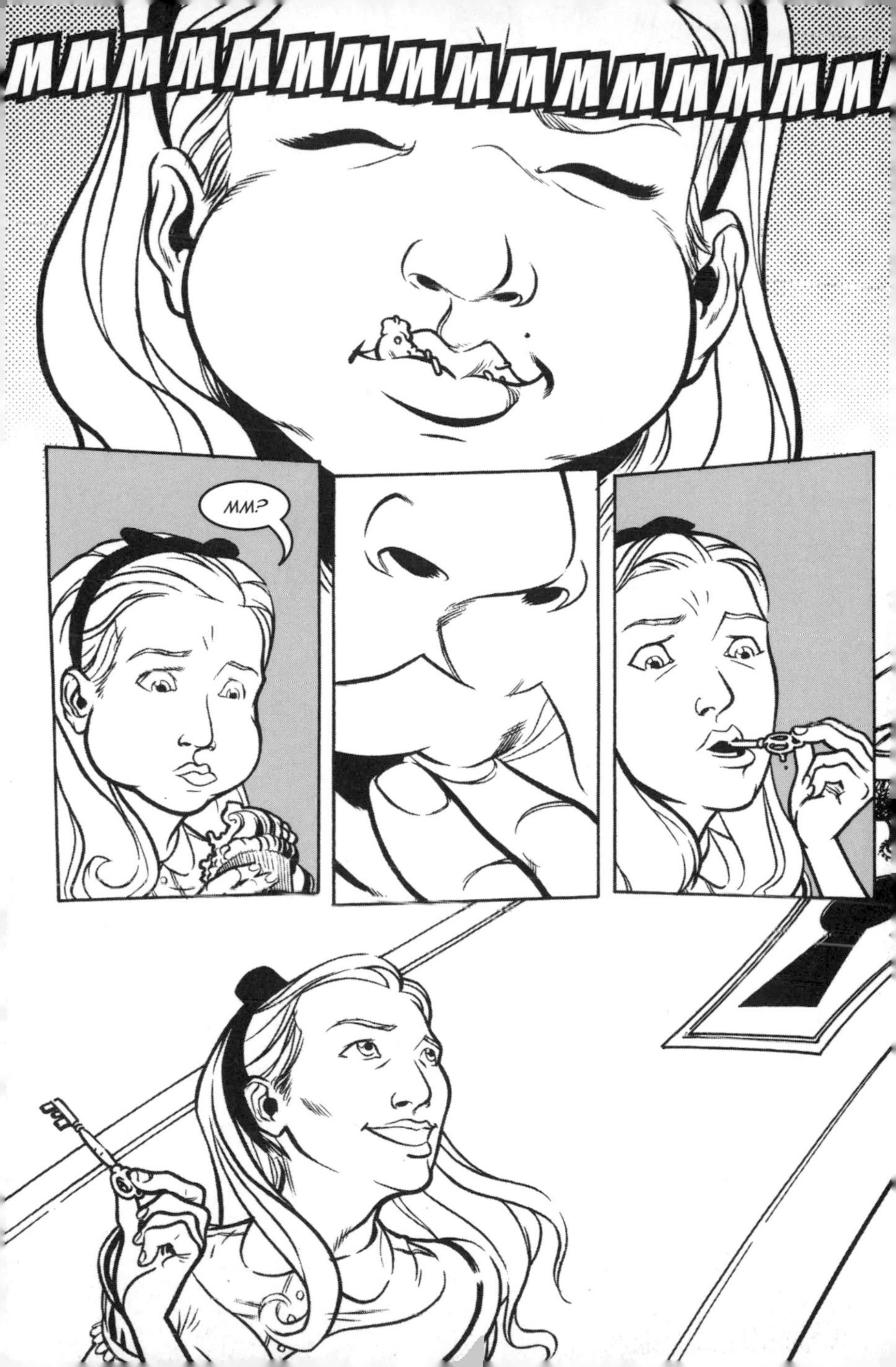
MMMMMMMMMMMMMMMM
MM?

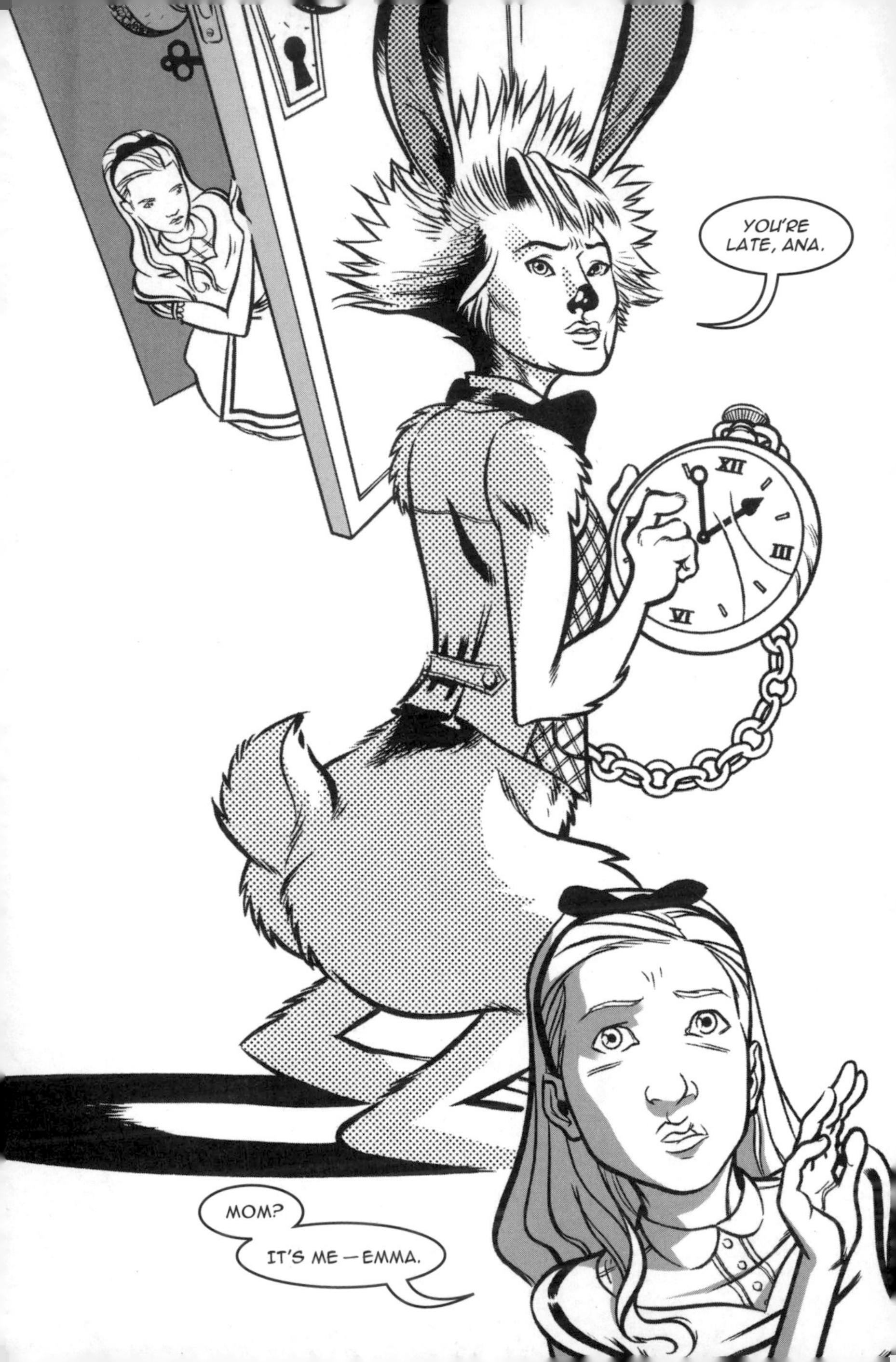
YOU'RE LATE, ANA.
MOM?
IT'S ME — EMMA.

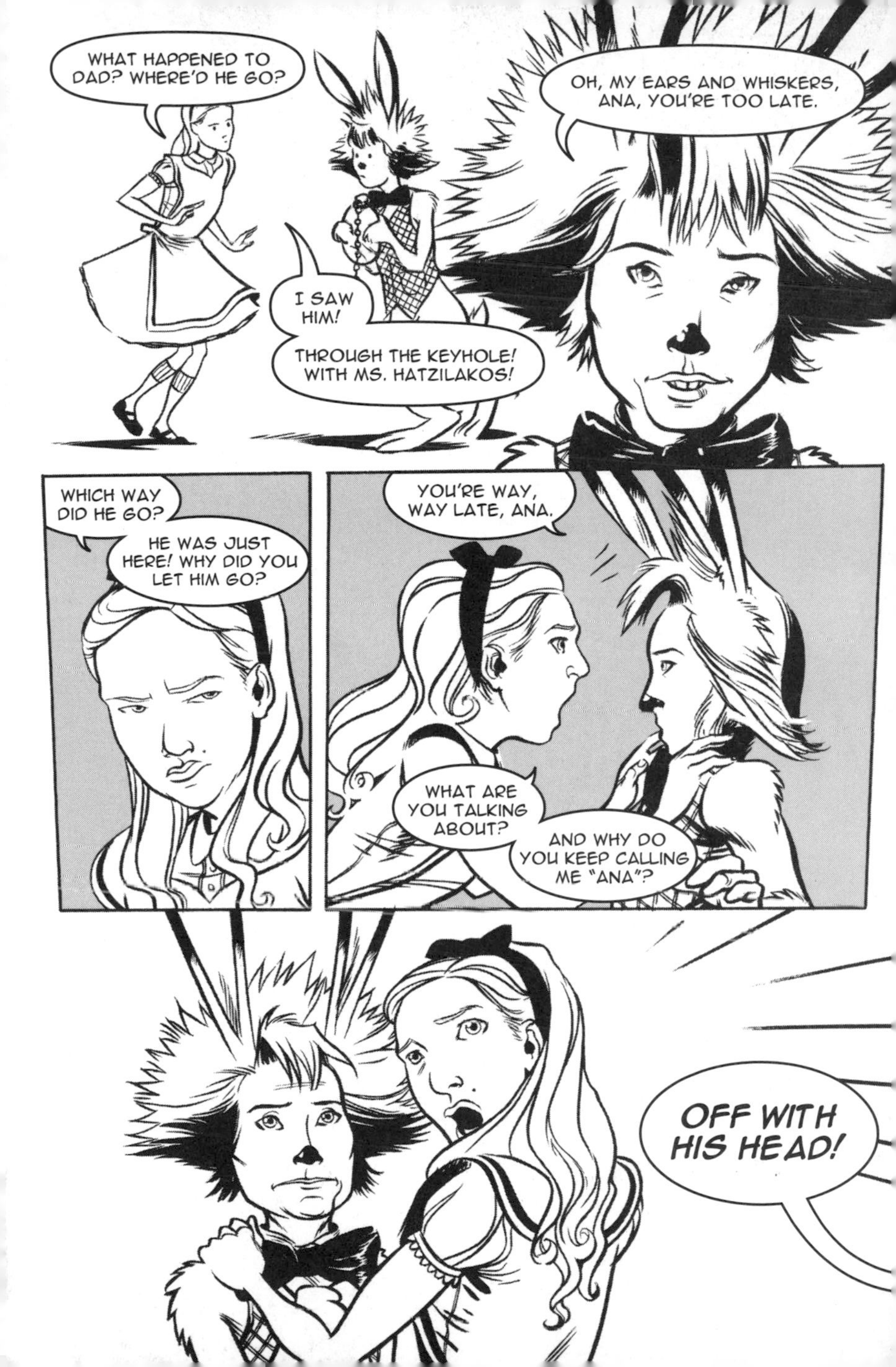
WHAT HAPPENED TO DAD? WHERE'D HE GO?
I SAW HIM!
THROUGH THE KEYHOLE! WITH MS. HATZILAKOS!
OH, MY EARS AND WHISKERS, ANA, YOU'RE TOO LATE.
WHICH WAY DID HE GO?
HE WAS JUST HERE! WHY DID YOU LET HIM GO?
YOU'RE WAY, WAY LATE, ANA.
WHAT ARE YOU TALKING ABOUT?
AND WHY DO YOU KEEP CALLING ME "ANA"?
OFF WITH HIS HEAD!

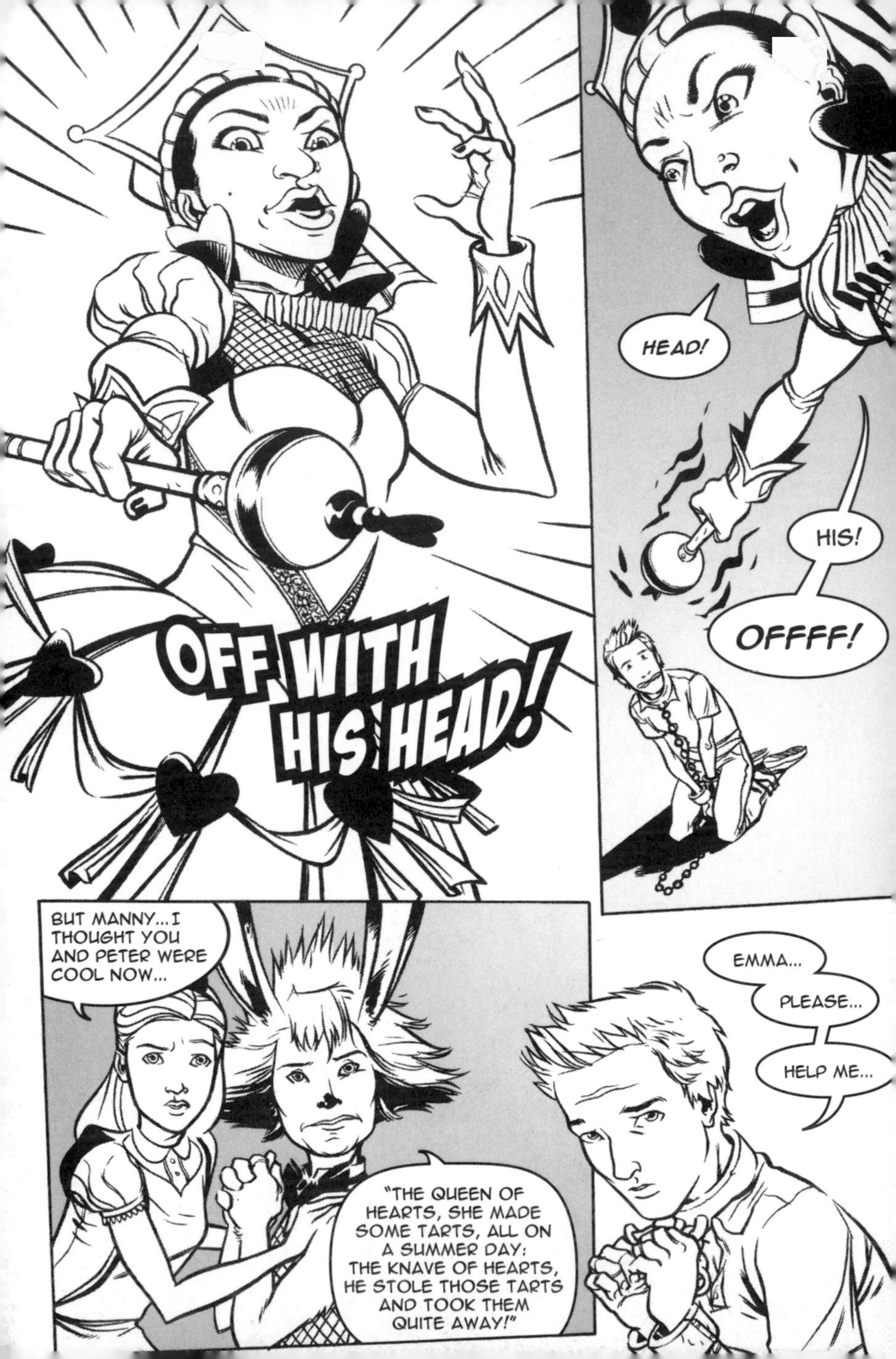
OFF WITH HIS HEAD!
HEAD!
HIS!
OFFFF!
BUT MANNY...I THOUGHT YOU AND PETER WERE COOL NOW...
"THE QUEEN OF HEARTS, SHE MADE SOME TARTS, ALL ON A SUMMER DAY: THE KNAVE OF HEARTS, HE STOLE THOSE TARTS AND TOOK THEM QUITE AWAY!"
EMMA...
PLEASE...
HELP ME...

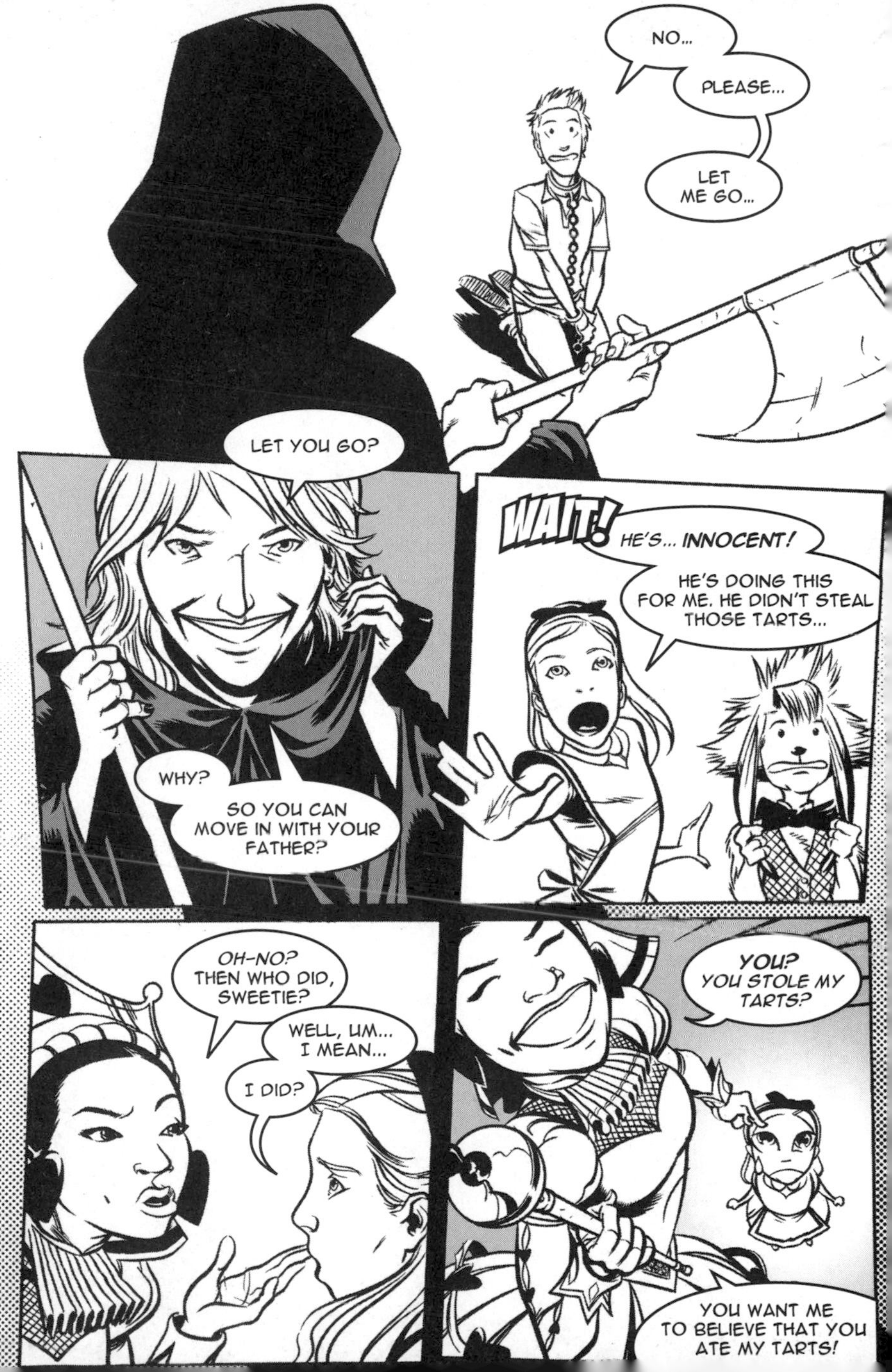
NO...
PLEASE...
LET ME GO...
LET YOU GO?
WHY?
SO YOU CAN MOVE IN WITH YOUR FATHER?
WAIT!
HE'S... INNOCENT!
HE'S DOING THIS FOR ME. HE DIDN'T STEAL THOSE TARTS...
OH-NO? THEN WHO DID, SWEETIE?
WELL, UM... I MEAN...
I DID?
YOU? YOU STOLE MY TARTS?
YOU WANT ME TO BELIEVE THAT YOU ATE MY TARTS!

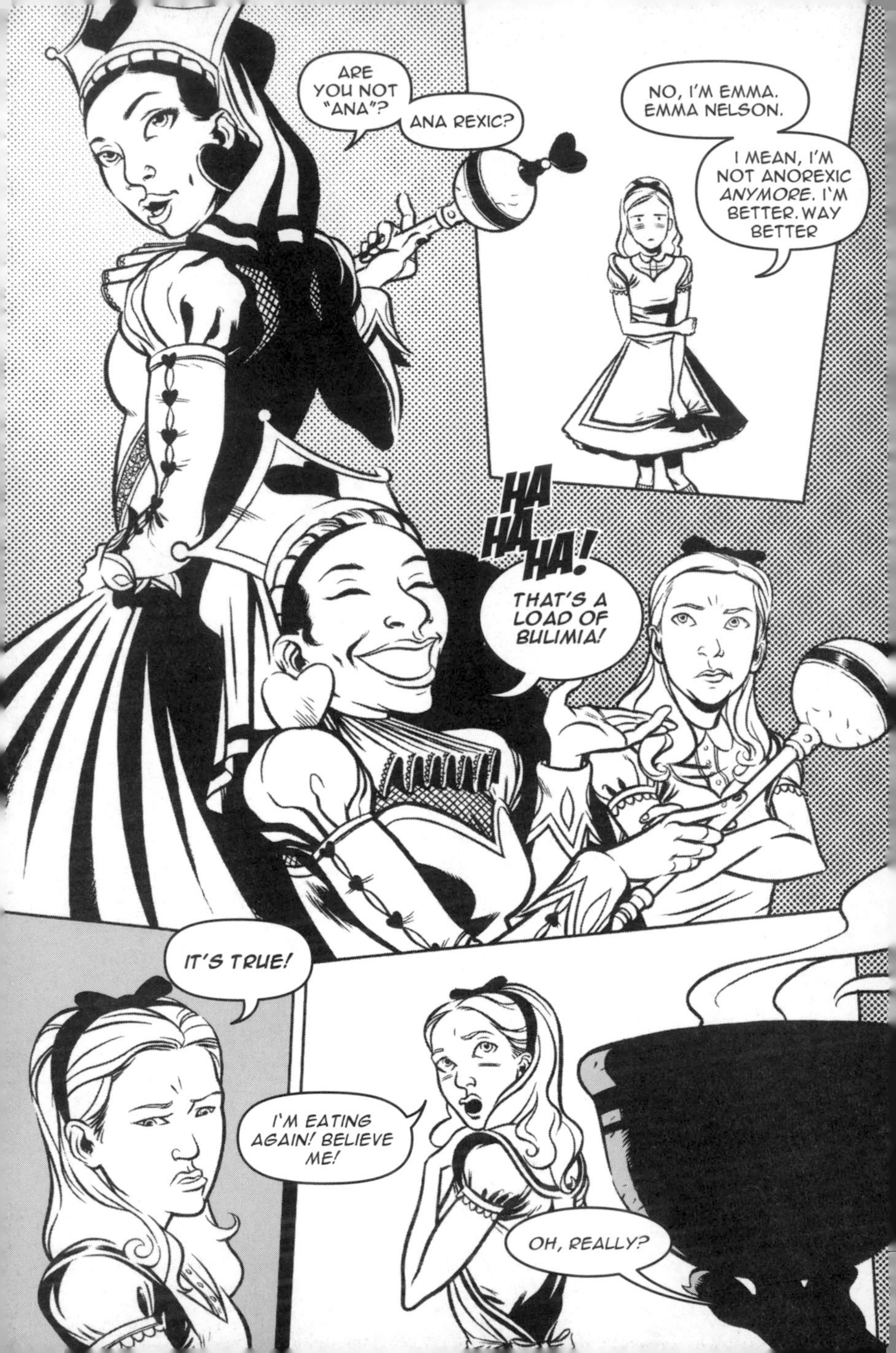
ARE YOU NOT "ANA"?
ANA REXIC?
NO, I'M EMMA. EMMA NELSON.
I MEAN, I'M NOT ANOREXIC ANYMORE. I'M BETTER. WAY BETTER
HA HA HA!
THAT'S A LOAD OF BULIMIA!
IT'S TRUE!
I'M EATING AGAIN! BELIEVE ME!
OH, REALLY?

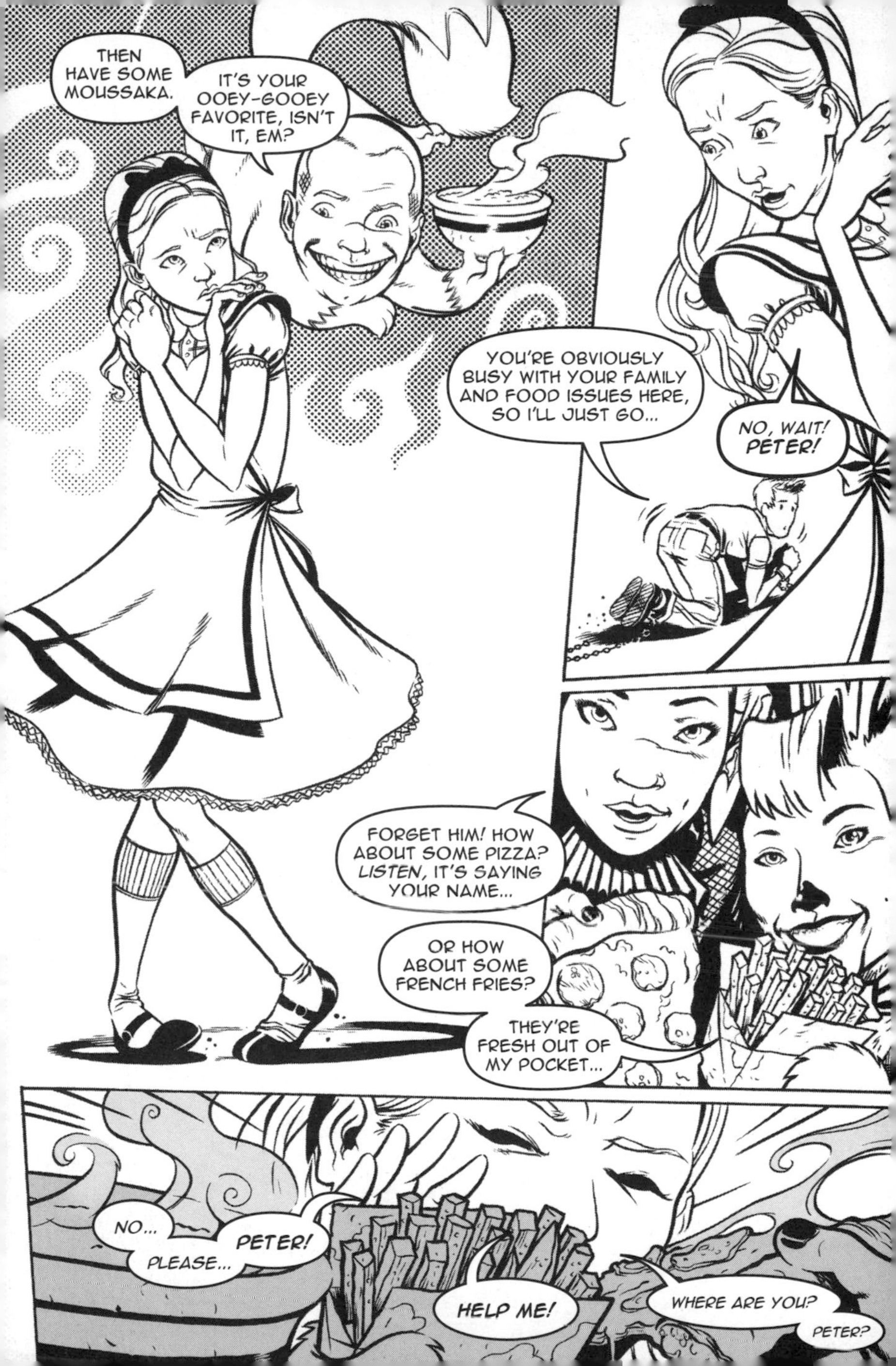
THEN HAVE SOME MOUSSAKA.
IT'S YOUR OOEY-GOOEY FAVORITE, ISN'T IT, EM?
YOU'RE OBVIOUSLY BUSY WITH YOUR FAMILY AND FOOD ISSUES HERE, SO I'LL JUST GO...
NO, WAIT! PETER!
FORGET HIM! HOW ABOUT SOME PIZZA? LISTEN, IT'S SAYING YOUR NAME...
OR HOW ABOUT SOME FRENCH FRIES?
THEY'RE FRESH OUT OF MY POCKET...
NO...
PETER!
PLEASE...
HELP ME!
WHERE ARE YOU?
PETER?

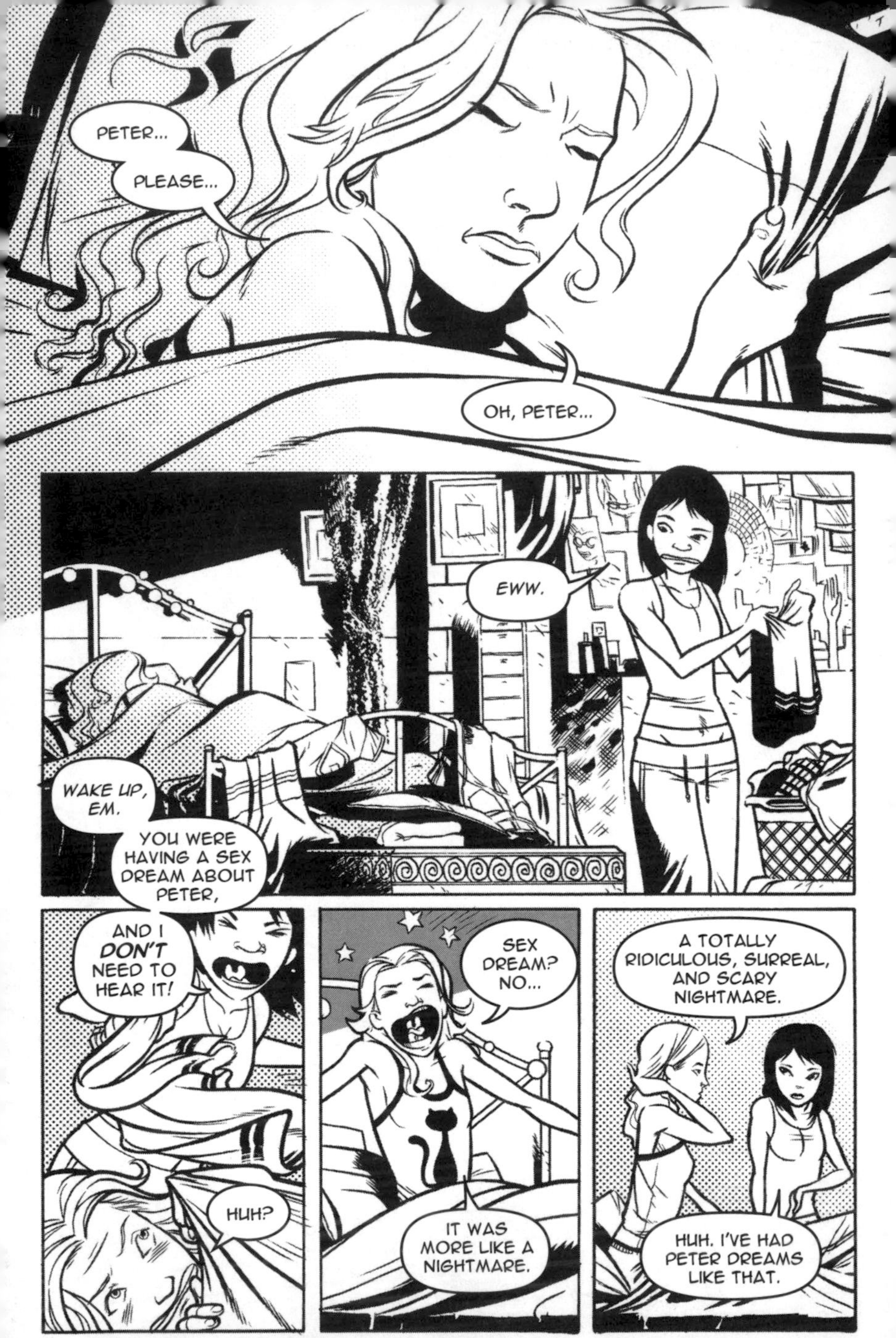
PETER...
PLEASE...
OH, PETER...
EWW.
WAKE UP, EM.
YOU WERE HAVING A SEX DREAM ABOUT PETER,
AND I ***DON'T*** NEED TO HEAR IT!
HUH?
SEX DREAM? NO...
IT WAS MORE LIKE A NIGHTMARE.
A TOTALLY RIDICULOUS, SURREAL, AND SCARY NIGHTMARE.
HUH. I'VE HAD PETER DREAMS LIKE THAT.

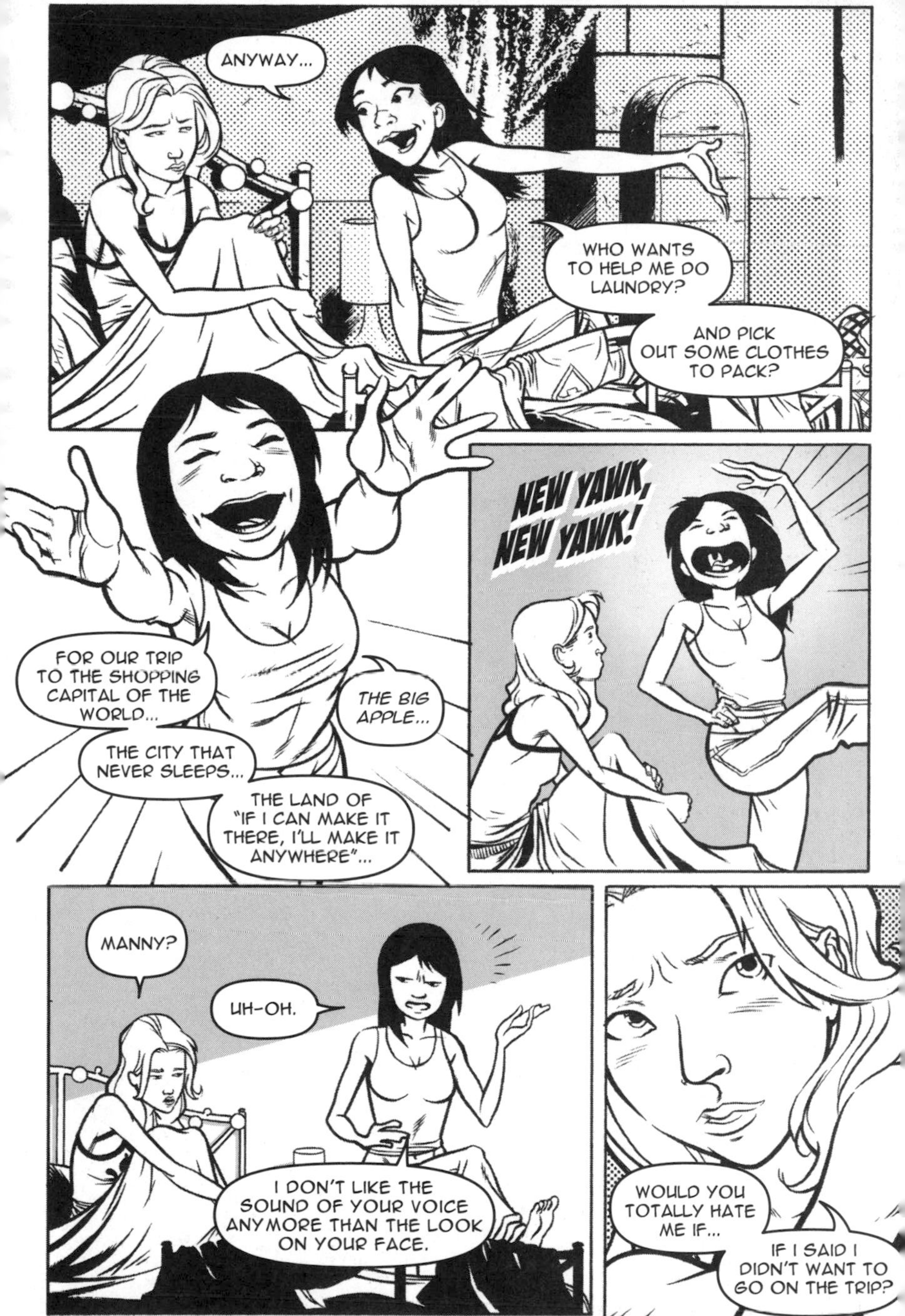
ANYWAY...
WHO WANTS TO HELP ME DO LAUNDRY?
AND PICK OUT SOME CLOTHES TO PACK?
FOR OUR TRIP TO THE SHOPPING CAPITAL OF THE WORLD...
THE BIG APPLE...
THE CITY THAT NEVER SLEEPS...
THE LAND OF "IF I CAN MAKE IT THERE, I'LL MAKE IT ANYWHERE"...
NEW YAWK, NEW YAWK!
MANNY?
UH-OH.
I DON'T LIKE THE SOUND OF YOUR VOICE ANYMORE THAN THE LOOK ON YOUR FACE.
WOULD YOU TOTALLY HATE ME IF...
IF I SAID I DIDN'T WANT TO GO ON THE TRIP?

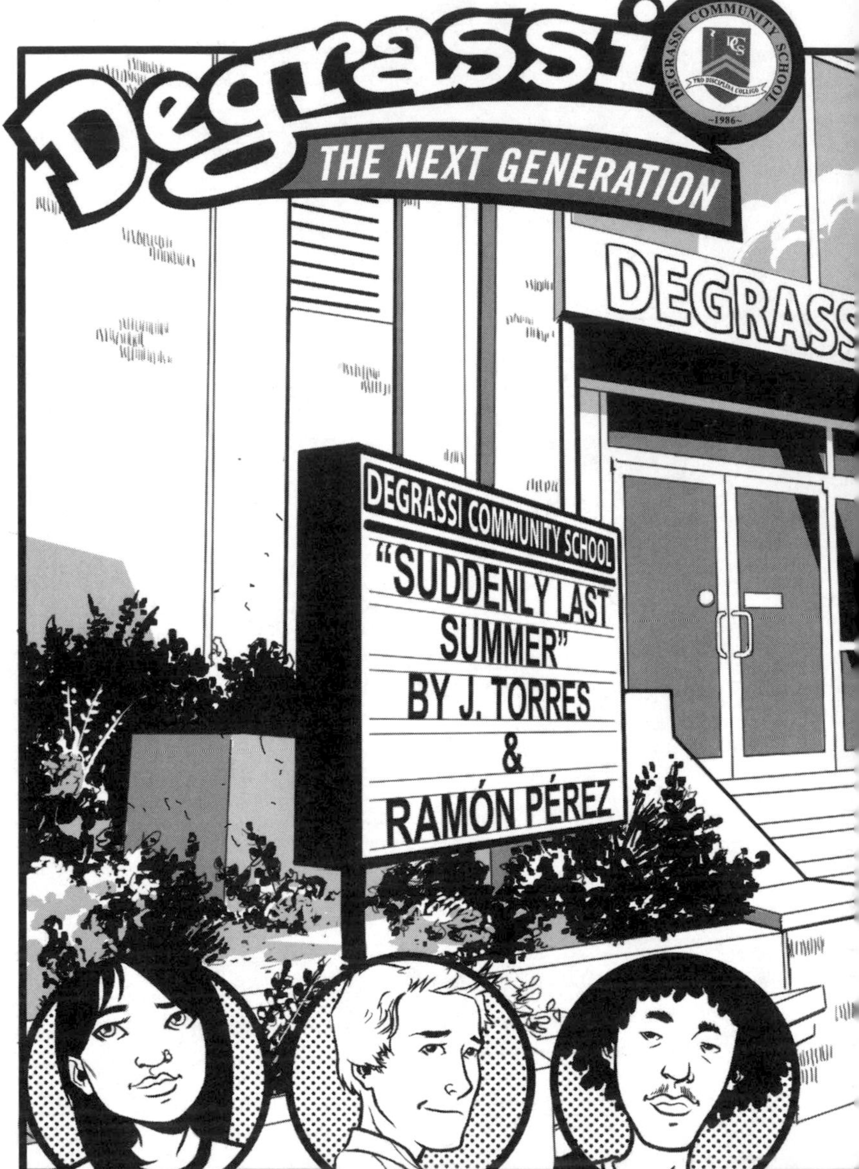
Degrassi
THE NEXT GENERATION
DEGRASSI COMMUNITY SCHOOL
PRO DISCIPLINA COLLIGO
~1986~
DEGRASS
DEGRASSI COMMUNITY SCHOOL
"SUDDENLY LAST SUMMER"
BY J. TORRES
&
RAMÓN PÉREZ
MANNY
PETER
DANNY

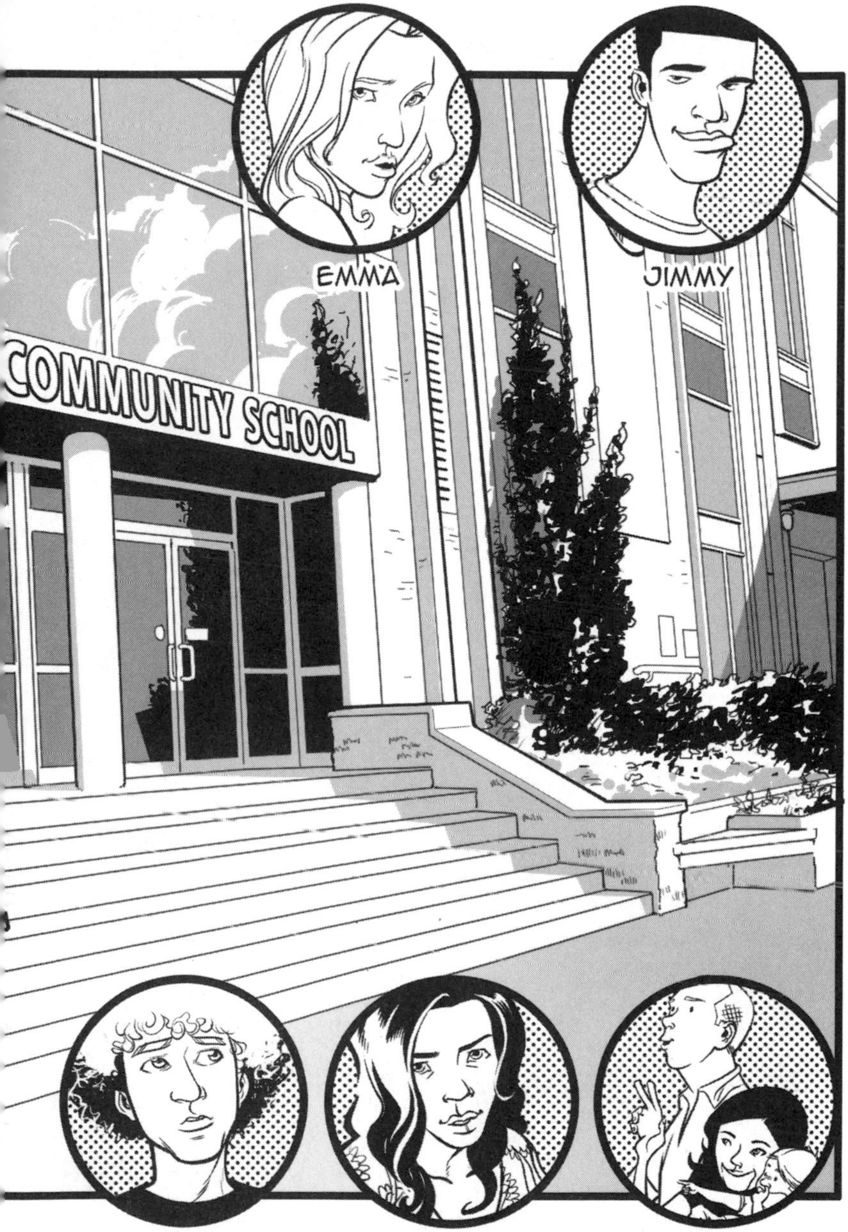
EMMA
JIMMY
COMMUNITY SCHOOL
DEREK
ASHLEY
SNAKE & SPIKE

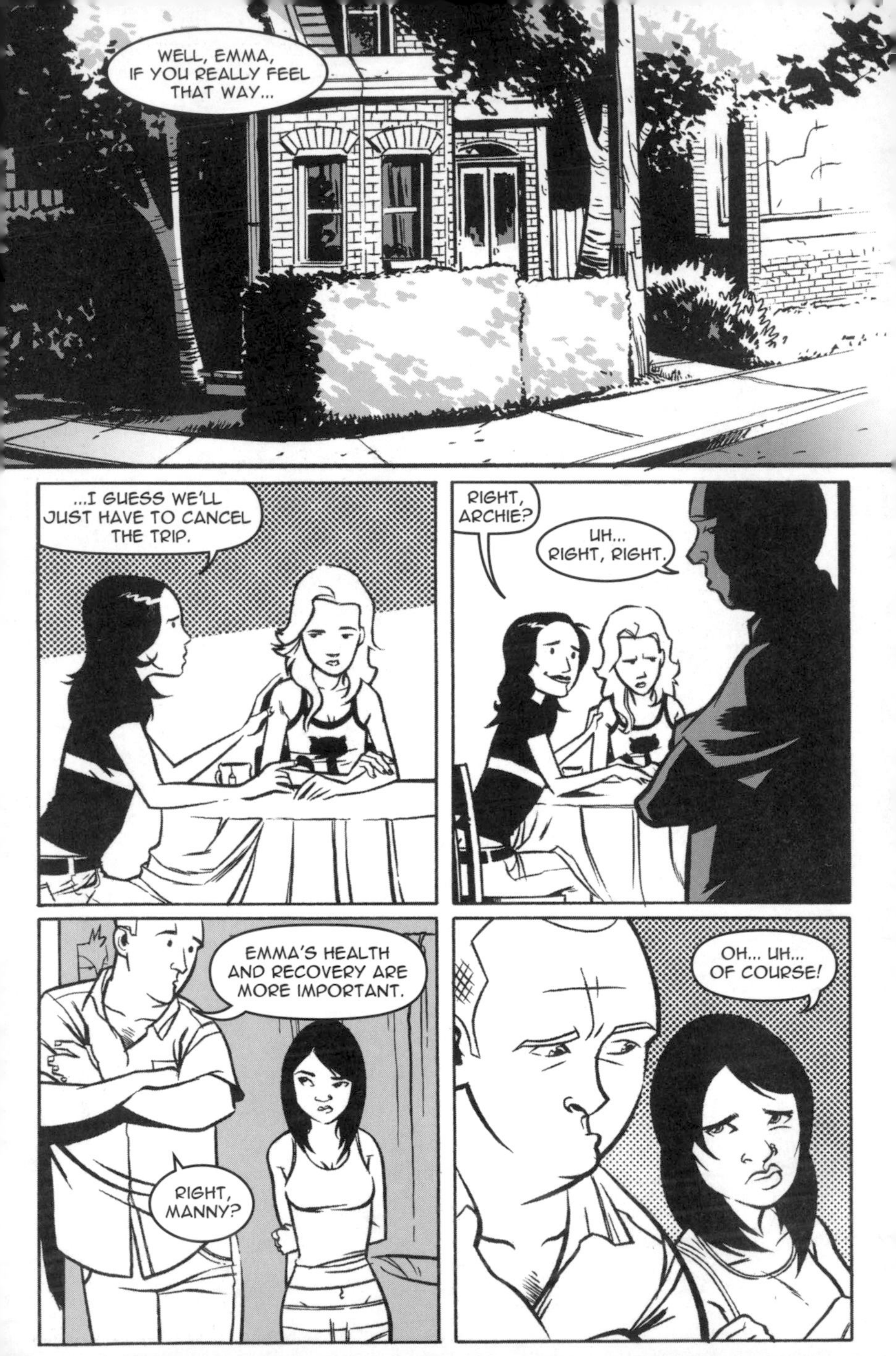
WELL, EMMA, IF YOU REALLY FEEL THAT WAY...
...I GUESS WE'LL JUST HAVE TO CANCEL THE TRIP.
RIGHT, ARCHIE?
UH... RIGHT, RIGHT.
EMMA'S HEALTH AND RECOVERY ARE MORE IMPORTANT.
RIGHT, MANNY?
OH... UH... OF COURSE!

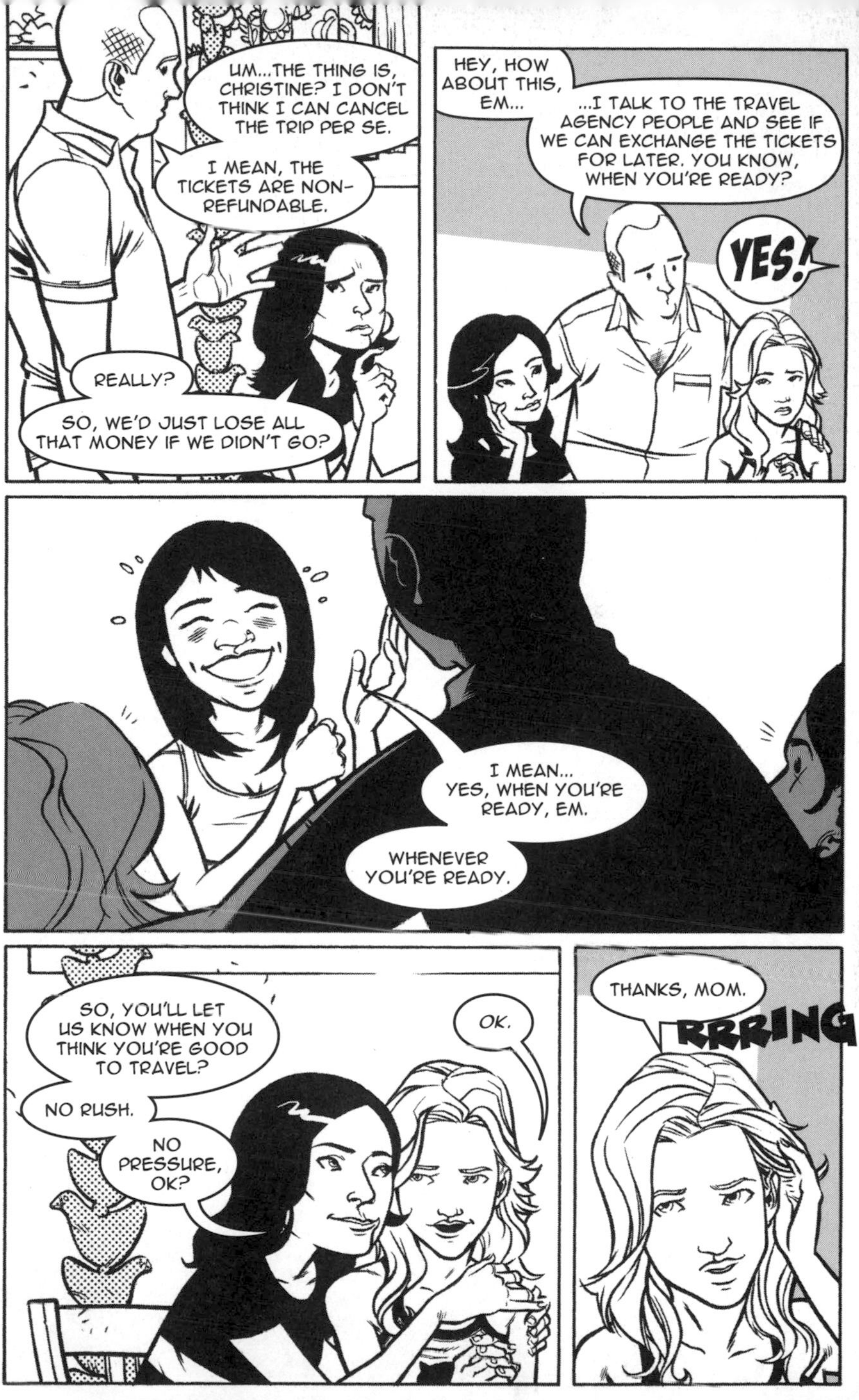
UM...THE THING IS, CHRISTINE? I DON'T THINK I CAN CANCEL THE TRIP PER SE.
I MEAN, THE TICKETS ARE NON-REFUNDABLE.
REALLY?
SO, WE'D JUST LOSE ALL THAT MONEY IF WE DIDN'T GO?
HEY, HOW ABOUT THIS, EM...
...I TALK TO THE TRAVEL AGENCY PEOPLE AND SEE IF WE CAN EXCHANGE THE TICKETS FOR LATER. YOU KNOW, WHEN YOU'RE READY?
YES!
I MEAN... YES, WHEN YOU'RE READY, EM.
WHENEVER YOU'RE READY.
SO, YOU'LL LET US KNOW WHEN YOU THINK YOU'RE GOOD TO TRAVEL?
NO RUSH.
NO PRESSURE, OK?
OK.
THANKS, MOM.
RRRING

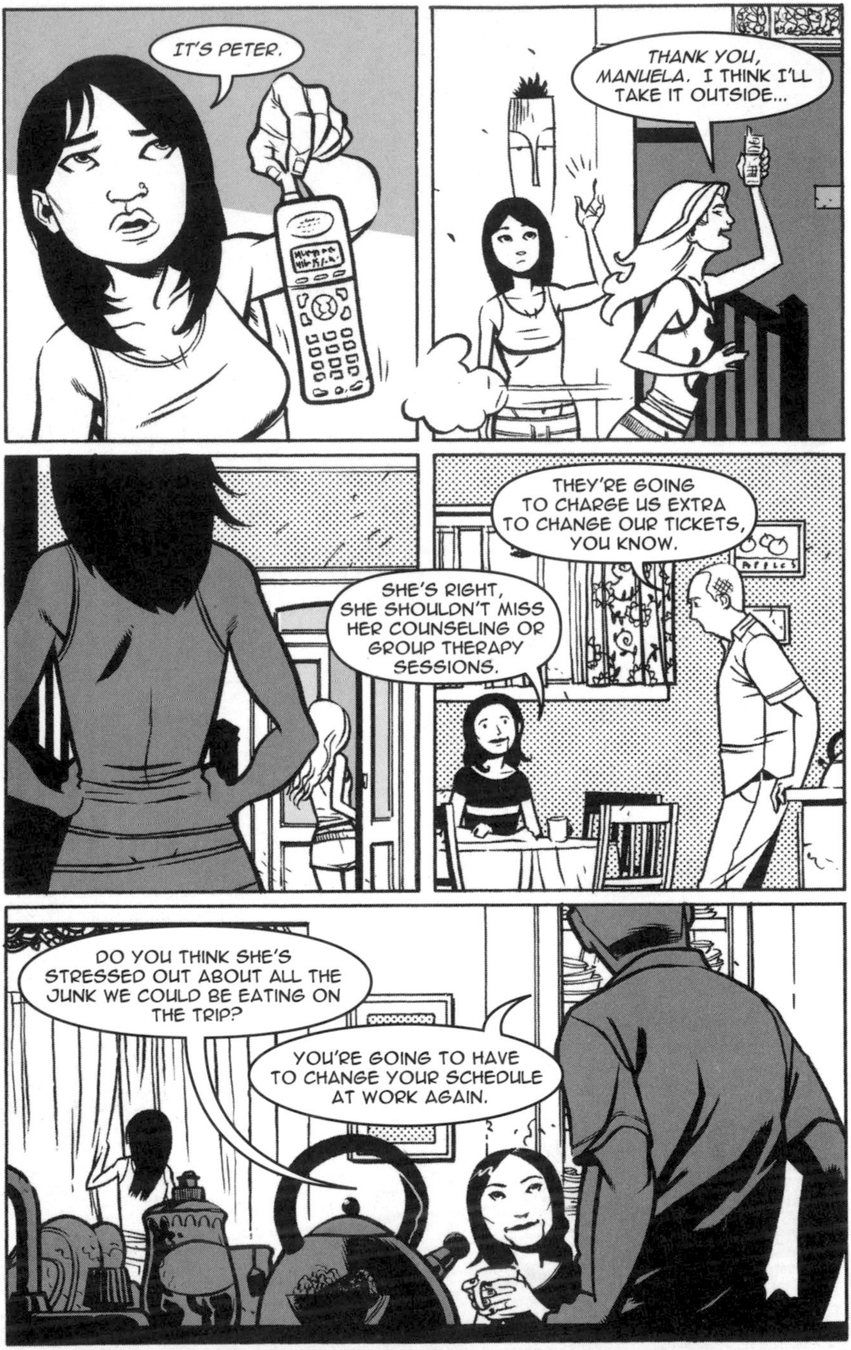
IT'S PETER.
THANK YOU, MANUELA. I THINK I'LL TAKE IT OUTSIDE...
SHE'S RIGHT, SHE SHOULDN'T MISS HER COUNSELING OR GROUP THERAPY SESSIONS.
THEY'RE GOING TO CHARGE US EXTRA TO CHANGE OUR TICKETS, YOU KNOW.
DO YOU THINK SHE'S STRESSED OUT ABOUT ALL THE JUNK WE COULD BE EATING ON THE TRIP?
YOU'RE GOING TO HAVE TO CHANGE YOUR SCHEDULE AT WORK AGAIN.

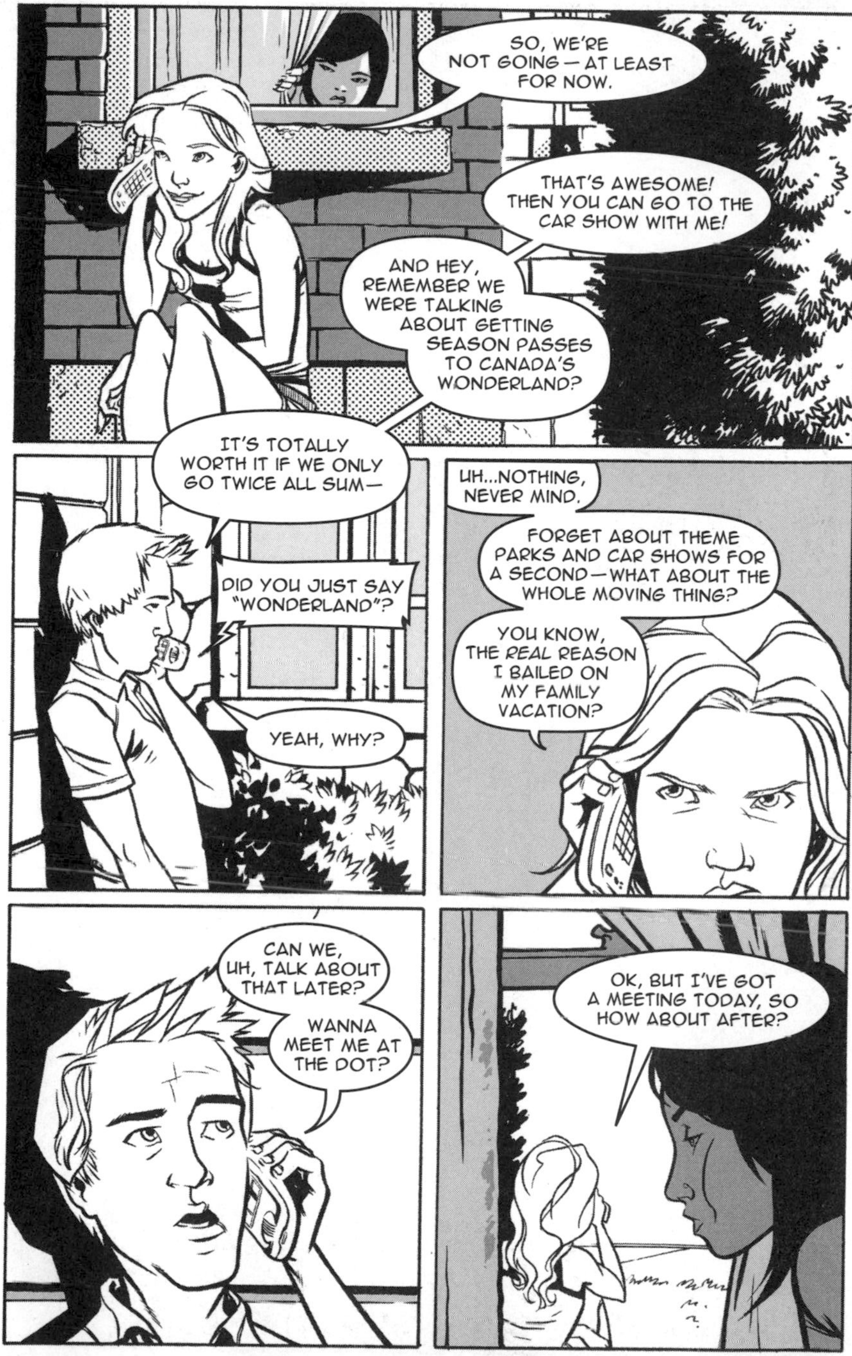
SO, WE'RE NOT GOING — AT LEAST FOR NOW.
THAT'S AWESOME! THEN YOU CAN GO TO THE CAR SHOW WITH ME!
AND HEY, REMEMBER WE WERE TALKING ABOUT GETTING SEASON PASSES TO CANADA'S WONDERLAND?
IT'S TOTALLY WORTH IT IF WE ONLY GO TWICE ALL SUM—
DID YOU JUST SAY "WONDERLAND"?
YEAH, WHY?
UH...NOTHING, NEVER MIND.
FORGET ABOUT THEME PARKS AND CAR SHOWS FOR A SECOND—WHAT ABOUT THE WHOLE MOVING THING?
YOU KNOW, THE *REAL* REASON I BAILED ON MY FAMILY VACATION?
CAN WE, UH, TALK ABOUT THAT LATER?
WANNA MEET ME AT THE DOT?
OK, BUT I'VE GOT A MEETING TODAY, SO HOW ABOUT AFTER?

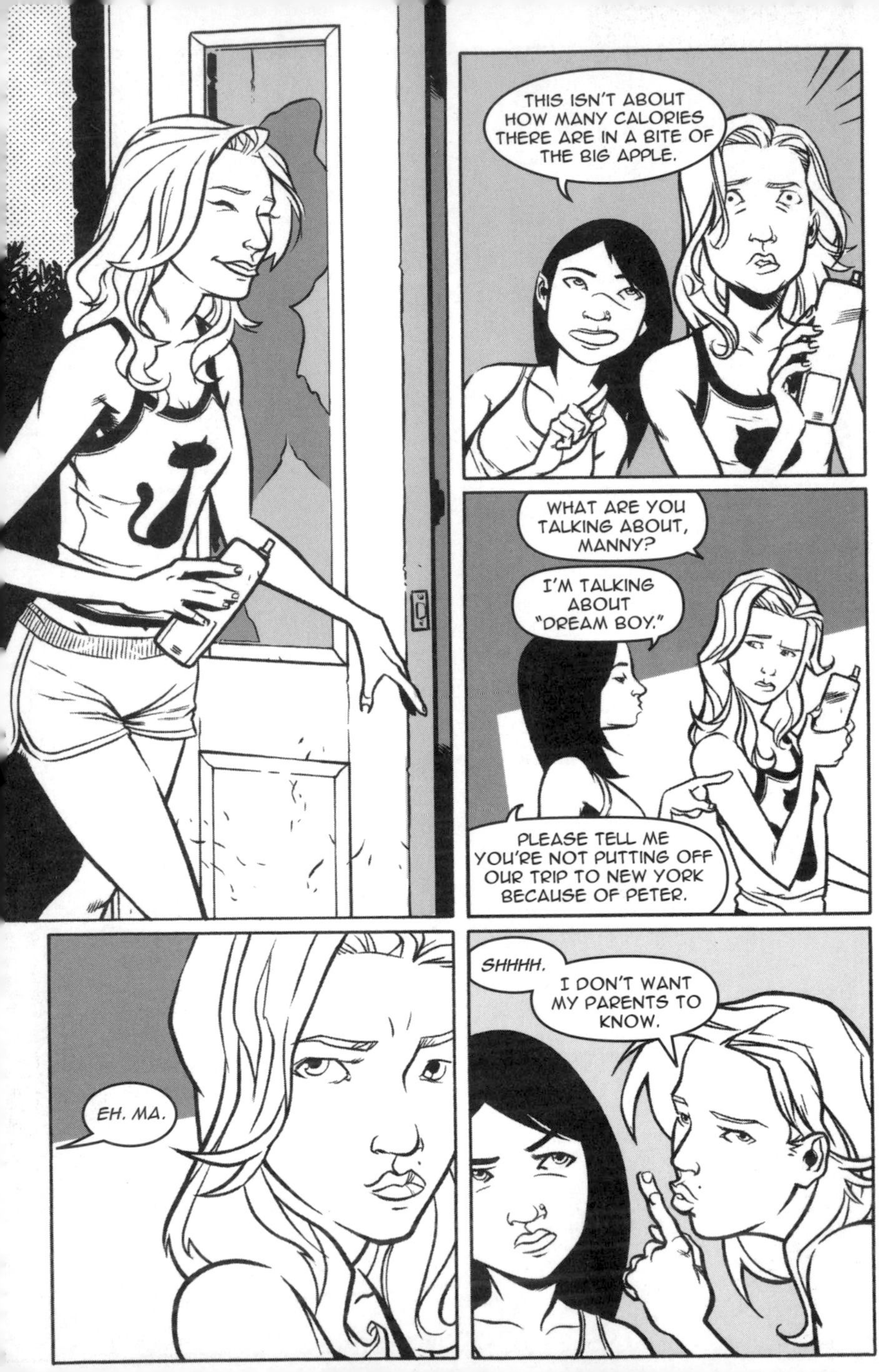
THIS ISN'T ABOUT HOW MANY CALORIES THERE ARE IN A BITE OF THE BIG APPLE.
WHAT ARE YOU TALKING ABOUT, MANNY?
I'M TALKING ABOUT "DREAM BOY."
PLEASE TELL ME YOU'RE NOT PUTTING OFF OUR TRIP TO NEW YORK BECAUSE OF PETER.
EH. MA.
SHHHH.
I DON'T WANT MY PARENTS TO KNOW.

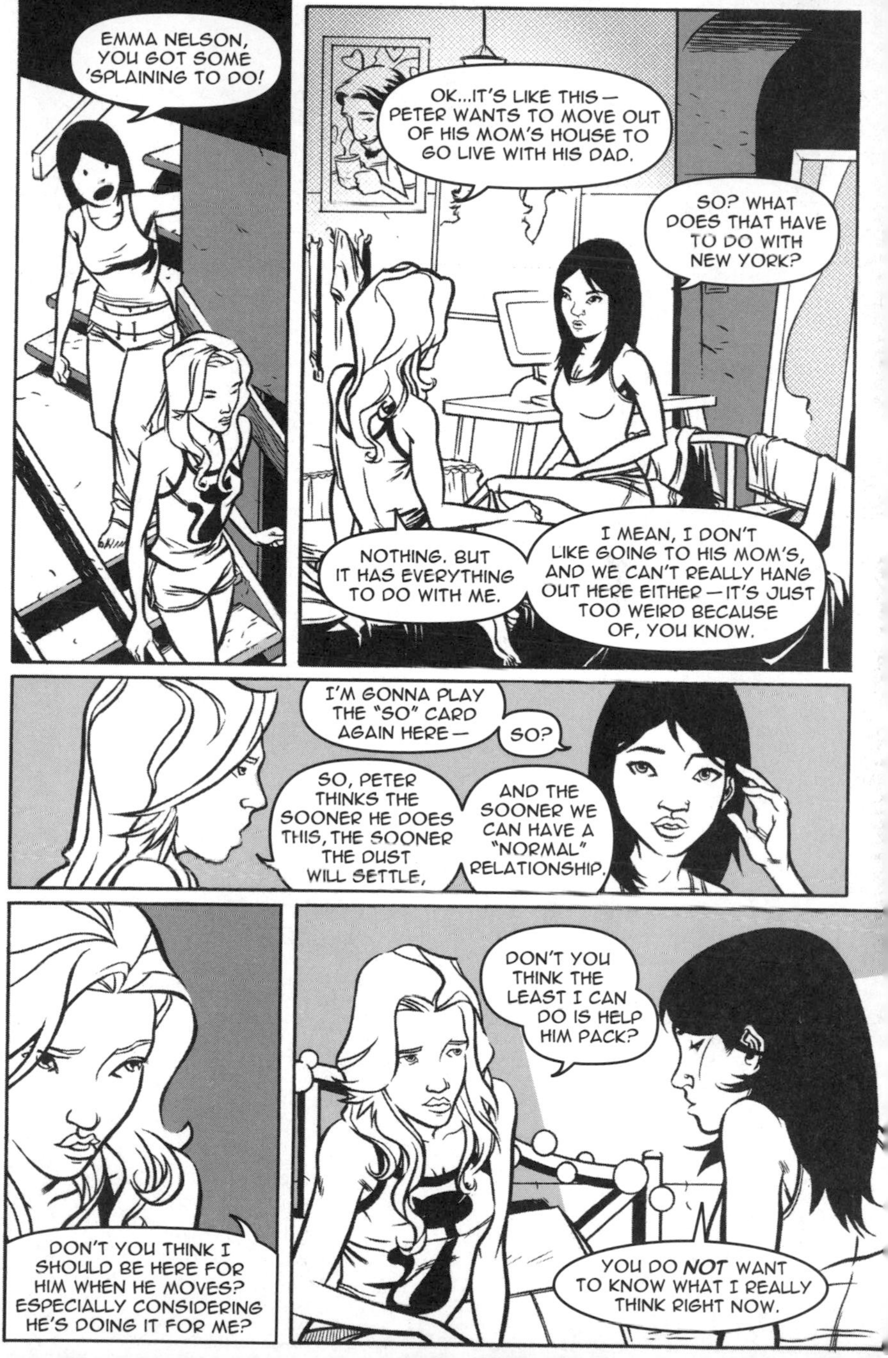
EMMA NELSON, YOU GOT SOME 'SPLAINING TO DO!
OK...IT'S LIKE THIS — PETER WANTS TO MOVE OUT OF HIS MOM'S HOUSE TO GO LIVE WITH HIS DAD.
SO? WHAT DOES THAT HAVE TO DO WITH NEW YORK?
NOTHING. BUT IT HAS EVERYTHING TO DO WITH ME.
I MEAN, I DON'T LIKE GOING TO HIS MOM'S, AND WE CAN'T REALLY HANG OUT HERE EITHER — IT'S JUST TOO WEIRD BECAUSE OF, YOU KNOW.
I'M GONNA PLAY THE "SO" CARD AGAIN HERE —
SO?
SO, PETER THINKS THE SOONER HE DOES THIS, THE SOONER THE DUST WILL SETTLE,
AND THE SOONER WE CAN HAVE A "NORMAL" RELATIONSHIP.
DON'T YOU THINK I SHOULD BE HERE FOR HIM WHEN HE MOVES? ESPECIALLY CONSIDERING HE'S DOING IT FOR ME?
DON'T YOU THINK THE LEAST I CAN DO IS HELP HIM PACK?
YOU DO **NOT** WANT TO KNOW WHAT I REALLY THINK RIGHT NOW.

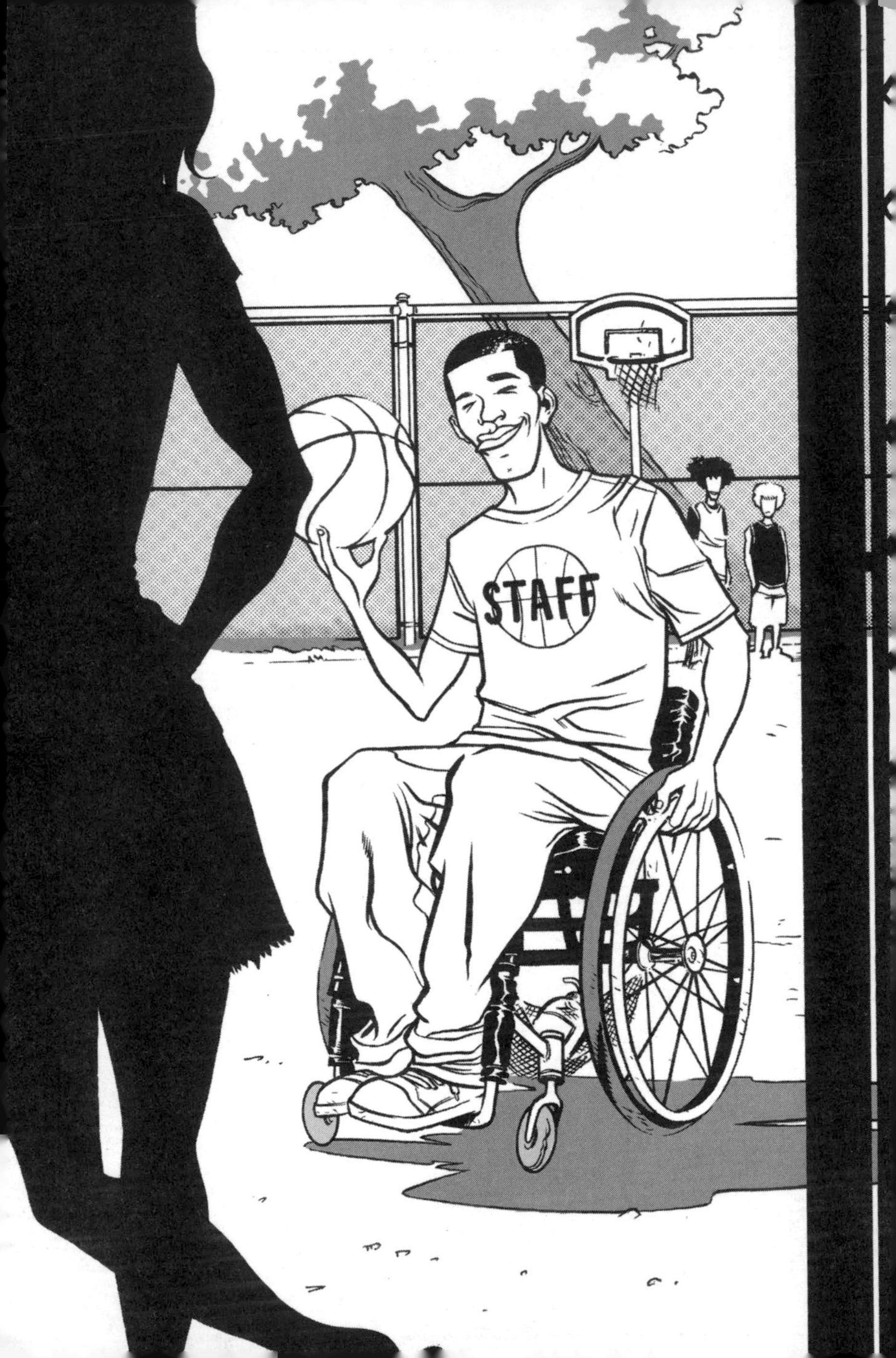
STAFF

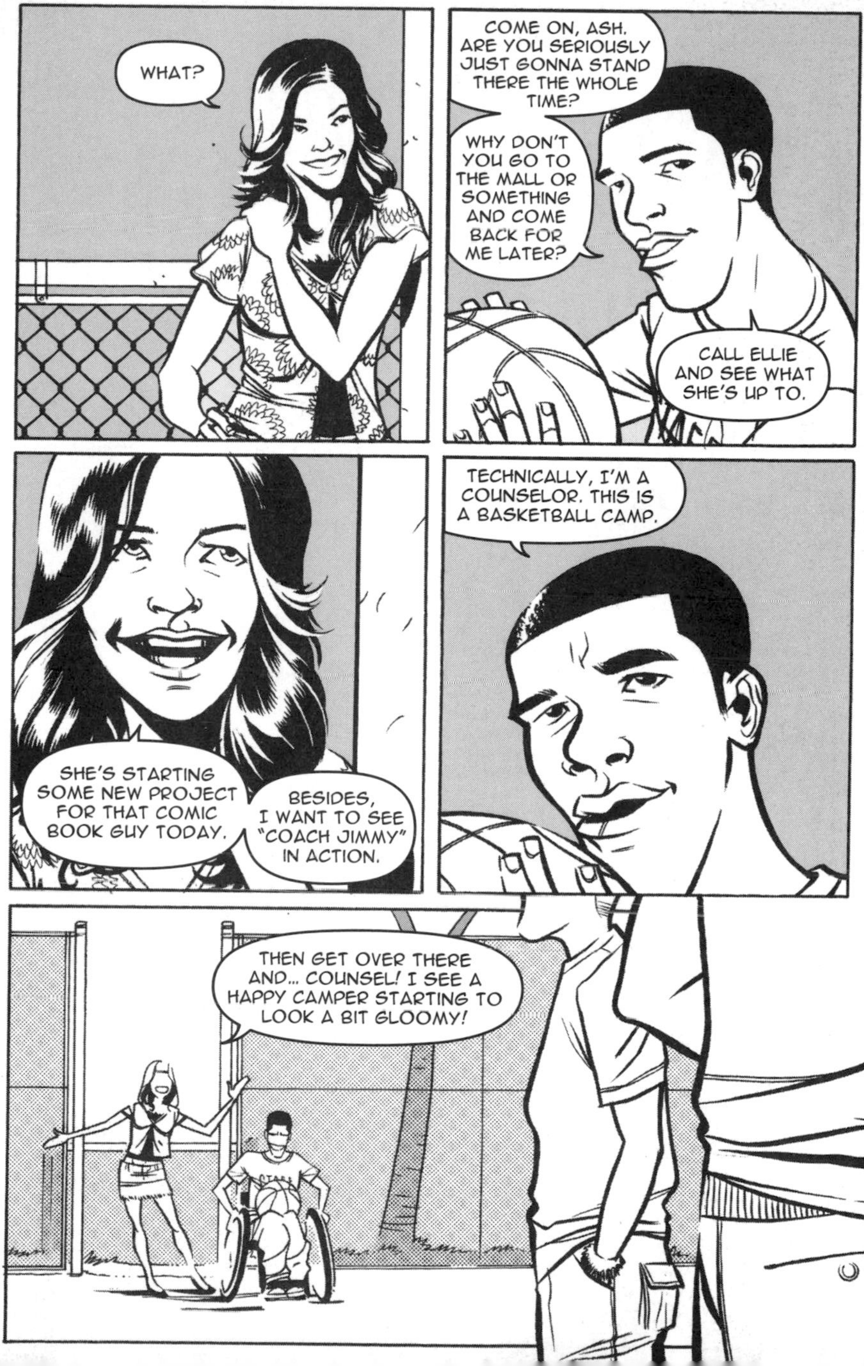
WHAT?
COME ON, ASH. ARE YOU SERIOUSLY JUST GONNA STAND THERE THE WHOLE TIME?
WHY DON'T YOU GO TO THE MALL OR SOMETHING AND COME BACK FOR ME LATER?
CALL ELLIE AND SEE WHAT SHE'S UP TO.
SHE'S STARTING SOME NEW PROJECT FOR THAT COMIC BOOK GUY TODAY.
BESIDES, I WANT TO SEE "COACH JIMMY" IN ACTION.
TECHNICALLY, I'M A COUNSELOR. THIS IS A BASKETBALL CAMP.
THEN GET OVER THERE AND... COUNSEL! I SEE A HAPPY CAMPER STARTING TO LOOK A BIT GLOOMY!

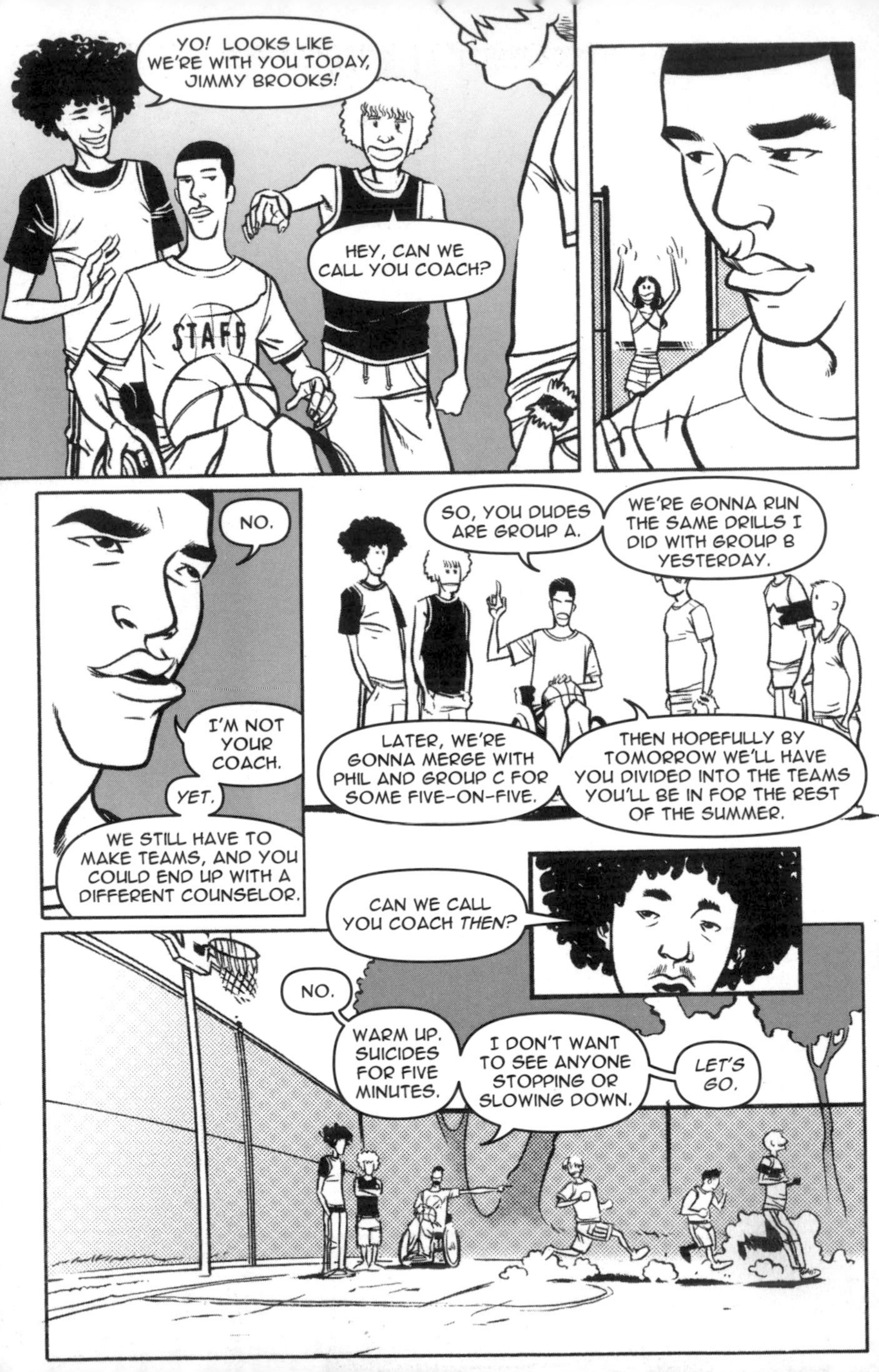
YO! LOOKS LIKE WE'RE WITH YOU TODAY, JIMMY BROOKS!
HEY, CAN WE CALL YOU COACH?
STAFF
NO.
I'M NOT YOUR COACH.
YET.
WE STILL HAVE TO MAKE TEAMS, AND YOU COULD END UP WITH A DIFFERENT COUNSELOR.
SO, YOU DUDES ARE GROUP A.
WE'RE GONNA RUN THE SAME DRILLS I DID WITH GROUP B YESTERDAY.
LATER, WE'RE GONNA MERGE WITH PHIL AND GROUP C FOR SOME FIVE-ON-FIVE.
THEN HOPEFULLY BY TOMORROW WE'LL HAVE YOU DIVIDED INTO THE TEAMS YOU'LL BE IN FOR THE REST OF THE SUMMER.
CAN WE CALL YOU COACH *THEN*?
NO.
WARM UP. SUICIDES FOR FIVE MINUTES.
I DON'T WANT TO SEE ANYONE STOPPING OR SLOWING DOWN.
LET'S GO.

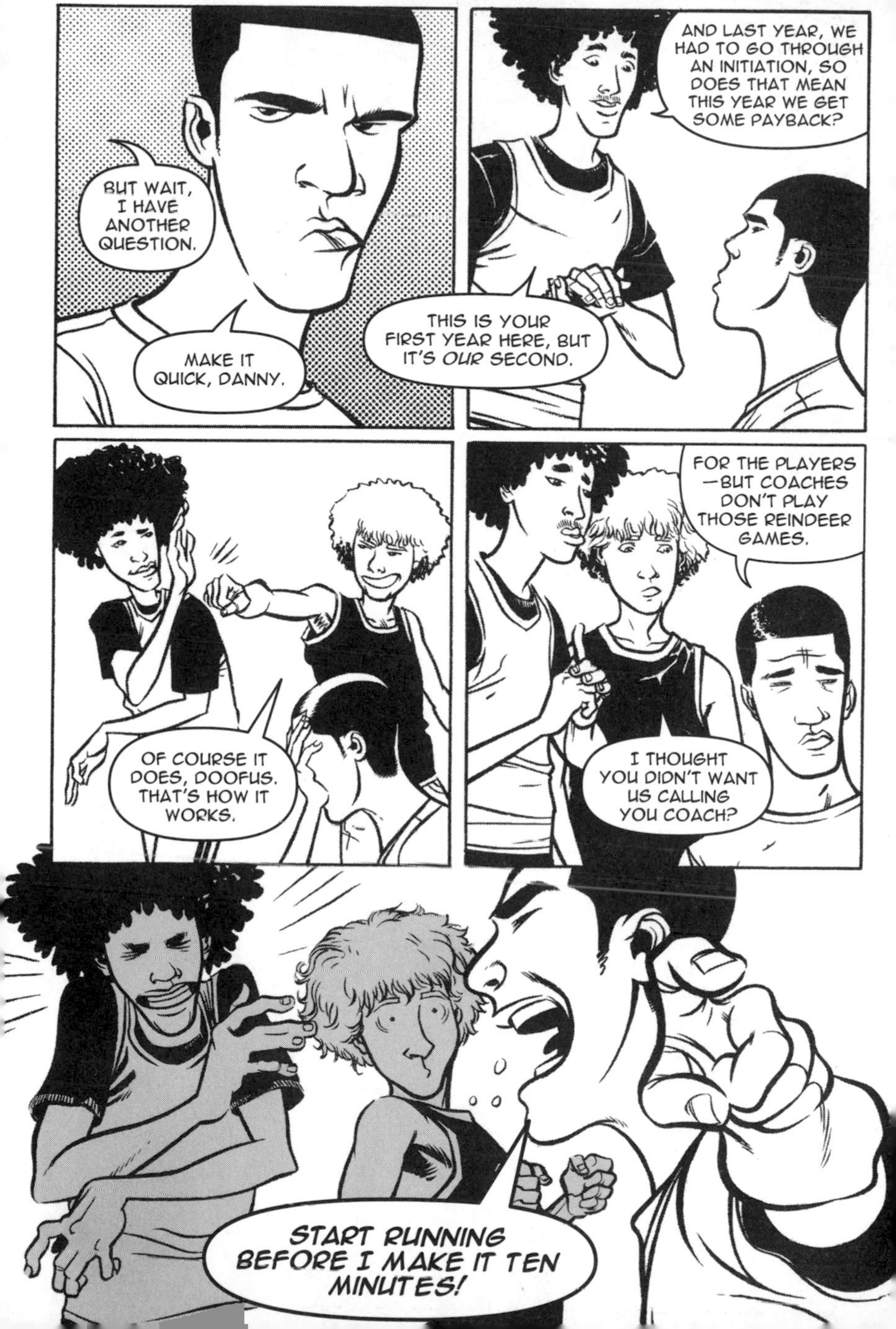
BUT WAIT, I HAVE ANOTHER QUESTION.
MAKE IT QUICK, DANNY.
THIS IS YOUR FIRST YEAR HERE, BUT IT'S *OUR* SECOND.
AND LAST YEAR, WE HAD TO GO THROUGH AN INITIATION, SO DOES THAT MEAN THIS YEAR WE GET SOME PAYBACK?
OF COURSE IT DOES, DOOFUS. THAT'S HOW IT WORKS.
FOR THE PLAYERS—BUT COACHES DON'T PLAY THOSE REINDEER GAMES.
I THOUGHT YOU DIDN'T WANT US CALLING YOU COACH?
START RUNNING BEFORE I MAKE IT TEN MINUTES!

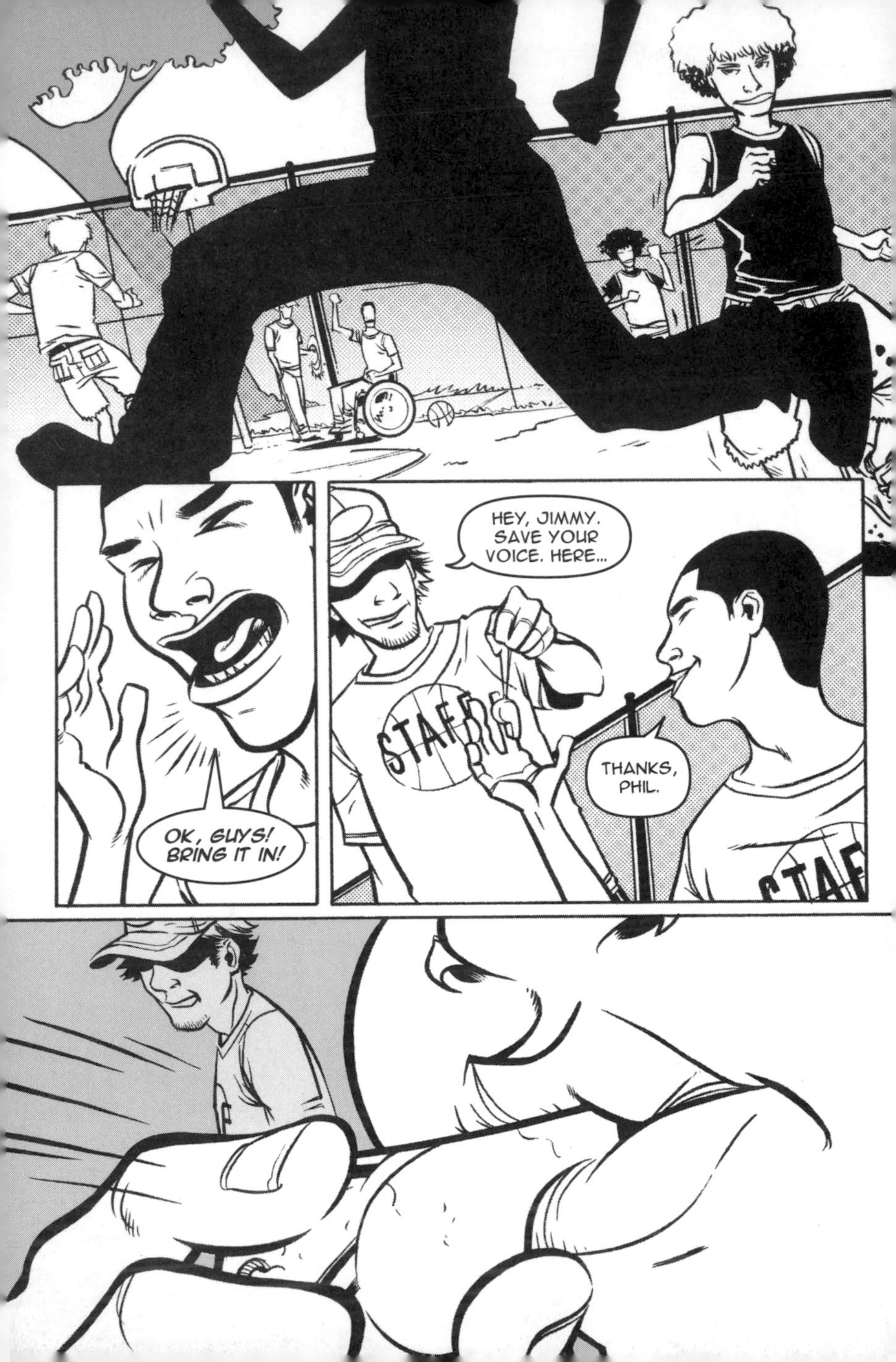
OK, GUYS! BRING IT IN!
HEY, JIMMY. SAVE YOUR VOICE. HERE...
STAFF
THANKS, PHIL.
STAF

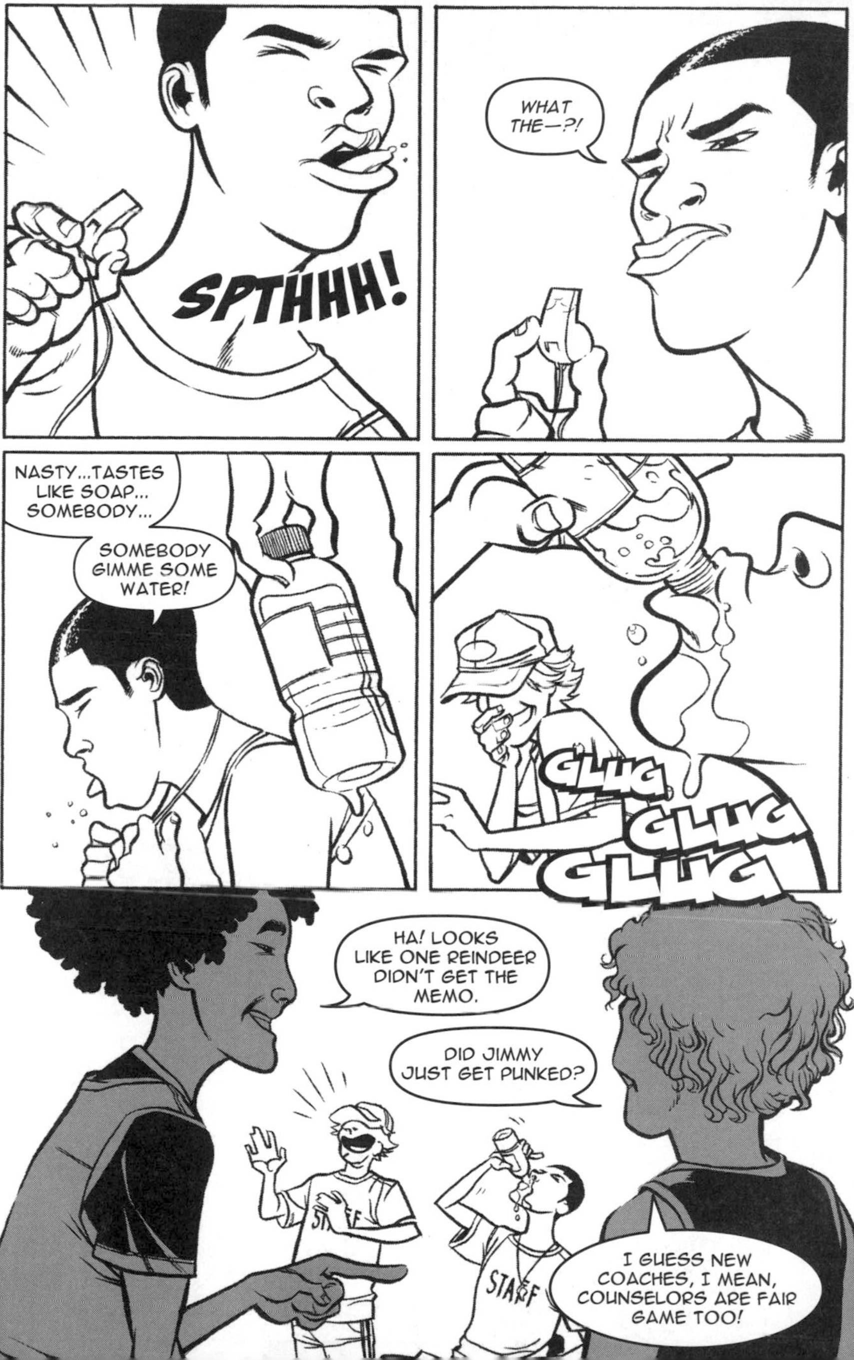
SPTHHH!
WHAT THE—?!
NASTY...TASTES LIKE SOAP... SOMEBODY...
SOMEBODY GIMME SOME WATER!
GLUG, GLUG GLUG
HA! LOOKS LIKE ONE REINDEER DIDN'T GET THE MEMO.
DID JIMMY JUST GET PUNKED?
I GUESS NEW COACHES, I MEAN, COUNSELORS ARE FAIR GAME TOO!

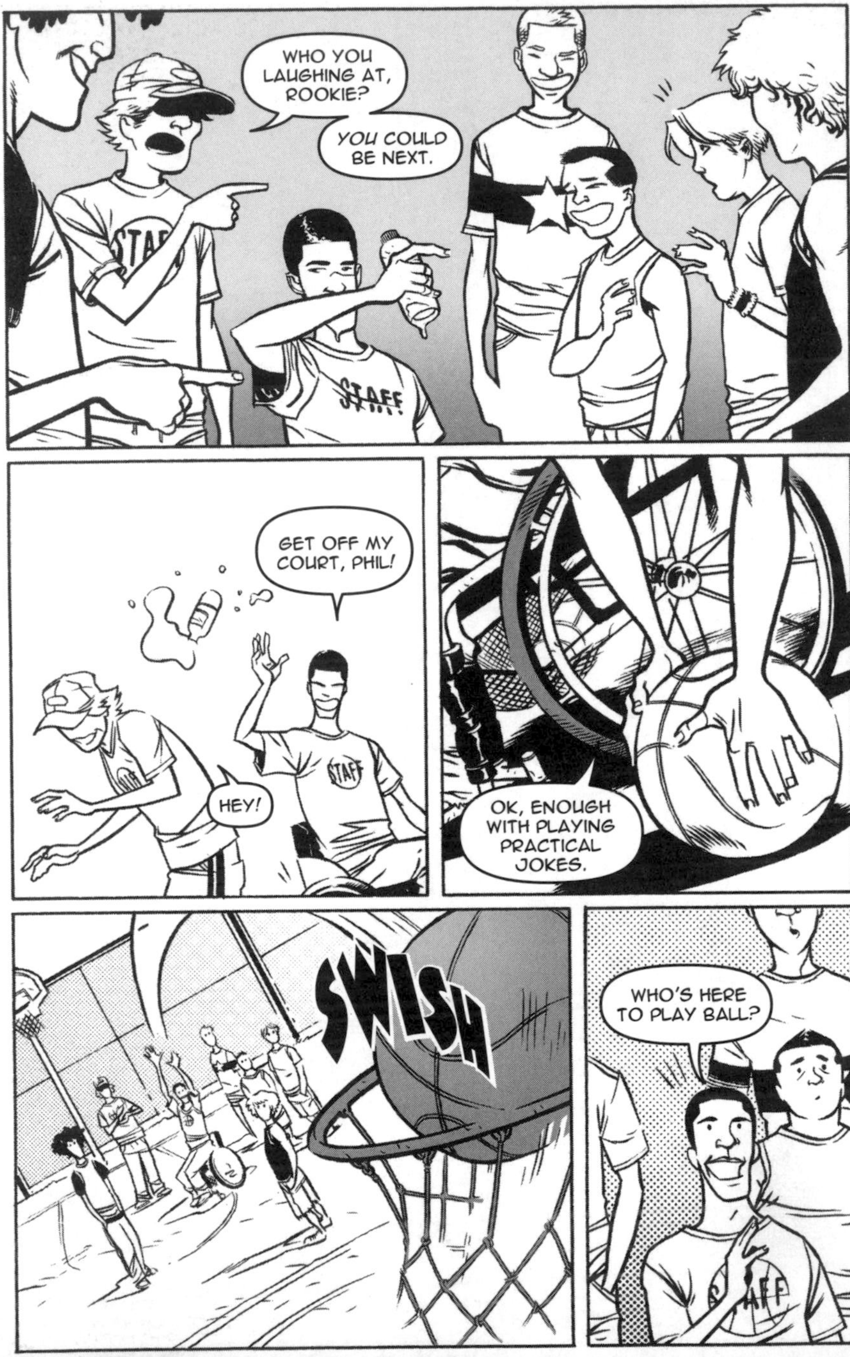
WHO YOU LAUGHING AT, ROOKIE?
YOU COULD BE NEXT.
GET OFF MY COURT, PHIL!
HEY!
OK, ENOUGH WITH PLAYING PRACTICAL JOKES.
SWISH
WHO'S HERE TO PLAY BALL?

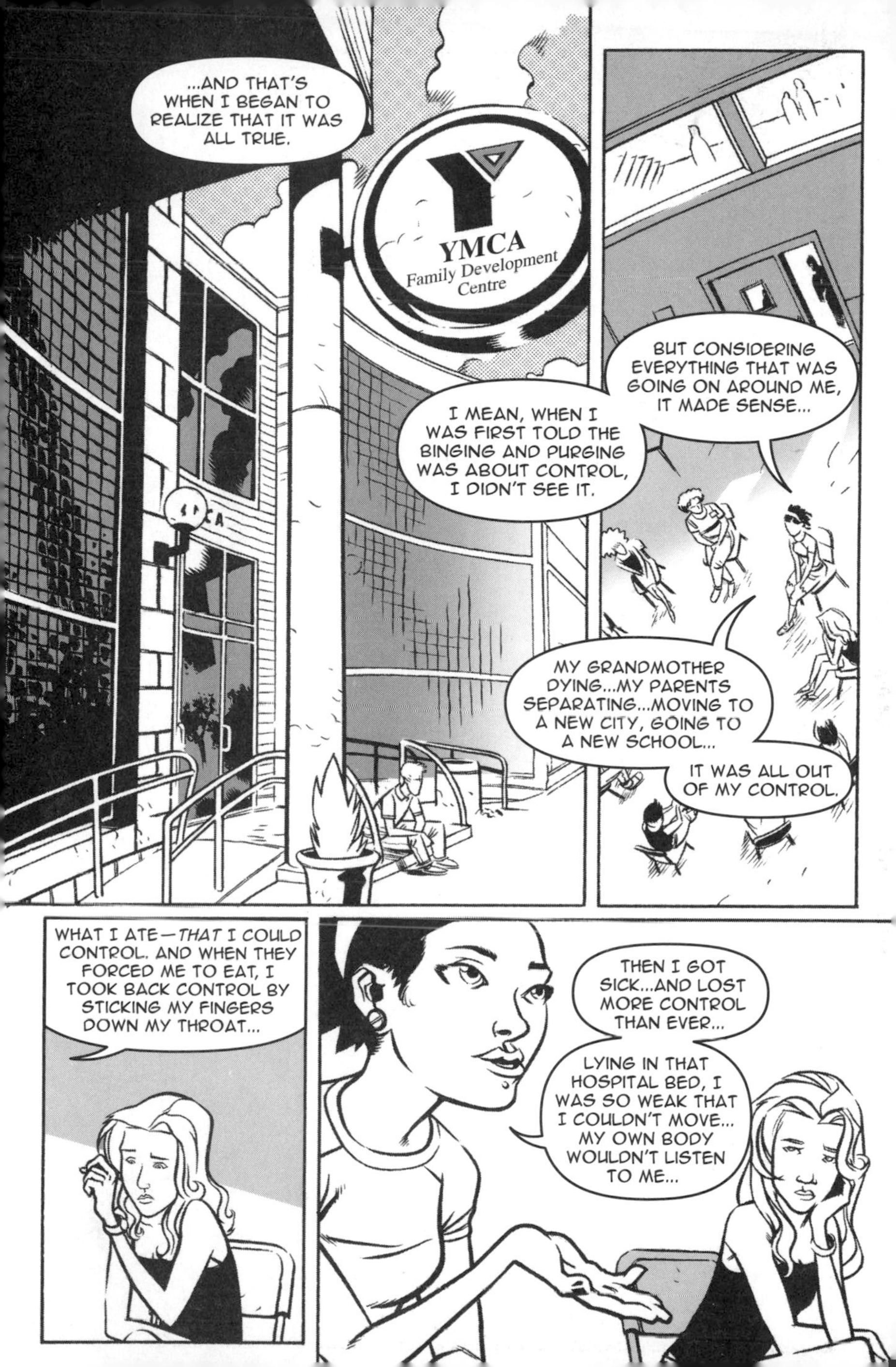
...AND THAT'S WHEN I BEGAN TO REALIZE THAT IT WAS ALL TRUE.
YMCA Family Development Centre
I MEAN, WHEN I WAS FIRST TOLD THE BINGING AND PURGING WAS ABOUT CONTROL, I DIDN'T SEE IT.
BUT CONSIDERING EVERYTHING THAT WAS GOING ON AROUND ME, IT MADE SENSE...
MY GRANDMOTHER DYING...MY PARENTS SEPARATING...MOVING TO A NEW CITY, GOING TO A NEW SCHOOL...
IT WAS ALL OUT OF MY CONTROL.
WHAT I ATE—*THAT* I COULD CONTROL. AND WHEN THEY FORCED ME TO EAT, I TOOK BACK CONTROL BY STICKING MY FINGERS DOWN MY THROAT...
THEN I GOT SICK...AND LOST MORE CONTROL THAN EVER...
LYING IN THAT HOSPITAL BED, I WAS SO WEAK THAT I COULDN'T MOVE... MY OWN BODY WOULDN'T LISTEN TO ME...

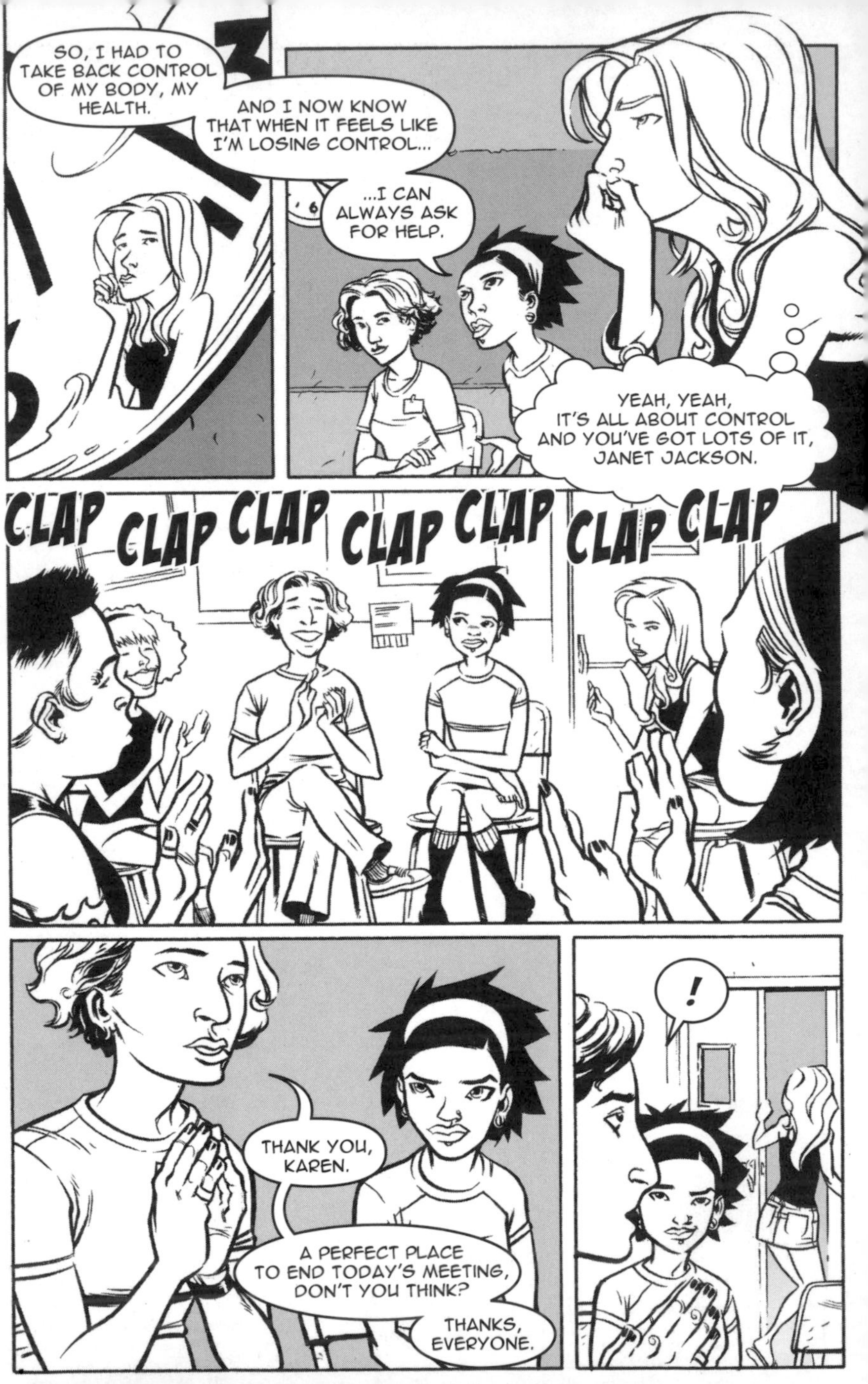
SO, I HAD TO TAKE BACK CONTROL OF MY BODY, MY HEALTH.
AND I NOW KNOW THAT WHEN IT FEELS LIKE I'M LOSING CONTROL...
...I CAN ALWAYS ASK FOR HELP.
YEAH, YEAH, IT'S ALL ABOUT CONTROL AND YOU'VE GOT LOTS OF IT, JANET JACKSON.
CLAP CLAP CLAP CLAP CLAP CLAP CLAP
THANK YOU, KAREN.
A PERFECT PLACE TO END TODAY'S MEETING, DON'T YOU THINK?
THANKS, EVERYONE.
!

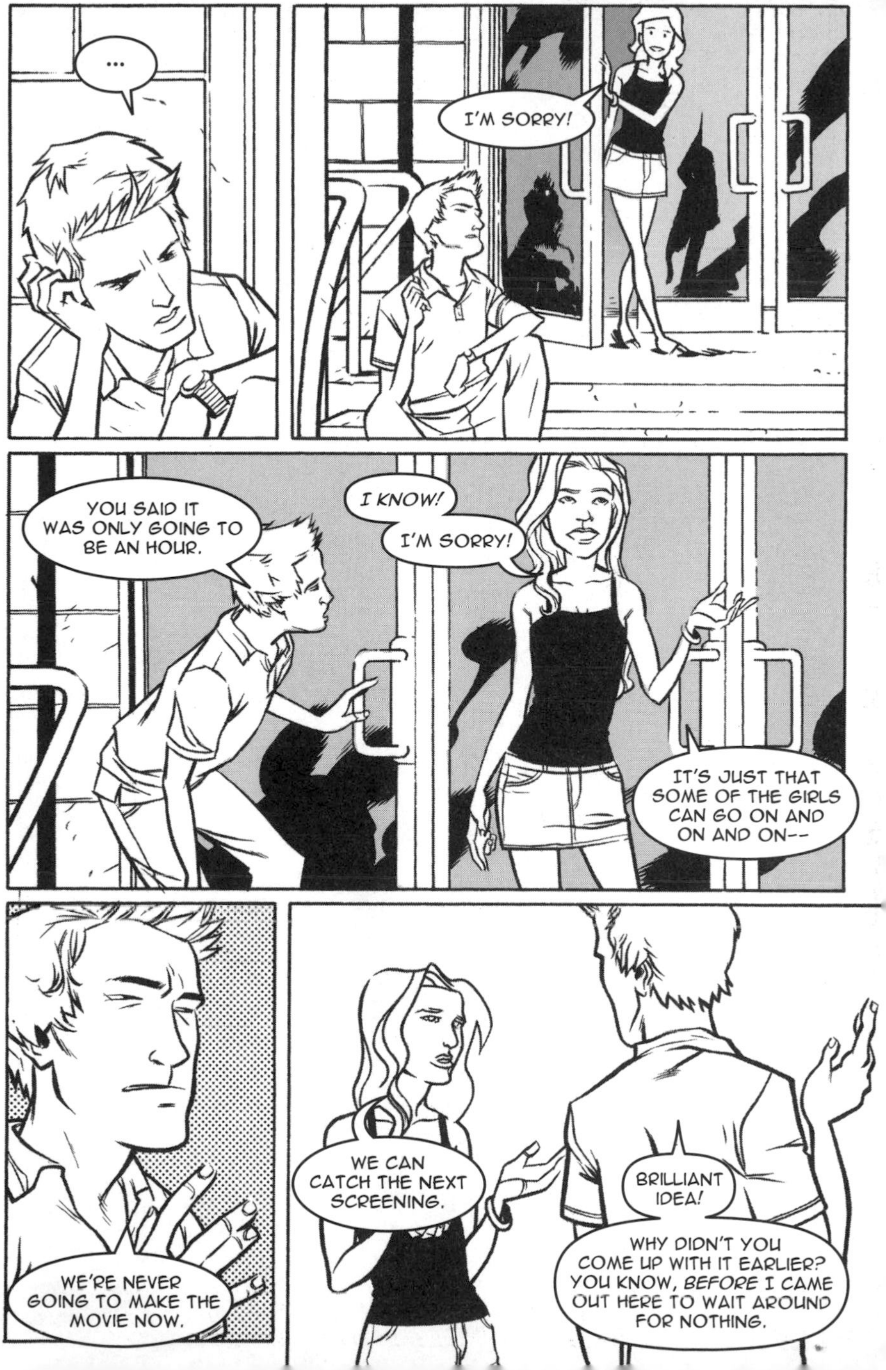
...
I'M SORRY!
YOU SAID IT WAS ONLY GOING TO BE AN HOUR.
I KNOW!
I'M SORRY!
IT'S JUST THAT SOME OF THE GIRLS CAN GO ON AND ON AND ON--
WE'RE NEVER GOING TO MAKE THE MOVIE NOW.
WE CAN CATCH THE NEXT SCREENING.
BRILLIANT IDEA!
WHY DIDN'T YOU COME UP WITH IT EARLIER? YOU KNOW, *BEFORE* I CAME OUT HERE TO WAIT AROUND FOR NOTHING.

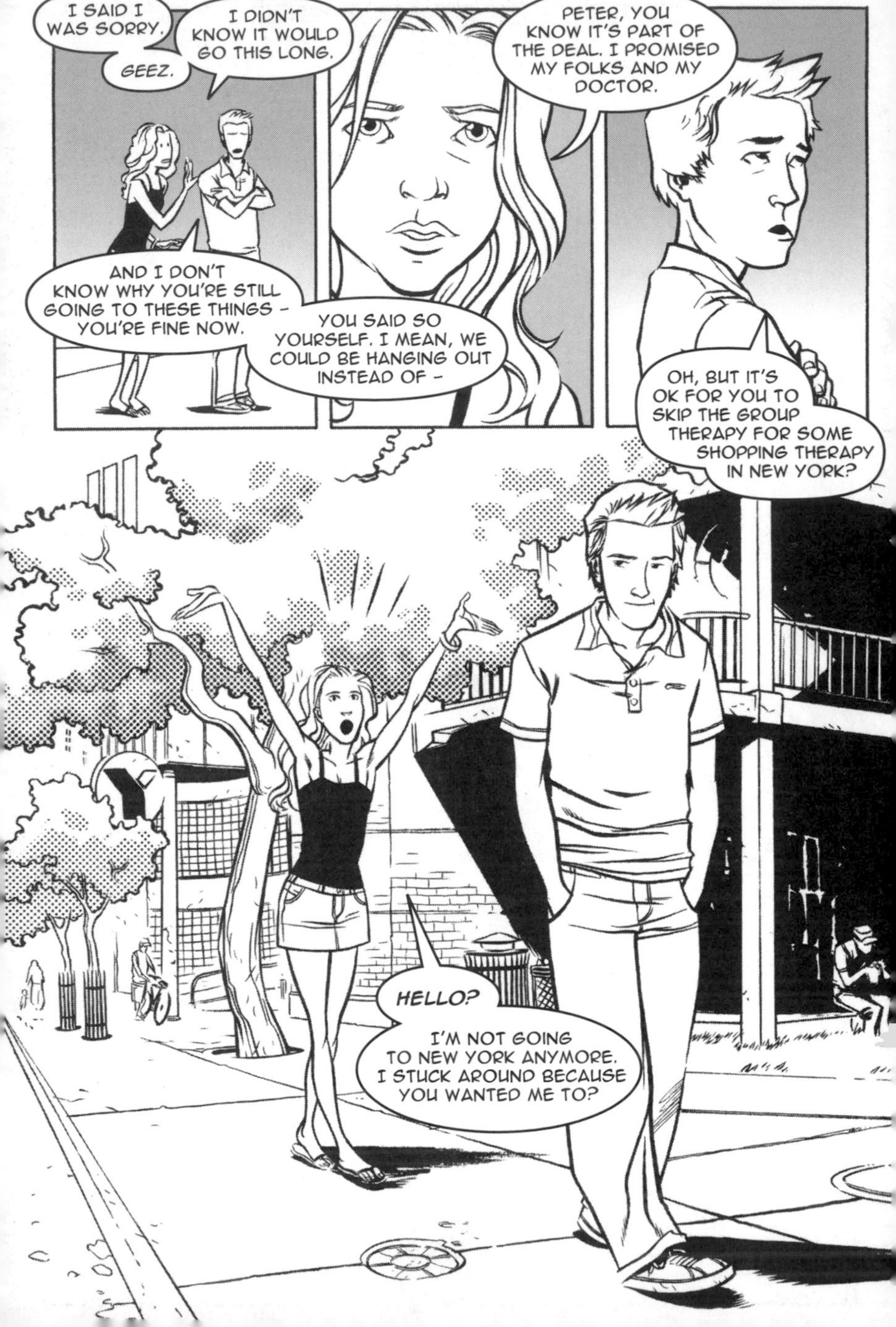
I SAID I WAS SORRY.
GEEZ.
I DIDN'T KNOW IT WOULD GO THIS LONG.
AND I DON'T KNOW WHY YOU'RE STILL GOING TO THESE THINGS - YOU'RE FINE NOW.
YOU SAID SO YOURSELF. I MEAN, WE COULD BE HANGING OUT INSTEAD OF -
PETER, YOU KNOW IT'S PART OF THE DEAL. I PROMISED MY FOLKS AND MY DOCTOR.
OH, BUT IT'S OK FOR YOU TO SKIP THE GROUP THERAPY FOR SOME SHOPPING THERAPY IN NEW YORK?
HELLO?
I'M NOT GOING TO NEW YORK ANYMORE. I STUCK AROUND BECAUSE YOU WANTED ME TO?

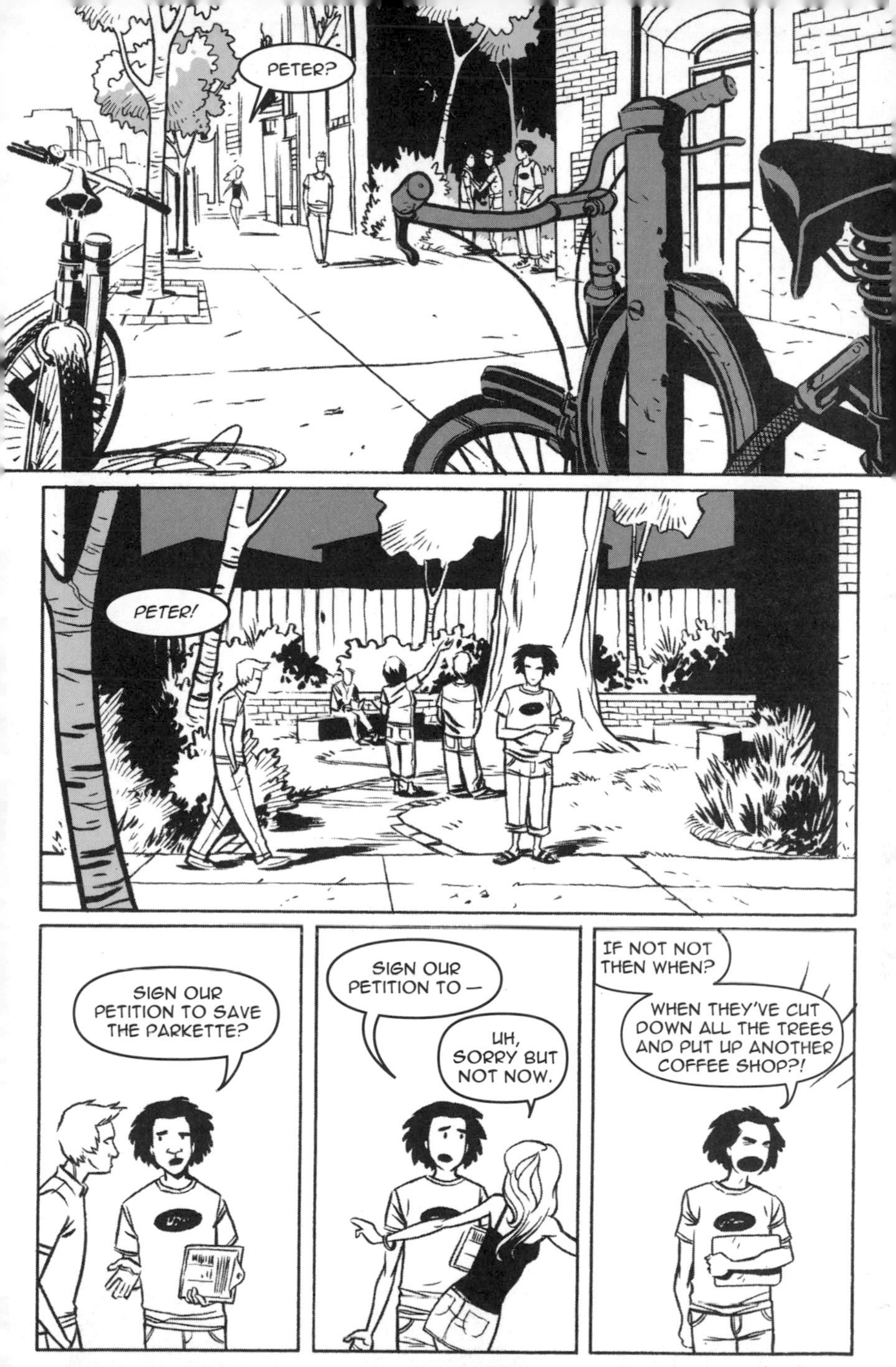
PETER?
PETER!
SIGN OUR PETITION TO SAVE THE PARKETTE?
SIGN OUR PETITION TO —
UH, SORRY BUT NOT NOW.
IF NOT NOT THEN WHEN?
WHEN THEY'VE CUT DOWN ALL THE TREES AND PUT UP ANOTHER COFFEE SHOP?!

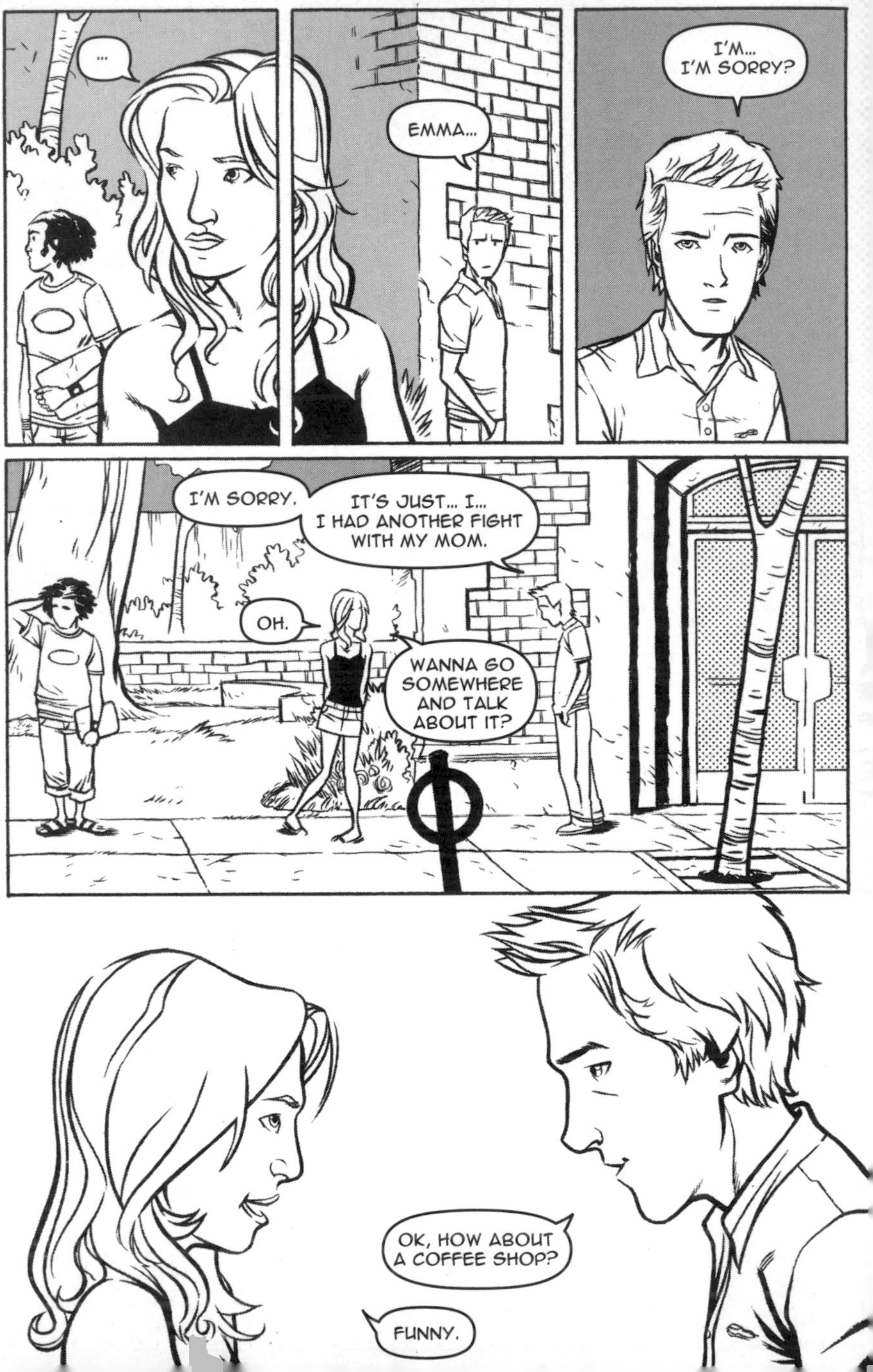
...
EMMA...
I'M... I'M SORRY?
I'M SORRY.
IT'S JUST... I... I HAD ANOTHER FIGHT WITH MY MOM.
OH.
WANNA GO SOMEWHERE AND TALK ABOUT IT?
OK, HOW ABOUT A COFFEE SHOP?
FUNNY.

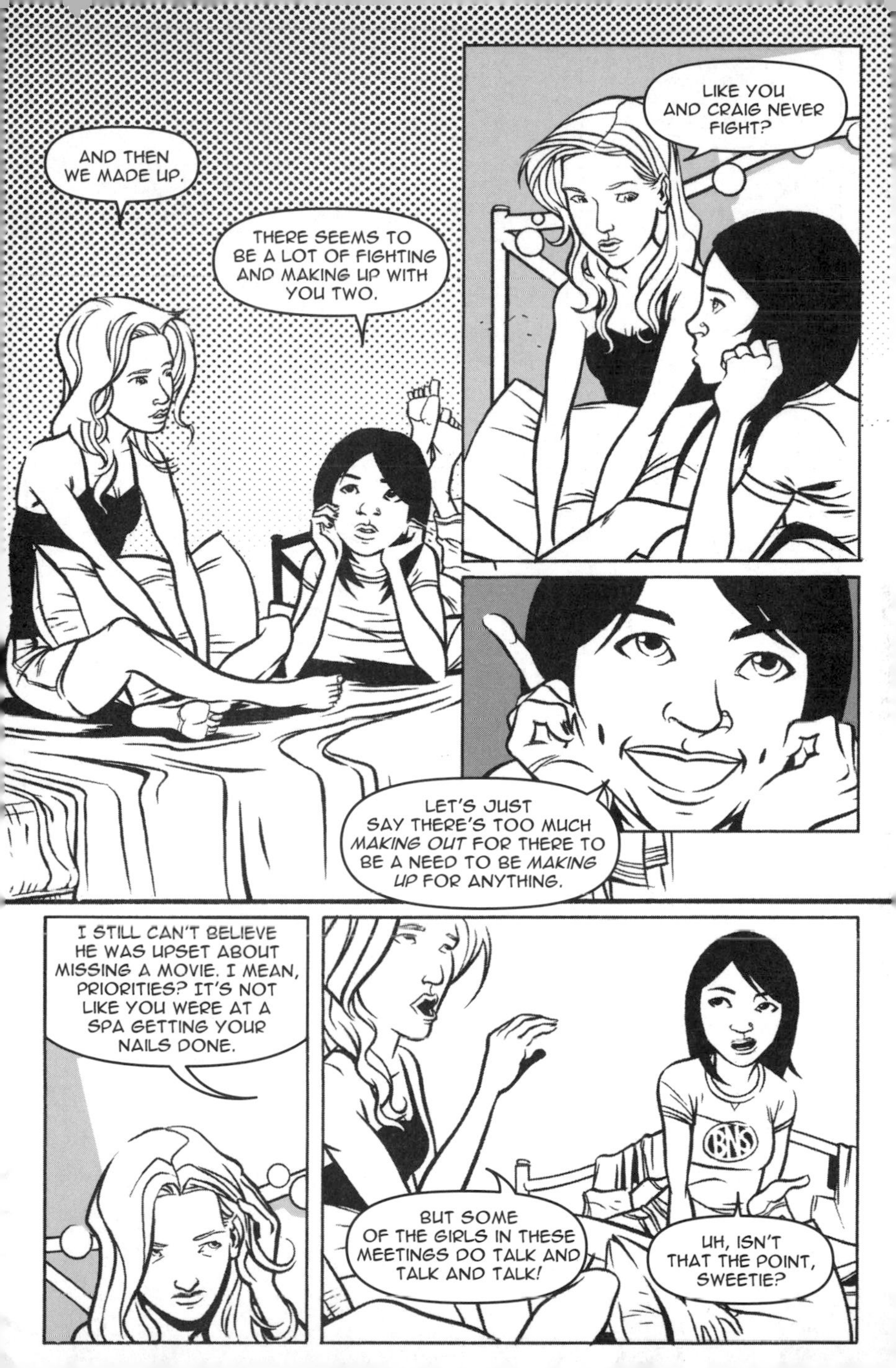
AND THEN WE MADE UP.
THERE SEEMS TO BE A LOT OF FIGHTING AND MAKING UP WITH YOU TWO.
LIKE YOU AND CRAIG NEVER FIGHT?
LET'S JUST SAY THERE'S TOO MUCH *MAKING OUT* FOR THERE TO BE A NEED TO BE *MAKING UP* FOR ANYTHING.
I STILL CAN'T BELIEVE HE WAS UPSET ABOUT MISSING A MOVIE. I MEAN, PRIORITIES? IT'S NOT LIKE YOU WERE AT A SPA GETTING YOUR NAILS DONE.
BUT SOME OF THE GIRLS IN THESE MEETINGS DO TALK AND TALK AND TALK!
UH, ISN'T THAT THE POINT, SWEETIE?

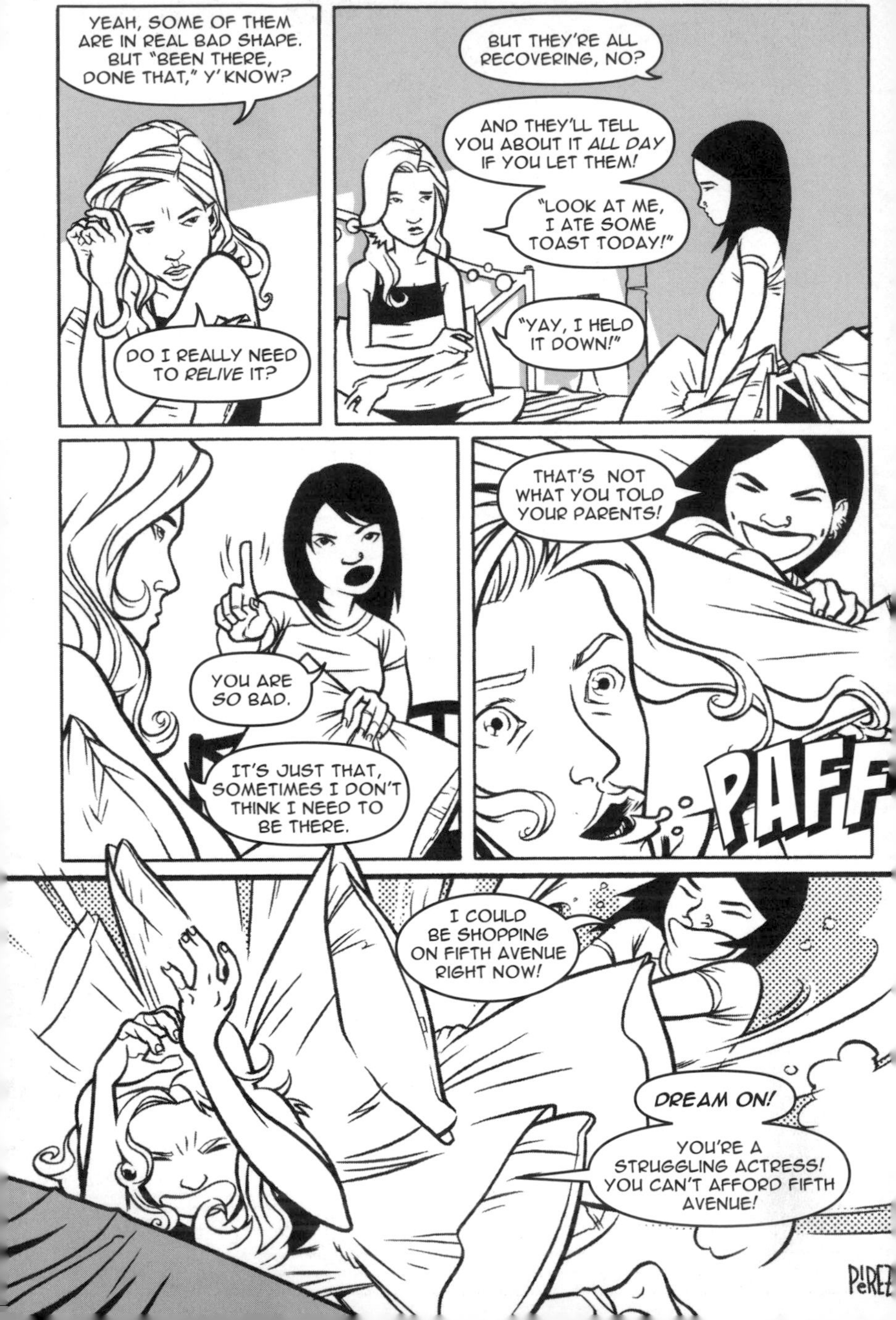
YEAH, SOME OF THEM ARE IN REAL BAD SHAPE. BUT "BEEN THERE, DONE THAT," Y'KNOW?
DO I REALLY NEED TO *RELIVE* IT?
BUT THEY'RE ALL RECOVERING, NO?
AND THEY'LL TELL YOU ABOUT IT *ALL DAY* IF YOU LET THEM!
"LOOK AT ME, I ATE SOME TOAST TODAY!"
"YAY, I HELD IT DOWN!"
YOU ARE *SO* BAD.
IT'S JUST THAT, SOMETIMES I DON'T THINK I NEED TO BE THERE.
THAT'S NOT WHAT YOU TOLD YOUR PARENTS!
PAFF
I COULD BE SHOPPING ON FIFTH AVENUE RIGHT NOW!
DREAM ON!
YOU'RE A STRUGGLING ACTRESS! YOU CAN'T AFFORD FIFTH AVENUE!
PéREZ

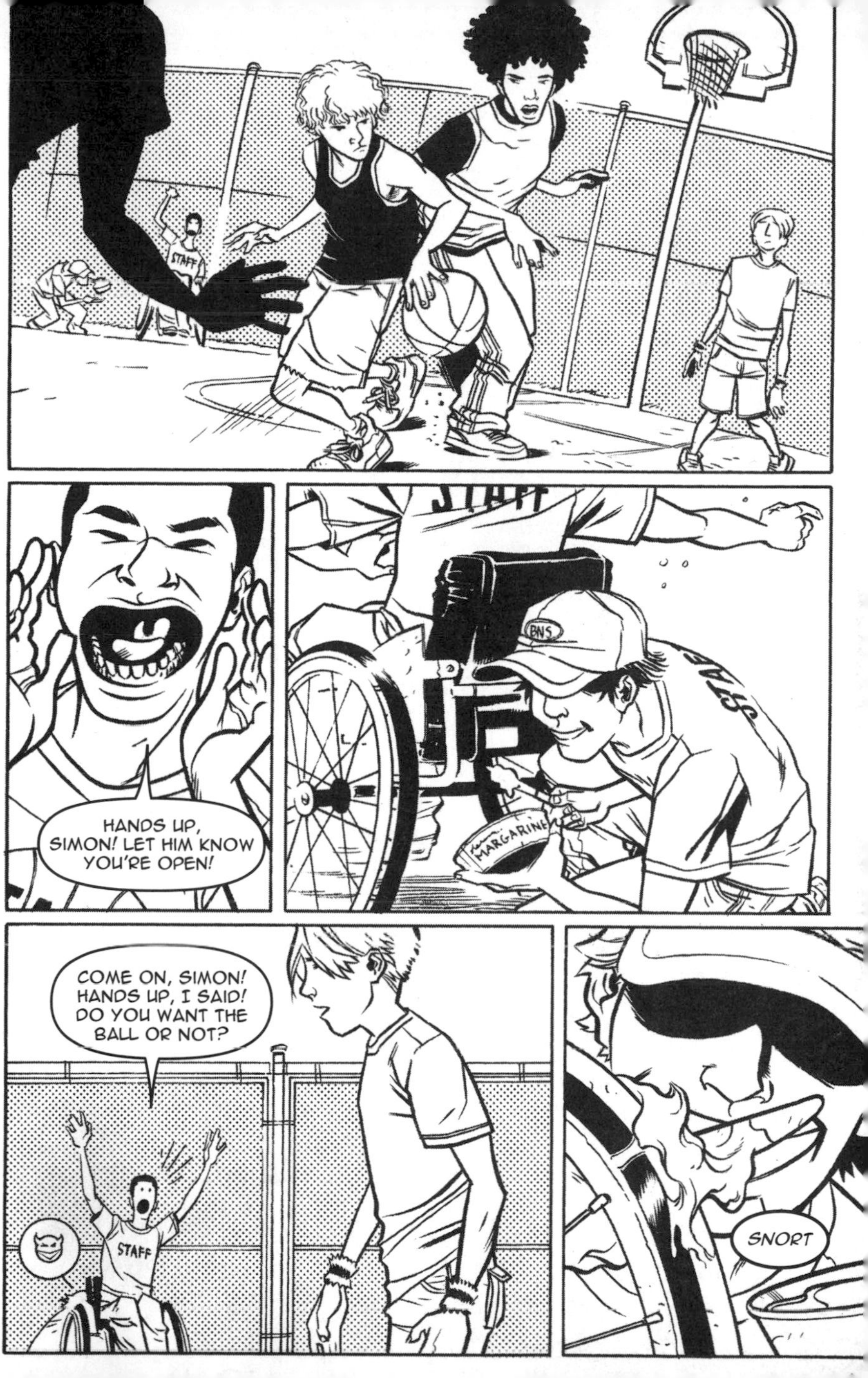
STAFF
HANDS UP, SIMON! LET HIM KNOW YOU'RE OPEN!
STAFF
BNS
MARGARINE
COME ON, SIMON! HANDS UP, I SAID! DO YOU WANT THE BALL OR NOT?
STAFF
SNORT

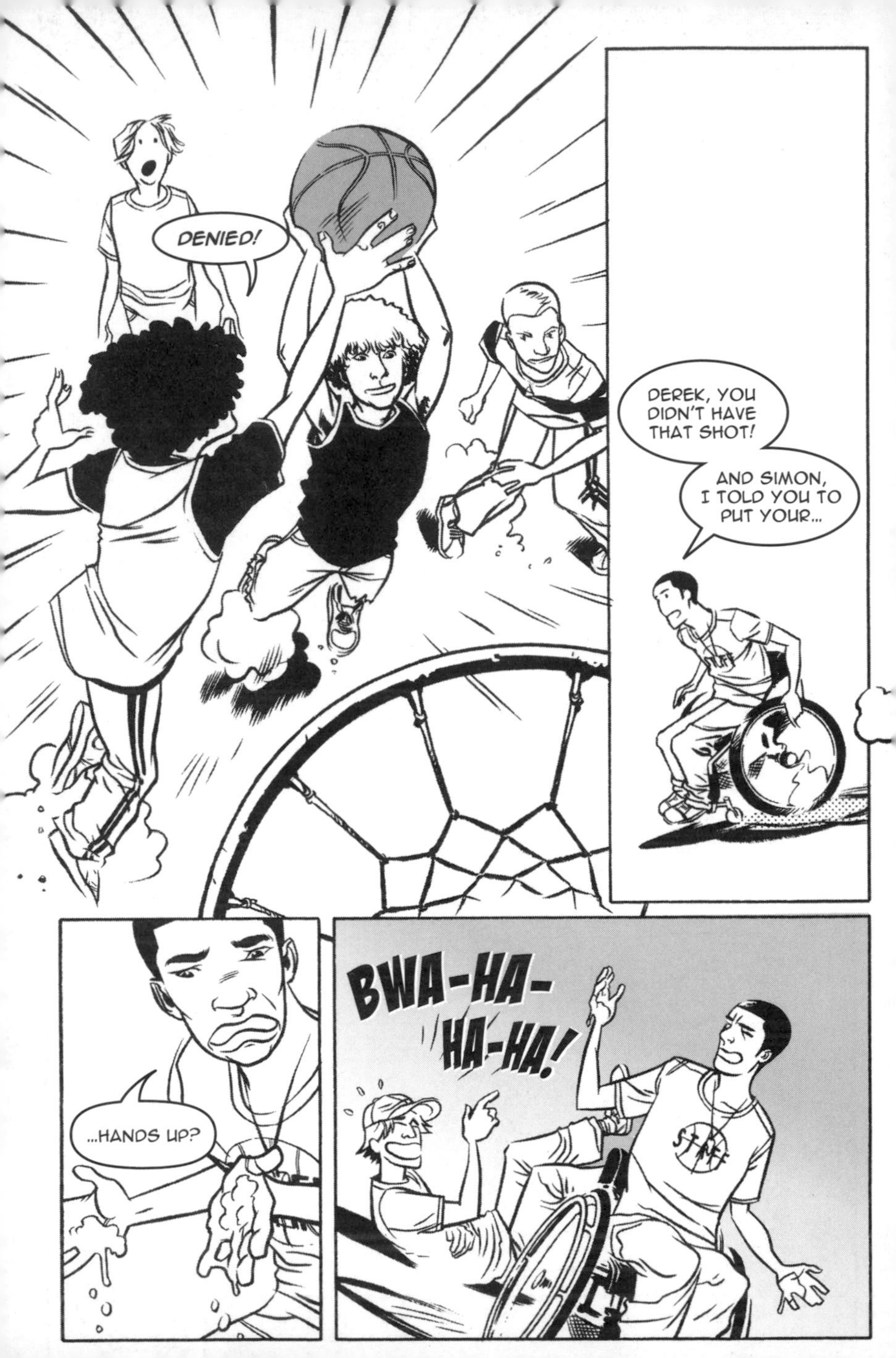
DENIED!
DEREK, YOU DIDN'T HAVE THAT SHOT!
AND SIMON, I TOLD YOU TO PUT YOUR...
...HANDS UP?
BWA-HA-HA-HA!

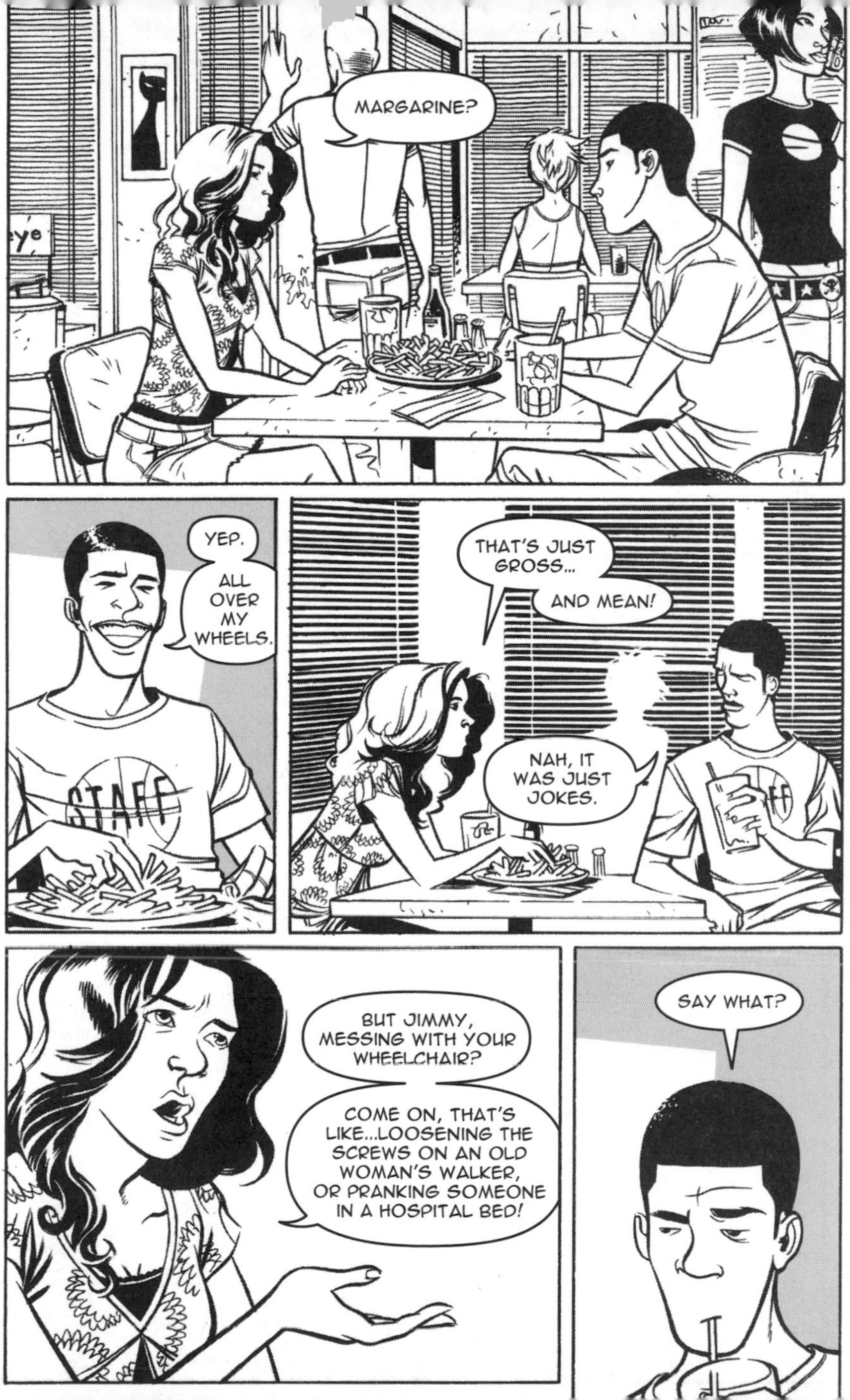
MARGARINE?
YEP.
ALL OVER MY WHEELS.
STAFF
THAT'S JUST GROSS...
AND MEAN!
NAH, IT WAS JUST JOKES.
BUT JIMMY, MESSING WITH YOUR WHEELCHAIR?
COME ON, THAT'S LIKE...LOOSENING THE SCREWS ON AN OLD WOMAN'S WALKER, OR PRANKING SOMEONE IN A HOSPITAL BED!
SAY WHAT?

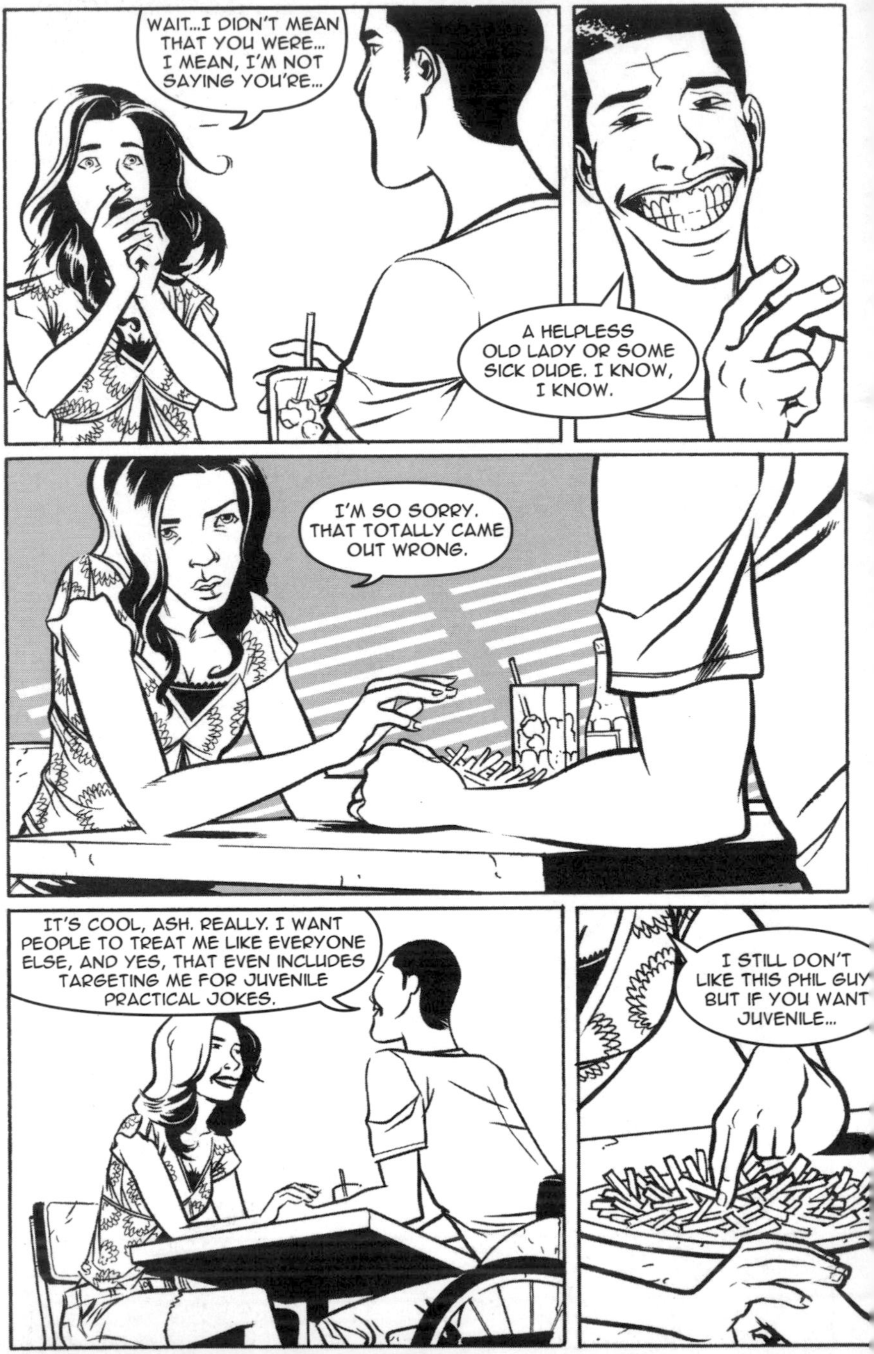
WAIT...I DIDN'T MEAN THAT YOU WERE... I MEAN, I'M NOT SAYING YOU'RE...
A HELPLESS OLD LADY OR SOME SICK DUDE. I KNOW, I KNOW.
I'M SO SORRY. THAT TOTALLY CAME OUT WRONG.
IT'S COOL, ASH. REALLY. I WANT PEOPLE TO TREAT ME LIKE EVERYONE ELSE, AND YES, THAT EVEN INCLUDES TARGETING ME FOR JUVENILE PRACTICAL JOKES.
I STILL DON'T LIKE THIS PHIL GUY BUT IF YOU WANT JUVENILE...

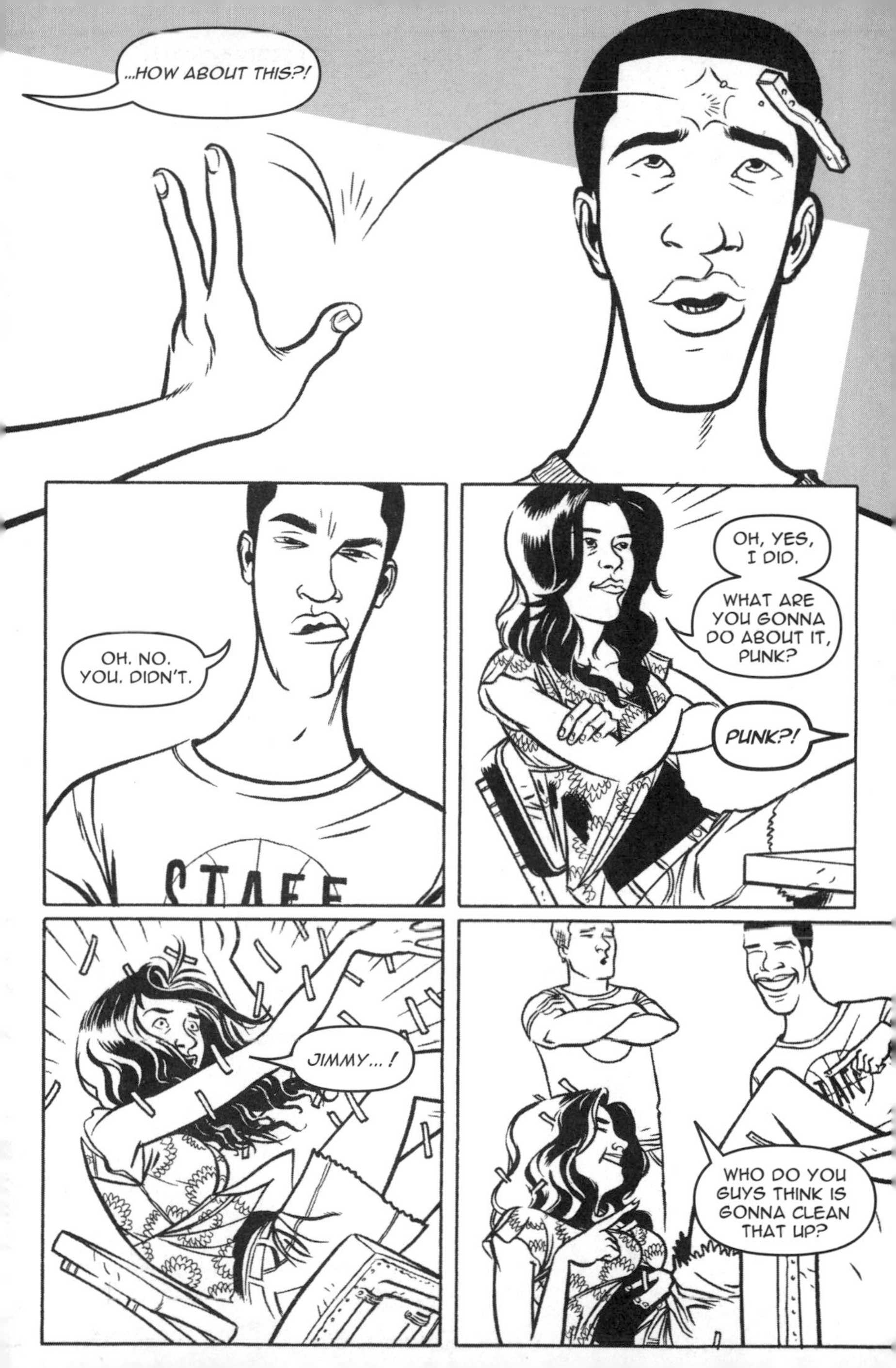
...HOW ABOUT THIS?!
OH. NO. YOU. DIDN'T.
OH, YES, I DID.
WHAT ARE YOU GONNA DO ABOUT IT, PUNK?
PUNK?!
STAFF
JIMMY...!
WHO DO YOU GUYS THINK IS GONNA CLEAN THAT UP?

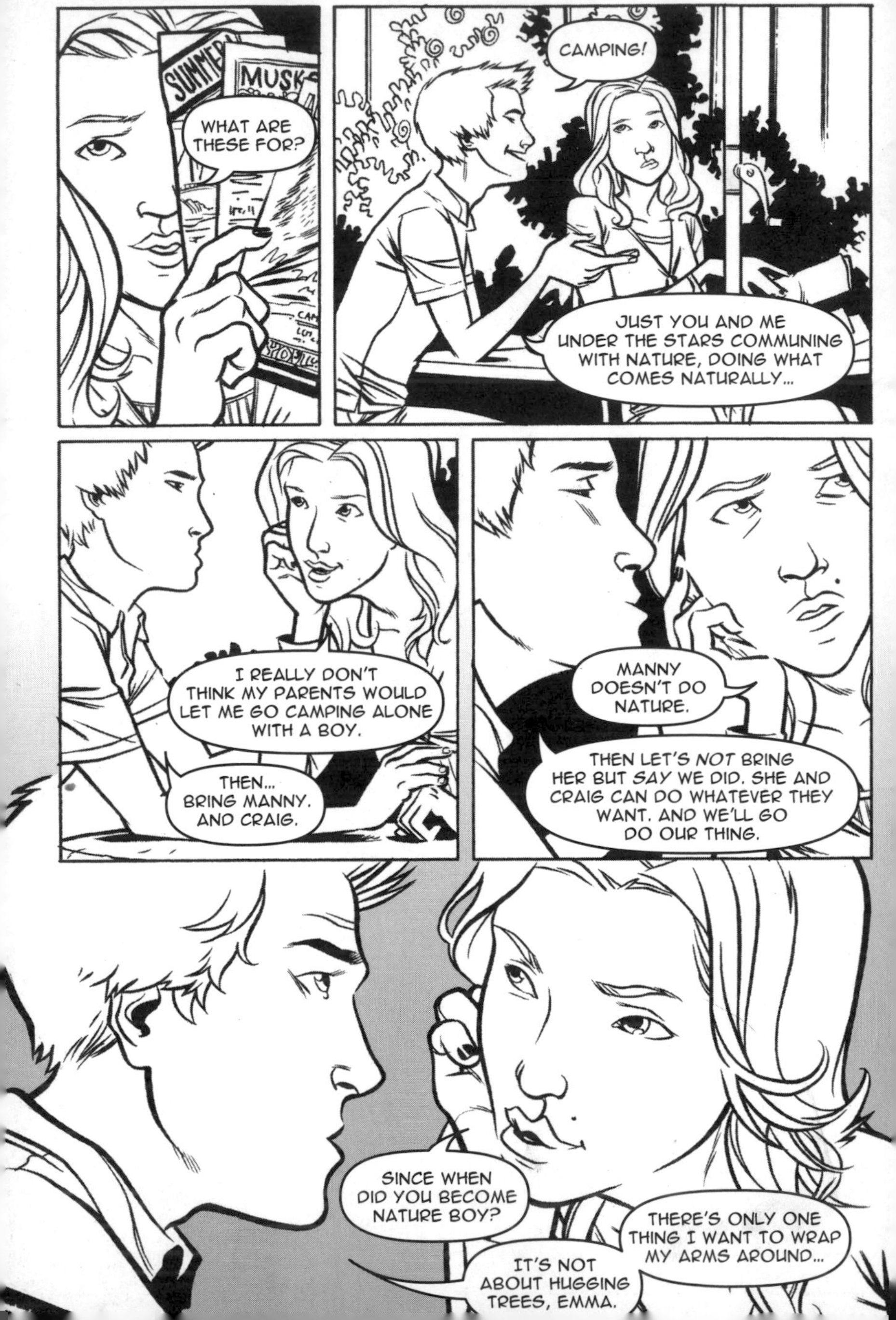
SUMMER
MUSK
WHAT ARE THESE FOR?
CAMPING!
JUST YOU AND ME UNDER THE STARS COMMUNING WITH NATURE, DOING WHAT COMES NATURALLY...
I REALLY DON'T THINK MY PARENTS WOULD LET ME GO CAMPING ALONE WITH A BOY.
THEN... BRING MANNY. AND CRAIG.
MANNY DOESN'T DO NATURE.
THEN LET'S *NOT* BRING HER BUT *SAY* WE DID. SHE AND CRAIG CAN DO WHATEVER THEY WANT. AND WE'LL GO DO OUR THING.
SINCE WHEN DID YOU BECOME NATURE BOY?
IT'S NOT ABOUT HUGGING TREES, EMMA.
THERE'S ONLY ONE THING I WANT TO WRAP MY ARMS AROUND...

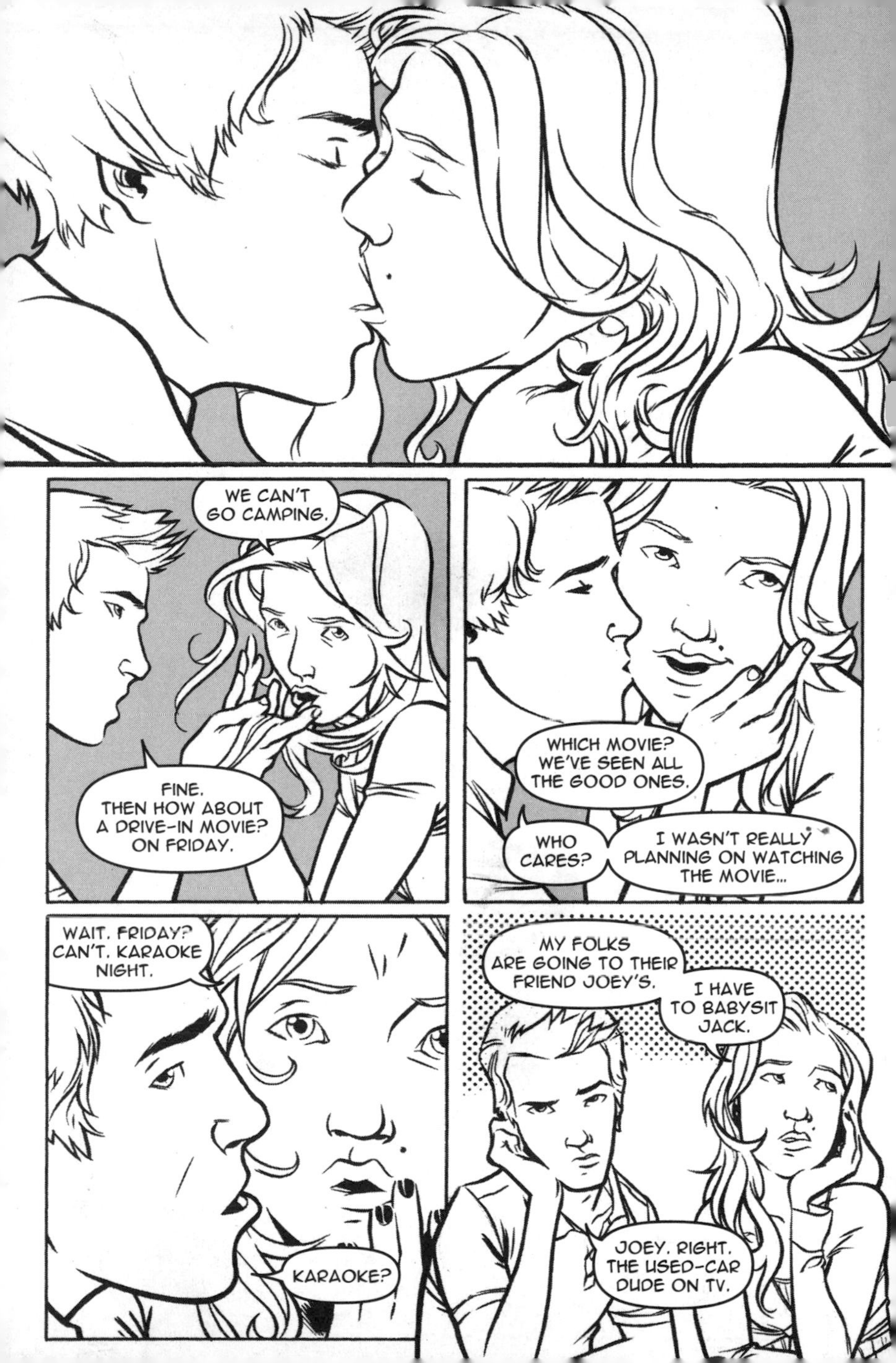
WE CAN'T GO CAMPING.
FINE. THEN HOW ABOUT A DRIVE-IN MOVIE? ON FRIDAY.
WHICH MOVIE? WE'VE SEEN ALL THE GOOD ONES.
WHO CARES?
I WASN'T REALLY PLANNING ON WATCHING THE MOVIE...
WAIT. FRIDAY? CAN'T. KARAOKE NIGHT.
KARAOKE?
MY FOLKS ARE GOING TO THEIR FRIEND JOEY'S.
I HAVE TO BABYSIT JACK.
JOEY. RIGHT. THE USED-CAR DUDE ON TV.

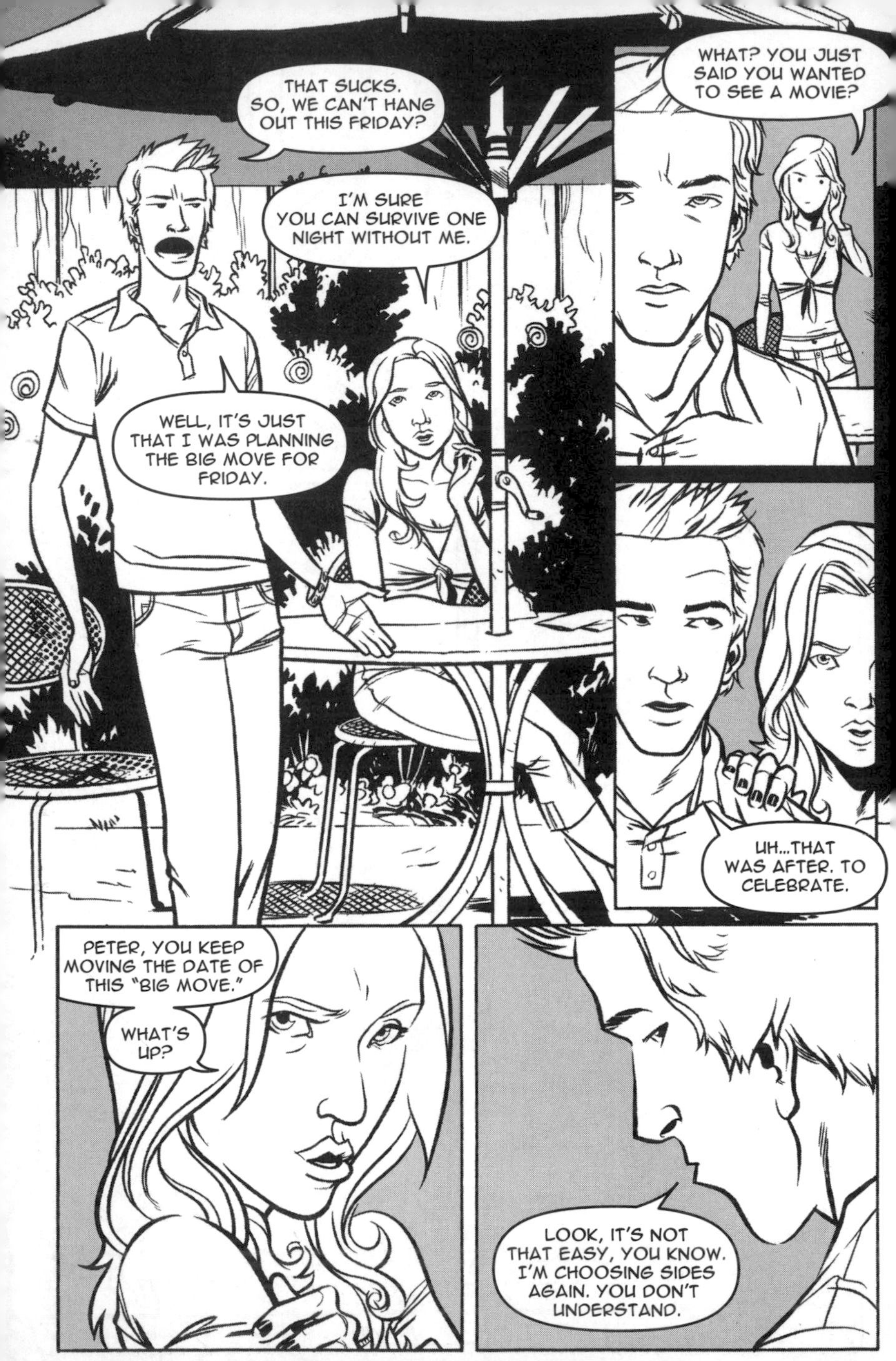
THAT SUCKS. SO, WE CAN'T HANG OUT THIS FRIDAY?
I'M SURE YOU CAN SURVIVE ONE NIGHT WITHOUT ME.
WELL, IT'S JUST THAT I WAS PLANNING THE BIG MOVE FOR FRIDAY.
WHAT? YOU JUST SAID YOU WANTED TO SEE A MOVIE?
UH...THAT WAS AFTER. TO CELEBRATE.
PETER, YOU KEEP MOVING THE DATE OF THIS "BIG MOVE."
WHAT'S UP?
LOOK, IT'S NOT THAT EASY, YOU KNOW. I'M CHOOSING SIDES AGAIN. YOU DON'T UNDERSTAND.

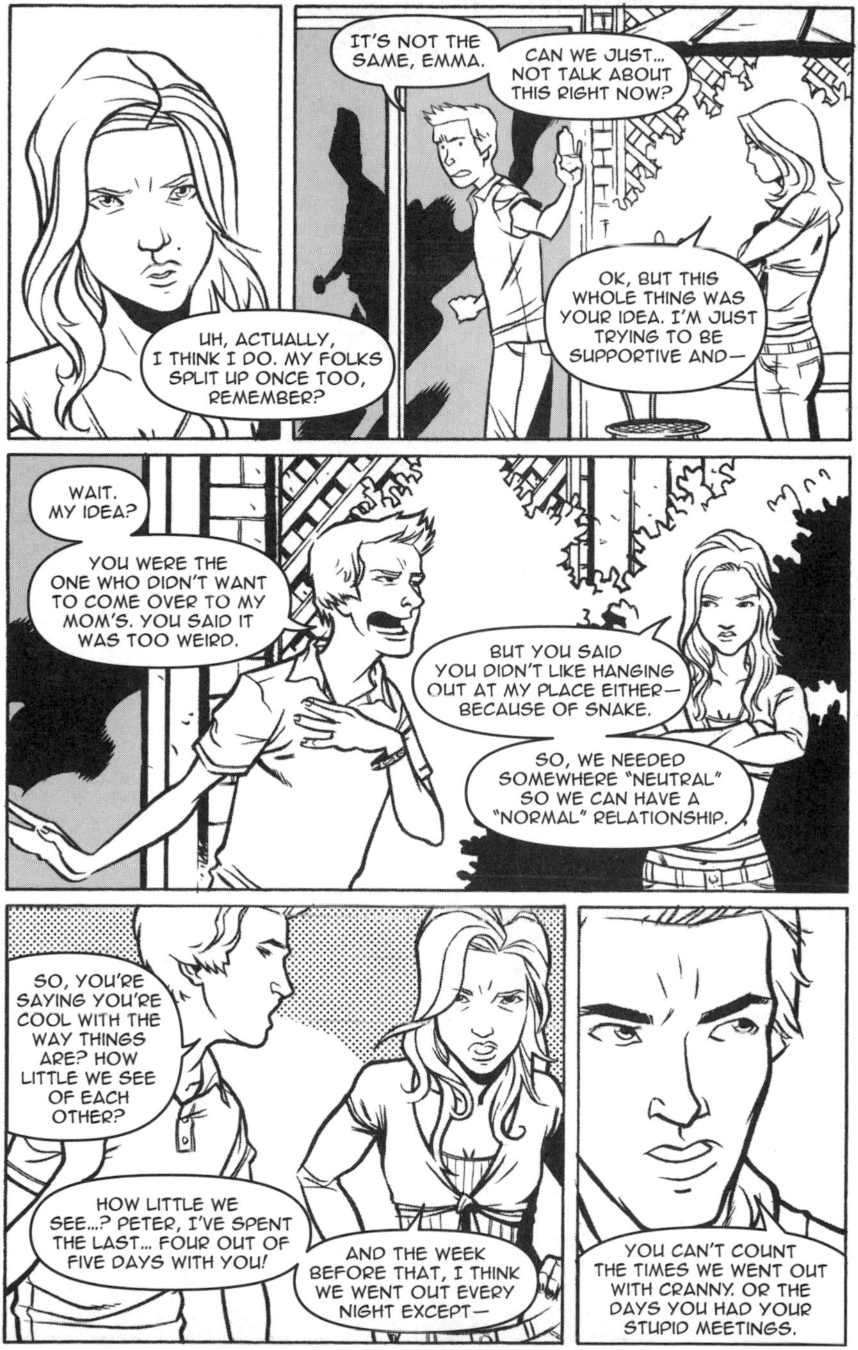
UH, ACTUALLY, I THINK I DO. MY FOLKS SPLIT UP ONCE TOO, REMEMBER?
IT'S NOT THE SAME, EMMA.
CAN WE JUST... NOT TALK ABOUT THIS RIGHT NOW?
OK, BUT THIS WHOLE THING WAS YOUR IDEA. I'M JUST TRYING TO BE SUPPORTIVE AND—
WAIT. MY IDEA?
YOU WERE THE ONE WHO DIDN'T WANT TO COME OVER TO MY MOM'S. YOU SAID IT WAS TOO WEIRD.
BUT YOU SAID YOU DIDN'T LIKE HANGING OUT AT MY PLACE EITHER— BECAUSE OF SNAKE.
SO, WE NEEDED SOMEWHERE "NEUTRAL" SO WE CAN HAVE A "NORMAL" RELATIONSHIP.
SO, YOU'RE SAYING YOU'RE COOL WITH THE WAY THINGS ARE? HOW LITTLE WE SEE OF EACH OTHER?
HOW LITTLE WE SEE...? PETER, I'VE SPENT THE LAST... FOUR OUT OF FIVE DAYS WITH YOU!
AND THE WEEK BEFORE THAT, I THINK WE WENT OUT EVERY NIGHT EXCEPT—
YOU CAN'T COUNT THE TIMES WE WENT OUT WITH CRANNY. OR THE DAYS YOU HAD YOUR STUPID MEETINGS.

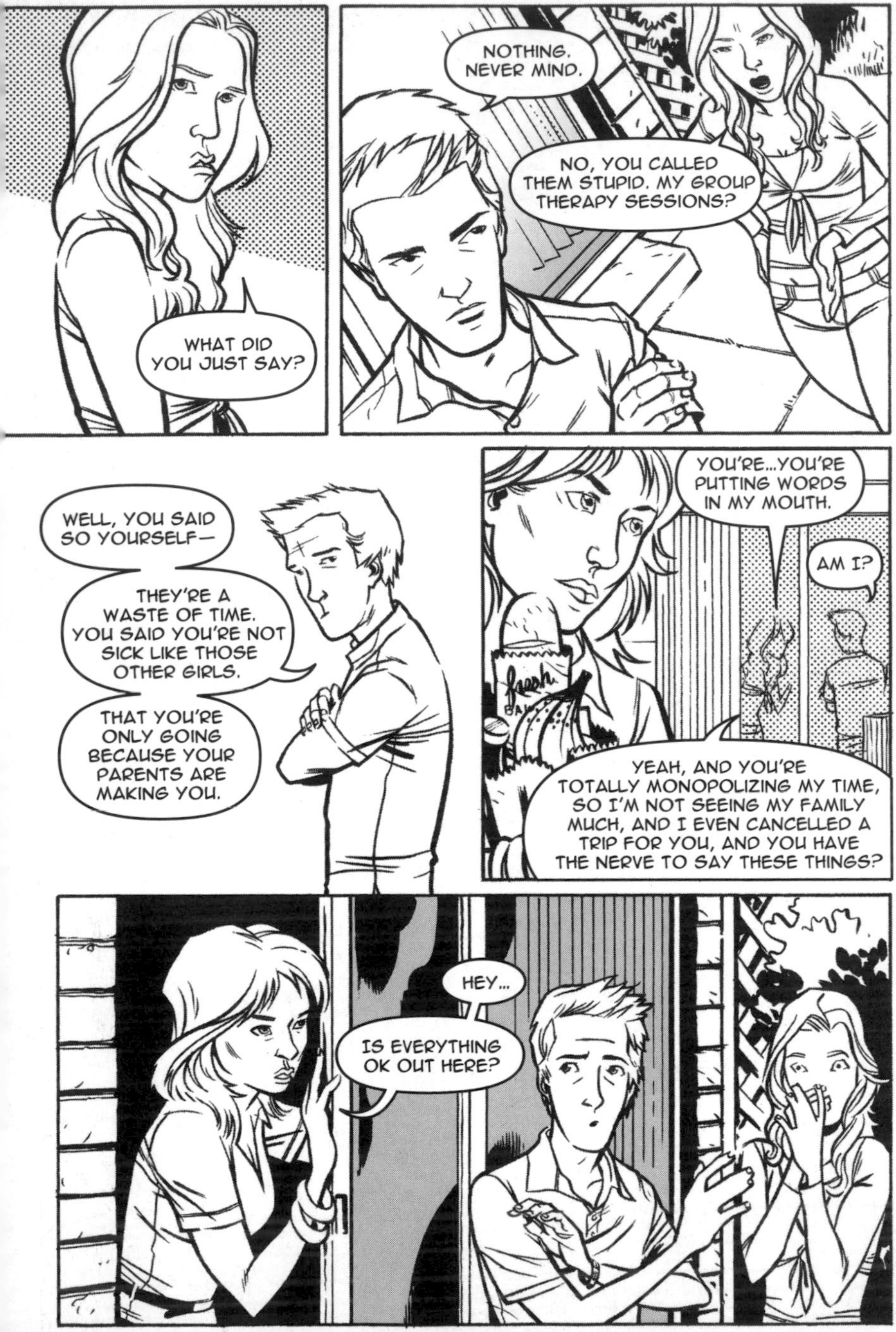
WHAT DID YOU JUST SAY?
NOTHING. NEVER MIND.
NO, YOU CALLED THEM STUPID. MY GROUP THERAPY SESSIONS?
WELL, YOU SAID SO YOURSELF—
THEY'RE A WASTE OF TIME. YOU SAID YOU'RE NOT SICK LIKE THOSE OTHER GIRLS.
THAT YOU'RE ONLY GOING BECAUSE YOUR PARENTS ARE MAKING YOU.
YOU'RE...YOU'RE PUTTING WORDS IN MY MOUTH.
AM I?
YEAH, AND YOU'RE TOTALLY MONOPOLIZING MY TIME, SO I'M NOT SEEING MY FAMILY MUCH, AND I EVEN CANCELLED A TRIP FOR YOU, AND YOU HAVE THE NERVE TO SAY THESE THINGS?
HEY...
IS EVERYTHING OK OUT HERE?

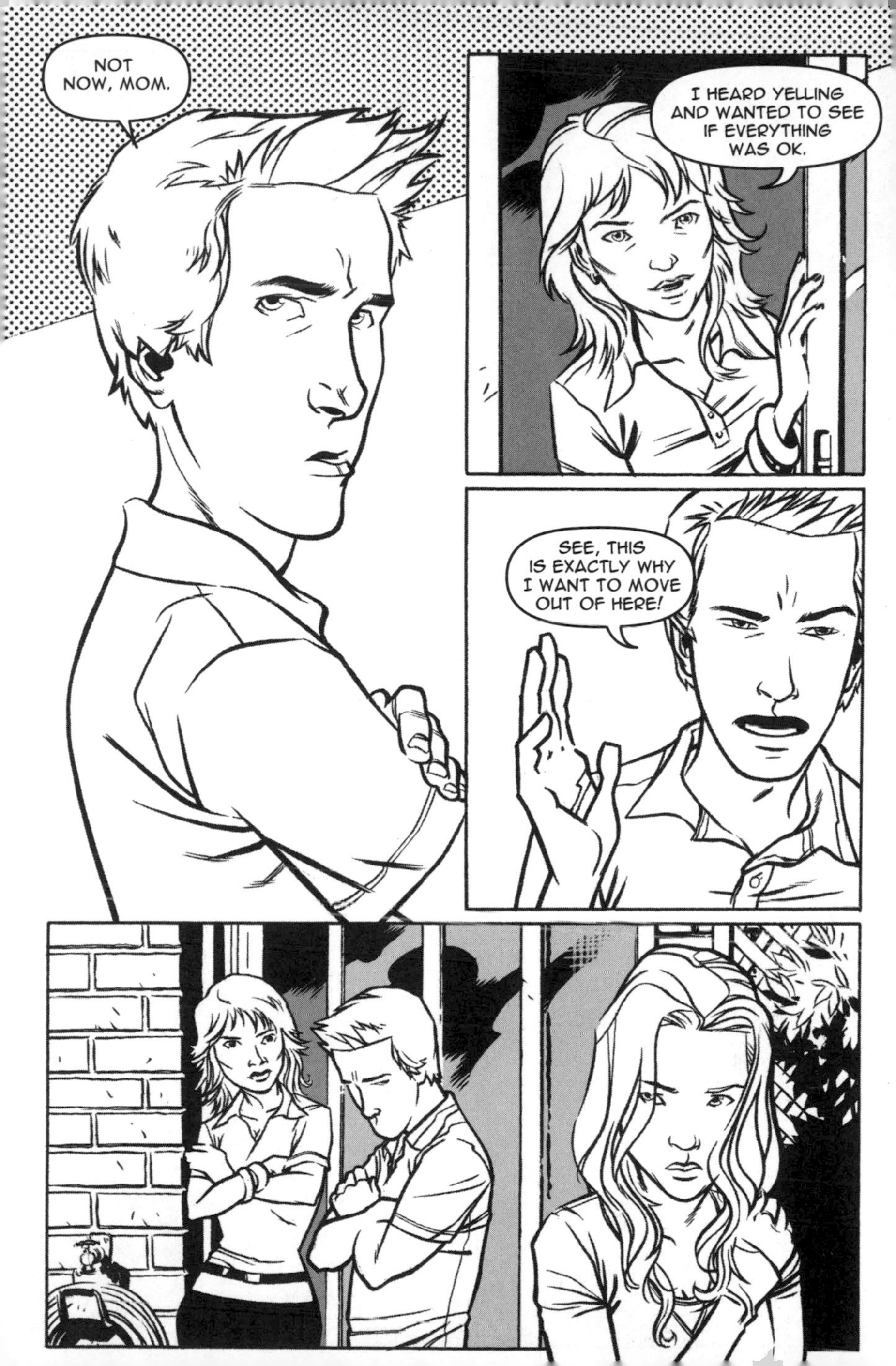
NOT NOW, MOM.
I HEARD YELLING AND WANTED TO SEE IF EVERYTHING WAS OK.
SEE, THIS IS EXACTLY WHY I WANT TO MOVE OUT OF HERE!

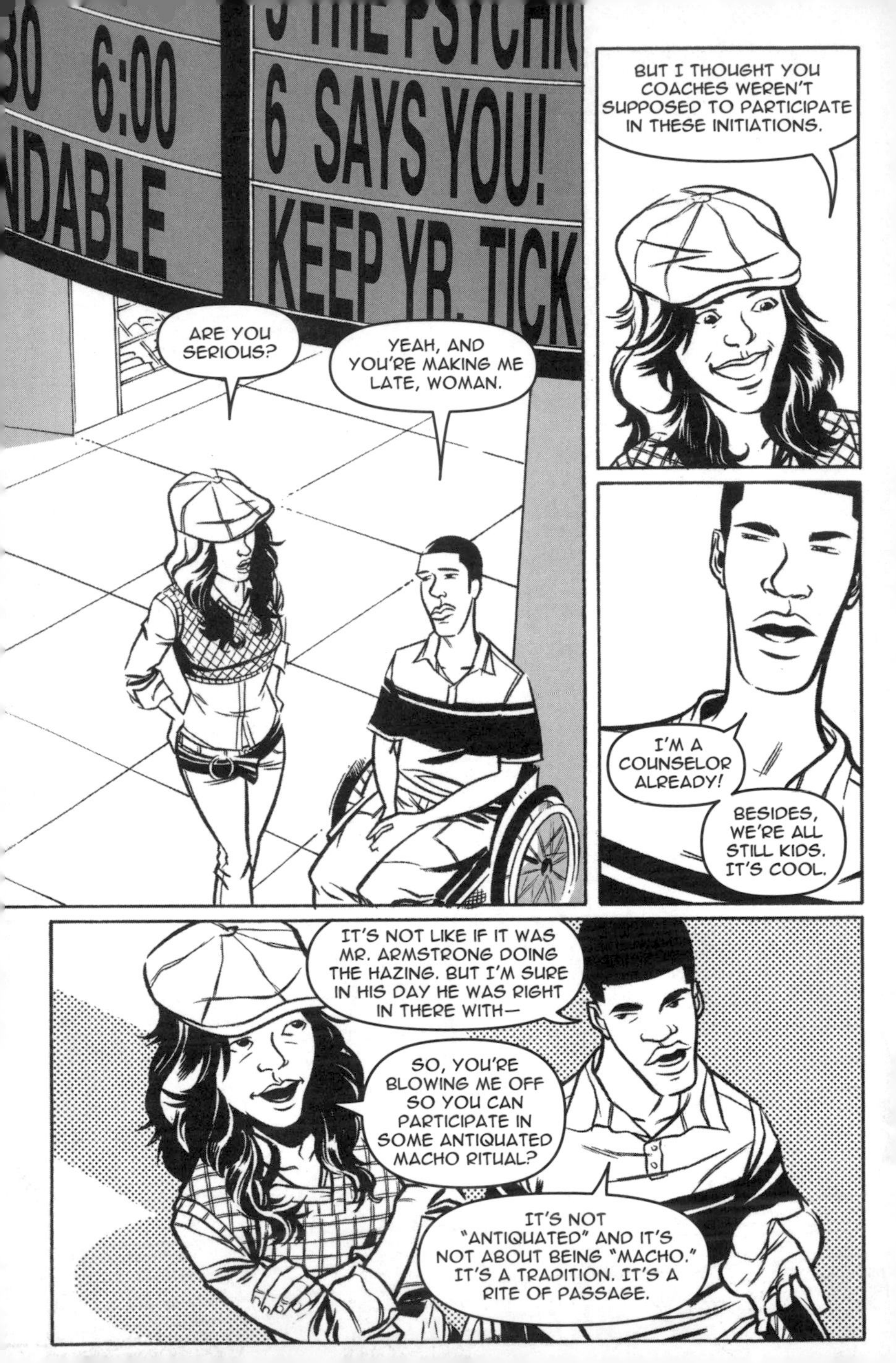
30 6:00
NDABLE
S THE PSYCHIC
6 SAYS YOU!
KEEP YR. TICK
ARE YOU SERIOUS?
YEAH, AND YOU'RE MAKING ME LATE, WOMAN.
BUT I THOUGHT YOU COACHES WEREN'T SUPPOSED TO PARTICIPATE IN THESE INITIATIONS.
I'M A COUNSELOR ALREADY!
BESIDES, WE'RE ALL STILL KIDS. IT'S COOL.
IT'S NOT LIKE IF IT WAS MR. ARMSTRONG DOING THE HAZING. BUT I'M SURE IN HIS DAY HE WAS RIGHT IN THERE WITH—
SO, YOU'RE BLOWING ME OFF SO YOU CAN PARTICIPATE IN SOME ANTIQUATED MACHO RITUAL?
IT'S NOT "ANTIQUATED" AND IT'S NOT ABOUT BEING "MACHO." IT'S A TRADITION. IT'S A RITE OF PASSAGE.

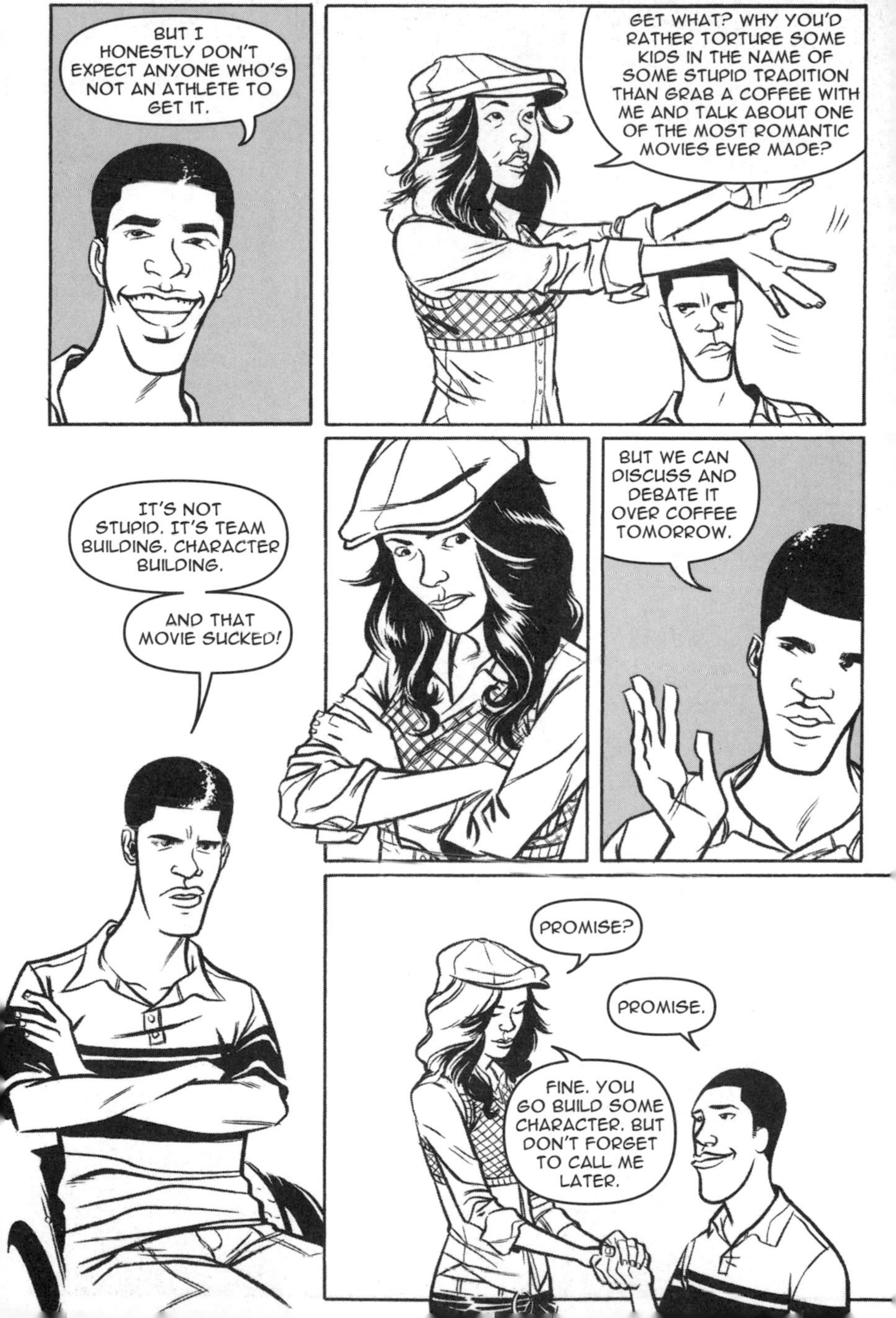
BUT I HONESTLY DON'T EXPECT ANYONE WHO'S NOT AN ATHLETE TO GET IT.
GET WHAT? WHY YOU'D RATHER TORTURE SOME KIDS IN THE NAME OF SOME STUPID TRADITION THAN GRAB A COFFEE WITH ME AND TALK ABOUT ONE OF THE MOST ROMANTIC MOVIES EVER MADE?
IT'S NOT STUPID. IT'S TEAM BUILDING. CHARACTER BUILDING.
AND THAT MOVIE SUCKED!
BUT WE CAN DISCUSS AND DEBATE IT OVER COFFEE TOMORROW.
PROMISE?
PROMISE.
FINE. YOU GO BUILD SOME CHARACTER. BUT DON'T FORGET TO CALL ME LATER.

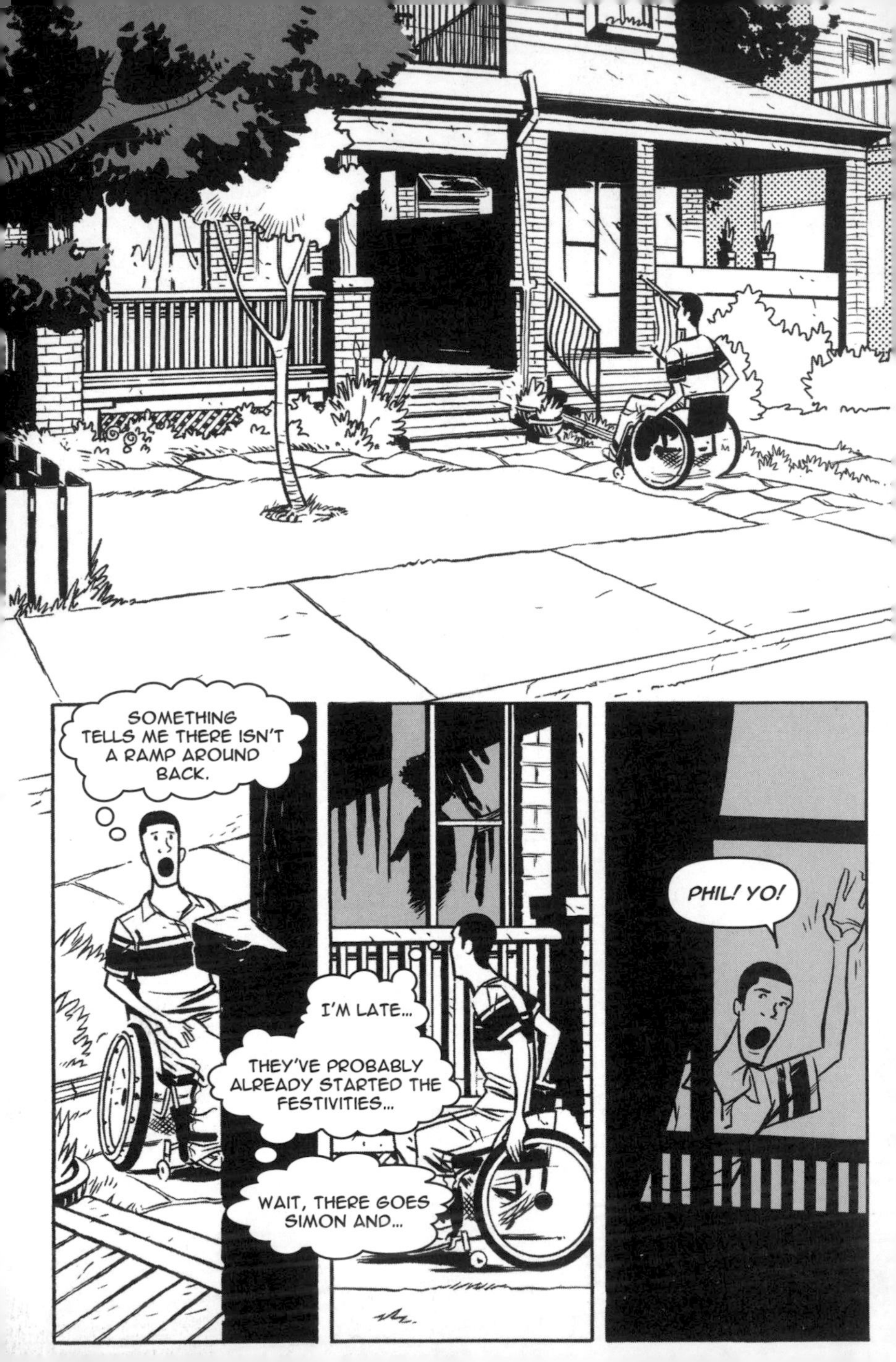
SOMETHING TELLS ME THERE ISN'T A RAMP AROUND BACK.
I'M LATE...
THEY'VE PROBABLY ALREADY STARTED THE FESTIVITIES...
WAIT, THERE GOES SIMON AND...
PHIL! YO!

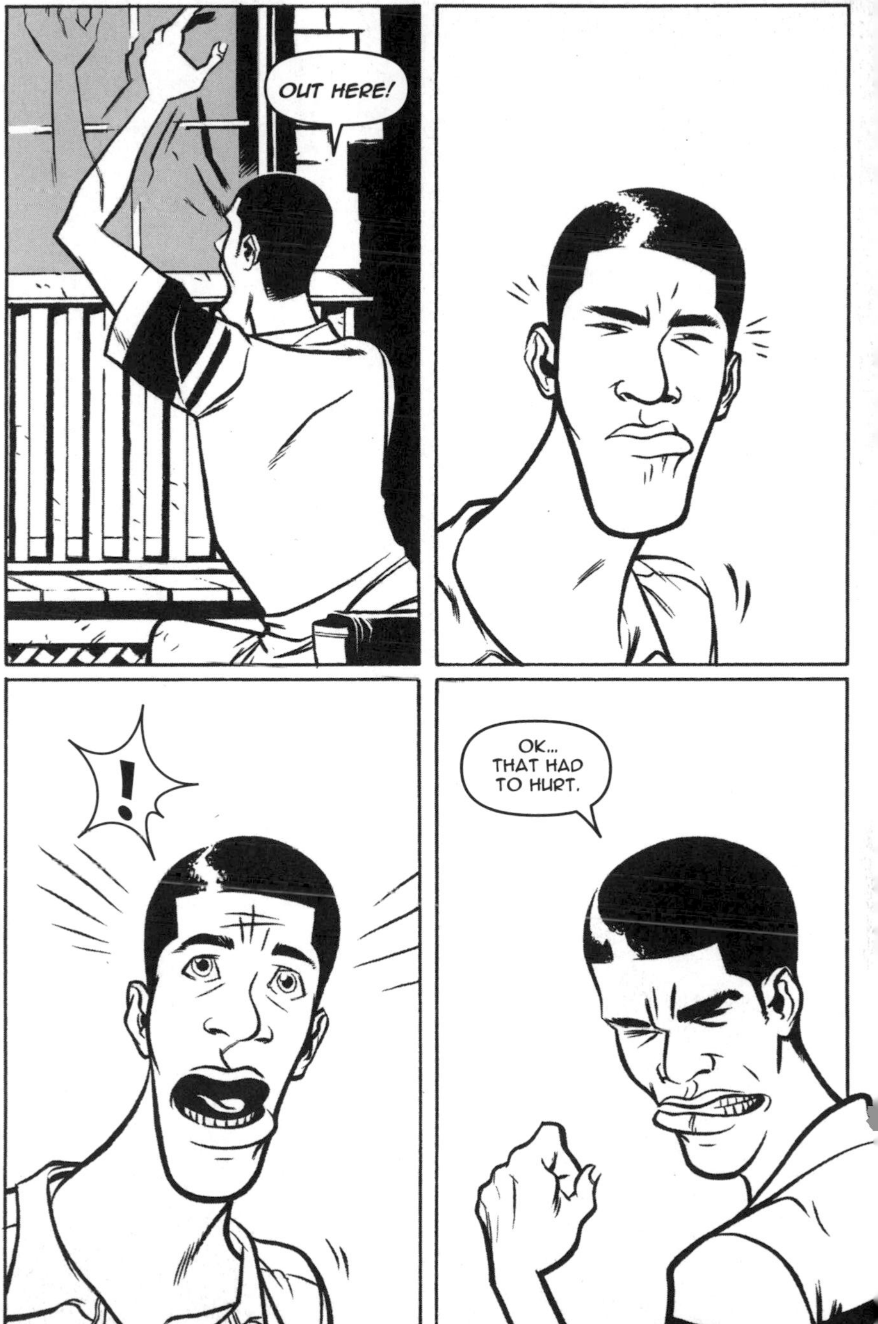
OUT HERE!
!
OK... THAT HAD TO HURT.

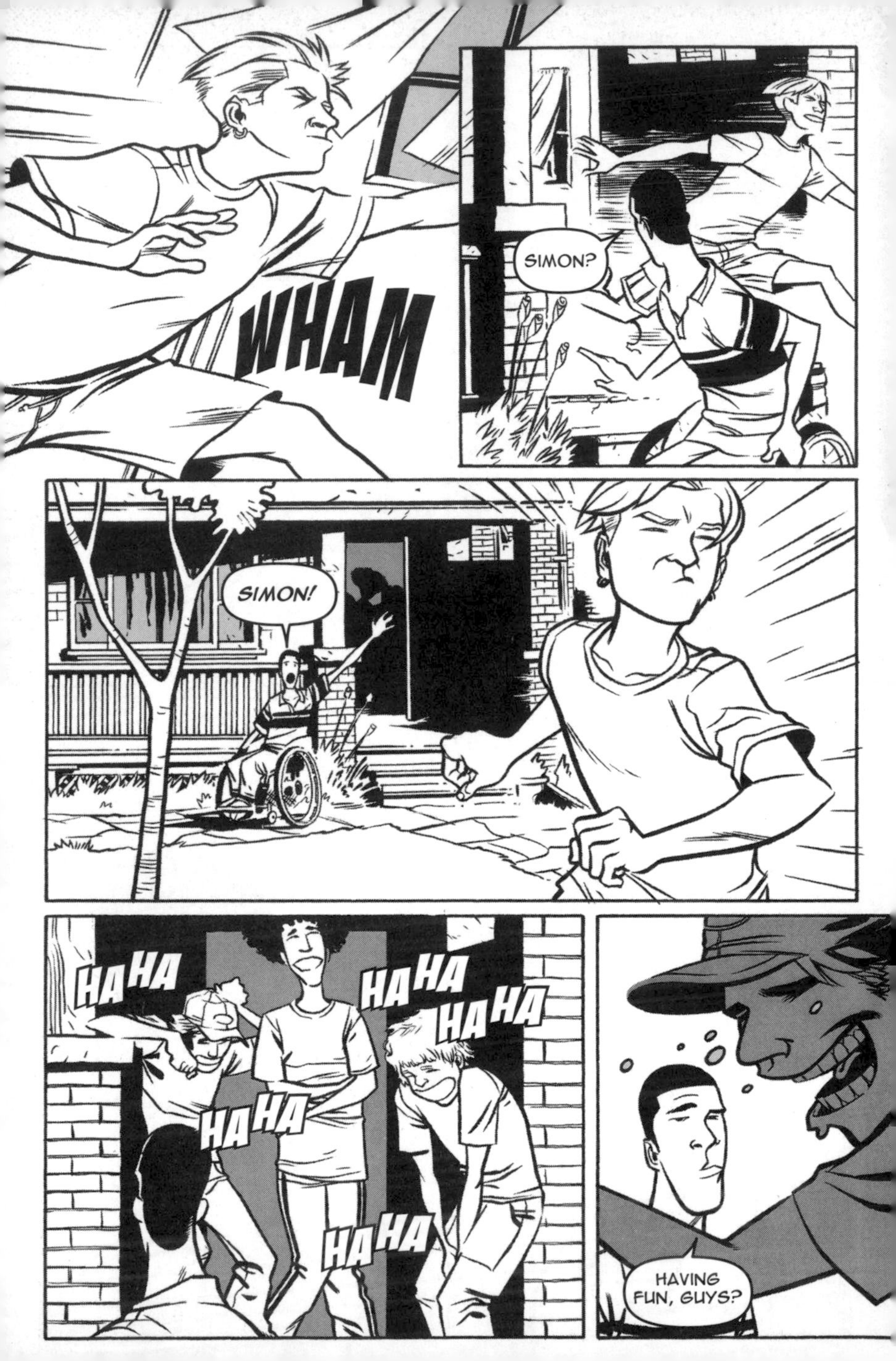
WHAM
SIMON?
SIMON!
HAHA
HAHA
HAHA
HAHA
HAHA
HAVING FUN, GUYS?

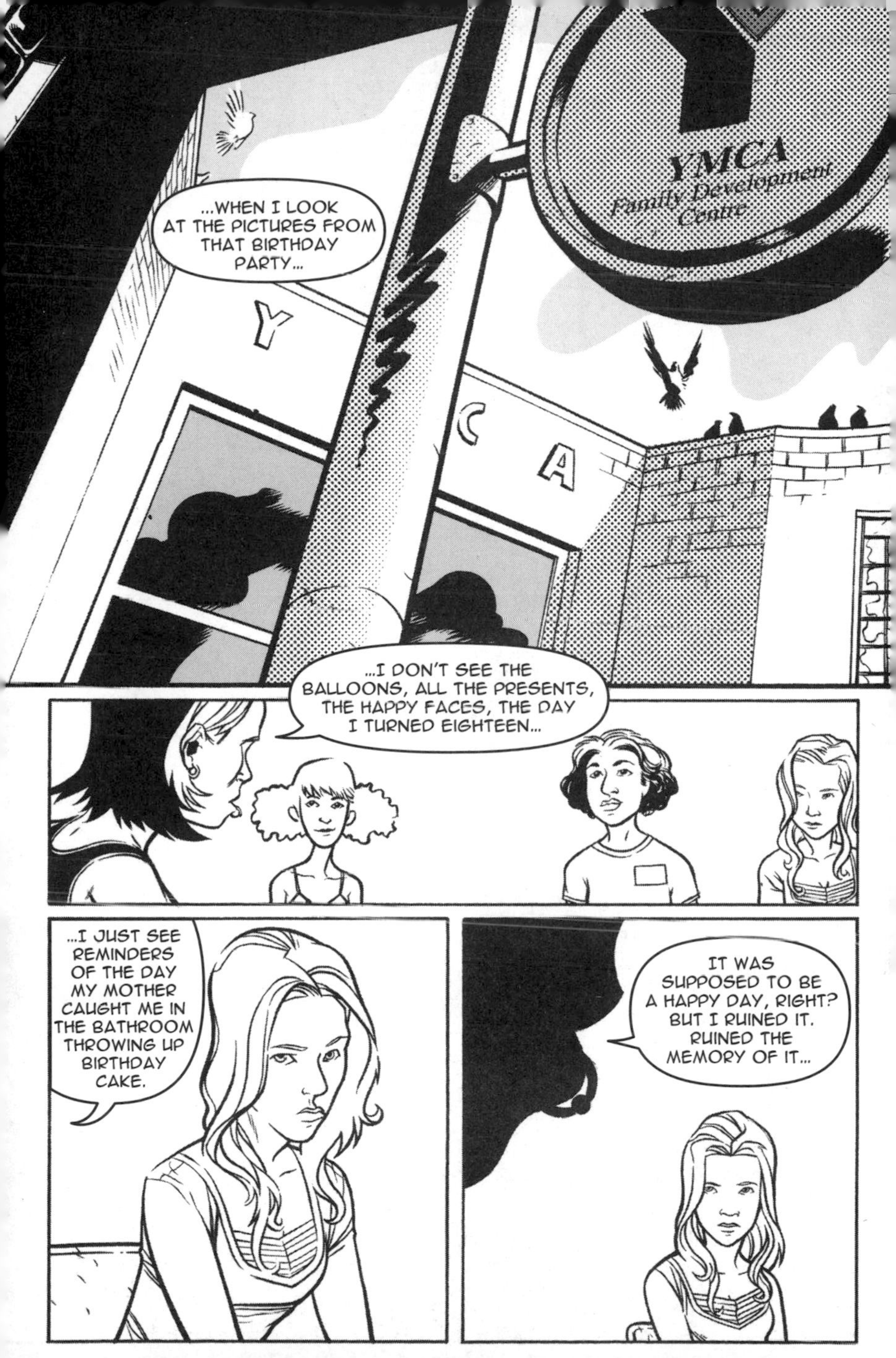
...WHEN I LOOK AT THE PICTURES FROM THAT BIRTHDAY PARTY...
YMCA Family Development Centre
Y C A
...I DON'T SEE THE BALLOONS, ALL THE PRESENTS, THE HAPPY FACES, THE DAY I TURNED EIGHTEEN...
...I JUST SEE REMINDERS OF THE DAY MY MOTHER CAUGHT ME IN THE BATHROOM THROWING UP BIRTHDAY CAKE.
IT WAS SUPPOSED TO BE A HAPPY DAY, RIGHT? BUT I RUINED IT. RUINED THE MEMORY OF IT...

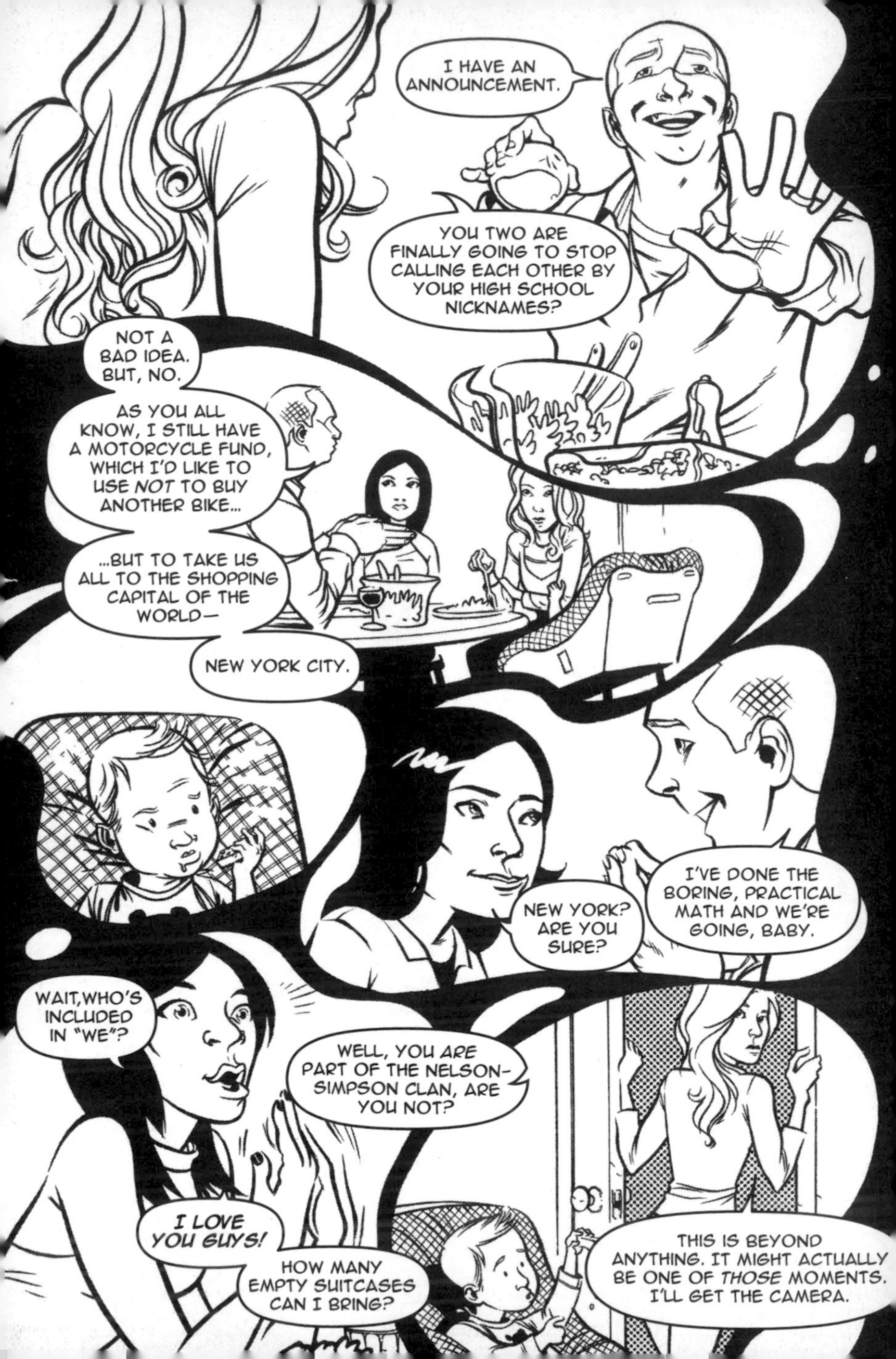
I HAVE AN ANNOUNCEMENT.
YOU TWO ARE FINALLY GOING TO STOP CALLING EACH OTHER BY YOUR HIGH SCHOOL NICKNAMES?
NOT A BAD IDEA. BUT, NO.
AS YOU ALL KNOW, I STILL HAVE A MOTORCYCLE FUND, WHICH I'D LIKE TO USE *NOT* TO BUY ANOTHER BIKE...
...BUT TO TAKE US ALL TO THE SHOPPING CAPITAL OF THE WORLD—
NEW YORK CITY.
NEW YORK? ARE YOU SURE?
I'VE DONE THE BORING, PRACTICAL MATH AND WE'RE GOING, BABY.
WAIT,WHO'S INCLUDED IN "WE"?
WELL, YOU *ARE* PART OF THE NELSON-SIMPSON CLAN, ARE YOU NOT?
I LOVE YOU GUYS!
HOW MANY EMPTY SUITCASES CAN I BRING?
THIS IS BEYOND ANYTHING. IT MIGHT ACTUALLY BE ONE OF *THOSE* MOMENTS. I'LL GET THE CAMERA.

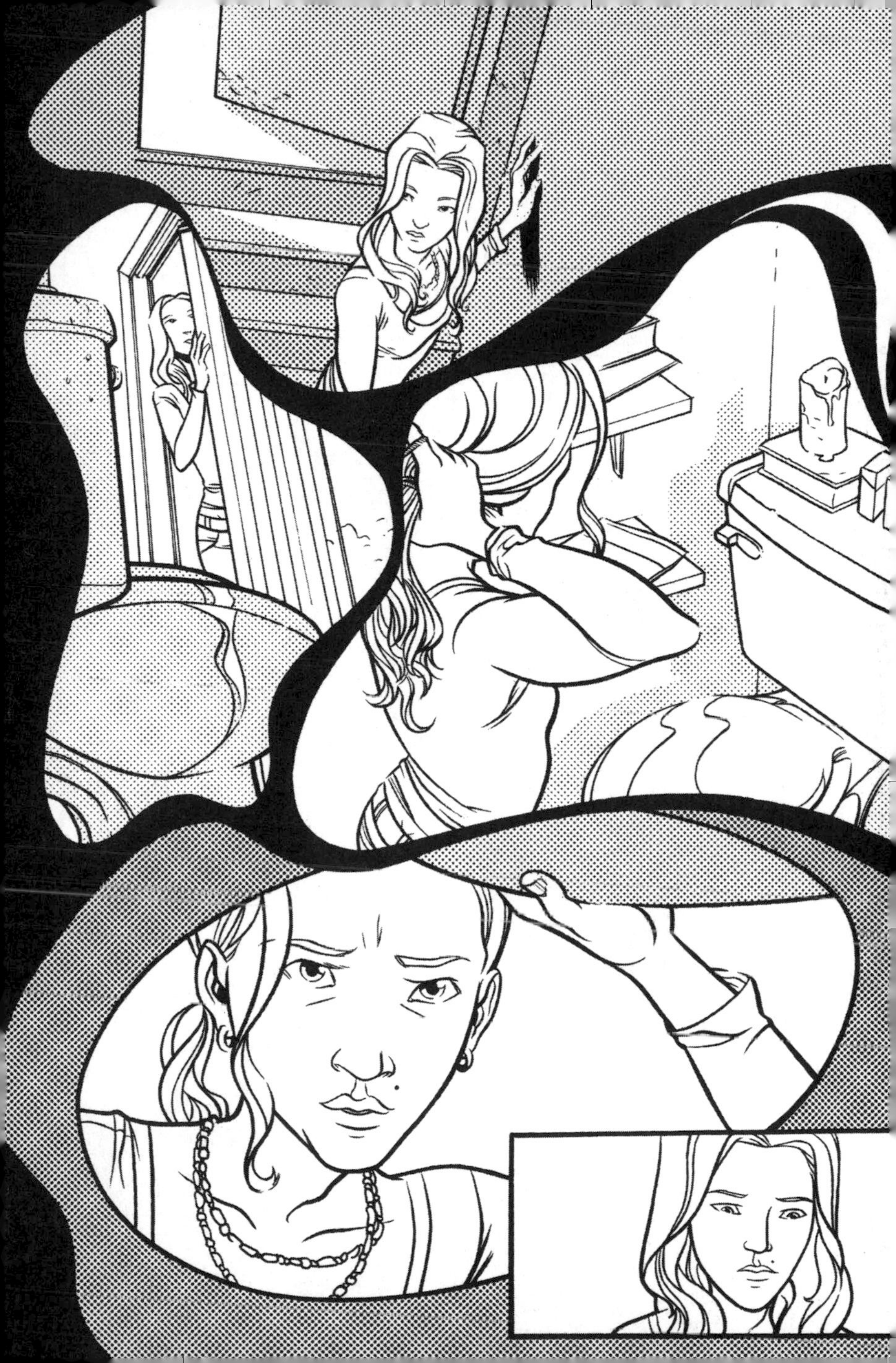

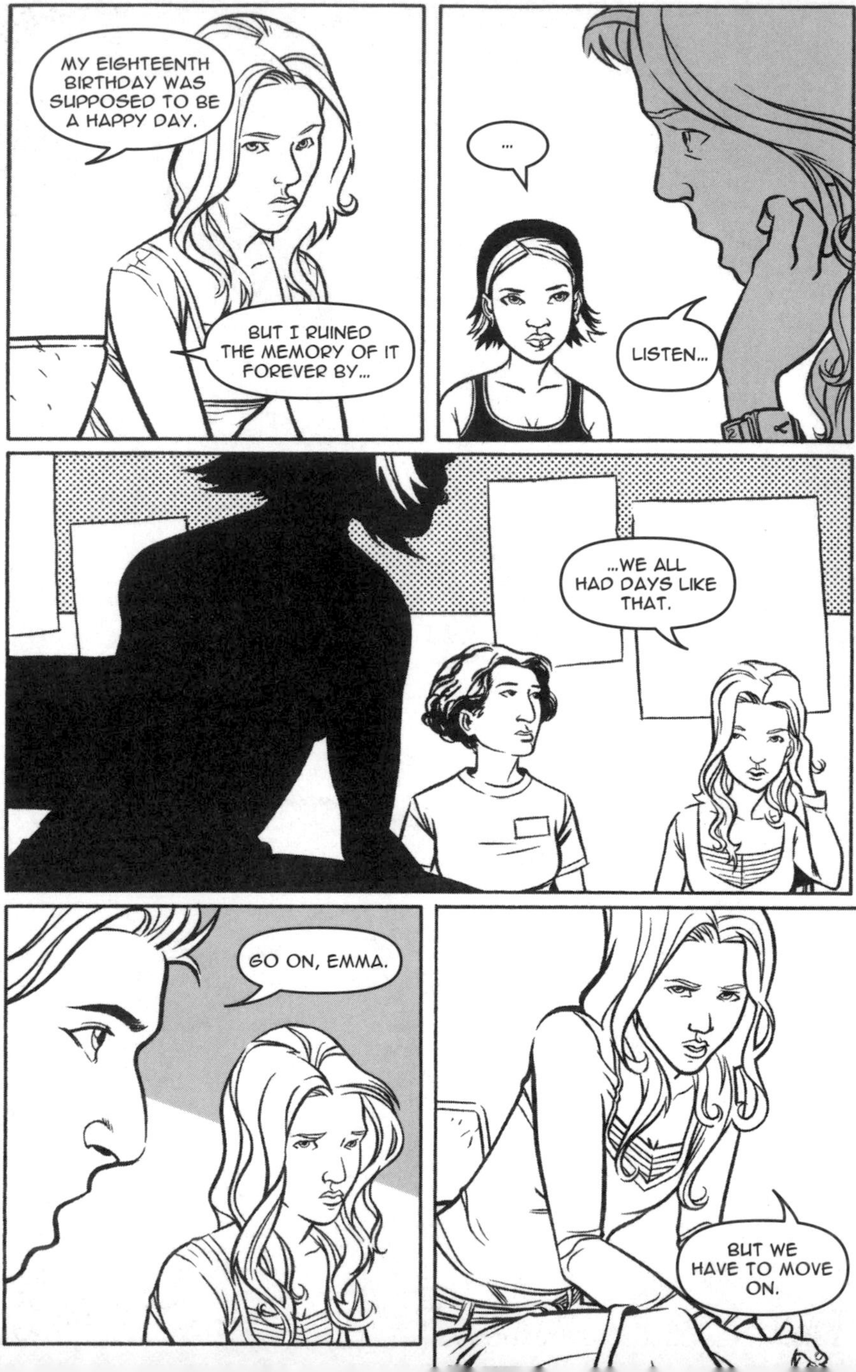
MY EIGHTEENTH BIRTHDAY WAS SUPPOSED TO BE A HAPPY DAY.
BUT I RUINED THE MEMORY OF IT FOREVER BY...
...
LISTEN...
...WE ALL HAD DAYS LIKE THAT.
GO ON, EMMA.
BUT WE HAVE TO MOVE ON.

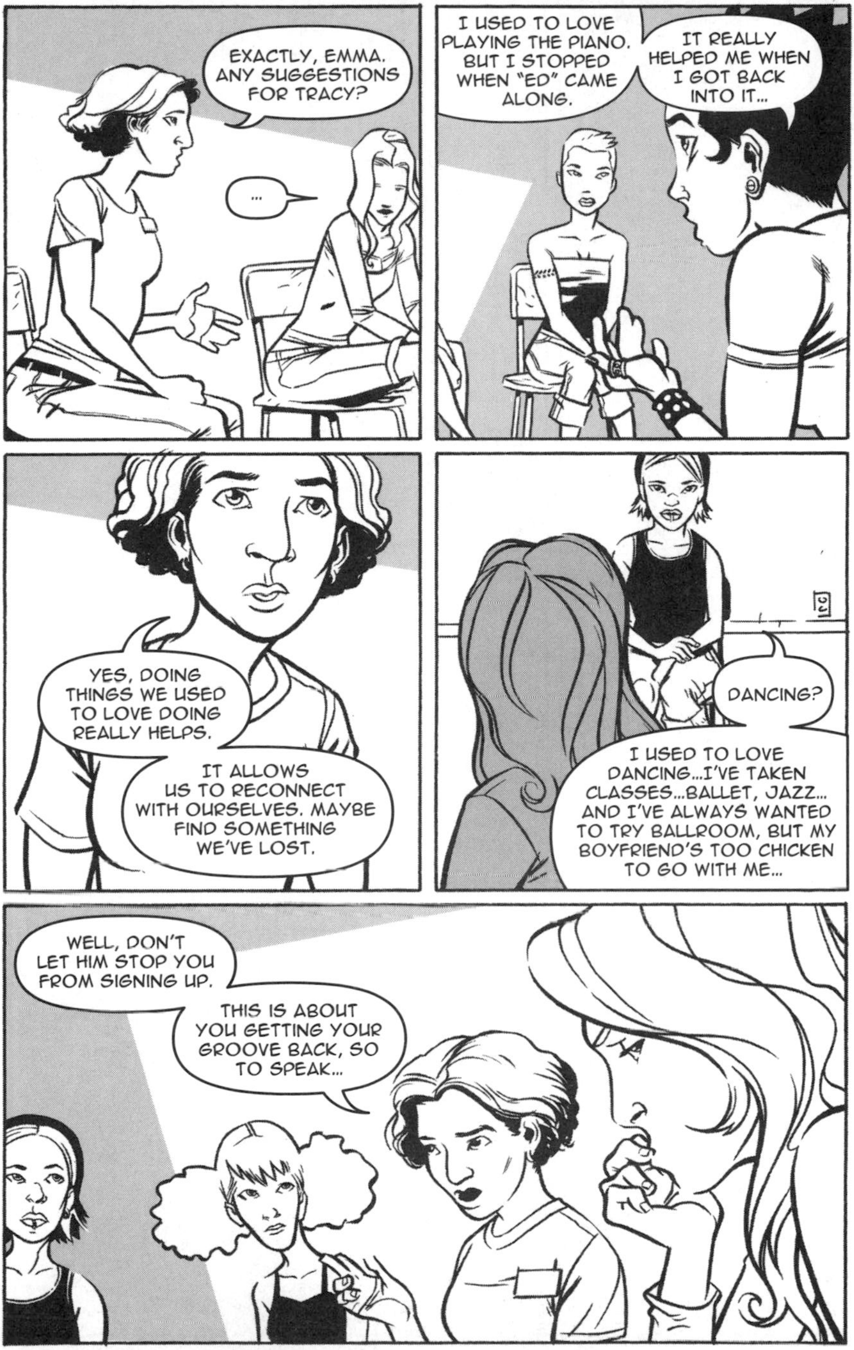
EXACTLY, EMMA. ANY SUGGESTIONS FOR TRACY?
...
I USED TO LOVE PLAYING THE PIANO. BUT I STOPPED WHEN "ED" CAME ALONG.
IT REALLY HELPED ME WHEN I GOT BACK INTO IT...
YES, DOING THINGS WE USED TO LOVE DOING REALLY HELPS.
IT ALLOWS US TO RECONNECT WITH OURSELVES. MAYBE FIND SOMETHING WE'VE LOST.
DANCING?
I USED TO LOVE DANCING...I'VE TAKEN CLASSES...BALLET, JAZZ... AND I'VE ALWAYS WANTED TO TRY BALLROOM, BUT MY BOYFRIEND'S TOO CHICKEN TO GO WITH ME...
WELL, DON'T LET HIM STOP YOU FROM SIGNING UP.
THIS IS ABOUT YOU GETTING YOUR GROOVE BACK, SO TO SPEAK...

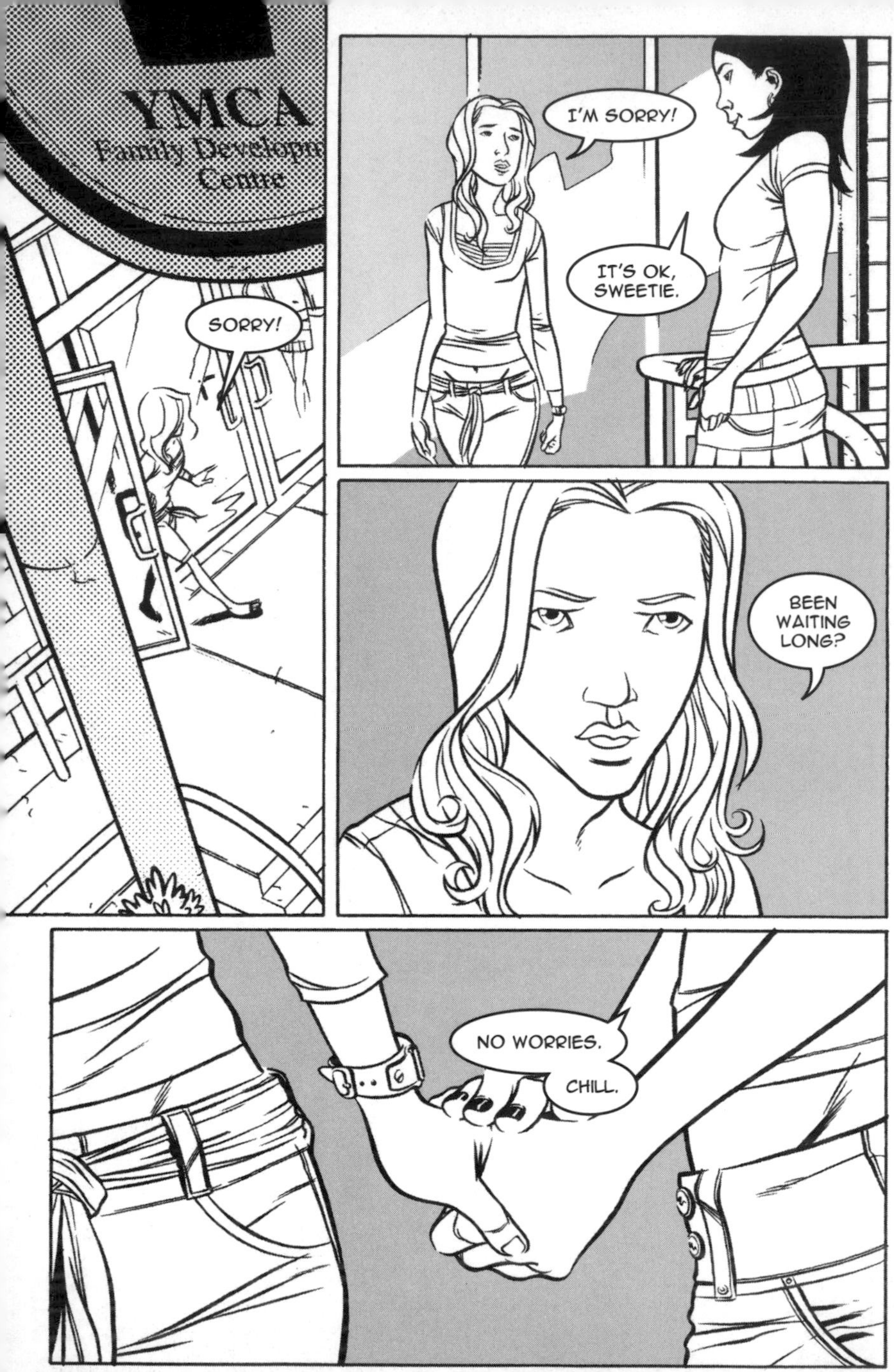
YMCA
Family Developm
Centre
SORRY!
I'M SORRY!
IT'S OK, SWEETIE.
BEEN WAITING LONG?
NO WORRIES.
CHILL.

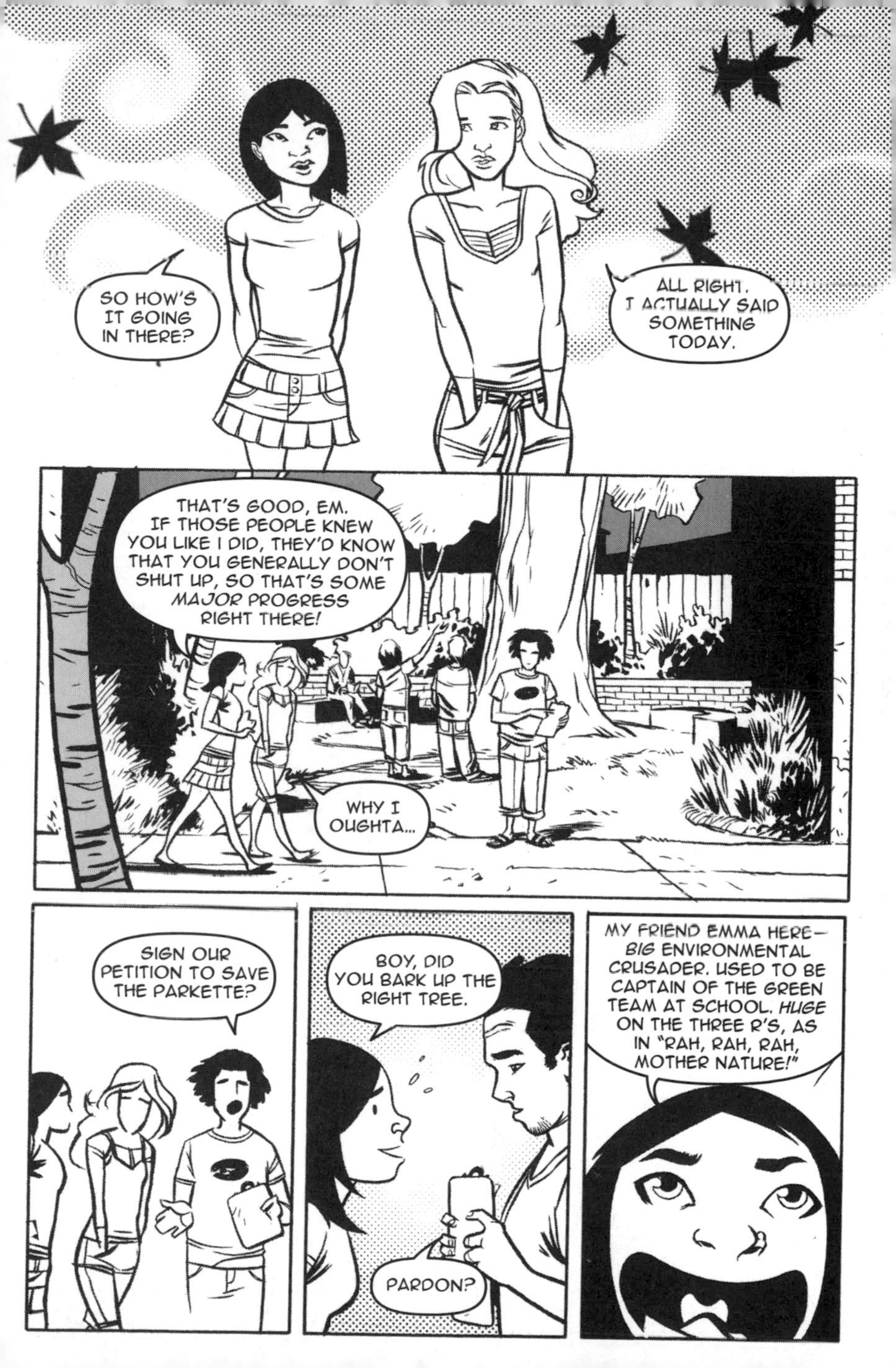

SO HOW'S IT GOING IN THERE?
ALL RIGHT. I ACTUALLY SAID SOMETHING TODAY.
THAT'S GOOD, EM. IF THOSE PEOPLE KNEW YOU LIKE I DID, THEY'D KNOW THAT YOU GENERALLY DON'T SHUT UP, SO THAT'S SOME *MAJOR* PROGRESS RIGHT THERE!
WHY I OUGHTA...
SIGN OUR PETITION TO SAVE THE PARKETTE?
BOY, DID YOU BARK UP THE RIGHT TREE.
PARDON?
MY FRIEND EMMA HERE— *BIG* ENVIRONMENTAL CRUSADER. USED TO BE CAPTAIN OF THE GREEN TEAM AT SCHOOL. *HUGE* ON THE THREE R'S, AS IN "RAH, RAH, RAH, MOTHER NATURE!"

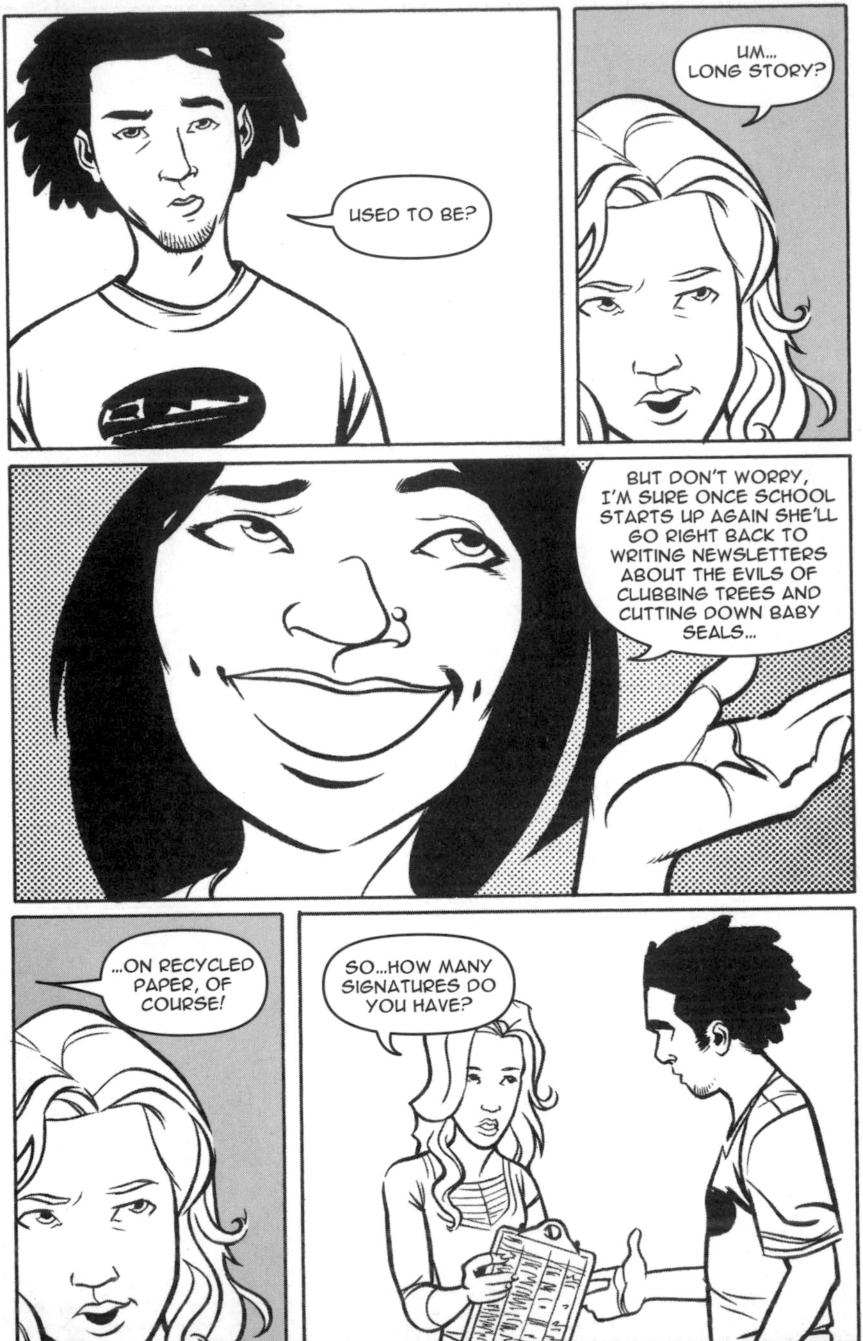
USED TO BE?
UM... LONG STORY?
BUT DON'T WORRY, I'M SURE ONCE SCHOOL STARTS UP AGAIN SHE'LL GO RIGHT BACK TO WRITING NEWSLETTERS ABOUT THE EVILS OF CLUBBING TREES AND CUTTING DOWN BABY SEALS...
...ON RECYCLED PAPER, OF COURSE!
SO...HOW MANY SIGNATURES DO YOU HAVE?

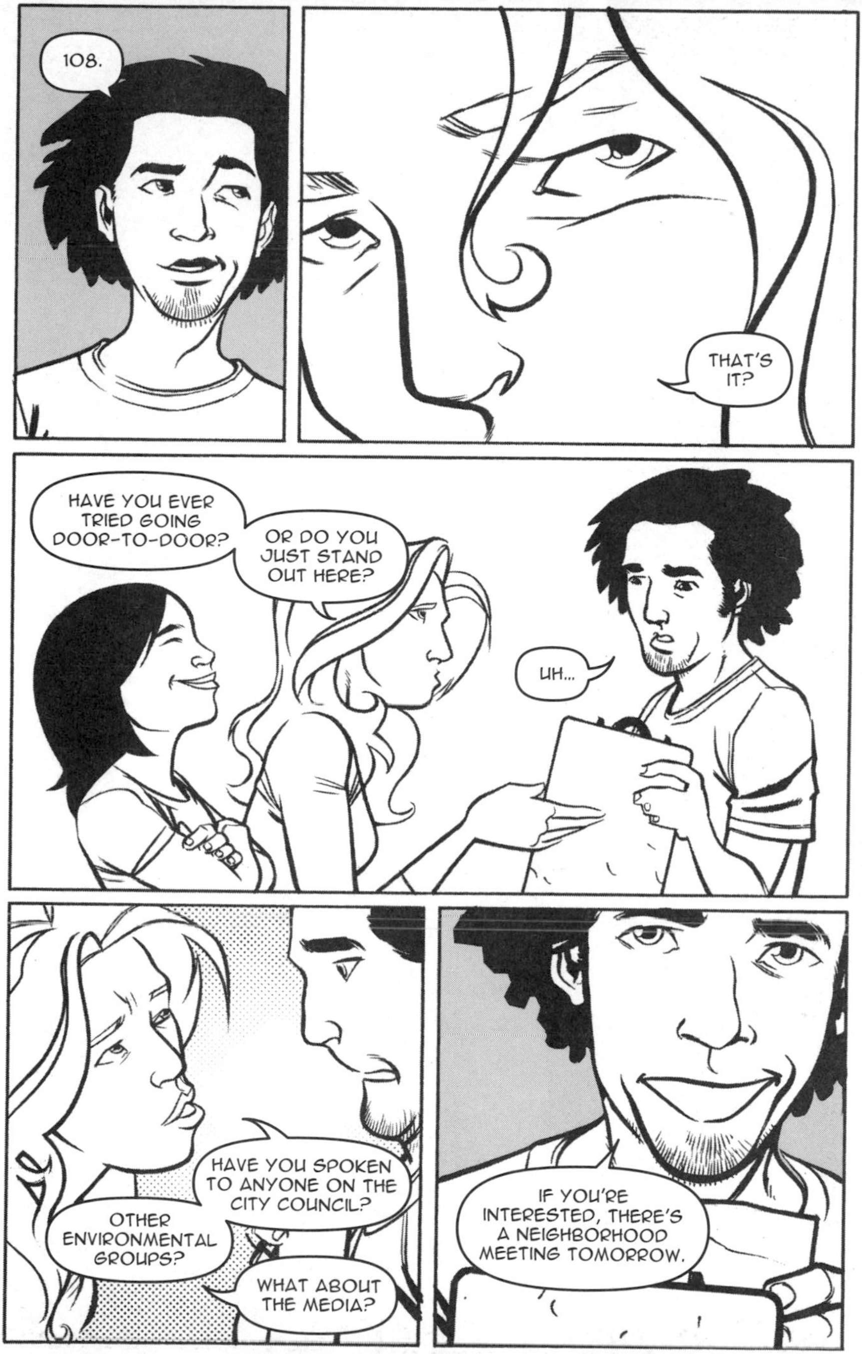
108.
THAT'S IT?
HAVE YOU EVER TRIED GOING DOOR-TO-DOOR?
OR DO YOU JUST STAND OUT HERE?
UH...
HAVE YOU SPOKEN TO ANYONE ON THE CITY COUNCIL?
OTHER ENVIRONMENTAL GROUPS?
WHAT ABOUT THE MEDIA?
IF YOU'RE INTERESTED, THERE'S A NEIGHBORHOOD MEETING TOMORROW.

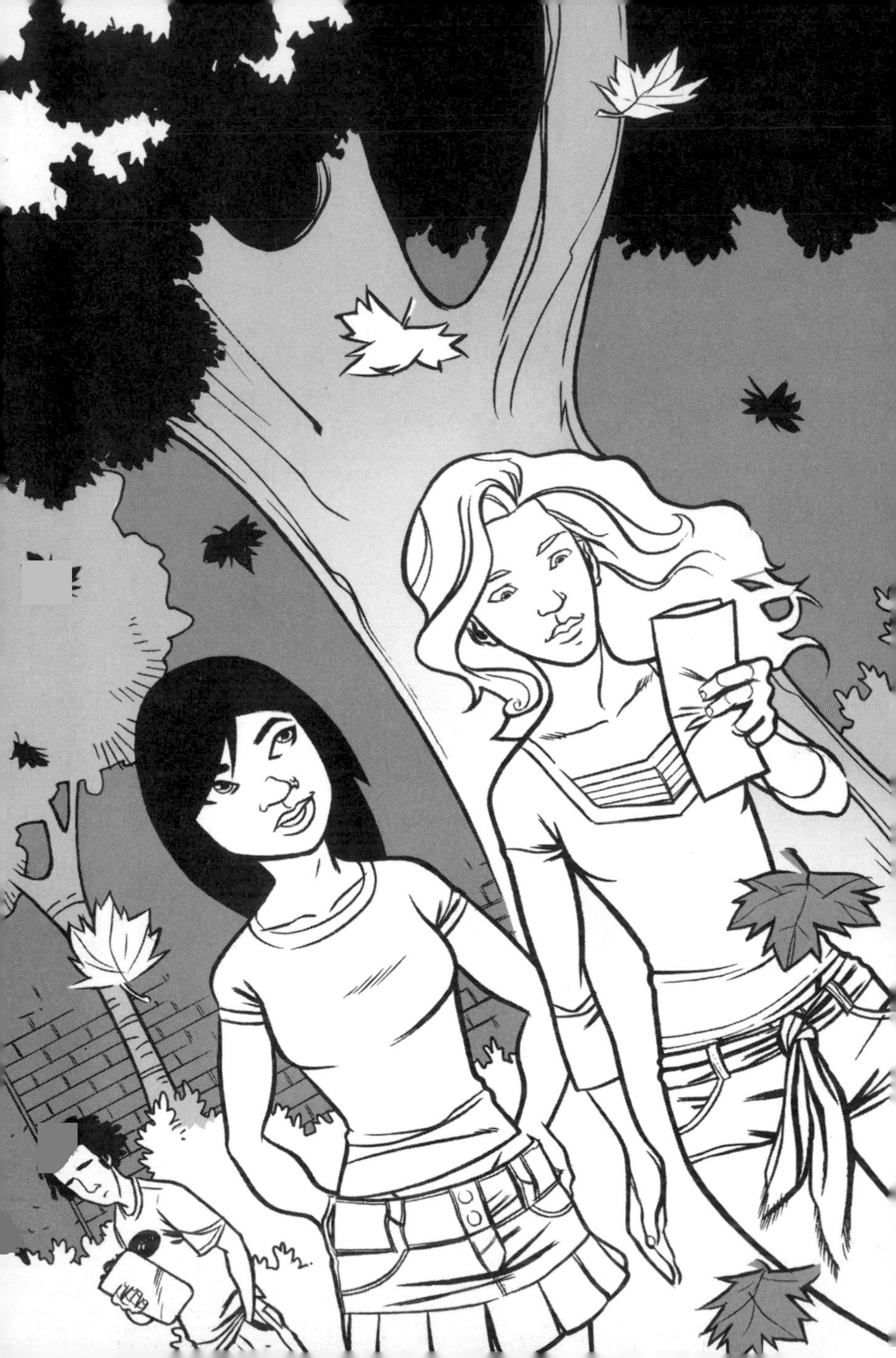

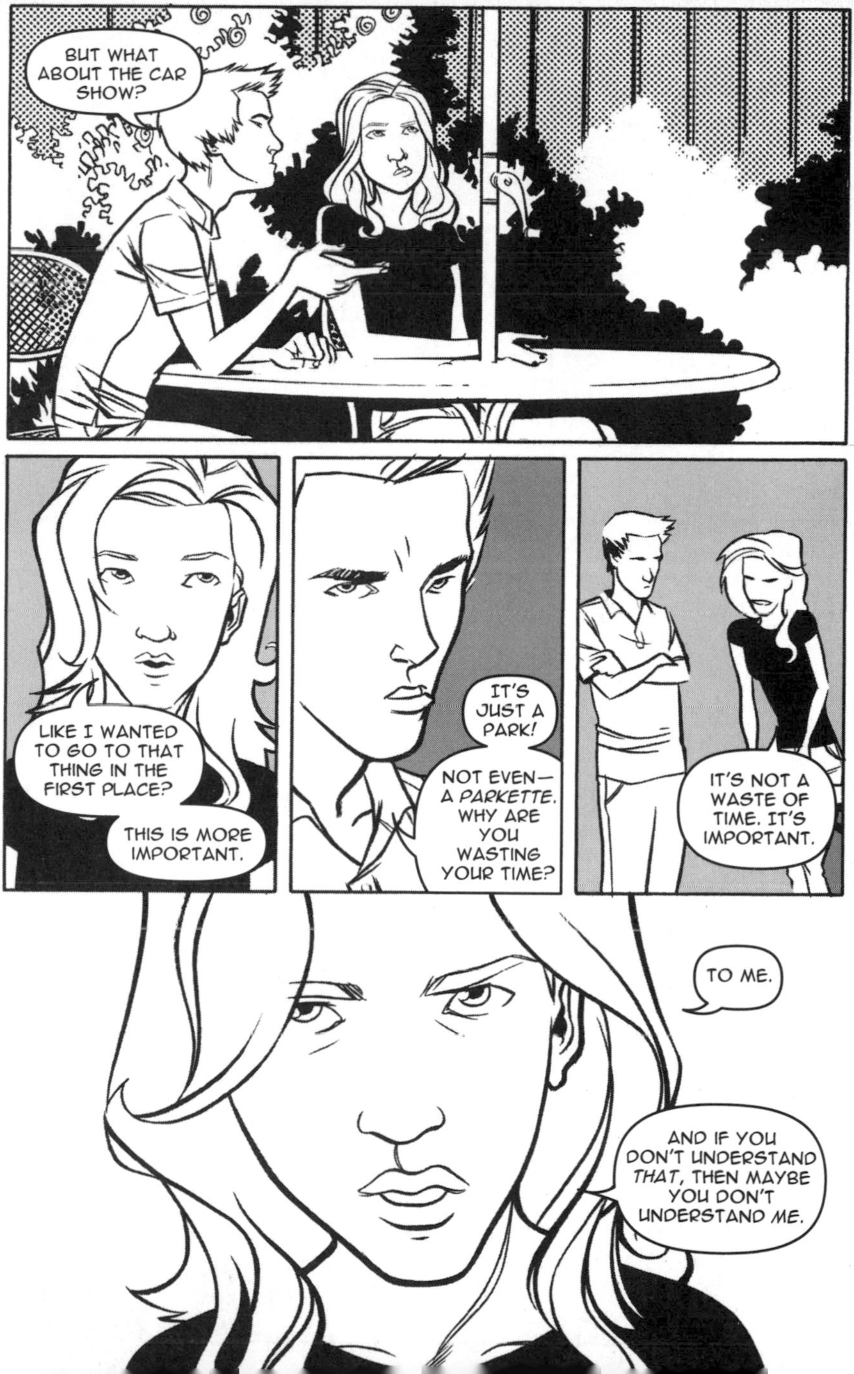
BUT WHAT ABOUT THE CAR SHOW?
LIKE I WANTED TO GO TO THAT THING IN THE FIRST PLACE?
THIS IS MORE IMPORTANT.
IT'S JUST A PARK!
NOT EVEN— A *PARKETTE*. WHY ARE YOU WASTING YOUR TIME?
IT'S NOT A WASTE OF TIME. IT'S IMPORTANT.
TO ME.
AND IF YOU DON'T UNDERSTAND *THAT*, THEN MAYBE YOU DON'T UNDERSTAND *ME*.

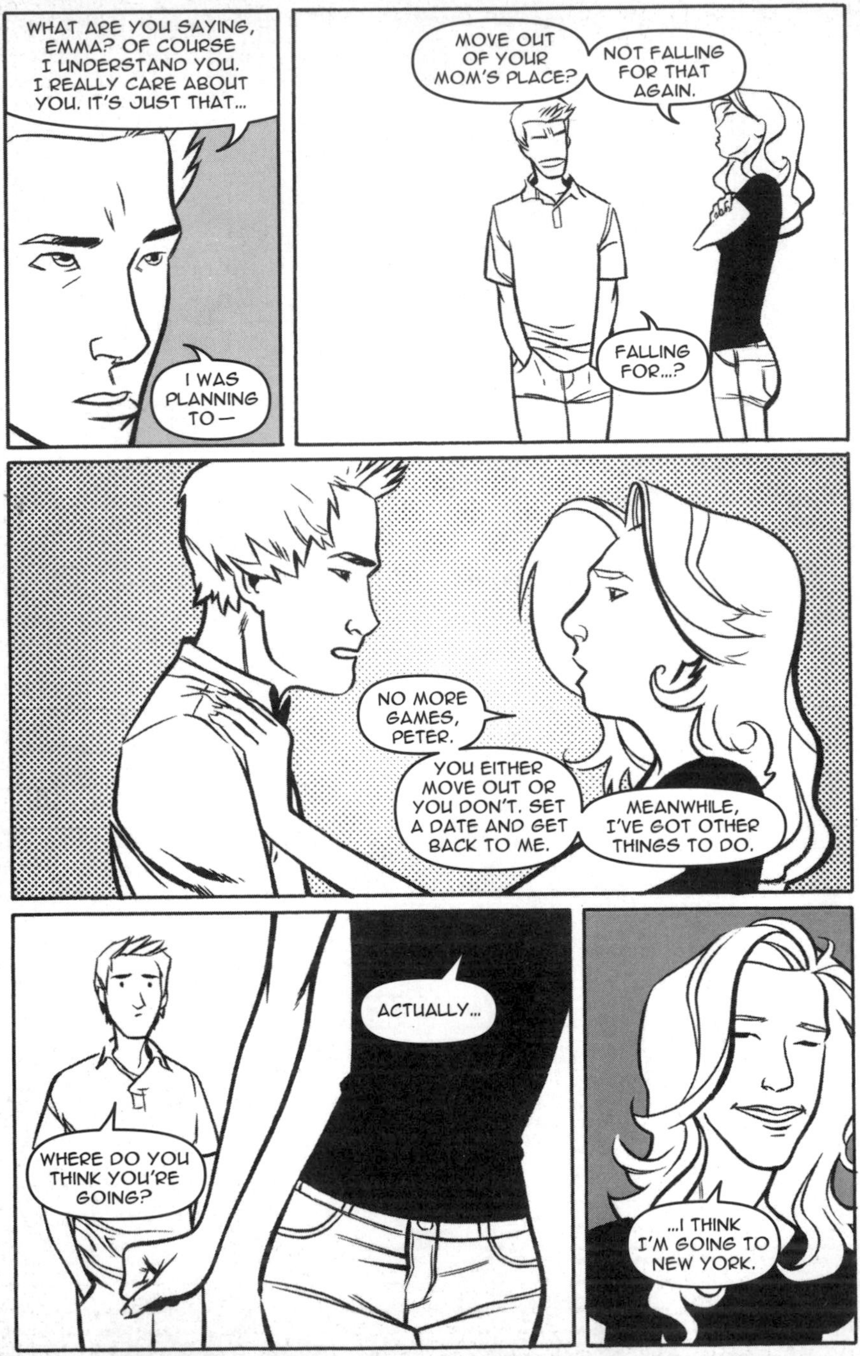
WHAT ARE YOU SAYING, EMMA? OF COURSE I UNDERSTAND YOU. I REALLY CARE ABOUT YOU. IT'S JUST THAT...
I WAS PLANNING TO—
MOVE OUT OF YOUR MOM'S PLACE?
NOT FALLING FOR THAT AGAIN.
FALLING FOR...?
NO MORE GAMES, PETER.
YOU EITHER MOVE OUT OR YOU DON'T. SET A DATE AND GET BACK TO ME.
MEANWHILE, I'VE GOT OTHER THINGS TO DO.
WHERE DO YOU THINK YOU'RE GOING?
ACTUALLY...
...I THINK I'M GOING TO NEW YORK.

ACT 2

"Sometimes I never leave, but sometimes I would.
Sometimes I stay too long, sometimes I would.
Sometimes it frightens me, sometimes it would.
Sometimes I'm all alone and wish that I could..."

—The Motels

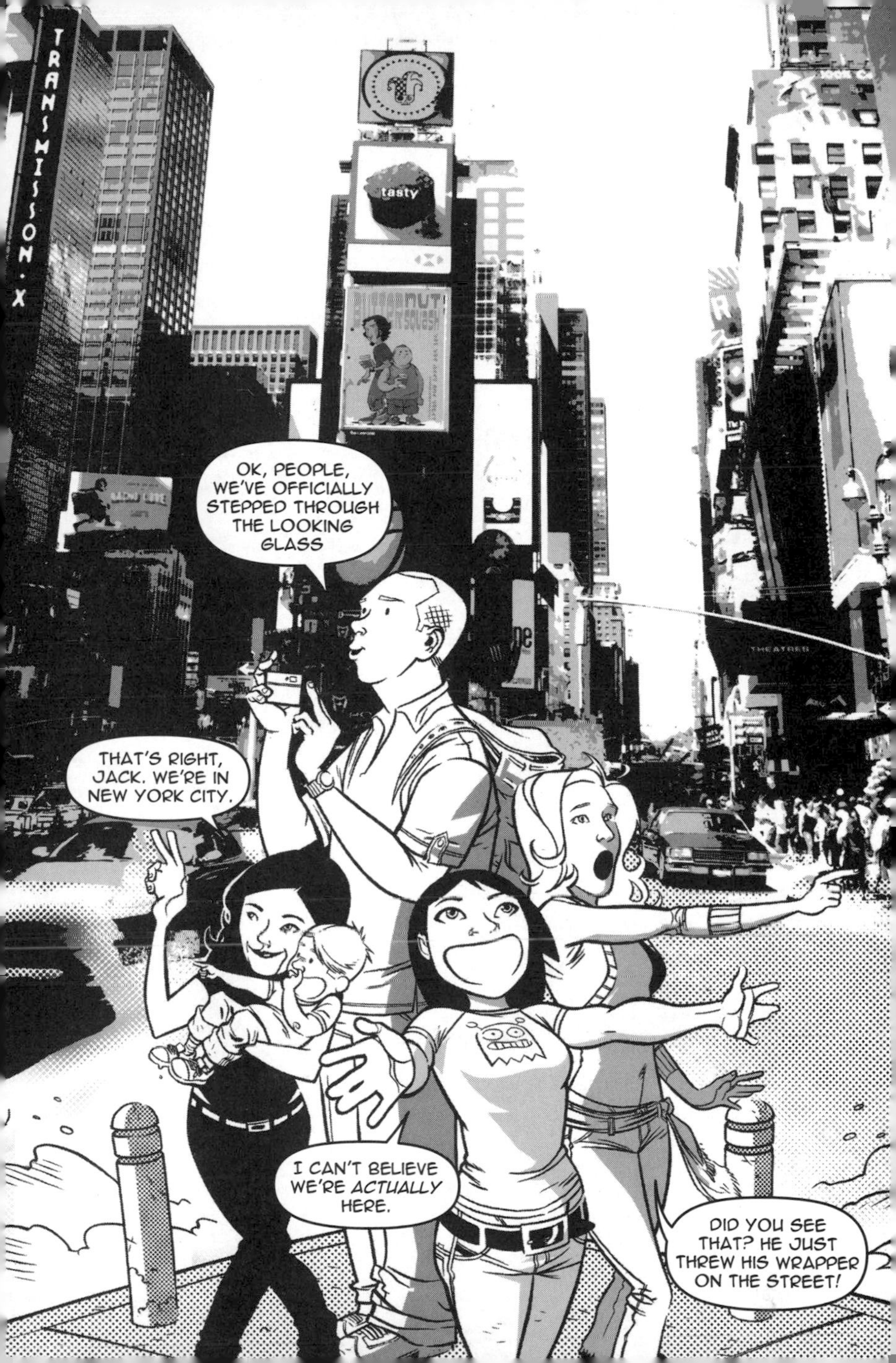
TRANSMISSION.X
tasty
OK, PEOPLE, WE'VE OFFICIALLY STEPPED THROUGH THE LOOKING GLASS
THAT'S RIGHT, JACK. WE'RE IN NEW YORK CITY.
I CAN'T BELIEVE WE'RE *ACTUALLY* HERE.
DID YOU SEE THAT? HE JUST THREW HIS WRAPPER ON THE STREET!

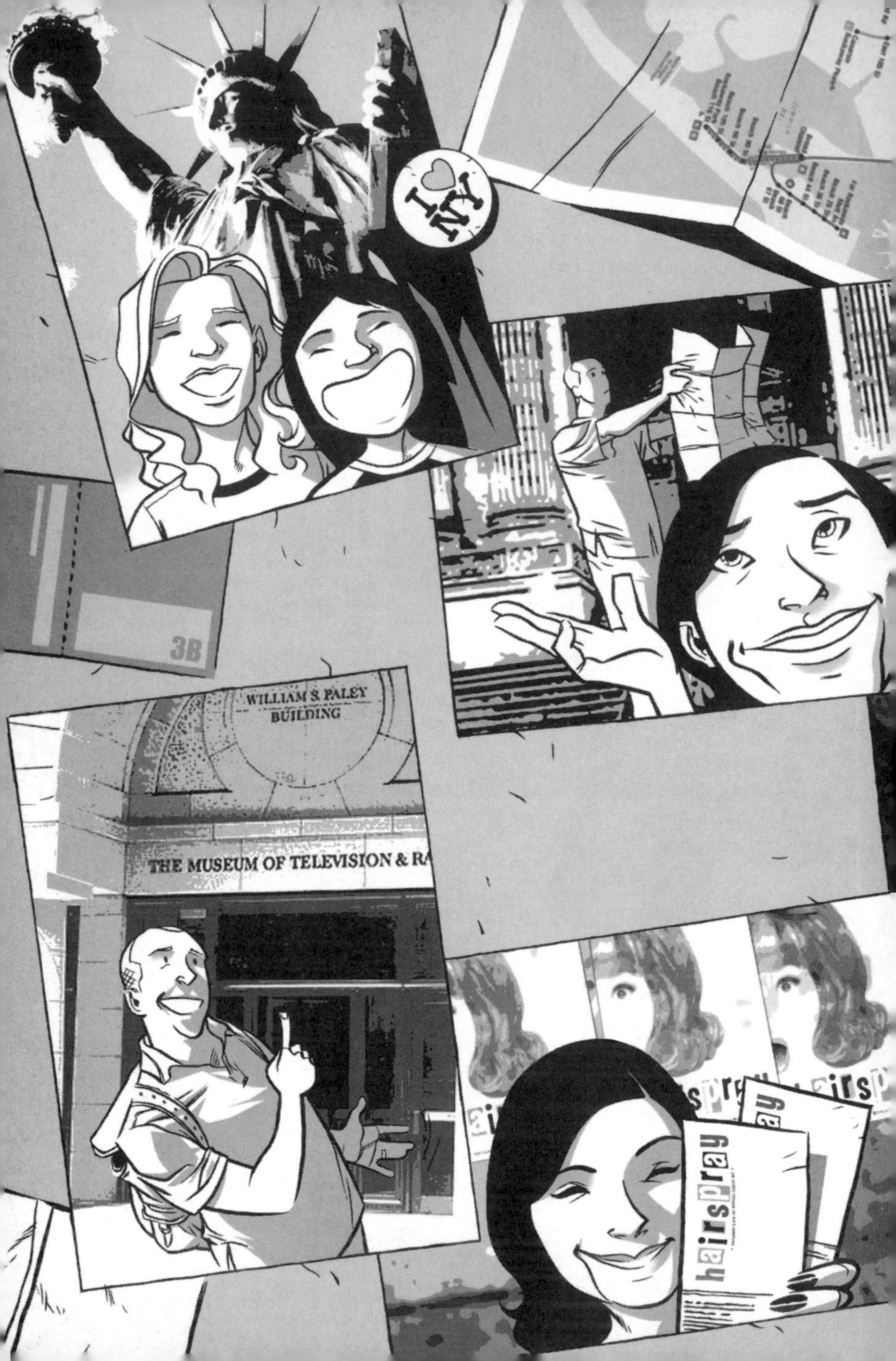

I ♥ NY
3B
WILLIAM S. PALEY
BUILDING
THE MUSEUM OF TELEVISION & RA
hairspray

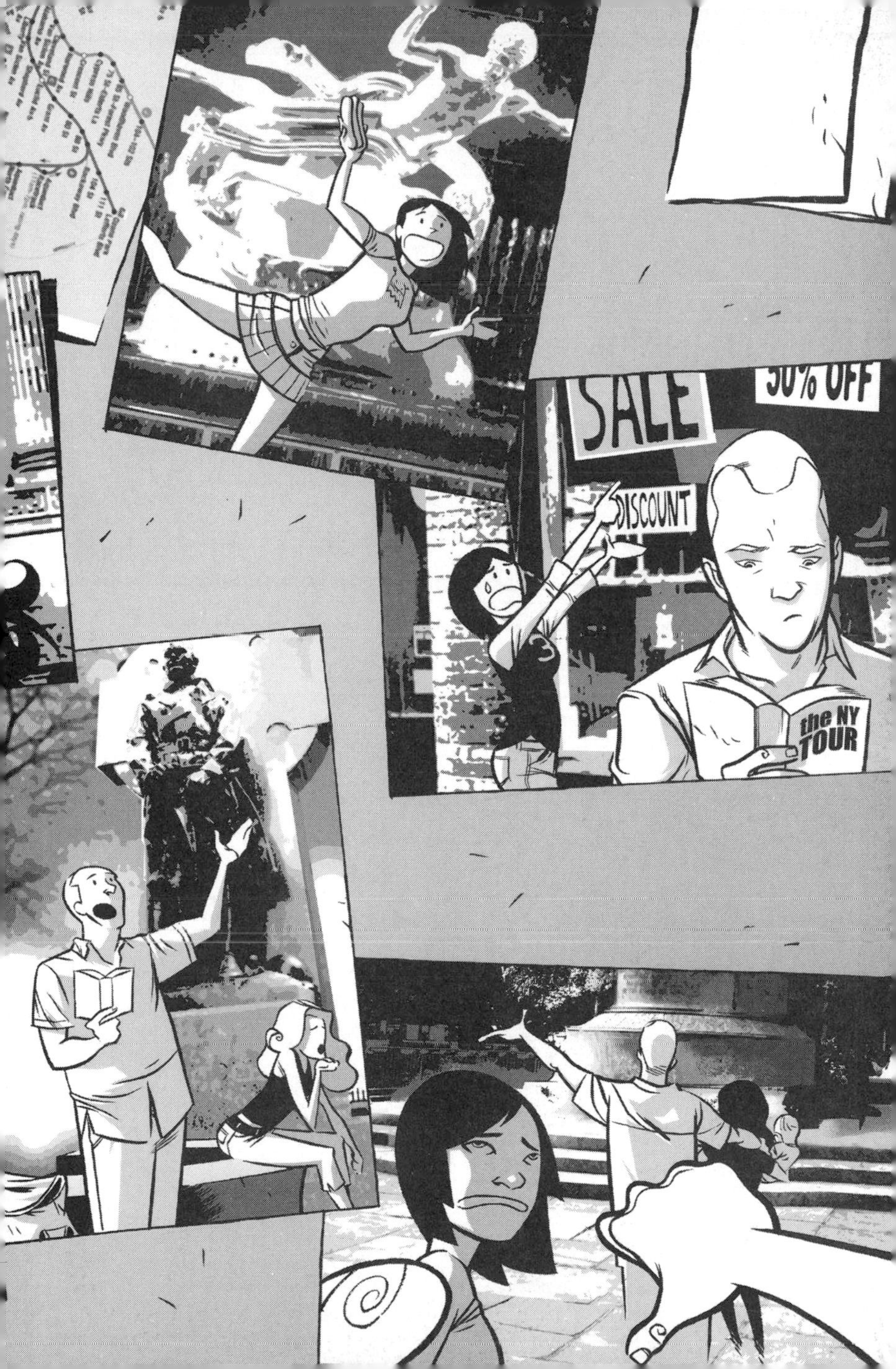
SALE
% OFF
DISCOUNT
the NY TOUR

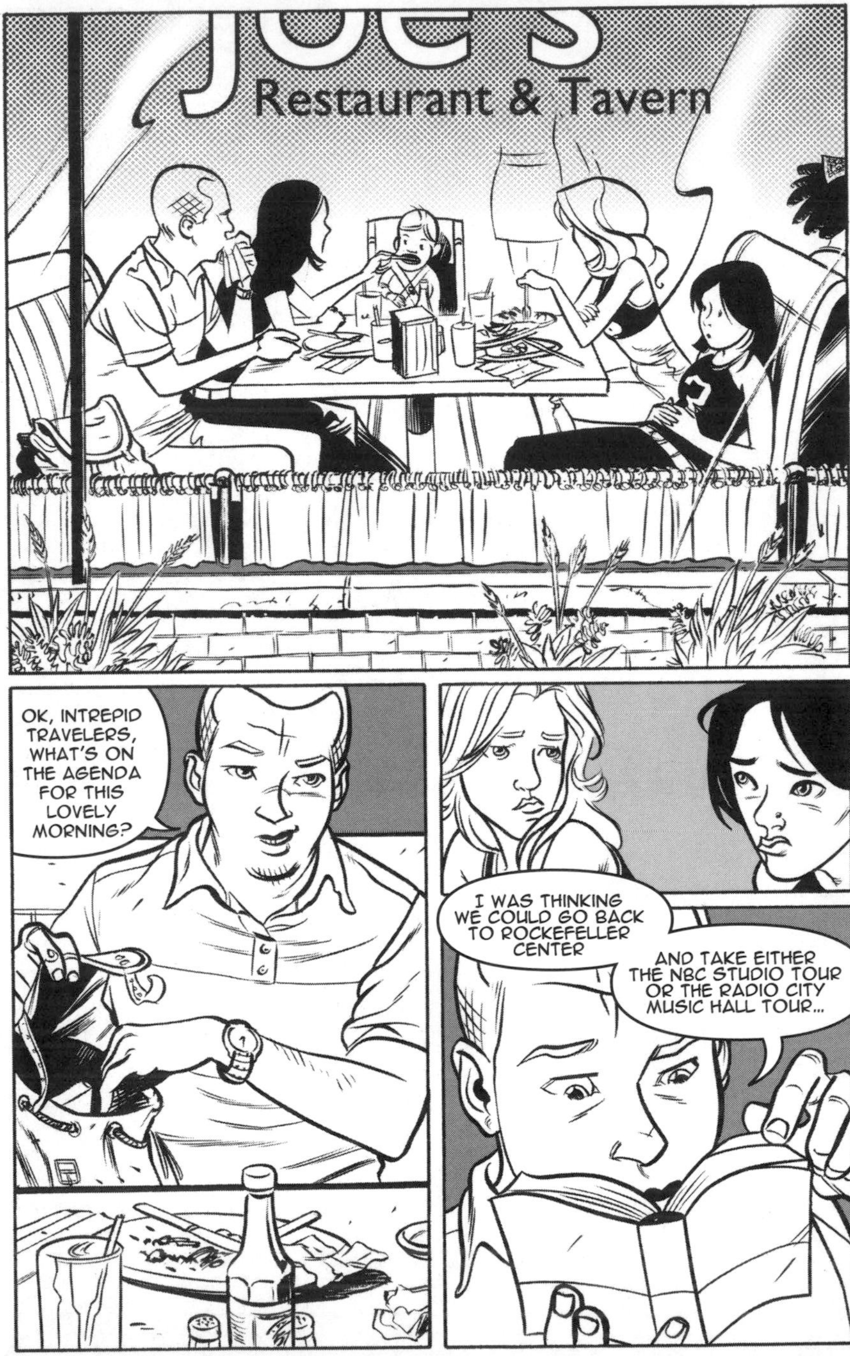
Restaurant & Tavern
OK, INTREPID TRAVELERS, WHAT'S ON THE AGENDA FOR THIS LOVELY MORNING?
I WAS THINKING WE COULD GO BACK TO ROCKEFELLER CENTER
AND TAKE EITHER THE NBC STUDIO TOUR OR THE RADIO CITY MUSIC HALL TOUR...

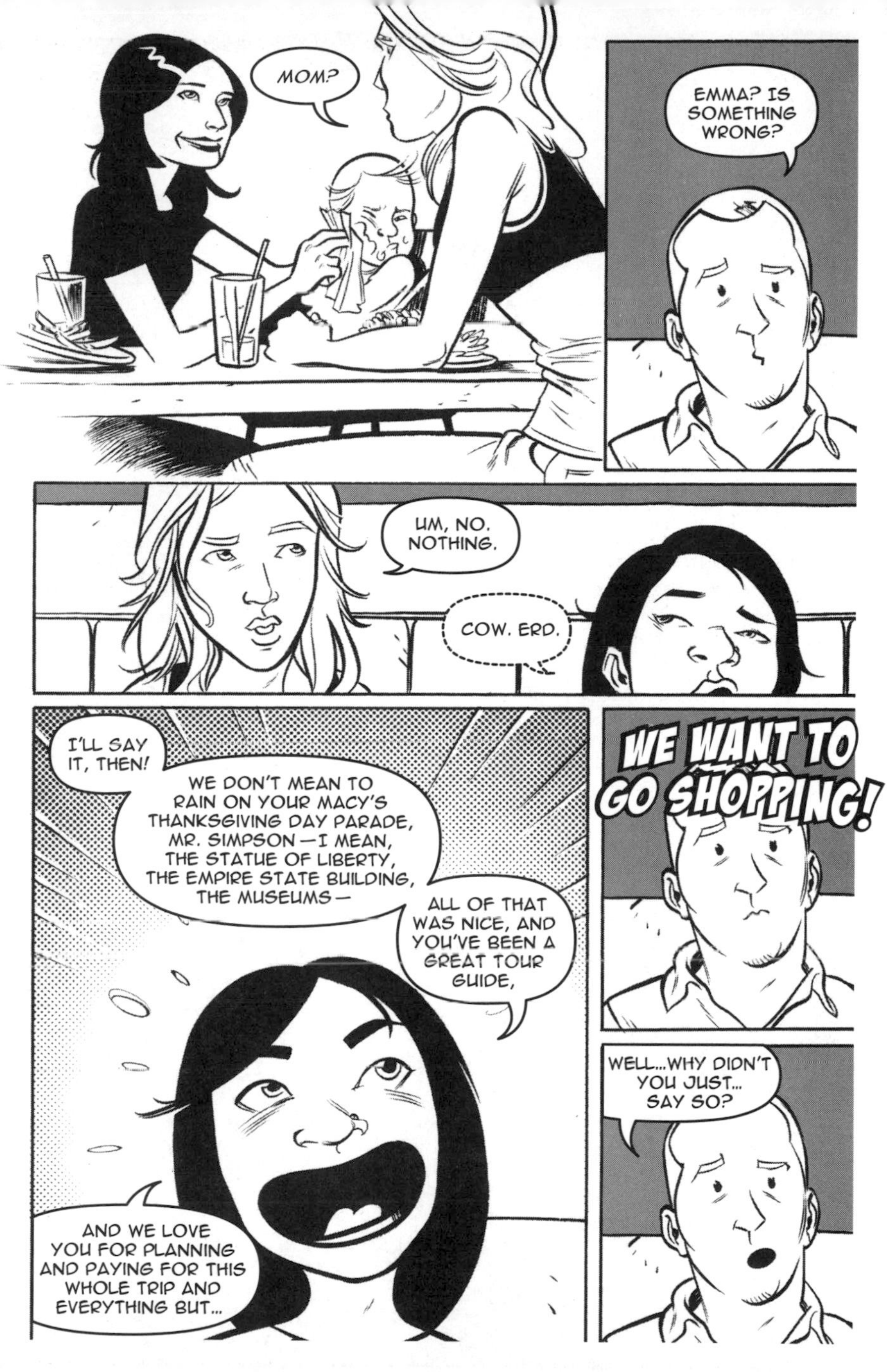
MOM?
EMMA? IS SOMETHING WRONG?
UM, NO. NOTHING.
COW. ERD.
I'LL SAY IT, THEN!
WE DON'T MEAN TO RAIN ON YOUR MACY'S THANKSGIVING DAY PARADE, MR. SIMPSON—I MEAN, THE STATUE OF LIBERTY, THE EMPIRE STATE BUILDING, THE MUSEUMS—
ALL OF THAT WAS NICE, AND YOU'VE BEEN A GREAT TOUR GUIDE,
AND WE LOVE YOU FOR PLANNING AND PAYING FOR THIS WHOLE TRIP AND EVERYTHING BUT...
WE WANT TO GO SHOPPING!
WELL...WHY DIDN'T YOU JUST... SAY SO?

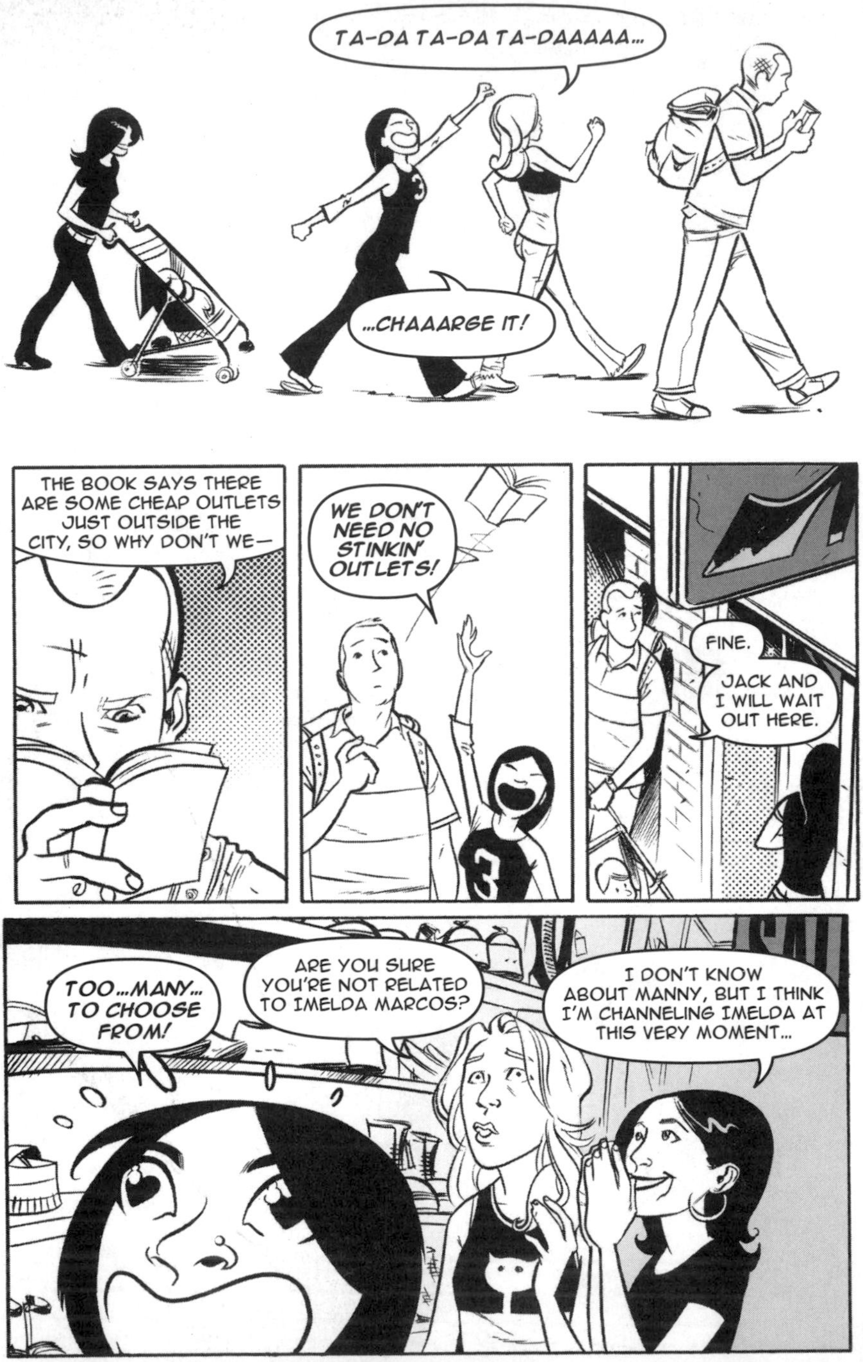
TA-DA TA-DA TA-DAAAAA...
...CHAAARGE IT!
THE BOOK SAYS THERE ARE SOME CHEAP OUTLETS JUST OUTSIDE THE CITY, SO WHY DON'T WE—
WE DON'T NEED NO STINKIN' OUTLETS!
FINE.
JACK AND I WILL WAIT OUT HERE.
TOO...MANY... TO CHOOSE FROM!
ARE YOU SURE YOU'RE NOT RELATED TO IMELDA MARCOS?
I DON'T KNOW ABOUT MANNY, BUT I THINK I'M CHANNELING IMELDA AT THIS VERY MOMENT...

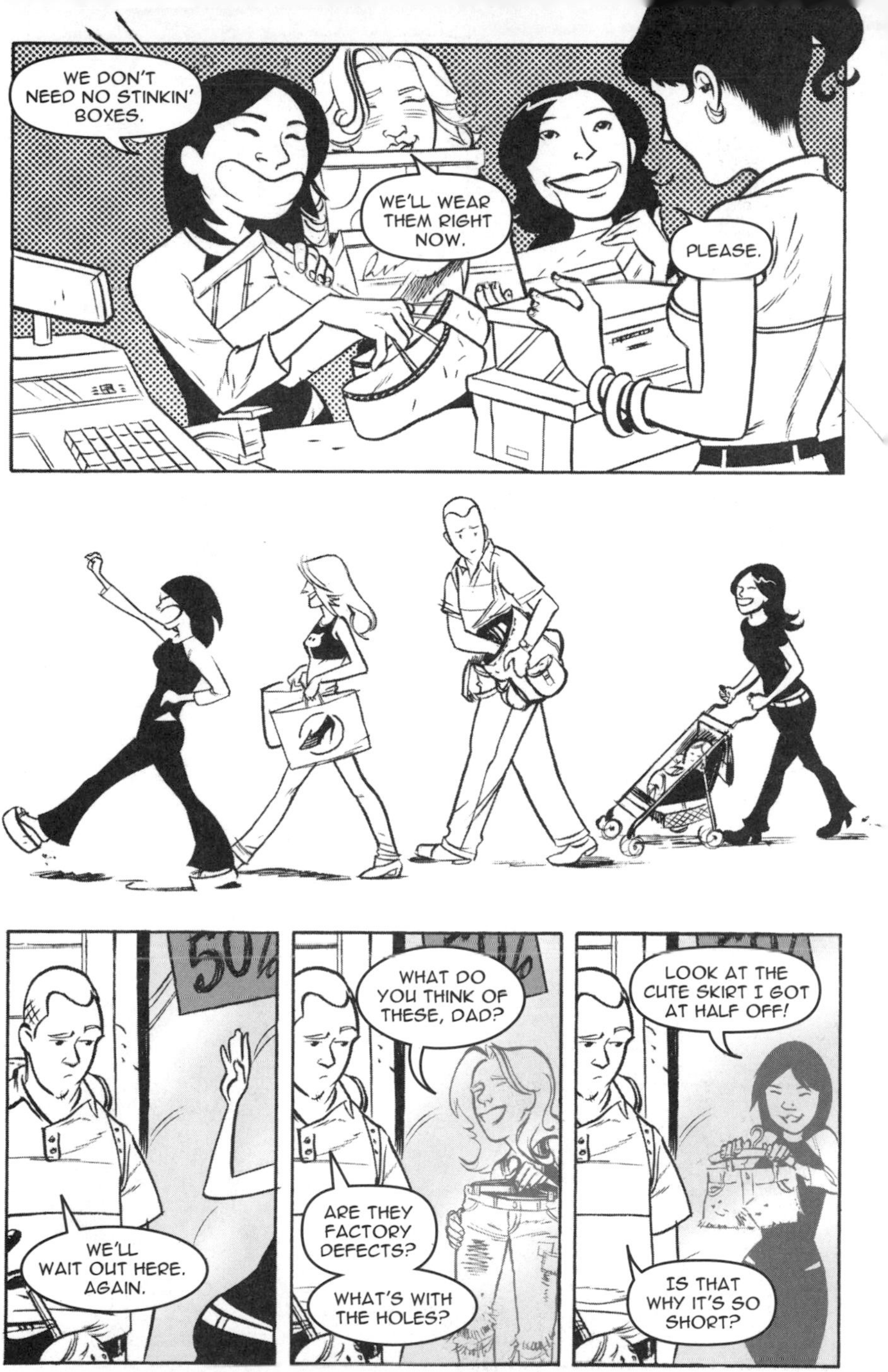
WE DON'T NEED NO STINKIN' BOXES.
WE'LL WEAR THEM RIGHT NOW.
PLEASE.
WE'LL WAIT OUT HERE. AGAIN.
WHAT DO YOU THINK OF THESE, DAD?
ARE THEY FACTORY DEFECTS?
WHAT'S WITH THE HOLES?
LOOK AT THE CUTE SKIRT I GOT AT HALF OFF!
IS THAT WHY IT'S SO SHORT?

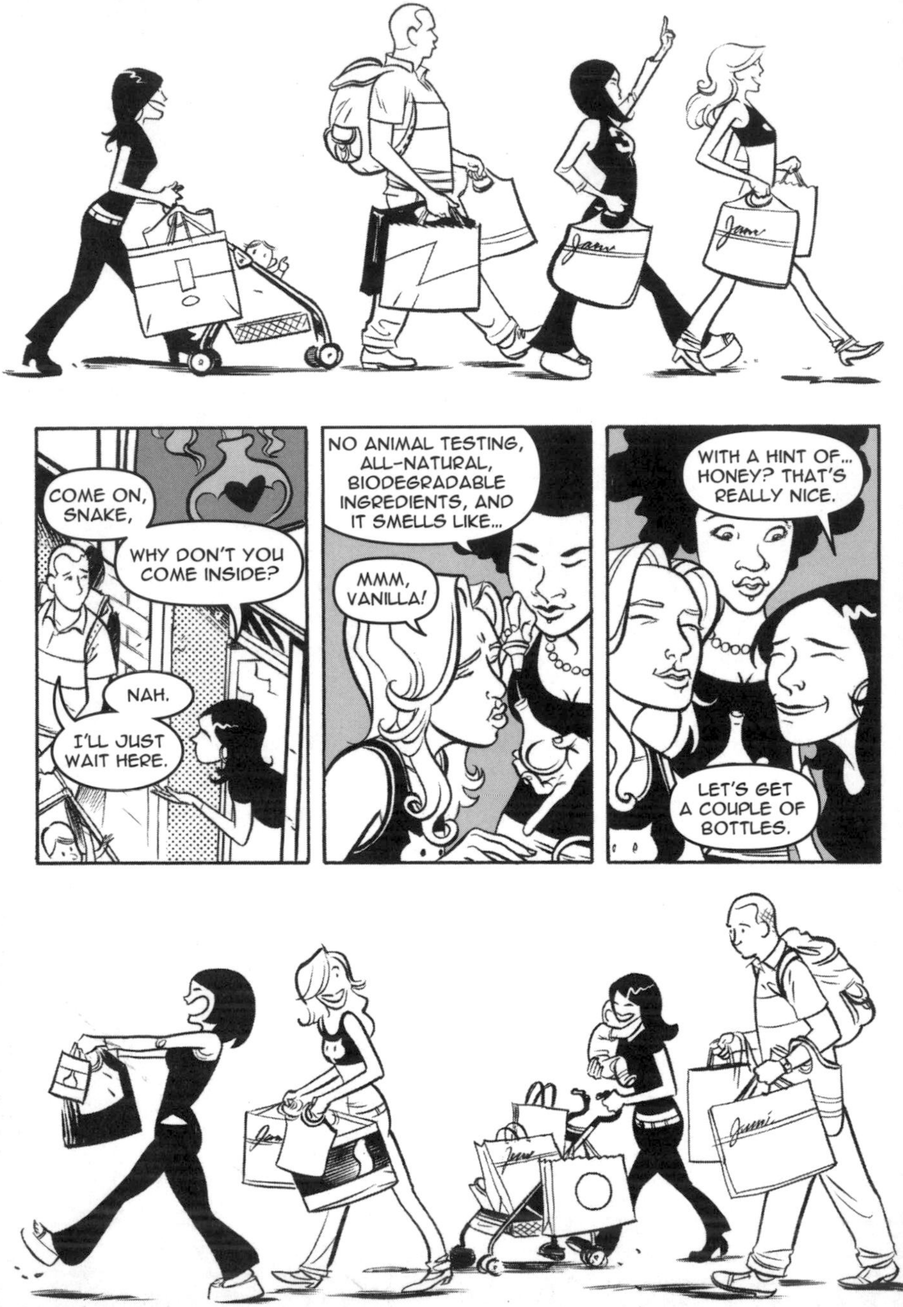
COME ON, SNAKE,
WHY DON'T YOU COME INSIDE?
NAH.
I'LL JUST WAIT HERE.
NO ANIMAL TESTING, ALL-NATURAL, BIODEGRADABLE INGREDIENTS, AND IT SMELLS LIKE...
MMM, VANILLA!
WITH A HINT OF... HONEY? THAT'S REALLY NICE.
LET'S GET A COUPLE OF BOTTLES.

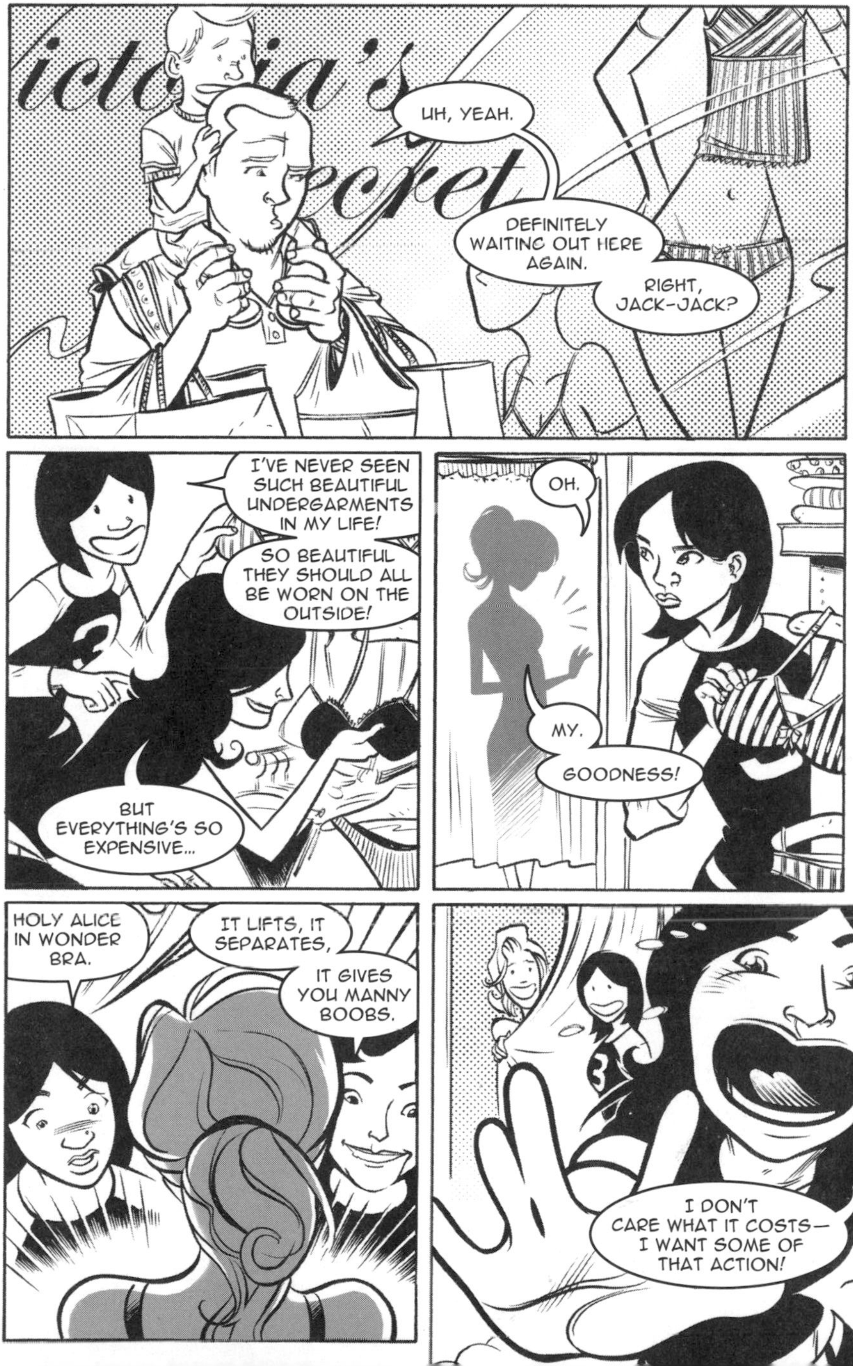
UH, YEAH.
DEFINITELY WAITING OUT HERE AGAIN.
RIGHT, JACK-JACK?
I'VE NEVER SEEN SUCH BEAUTIFUL UNDERGARMENTS IN MY LIFE!
SO BEAUTIFUL THEY SHOULD ALL BE WORN ON THE OUTSIDE!
BUT EVERYTHING'S SO EXPENSIVE...
OH.
MY.
GOODNESS!
HOLY ALICE IN WONDER BRA.
IT LIFTS, IT SEPARATES,
IT GIVES YOU MANNY BOOBS.
I DON'T CARE WHAT IT COSTS— I WANT SOME OF THAT ACTION!

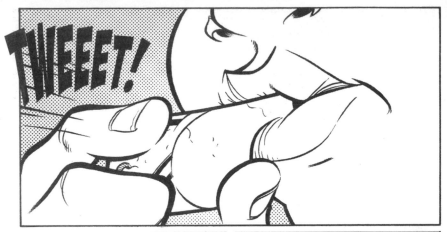

TWEEEET!

TIME FOR LUNCH, LADIES!

MAKE SURE TO DRINK LOTS OF WATER. NO DEHYDRATION ON MY WATCH.

HEY, WHAT'S GOING ON OVER THERE?

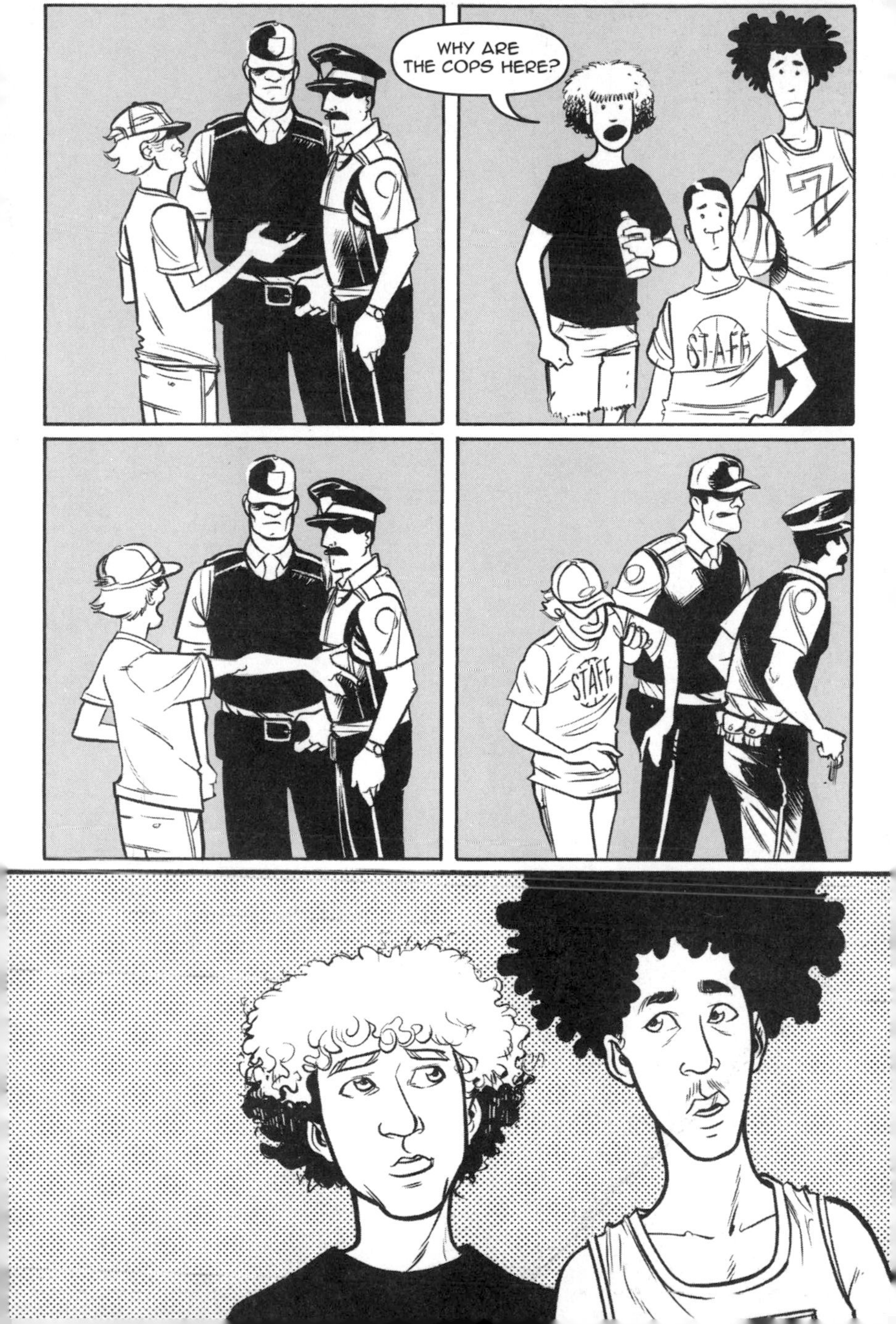
WHY ARE THE COPS HERE?

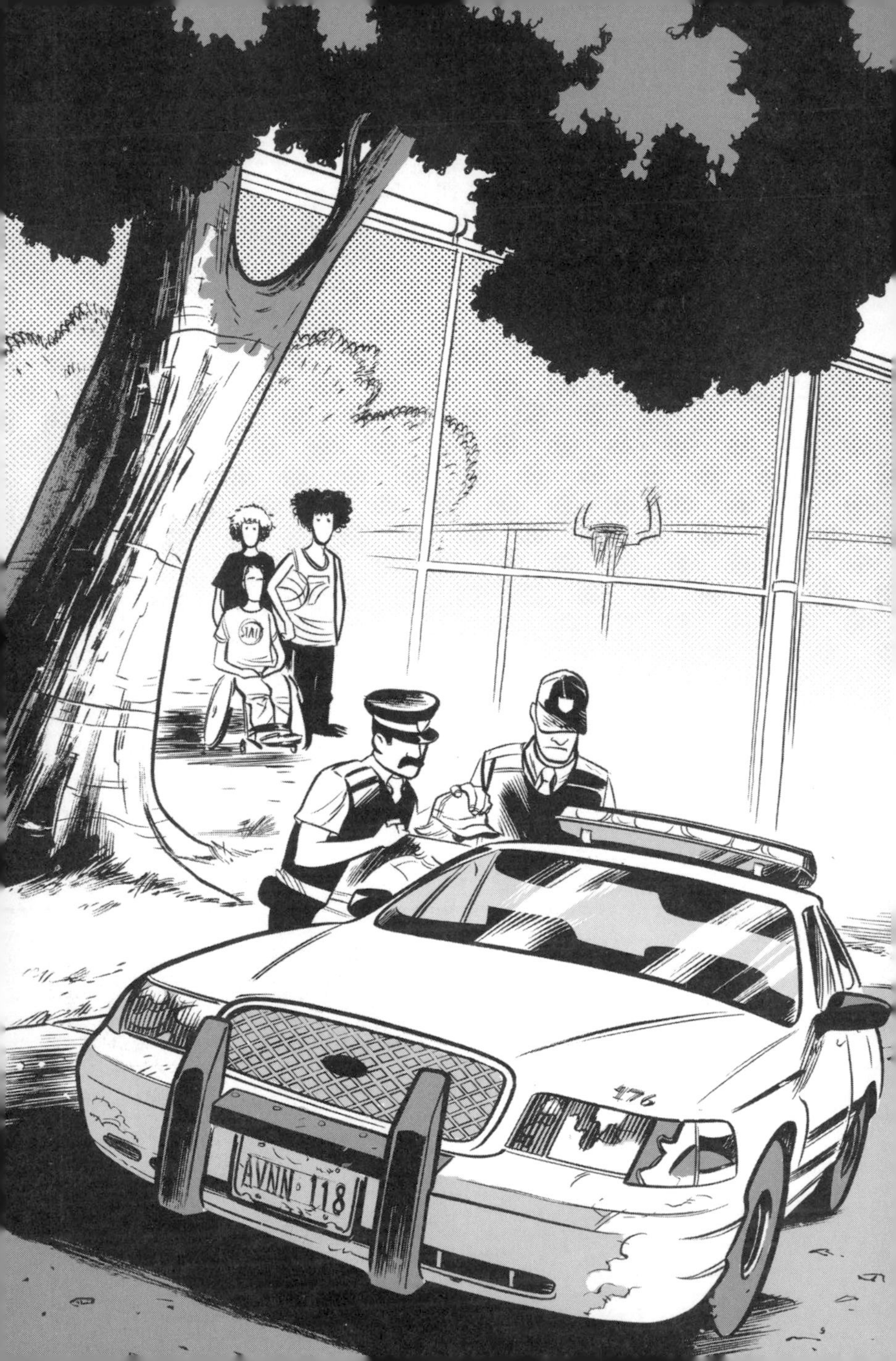
176
AVNN 118

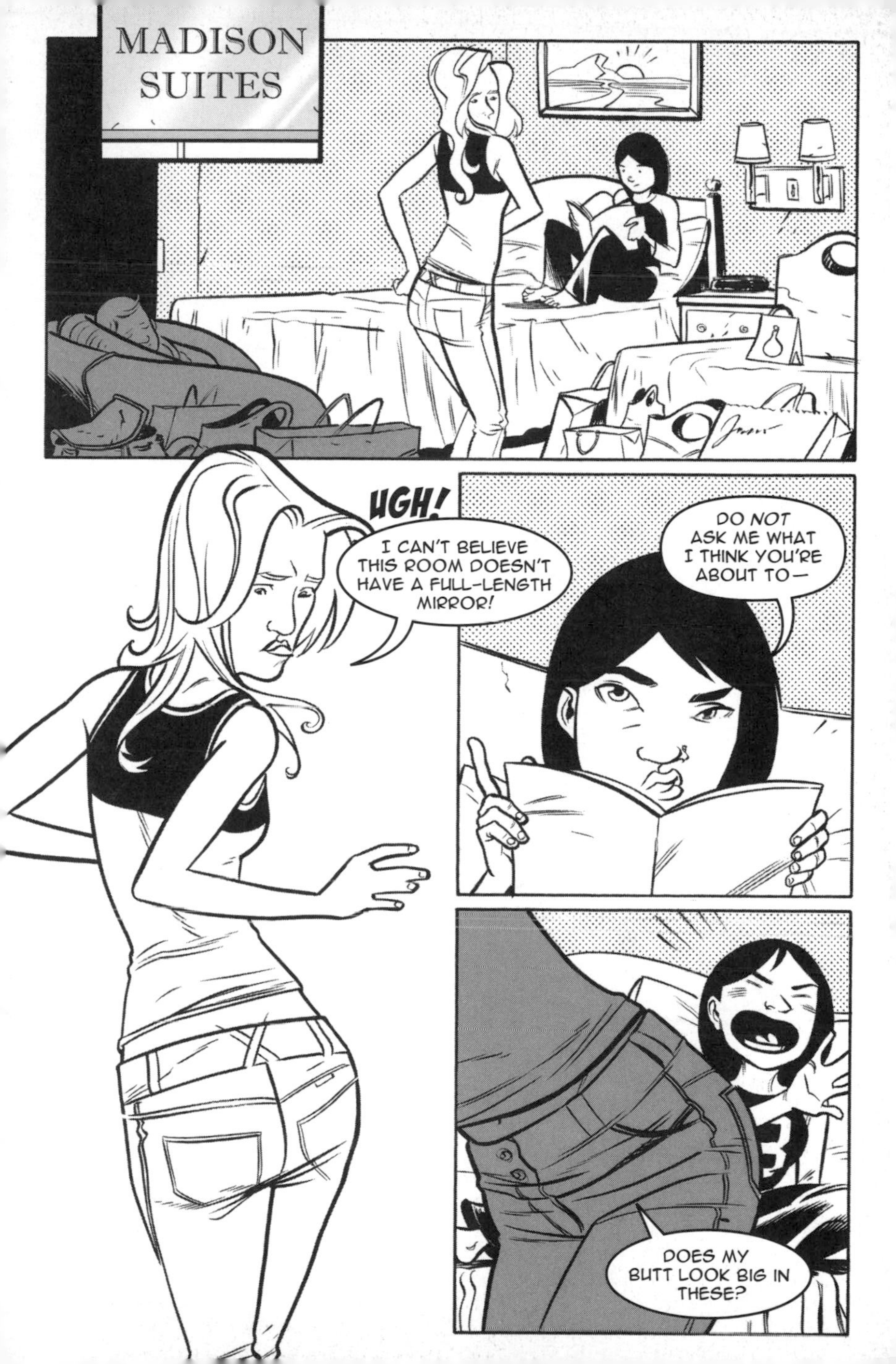
MADISON SUITES
UGH!
I CAN'T BELIEVE THIS ROOM DOESN'T HAVE A FULL-LENGTH MIRROR!
DO *NOT* ASK ME WHAT I THINK YOU'RE ABOUT TO—
DOES MY BUTT LOOK BIG IN THESE?

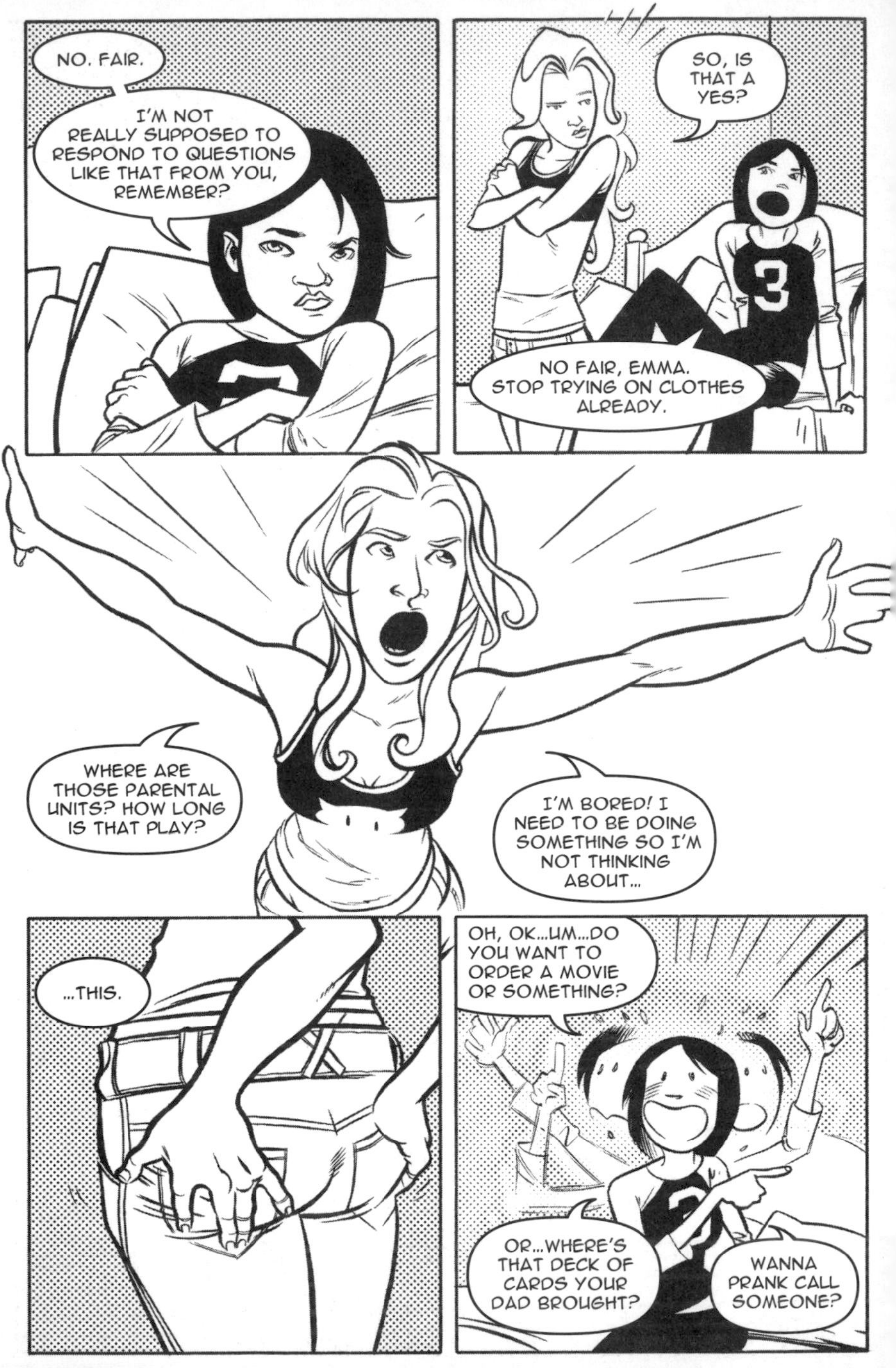
NO. FAIR.
I'M NOT REALLY SUPPOSED TO RESPOND TO QUESTIONS LIKE THAT FROM YOU, REMEMBER?
SO, IS THAT A YES?
NO FAIR, EMMA. STOP TRYING ON CLOTHES ALREADY.
WHERE ARE THOSE PARENTAL UNITS? HOW LONG IS THAT PLAY?
I'M BORED! I NEED TO BE DOING SOMETHING SO I'M NOT THINKING ABOUT...
...THIS.
OH, OK...UM...DO YOU WANT TO ORDER A MOVIE OR SOMETHING?
OR...WHERE'S THAT DECK OF CARDS YOUR DAD BROUGHT?
WANNA PRANK CALL SOMEONE?

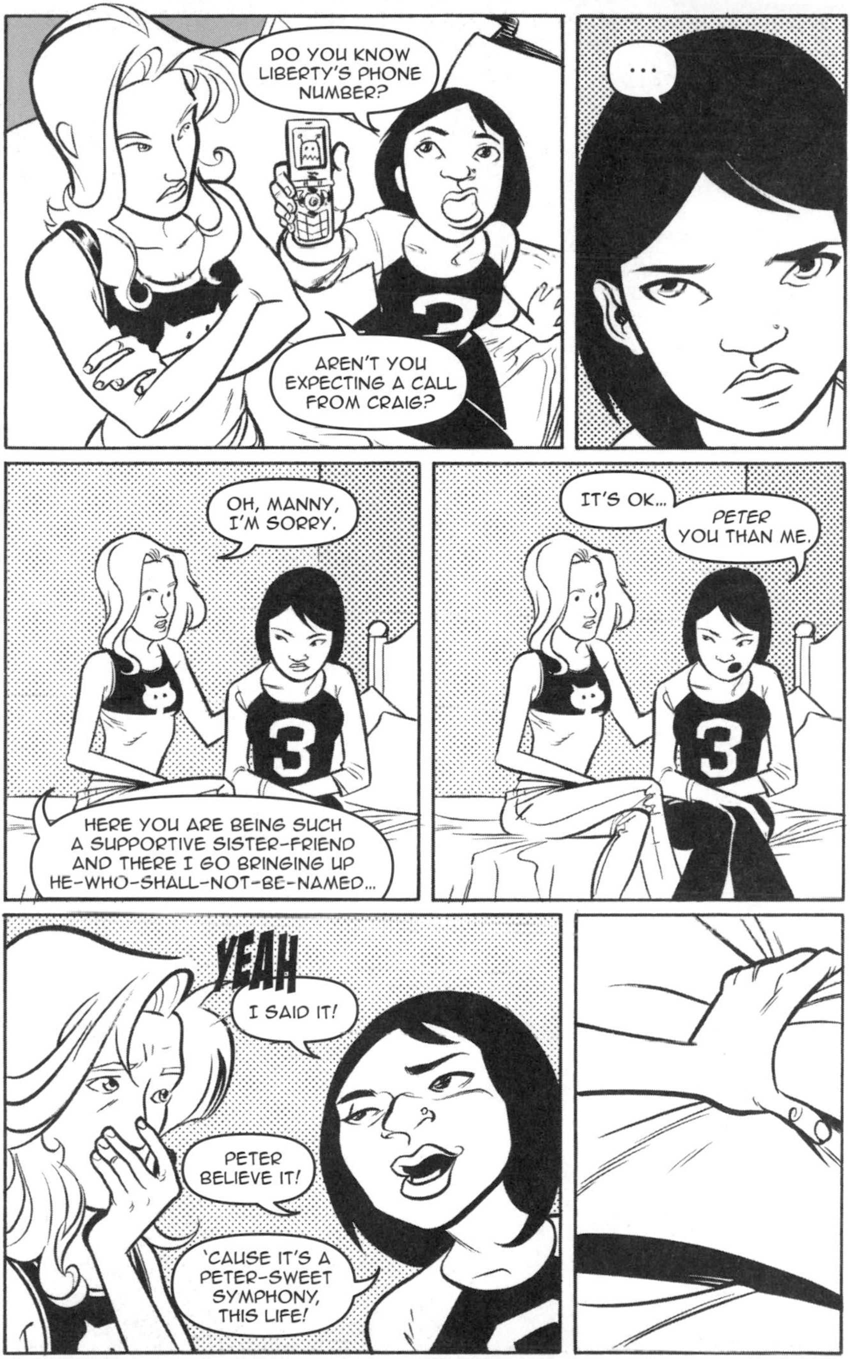
DO YOU KNOW LIBERTY'S PHONE NUMBER?
AREN'T YOU EXPECTING A CALL FROM CRAIG?
...
OH, MANNY, I'M SORRY.
HERE YOU ARE BEING SUCH A SUPPORTIVE SISTER-FRIEND AND THERE I GO BRINGING UP HE-WHO-SHALL-NOT-BE-NAMED...
IT'S OK...
PETER YOU THAN ME.
YEAH
I SAID IT!
PETER BELIEVE IT!
'CAUSE IT'S A PETER-SWEET SYMPHONY, THIS LIFE!

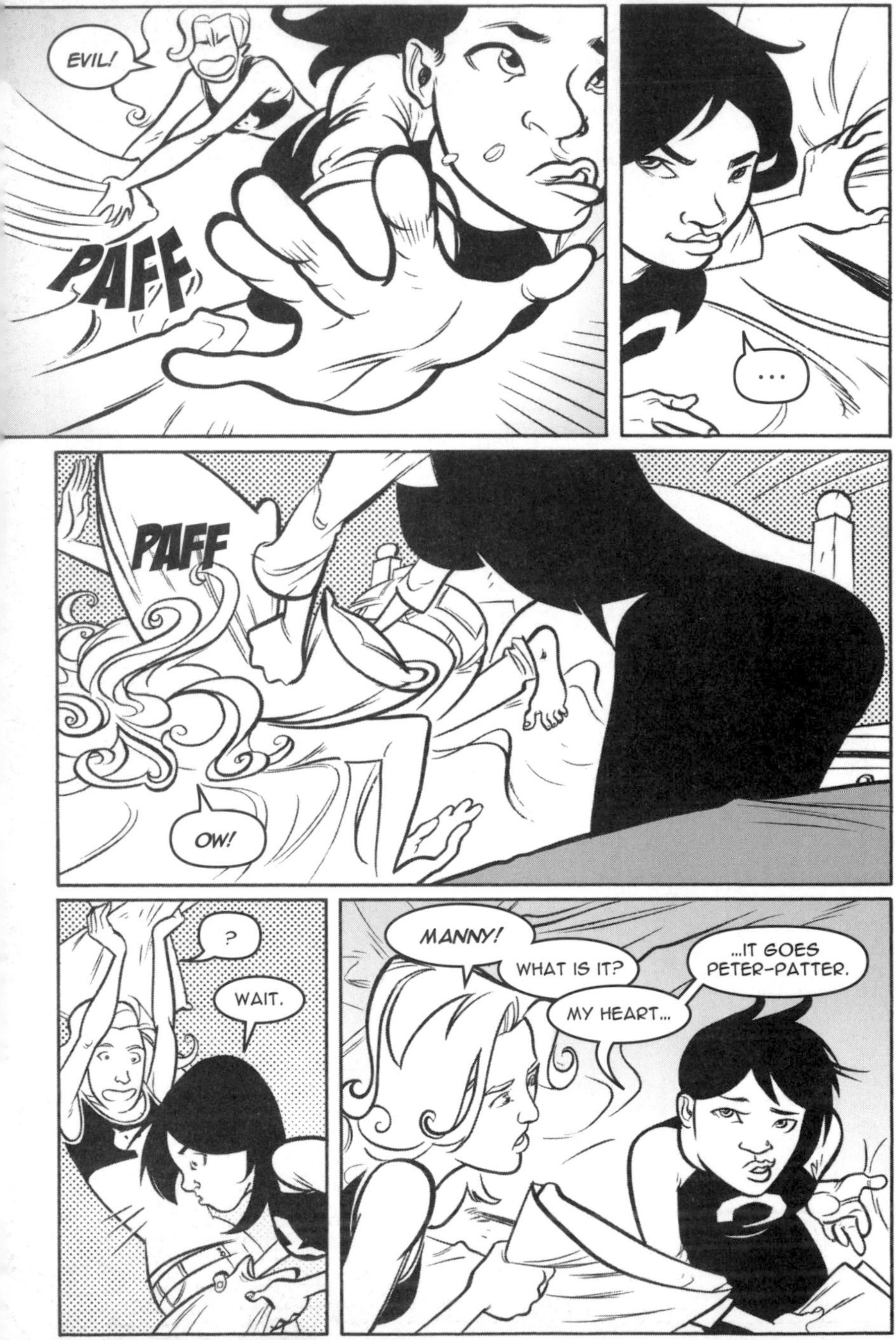

EVIL!
PAFF
...
PAFF
OW!
?
WAIT.
MANNY!
WHAT IS IT?
MY HEART...
...IT GOES PETER-PATTER.

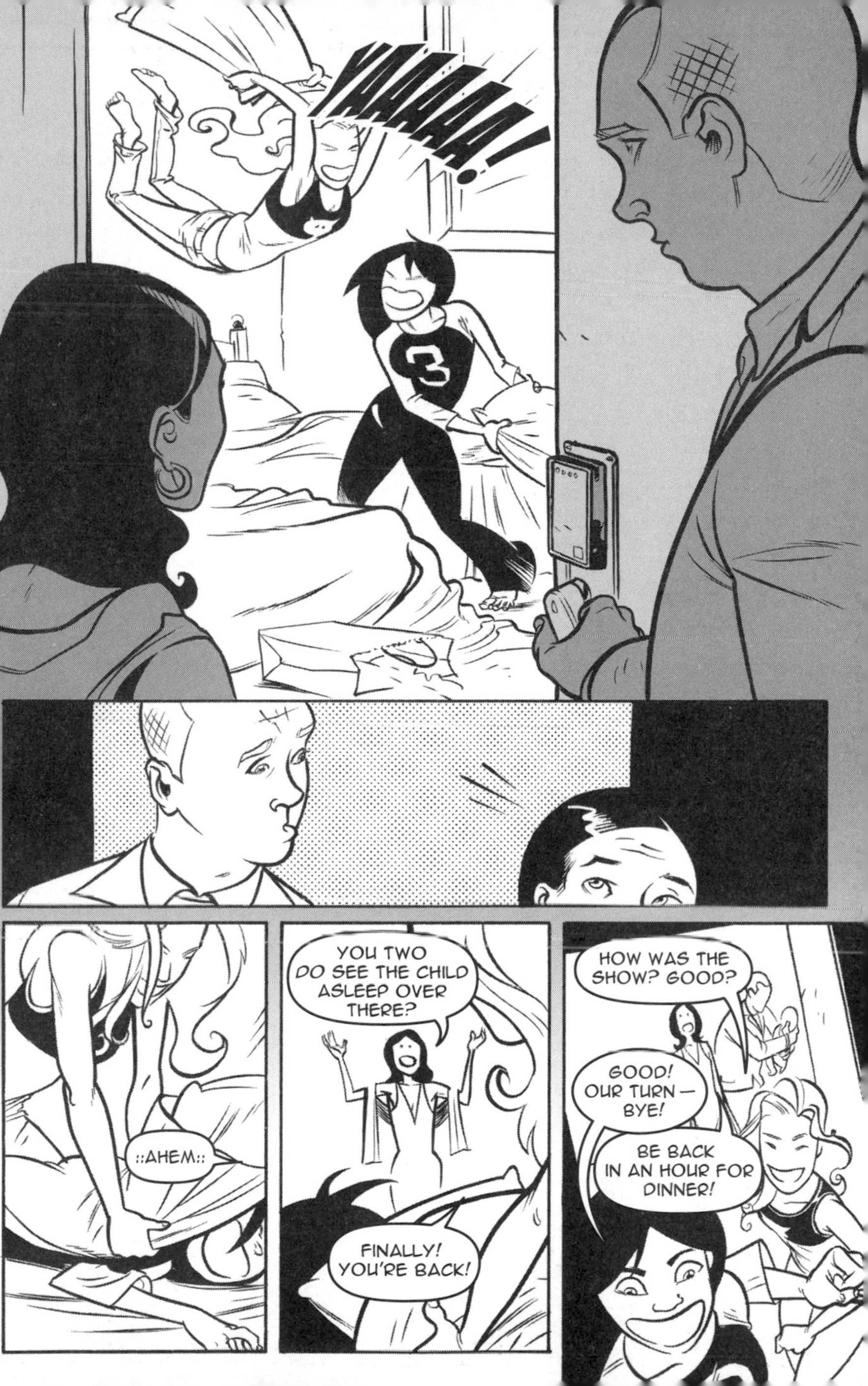
YAAAAA!
::AHEM::
YOU TWO DO SEE THE CHILD ASLEEP OVER THERE?
FINALLY! YOU'RE BACK!
HOW WAS THE SHOW? GOOD?
GOOD! OUR TURN— BYE!
BE BACK IN AN HOUR FOR DINNER!

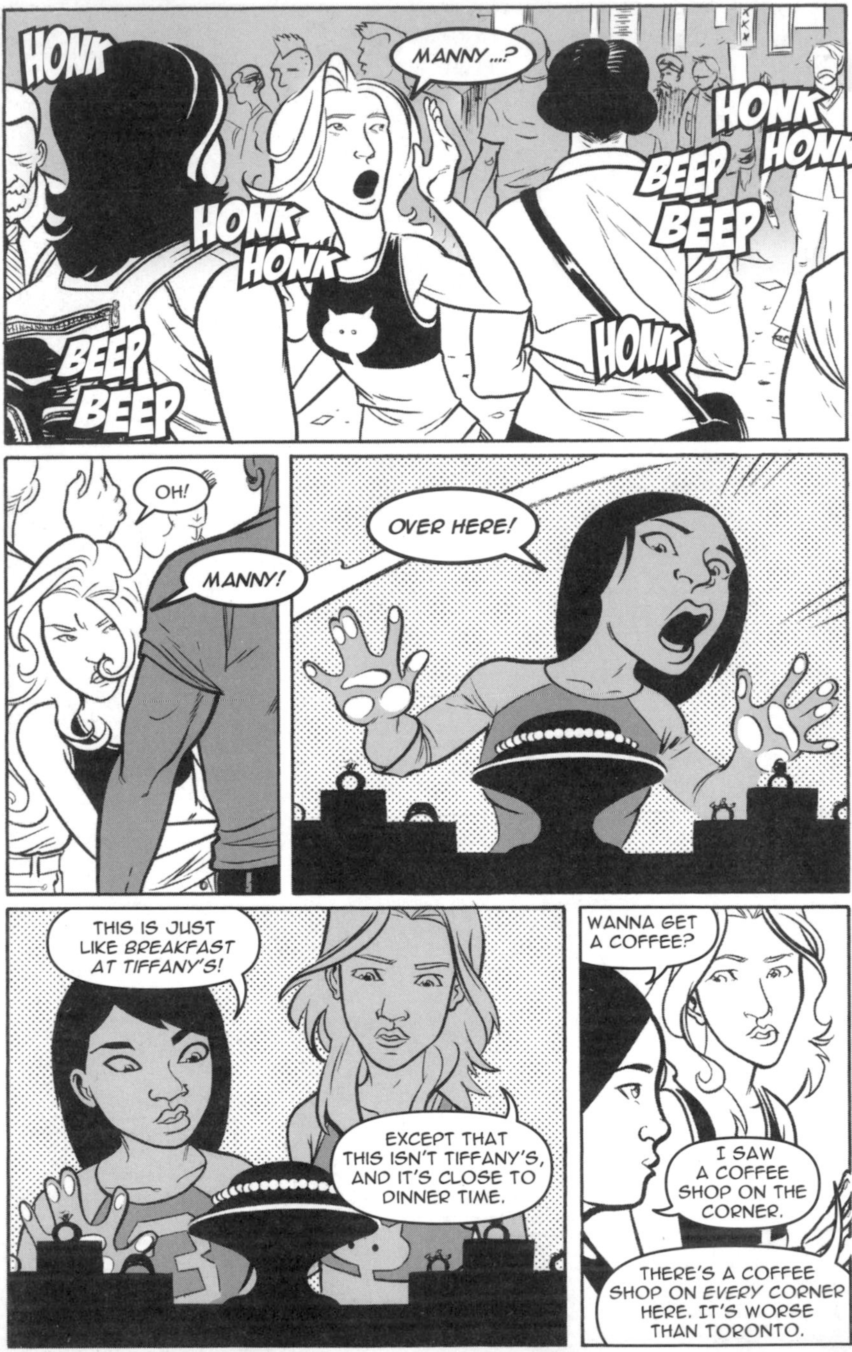
HONK
MANNY...?
HONK
HONK
BEEP
BEEP
HONK
HONK
HONK
BEEP
BEEP
HONK
HONK
OH!
MANNY!
OVER HERE!
THIS IS JUST LIKE BREAKFAST AT TIFFANY'S!
EXCEPT THAT THIS ISN'T TIFFANY'S, AND IT'S CLOSE TO DINNER TIME.
WANNA GET A COFFEE?
I SAW A COFFEE SHOP ON THE CORNER.
THERE'S A COFFEE SHOP ON EVERY CORNER HERE. IT'S WORSE THAN TORONTO.

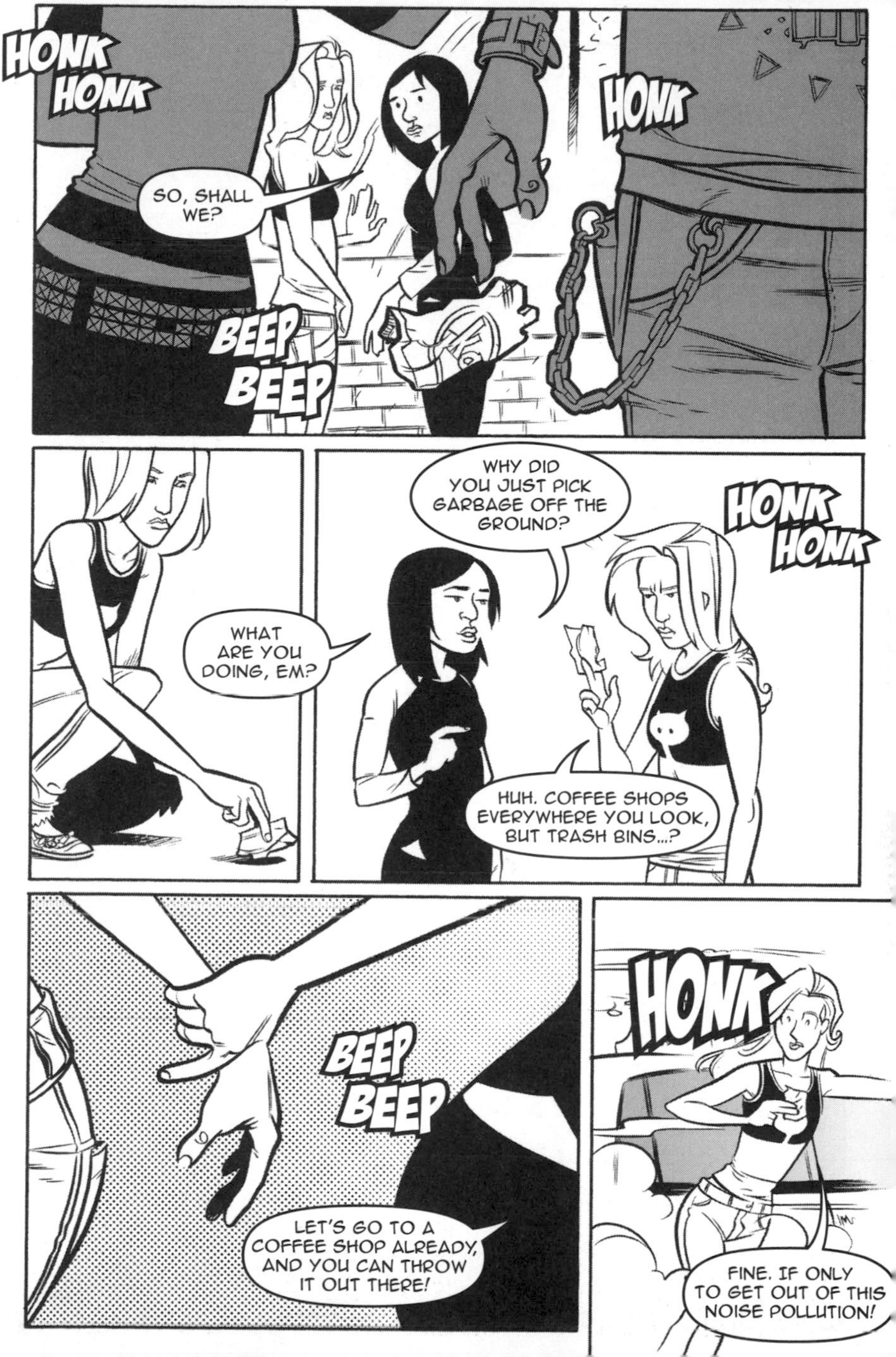
HONK
HONK
HONK
SO, SHALL WE?
BEEP
BEEP
WHAT ARE YOU DOING, EM?
WHY DID YOU JUST PICK GARBAGE OFF THE GROUND?
HONK
HONK
HUH. COFFEE SHOPS EVERYWHERE YOU LOOK, BUT TRASH BINS...?
BEEP
BEEP
LET'S GO TO A COFFEE SHOP ALREADY, AND YOU CAN THROW IT OUT THERE!
HONK
FINE. IF ONLY TO GET OUT OF THIS NOISE POLLUTION!

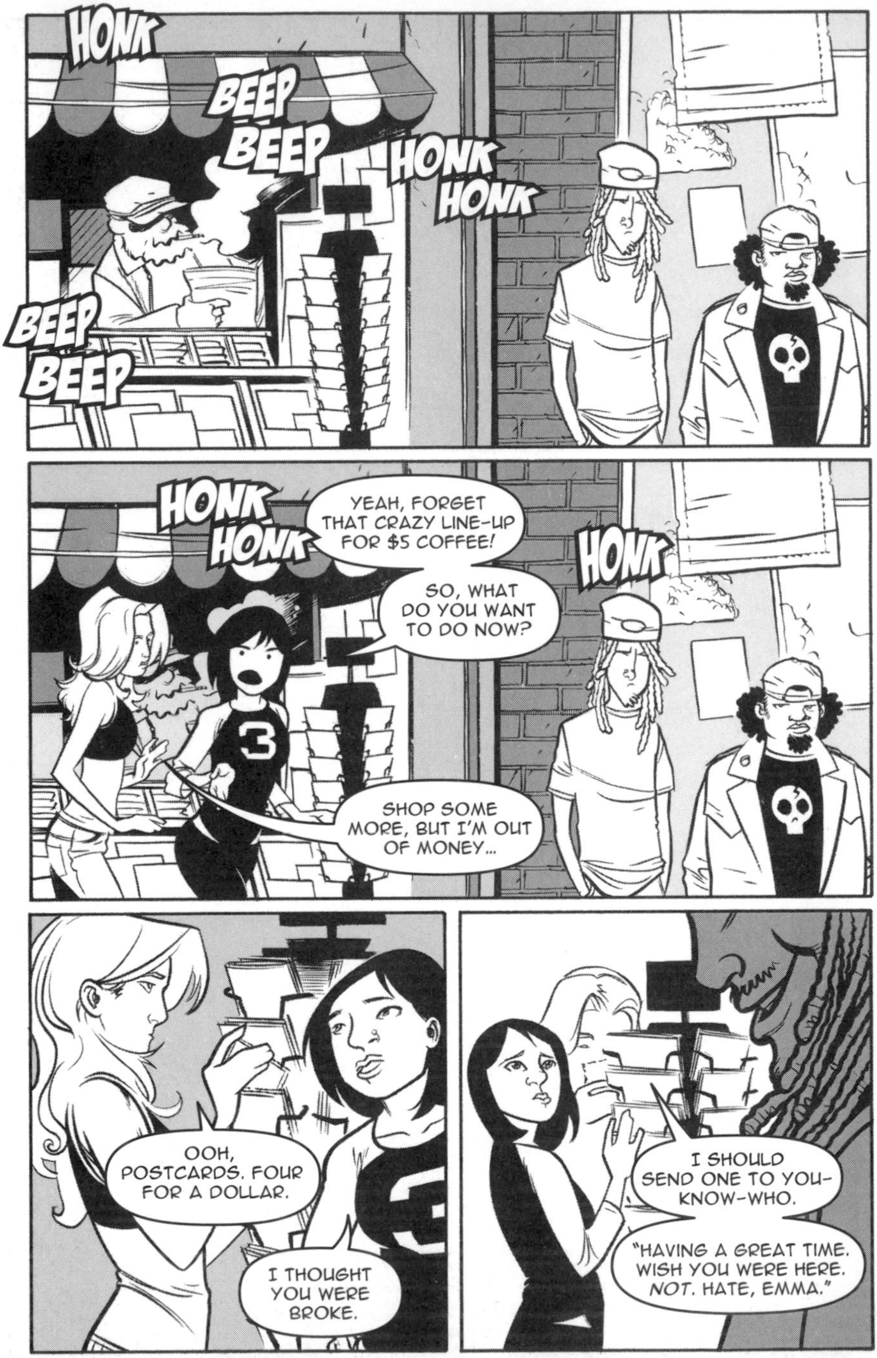

HONK
BEEP BEEP
HONK HONK
BEEP BEEP
HONK HONK
YEAH, FORGET THAT CRAZY LINE-UP FOR $5 COFFEE!
SO, WHAT DO YOU WANT TO DO NOW?
HONK
SHOP SOME MORE, BUT I'M OUT OF MONEY...
OOH, POSTCARDS. FOUR FOR A DOLLAR.
I THOUGHT YOU WERE BROKE.
I SHOULD SEND ONE TO YOU-KNOW-WHO.
"HAVING A GREAT TIME. WISH YOU WERE HERE. *NOT*. HATE, EMMA."

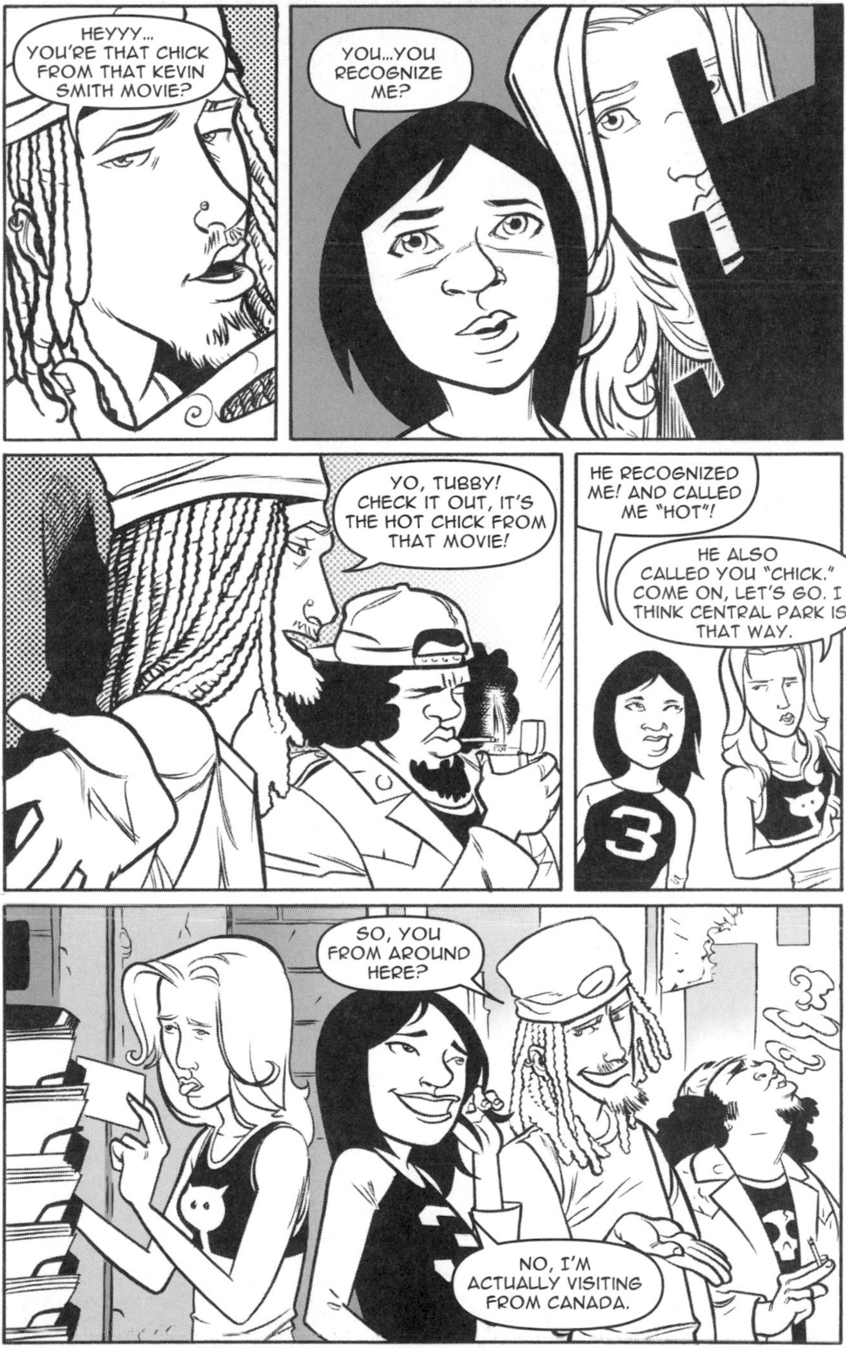
HEYYY... YOU'RE THAT CHICK FROM THAT KEVIN SMITH MOVIE?
YOU...YOU RECOGNIZE ME?
YO, TUBBY! CHECK IT OUT, IT'S THE HOT CHICK FROM THAT MOVIE!
HE RECOGNIZED ME! AND CALLED ME "HOT"!
HE ALSO CALLED YOU "CHICK." COME ON, LET'S GO. I THINK CENTRAL PARK IS THAT WAY.
SO, YOU FROM AROUND HERE?
NO, I'M ACTUALLY VISITING FROM CANADA.

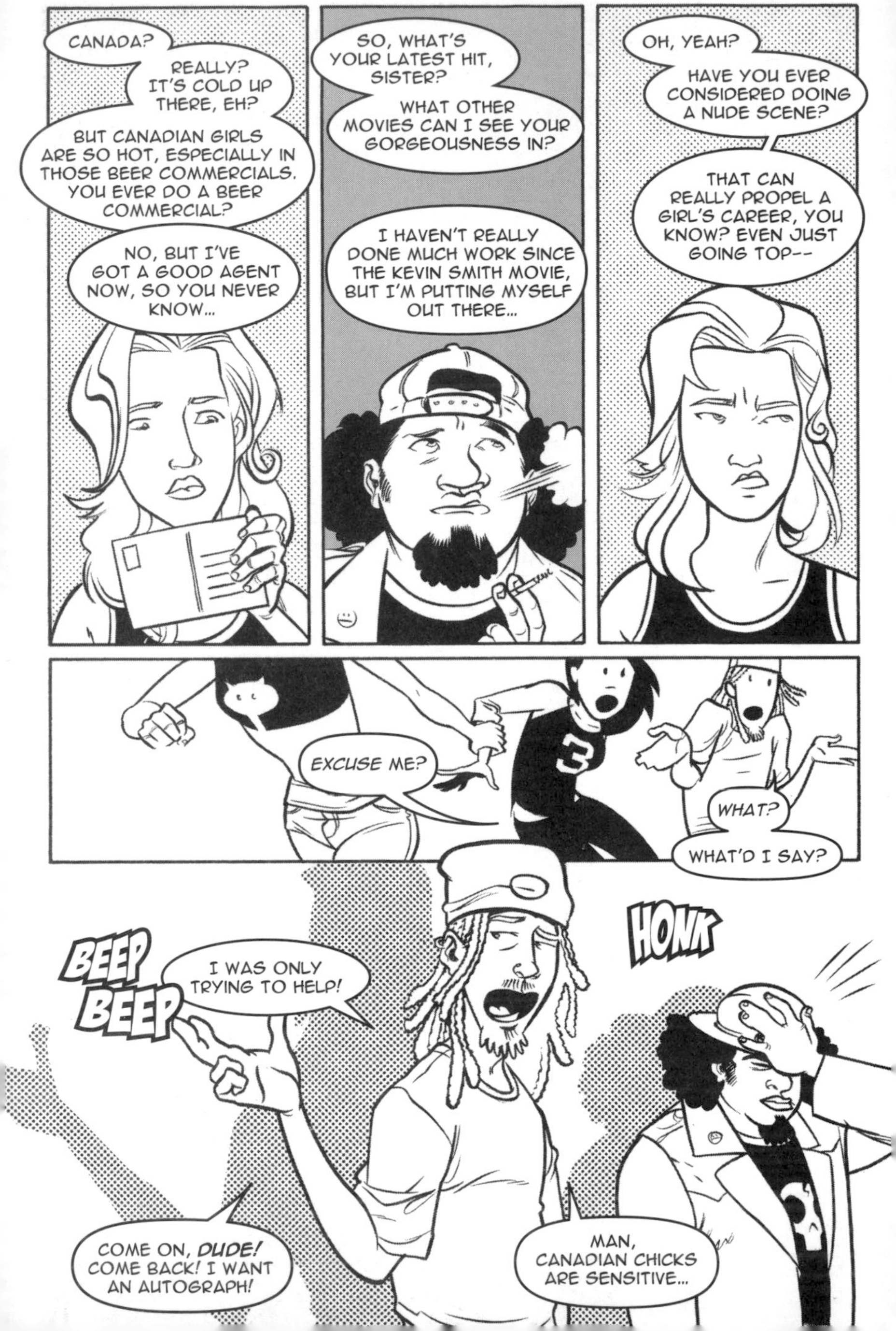
CANADA?
REALLY? IT'S COLD UP THERE, EH?
BUT CANADIAN GIRLS ARE SO HOT, ESPECIALLY IN THOSE BEER COMMERCIALS. YOU EVER DO A BEER COMMERCIAL?
NO, BUT I'VE GOT A GOOD AGENT NOW, SO YOU NEVER KNOW...
SO, WHAT'S YOUR LATEST HIT, SISTER?
WHAT OTHER MOVIES CAN I SEE YOUR GORGEOUSNESS IN?
I HAVEN'T REALLY DONE MUCH WORK SINCE THE KEVIN SMITH MOVIE, BUT I'M PUTTING MYSELF OUT THERE...
OH, YEAH?
HAVE YOU EVER CONSIDERED DOING A NUDE SCENE?
THAT CAN REALLY PROPEL A GIRL'S CAREER, YOU KNOW? EVEN JUST GOING TOP--
EXCUSE ME?
WHAT?
WHAT'D I SAY?
BEEP BEEP
I WAS ONLY TRYING TO HELP!
HONK
COME ON, DUDE! COME BACK! I WANT AN AUTOGRAPH!
MAN, CANADIAN CHICKS ARE SENSITIVE...

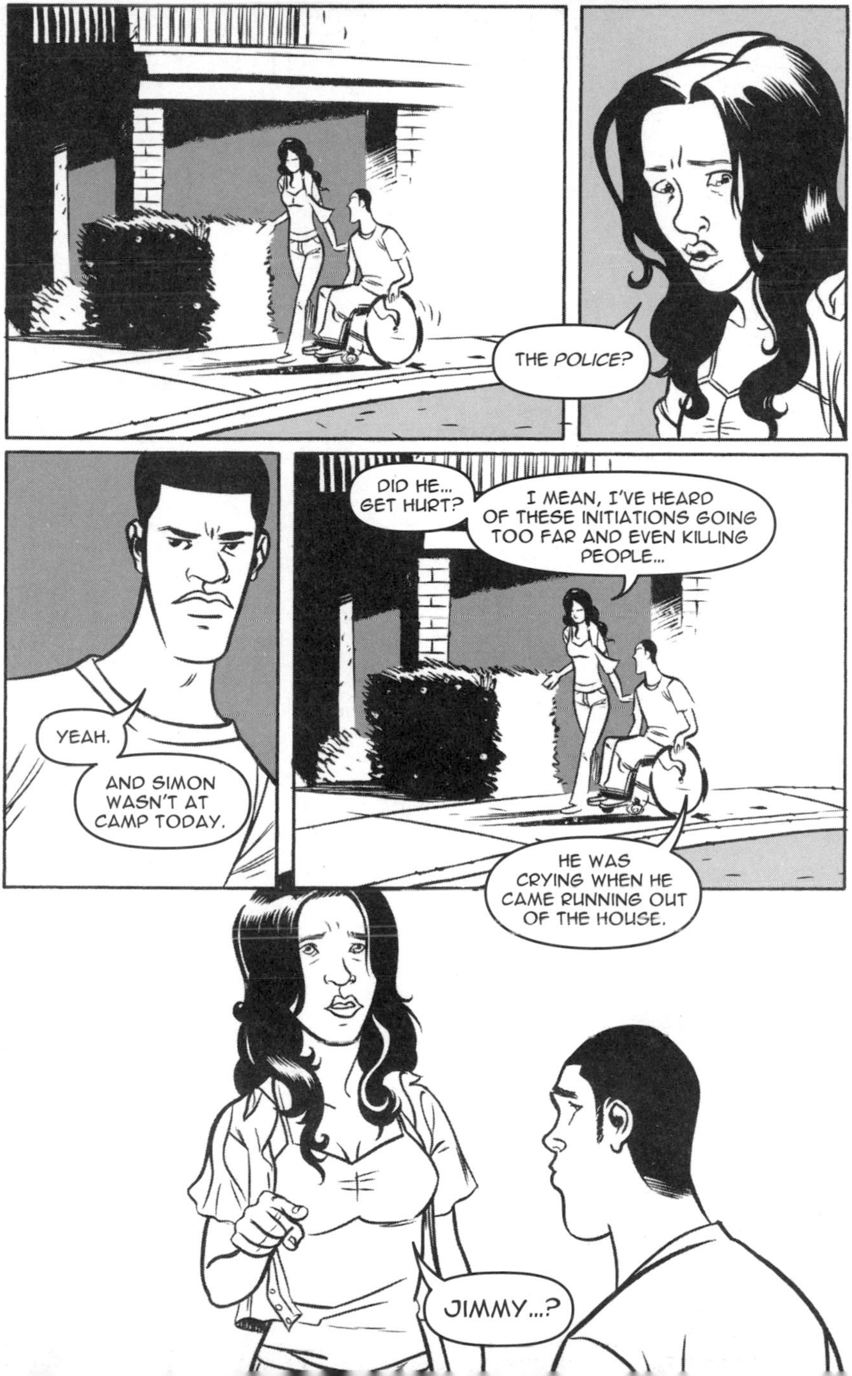
THE POLICE?
YEAH.
AND SIMON WASN'T AT CAMP TODAY.
DID HE... GET HURT?
I MEAN, I'VE HEARD OF THESE INITIATIONS GOING TOO FAR AND EVEN KILLING PEOPLE...
HE WAS CRYING WHEN HE CAME RUNNING OUT OF THE HOUSE.
JIMMY...?

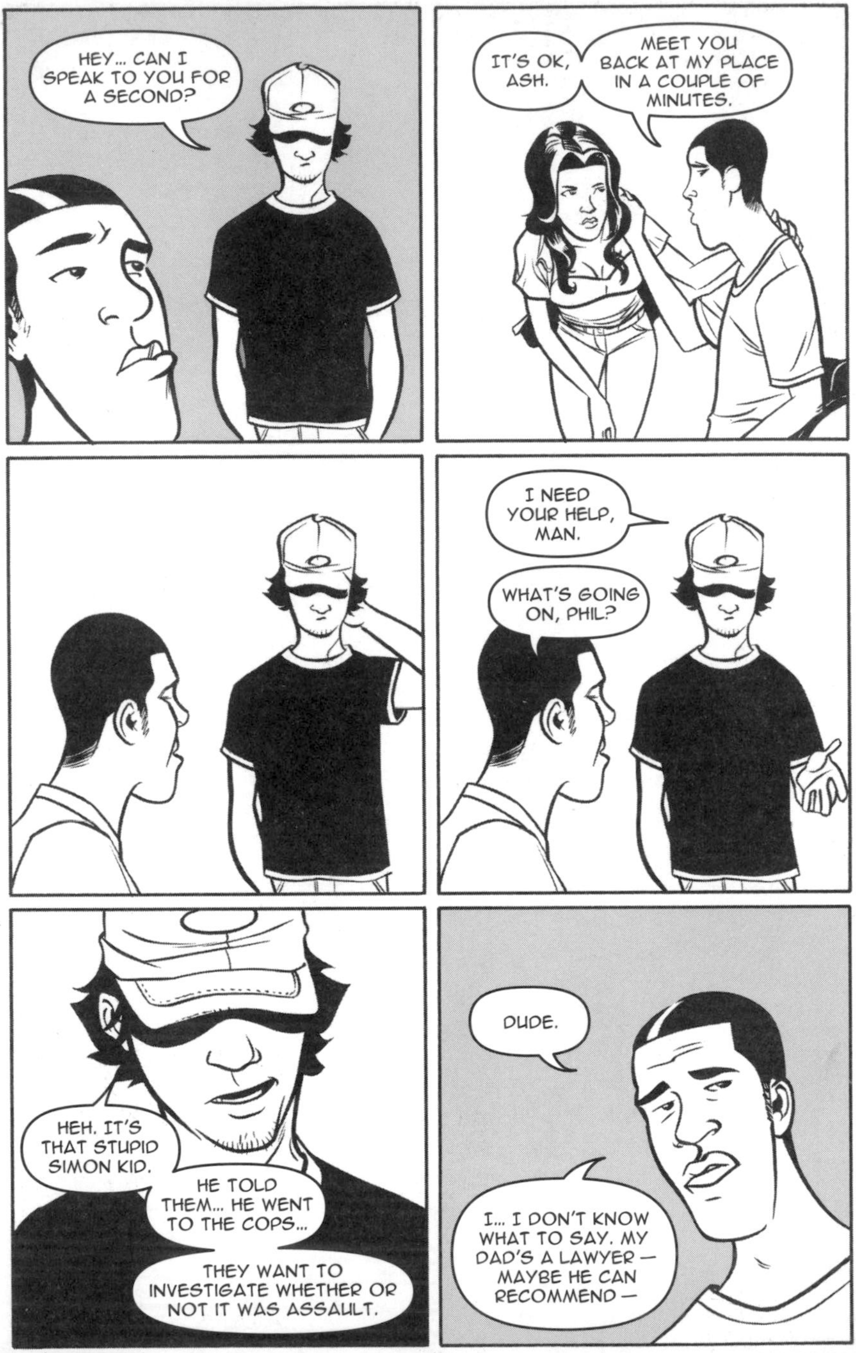
HEY... CAN I SPEAK TO YOU FOR A SECOND?
IT'S OK, ASH.
MEET YOU BACK AT MY PLACE IN A COUPLE OF MINUTES.
I NEED YOUR HELP, MAN.
WHAT'S GOING ON, PHIL?
HEH. IT'S THAT STUPID SIMON KID.
HE TOLD THEM... HE WENT TO THE COPS...
THEY WANT TO INVESTIGATE WHETHER OR NOT IT WAS ASSAULT.
DUDE.
I... I DON'T KNOW WHAT TO SAY. MY DAD'S A LAWYER — MAYBE HE CAN RECOMMEND —

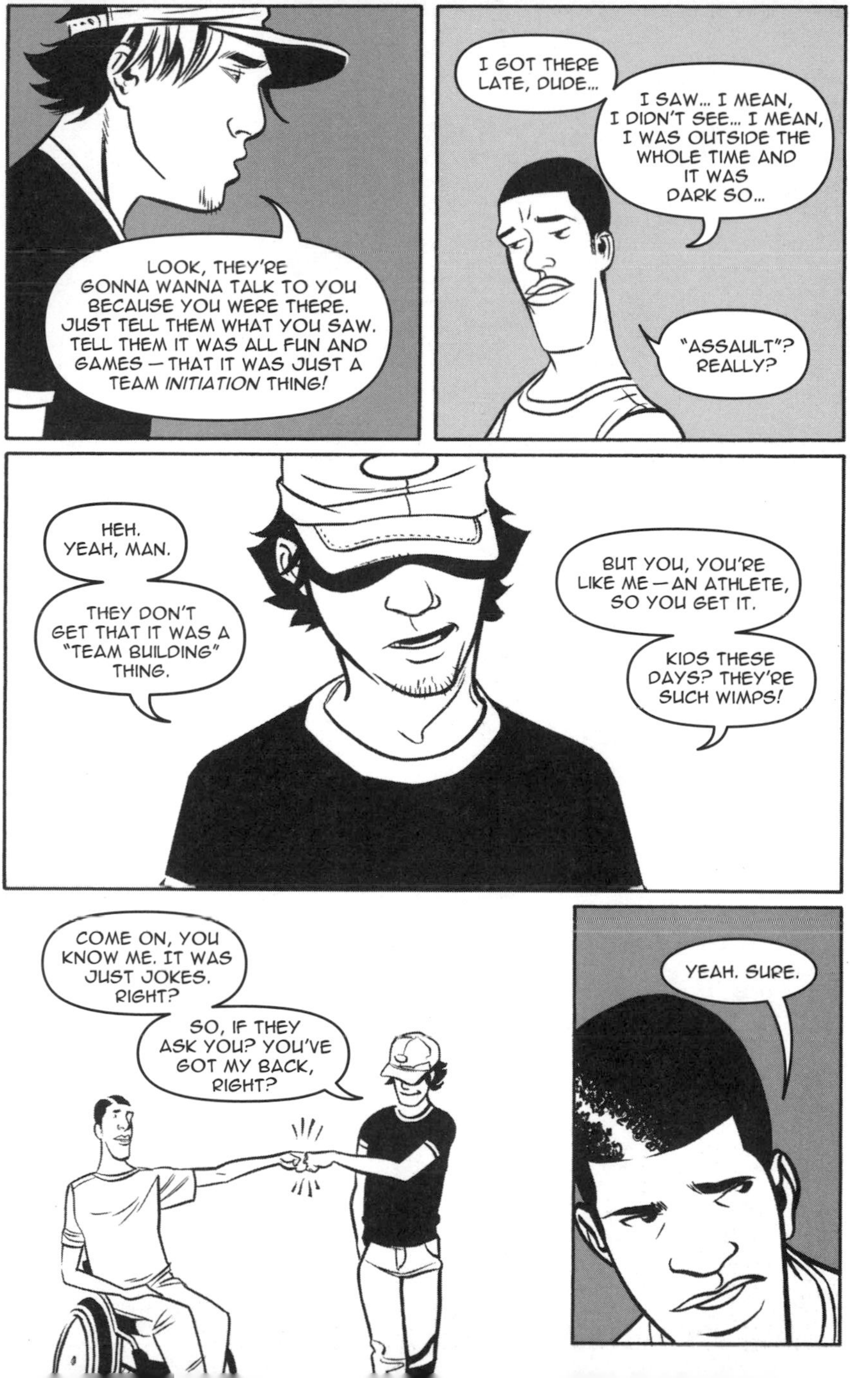
LOOK, THEY'RE GONNA WANNA TALK TO YOU BECAUSE YOU WERE THERE. JUST TELL THEM WHAT YOU SAW. TELL THEM IT WAS ALL FUN AND GAMES — THAT IT WAS JUST A TEAM *INITIATION* THING!
I GOT THERE LATE, DUDE...
I SAW... I MEAN, I DIDN'T SEE... I MEAN, I WAS OUTSIDE THE WHOLE TIME AND IT WAS DARK SO...
"ASSAULT"? REALLY?
HEH. YEAH, MAN.
THEY DON'T GET THAT IT WAS A "TEAM BUILDING" THING.
BUT YOU, YOU'RE LIKE ME — AN ATHLETE, SO YOU GET IT.
KIDS THESE DAYS? THEY'RE SUCH WIMPS!
COME ON, YOU KNOW ME. IT WAS JUST JOKES. RIGHT?
SO, IF THEY ASK YOU? YOU'VE GOT MY BACK, RIGHT?
YEAH. SURE.

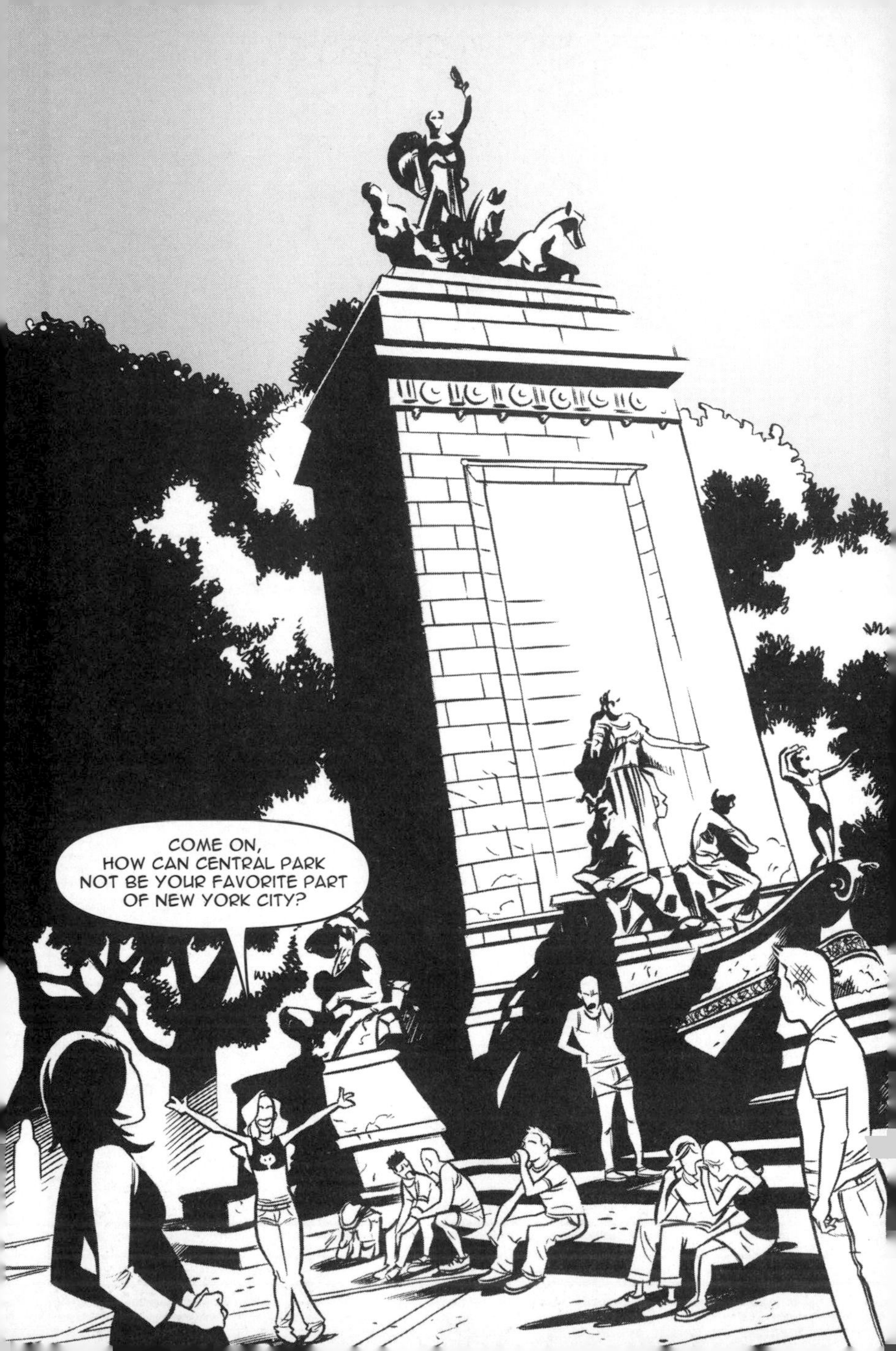
COME ON, HOW CAN CENTRAL PARK NOT BE YOUR FAVORITE PART OF NEW YORK CITY?

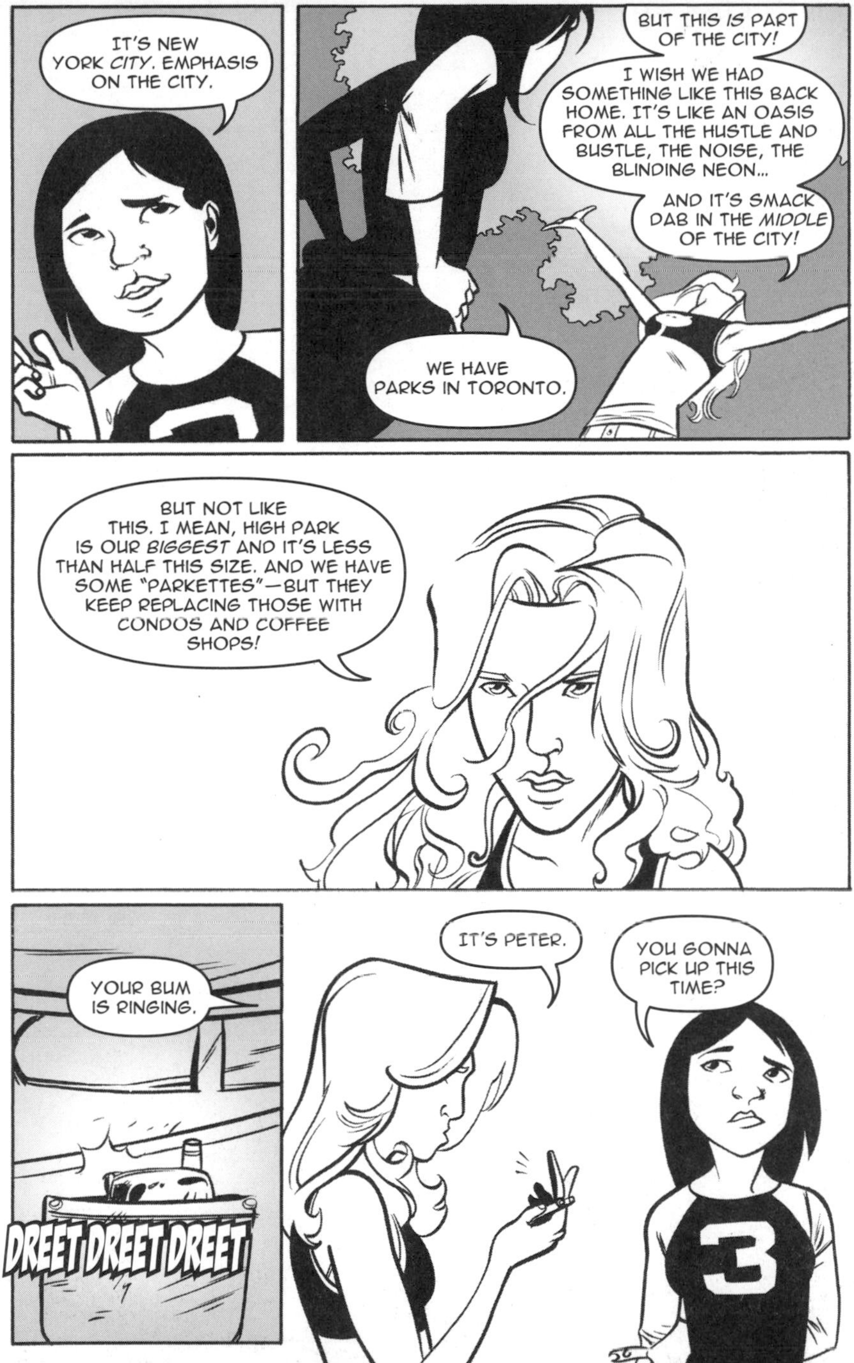

IT'S NEW YORK *CITY*. EMPHASIS ON THE CITY.
BUT THIS *IS* PART OF THE CITY!
I WISH WE HAD SOMETHING LIKE THIS BACK HOME. IT'S LIKE AN OASIS FROM ALL THE HUSTLE AND BUSTLE, THE NOISE, THE BLINDING NEON...
AND IT'S SMACK DAB IN THE *MIDDLE* OF THE CITY!
WE HAVE PARKS IN TORONTO.
BUT NOT LIKE THIS. I MEAN, HIGH PARK IS OUR *BIGGEST* AND IT'S LESS THAN HALF THIS SIZE. AND WE HAVE SOME "PARKETTES"—BUT THEY KEEP REPLACING THOSE WITH CONDOS AND COFFEE SHOPS!
YOUR BUM IS RINGING.
DREET DREET DREET
IT'S PETER.
YOU GONNA PICK UP THIS TIME?

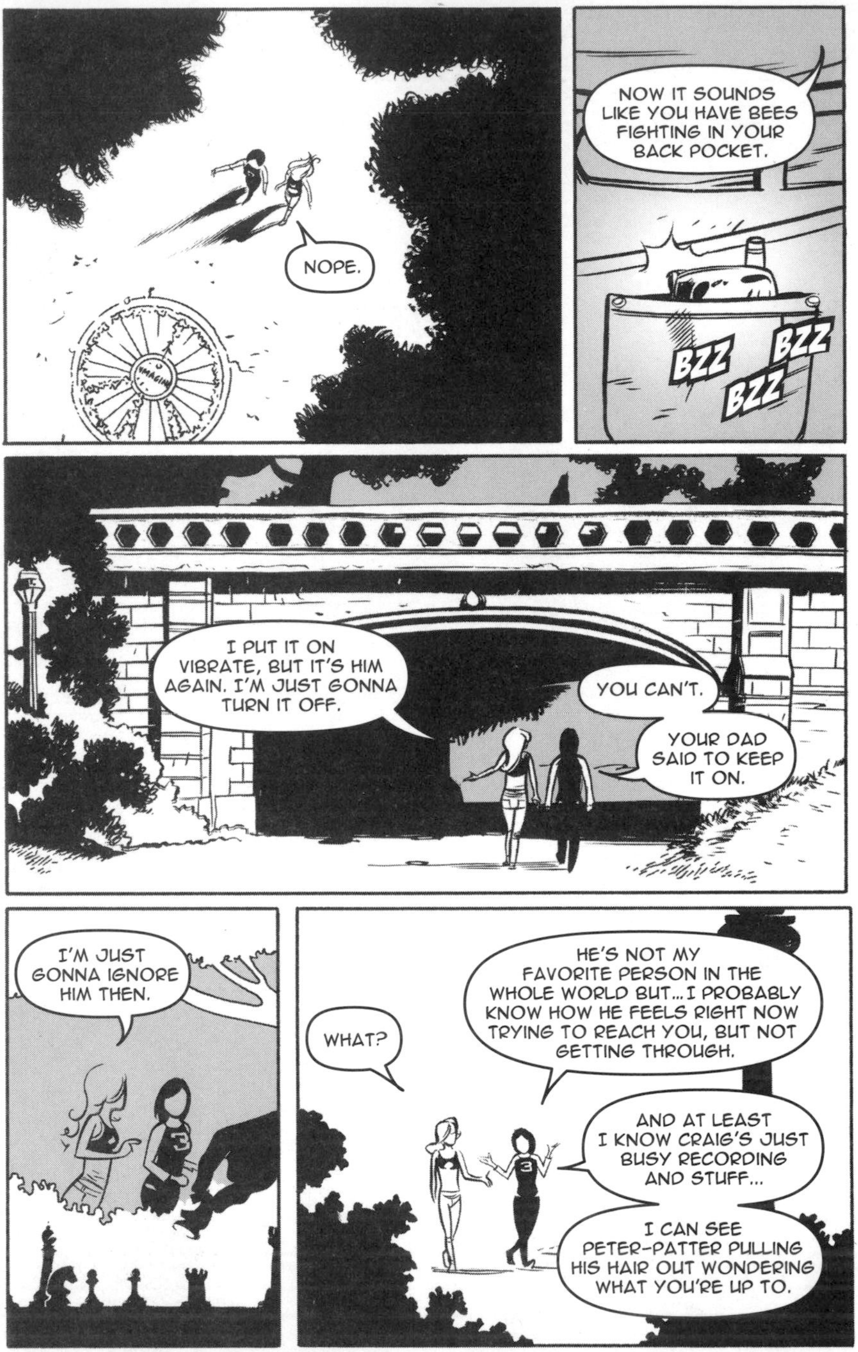
NOPE.
NOW IT SOUNDS LIKE YOU HAVE BEES FIGHTING IN YOUR BACK POCKET.
BZZ
BZZ
BZZ
I PUT IT ON VIBRATE, BUT IT'S HIM AGAIN. I'M JUST GONNA TURN IT OFF.
YOU CAN'T.
YOUR DAD SAID TO KEEP IT ON.
I'M JUST GONNA IGNORE HIM THEN.
WHAT?
HE'S NOT MY FAVORITE PERSON IN THE WHOLE WORLD BUT...I PROBABLY KNOW HOW HE FEELS RIGHT NOW TRYING TO REACH YOU, BUT NOT GETTING THROUGH.
AND AT LEAST I KNOW CRAIG'S JUST BUSY RECORDING AND STUFF...
I CAN SEE PETER-PATTER PULLING HIS HAIR OUT WONDERING WHAT YOU'RE UP TO.

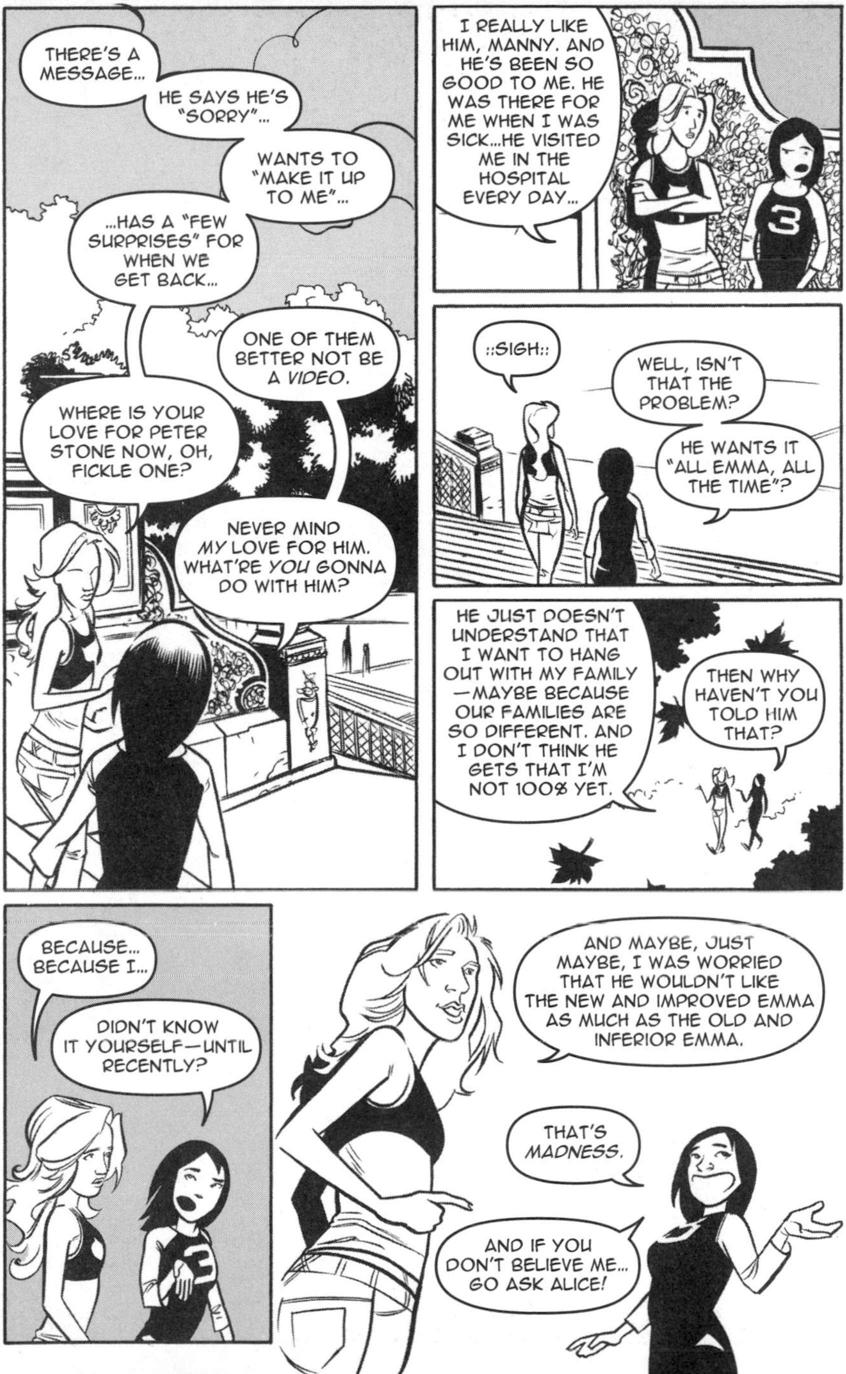
THERE'S A MESSAGE...
HE SAYS HE'S "SORRY"...
WANTS TO "MAKE IT UP TO ME"...
...HAS A "FEW SURPRISES" FOR WHEN WE GET BACK...
ONE OF THEM BETTER NOT BE A *VIDEO*.
WHERE IS YOUR LOVE FOR PETER STONE NOW, OH, FICKLE ONE?
NEVER MIND *MY* LOVE FOR HIM. WHAT'RE *YOU* GONNA DO WITH HIM?
I REALLY LIKE HIM, MANNY. AND HE'S BEEN SO GOOD TO ME. HE WAS THERE FOR ME WHEN I WAS SICK...HE VISITED ME IN THE HOSPITAL EVERY DAY...
::SIGH::
WELL, ISN'T THAT THE PROBLEM?
HE WANTS IT "ALL EMMA, ALL THE TIME"?
HE JUST DOESN'T UNDERSTAND THAT I WANT TO HANG OUT WITH MY FAMILY—MAYBE BECAUSE OUR FAMILIES ARE SO DIFFERENT. AND I DON'T THINK HE GETS THAT I'M NOT 100% YET.
THEN WHY HAVEN'T YOU TOLD HIM THAT?
BECAUSE... BECAUSE I...
DIDN'T KNOW IT YOURSELF—UNTIL RECENTLY?
AND MAYBE, JUST MAYBE, I WAS WORRIED THAT HE WOULDN'T LIKE THE NEW AND IMPROVED EMMA AS MUCH AS THE OLD AND INFERIOR EMMA.
THAT'S *MADNESS*.
AND IF YOU DON'T BELIEVE ME... GO ASK ALICE!

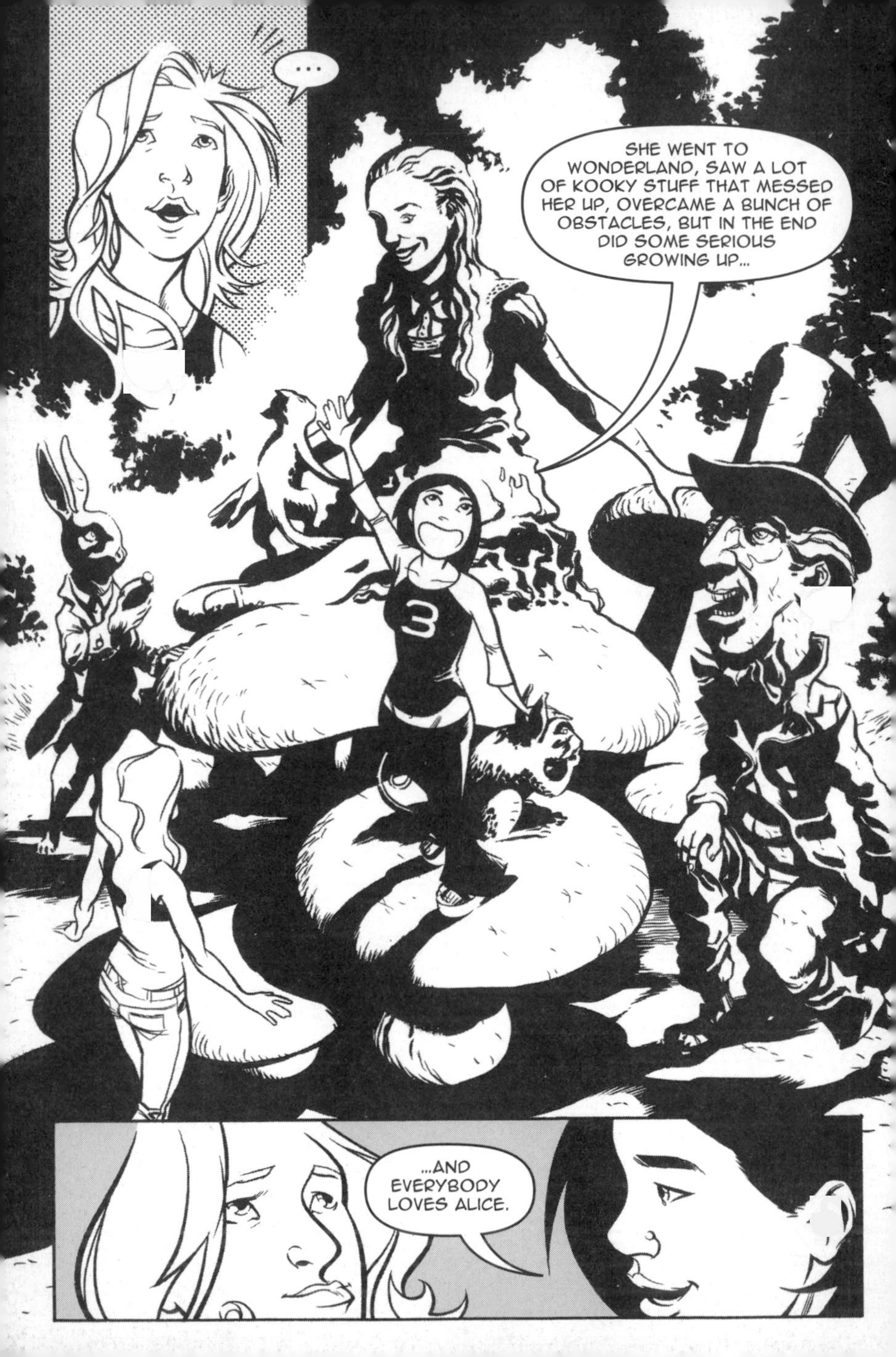
...
SHE WENT TO WONDERLAND, SAW A LOT OF KOOKY STUFF THAT MESSED HER UP, OVERCAME A BUNCH OF OBSTACLES, BUT IN THE END DID SOME SERIOUS GROWING UP...
...AND EVERYBODY LOVES ALICE.

ACT 3

"I speak for the trees."

—The Lorax

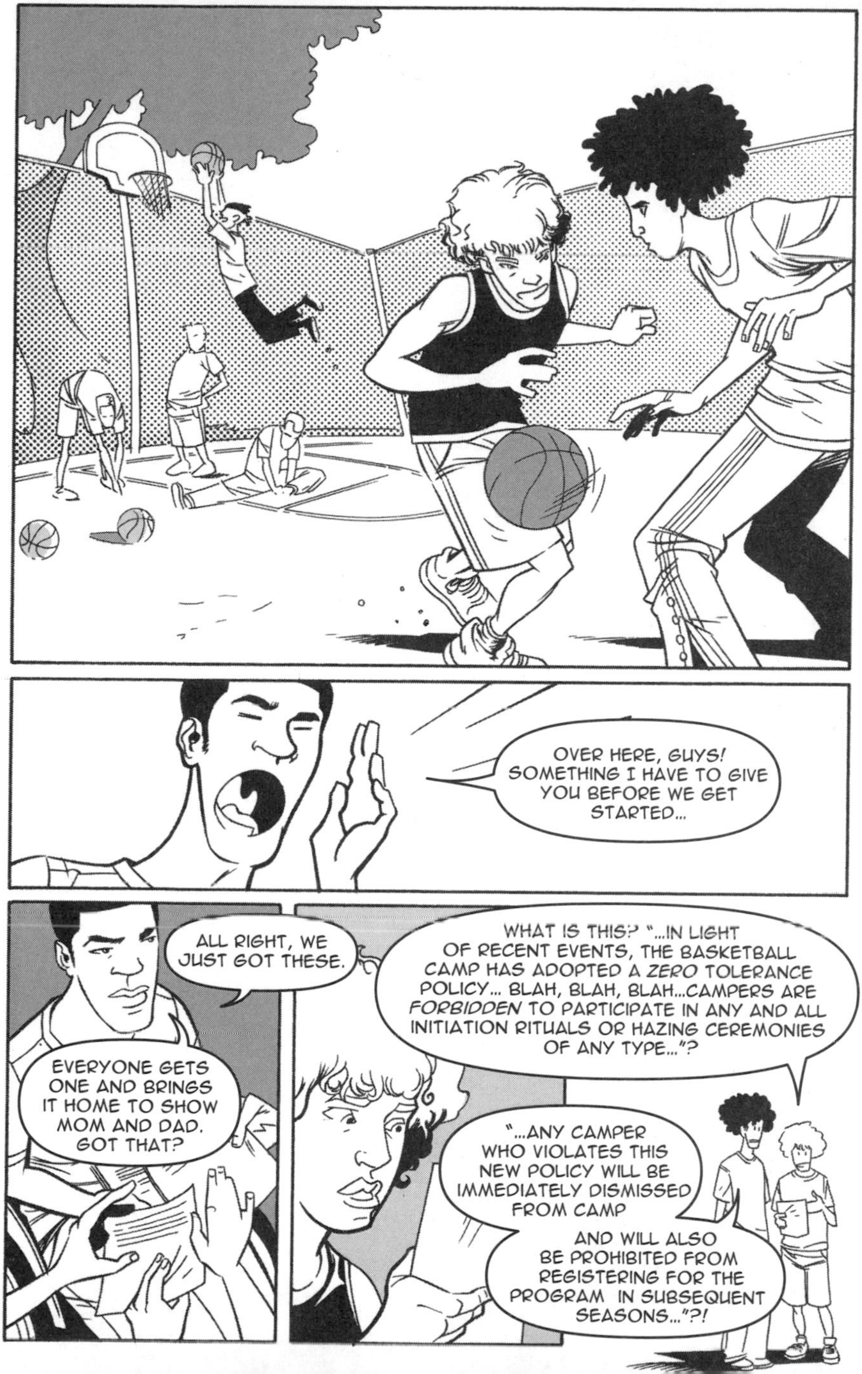
OVER HERE, GUYS! SOMETHING I HAVE TO GIVE YOU BEFORE WE GET STARTED...
ALL RIGHT, WE JUST GOT THESE.
EVERYONE GETS ONE AND BRINGS IT HOME TO SHOW MOM AND DAD. GOT THAT?
WHAT IS THIS? "...IN LIGHT OF RECENT EVENTS, THE BASKETBALL CAMP HAS ADOPTED A *ZERO* TOLERANCE POLICY... BLAH, BLAH, BLAH...CAMPERS ARE *FORBIDDEN* TO PARTICIPATE IN ANY AND ALL INITIATION RITUALS OR HAZING CEREMONIES OF ANY TYPE..."?
"...ANY CAMPER WHO VIOLATES THIS NEW POLICY WILL BE IMMEDIATELY DISMISSED FROM CAMP
AND WILL ALSO BE PROHIBITED FROM REGISTERING FOR THE PROGRAM IN SUBSEQUENT SEASONS..."?!

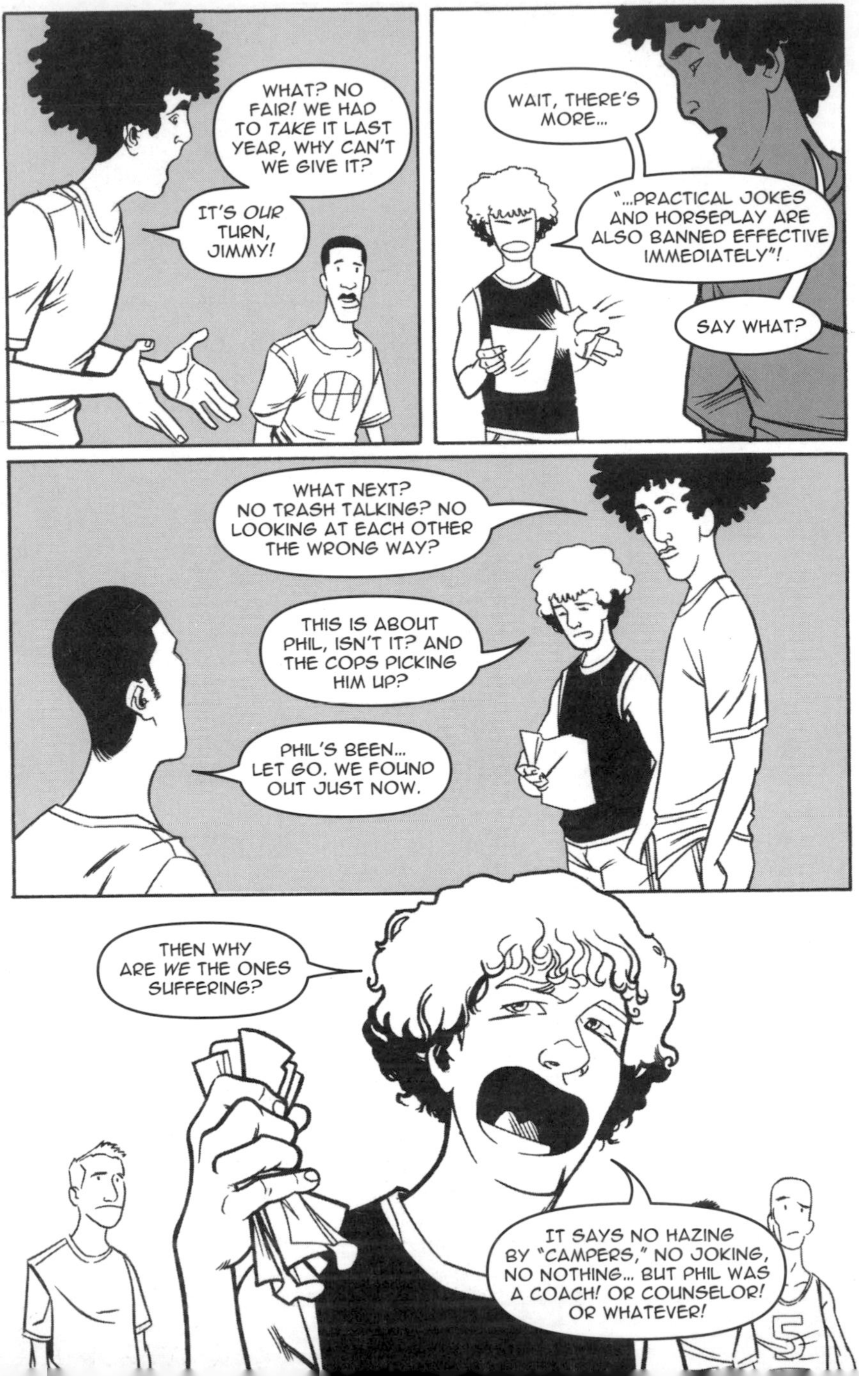
WHAT? NO FAIR! WE HAD TO *TAKE* IT LAST YEAR, WHY CAN'T WE GIVE IT?
IT'S *OUR* TURN, JIMMY!
WAIT, THERE'S MORE...
"...PRACTICAL JOKES AND HORSEPLAY ARE ALSO BANNED EFFECTIVE IMMEDIATELY"!
SAY WHAT?
WHAT NEXT? NO TRASH TALKING? NO LOOKING AT EACH OTHER THE WRONG WAY?
THIS IS ABOUT PHIL, ISN'T IT? AND THE COPS PICKING HIM UP?
PHIL'S BEEN... LET GO. WE FOUND OUT JUST NOW.
THEN WHY ARE *WE* THE ONES SUFFERING?
IT SAYS NO HAZING BY "CAMPERS," NO JOKING, NO NOTHING... BUT PHIL WAS A COACH! OR COUNSELOR! OR WHATEVER!

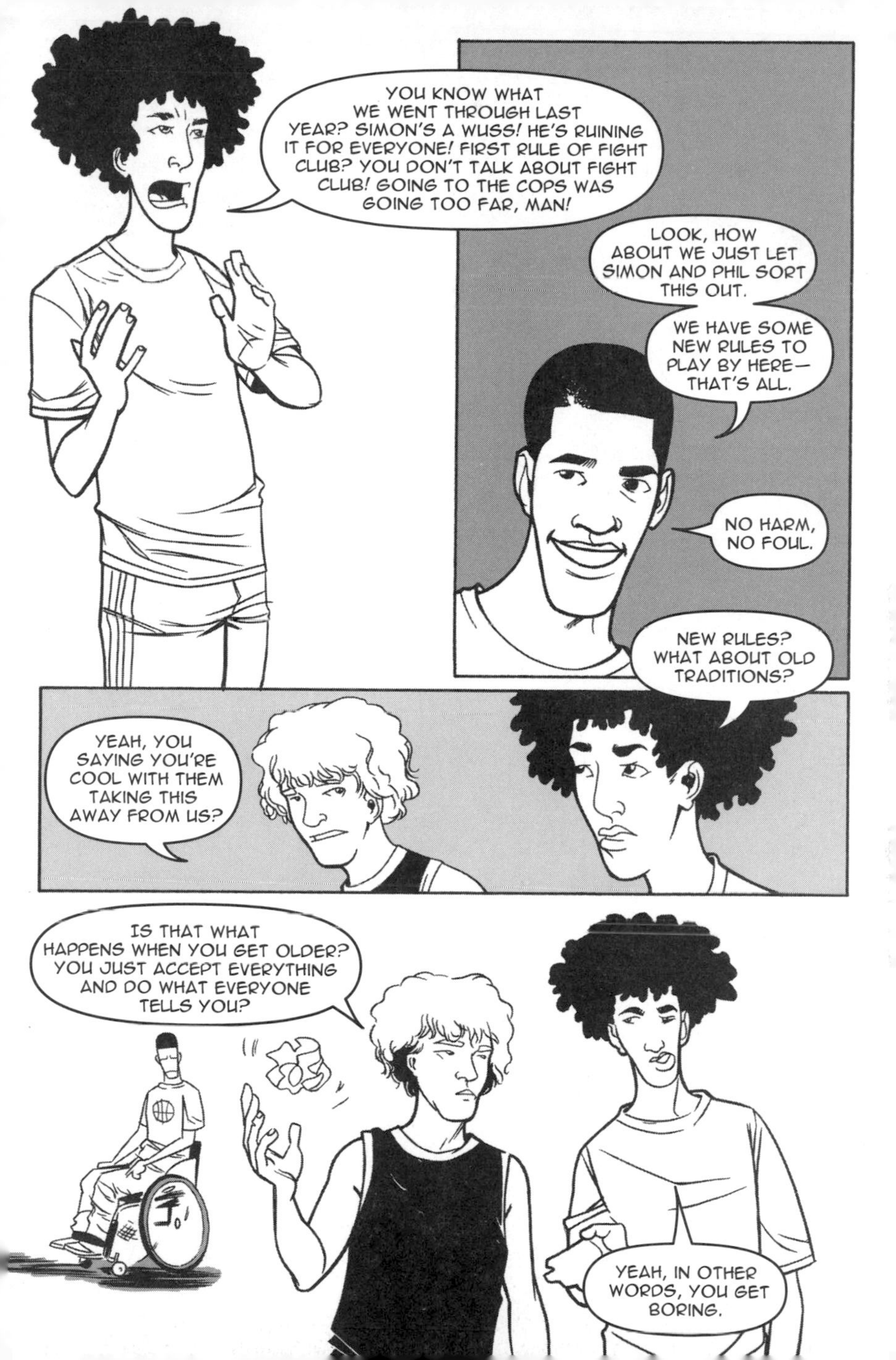
YOU KNOW WHAT WE WENT THROUGH LAST YEAR? SIMON'S A WUSS! HE'S RUINING IT FOR EVERYONE! FIRST RULE OF FIGHT CLUB? YOU DON'T TALK ABOUT FIGHT CLUB! GOING TO THE COPS WAS GOING TOO FAR, MAN!
LOOK, HOW ABOUT WE JUST LET SIMON AND PHIL SORT THIS OUT.
WE HAVE SOME NEW RULES TO PLAY BY HERE—THAT'S ALL.
NO HARM, NO FOUL.
NEW RULES? WHAT ABOUT OLD TRADITIONS?
YEAH, YOU SAYING YOU'RE COOL WITH THEM TAKING THIS AWAY FROM US?
IS THAT WHAT HAPPENS WHEN YOU GET OLDER? YOU JUST ACCEPT EVERYTHING AND DO WHAT EVERYONE TELLS YOU?
YEAH, IN OTHER WORDS, YOU GET BORING.

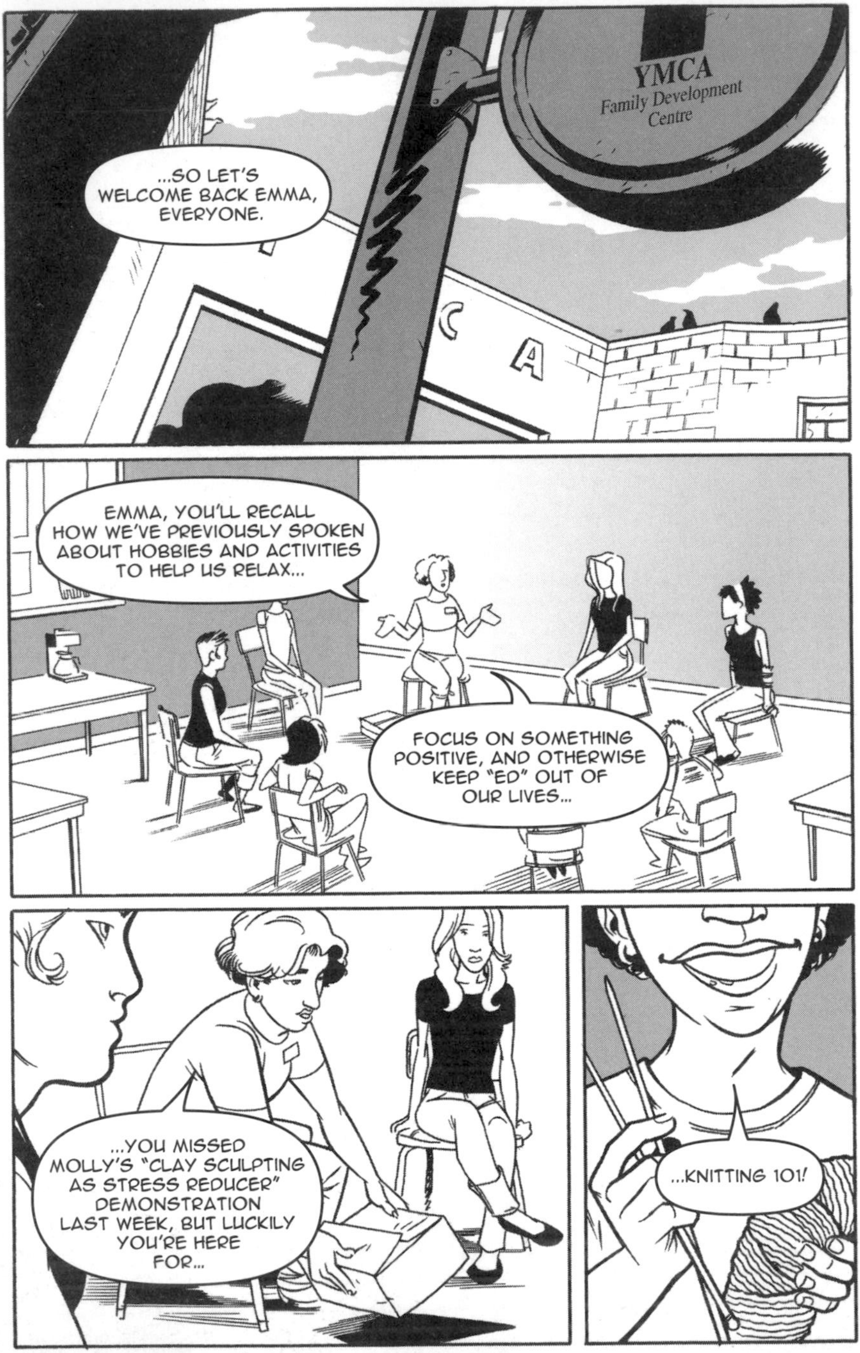
YMCA
Family Development
Centre
...SO LET'S WELCOME BACK EMMA, EVERYONE.
C A
EMMA, YOU'LL RECALL HOW WE'VE PREVIOUSLY SPOKEN ABOUT HOBBIES AND ACTIVITIES TO HELP US RELAX...
FOCUS ON SOMETHING POSITIVE, AND OTHERWISE KEEP "ED" OUT OF OUR LIVES...
...YOU MISSED MOLLY'S "CLAY SCULPTING AS STRESS REDUCER" DEMONSTRATION LAST WEEK, BUT LUCKILY YOU'RE HERE FOR...
...KNITTING 101!

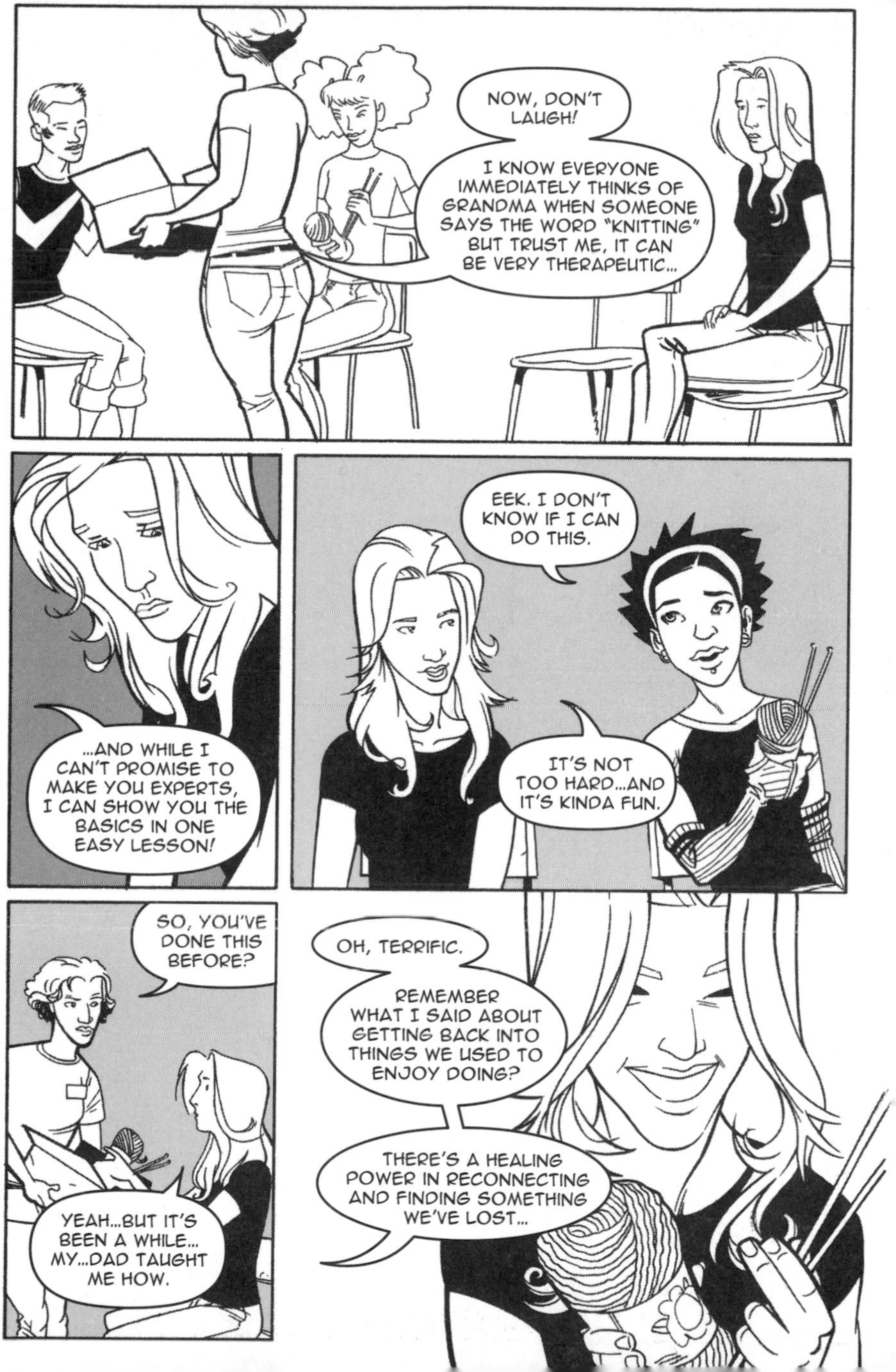
NOW, DON'T LAUGH!
I KNOW EVERYONE IMMEDIATELY THINKS OF GRANDMA WHEN SOMEONE SAYS THE WORD "KNITTING" BUT TRUST ME, IT CAN BE VERY THERAPEUTIC...
...AND WHILE I CAN'T PROMISE TO MAKE YOU EXPERTS, I CAN SHOW YOU THE BASICS IN ONE EASY LESSON!
EEK. I DON'T KNOW IF I CAN DO THIS.
IT'S NOT TOO HARD...AND IT'S KINDA FUN.
SO, YOU'VE DONE THIS BEFORE?
YEAH...BUT IT'S BEEN A WHILE... MY...DAD TAUGHT ME HOW.
OH, TERRIFIC.
REMEMBER WHAT I SAID ABOUT GETTING BACK INTO THINGS WE USED TO ENJOY DOING?
THERE'S A HEALING POWER IN RECONNECTING AND FINDING SOMETHING WE'VE LOST...

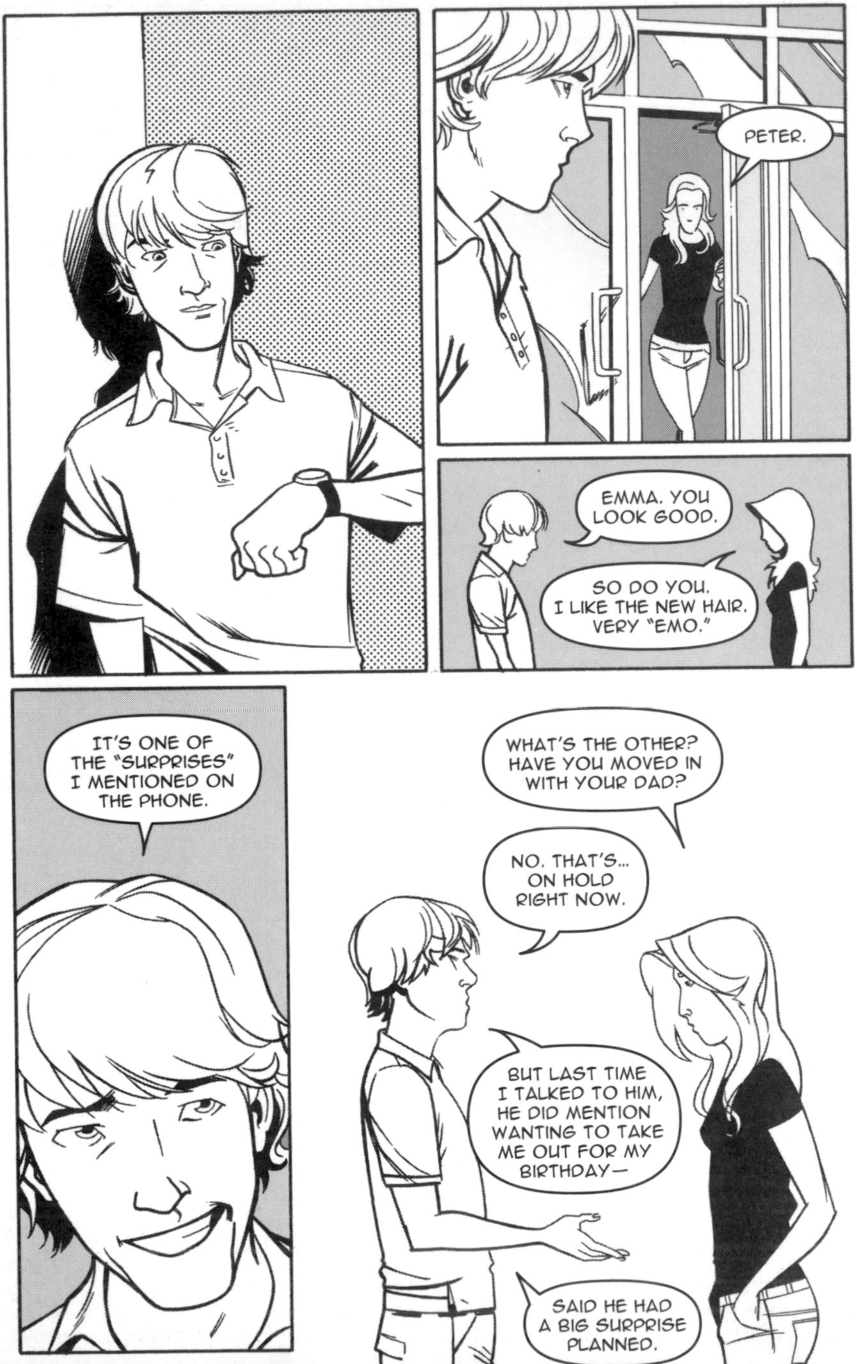
PETER.
EMMA. YOU LOOK GOOD.
SO DO YOU. I LIKE THE NEW HAIR. VERY "EMO."
IT'S ONE OF THE "SURPRISES" I MENTIONED ON THE PHONE.
WHAT'S THE OTHER? HAVE YOU MOVED IN WITH YOUR DAD?
NO. THAT'S... ON HOLD RIGHT NOW.
BUT LAST TIME I TALKED TO HIM, HE DID MENTION WANTING TO TAKE ME OUT FOR MY BIRTHDAY—
SAID HE HAD A BIG SURPRISE PLANNED.

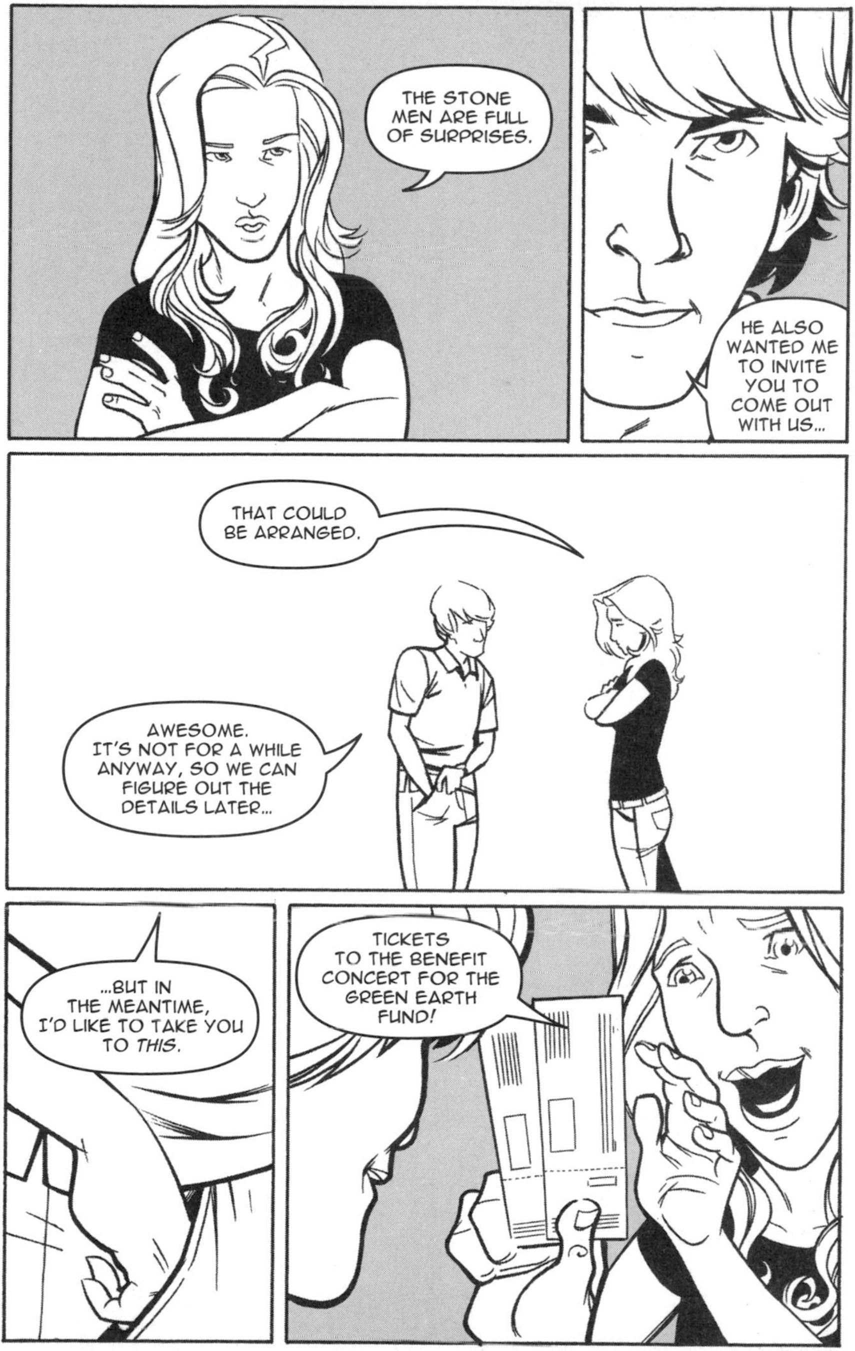
THE STONE MEN ARE FULL OF SURPRISES.
HE ALSO WANTED ME TO INVITE YOU TO COME OUT WITH US...
THAT COULD BE ARRANGED.
AWESOME. IT'S NOT FOR A WHILE ANYWAY, SO WE CAN FIGURE OUT THE DETAILS LATER...
...BUT IN THE MEANTIME, I'D LIKE TO TAKE YOU TO *THIS*.
TICKETS TO THE BENEFIT CONCERT FOR THE GREEN EARTH FUND!

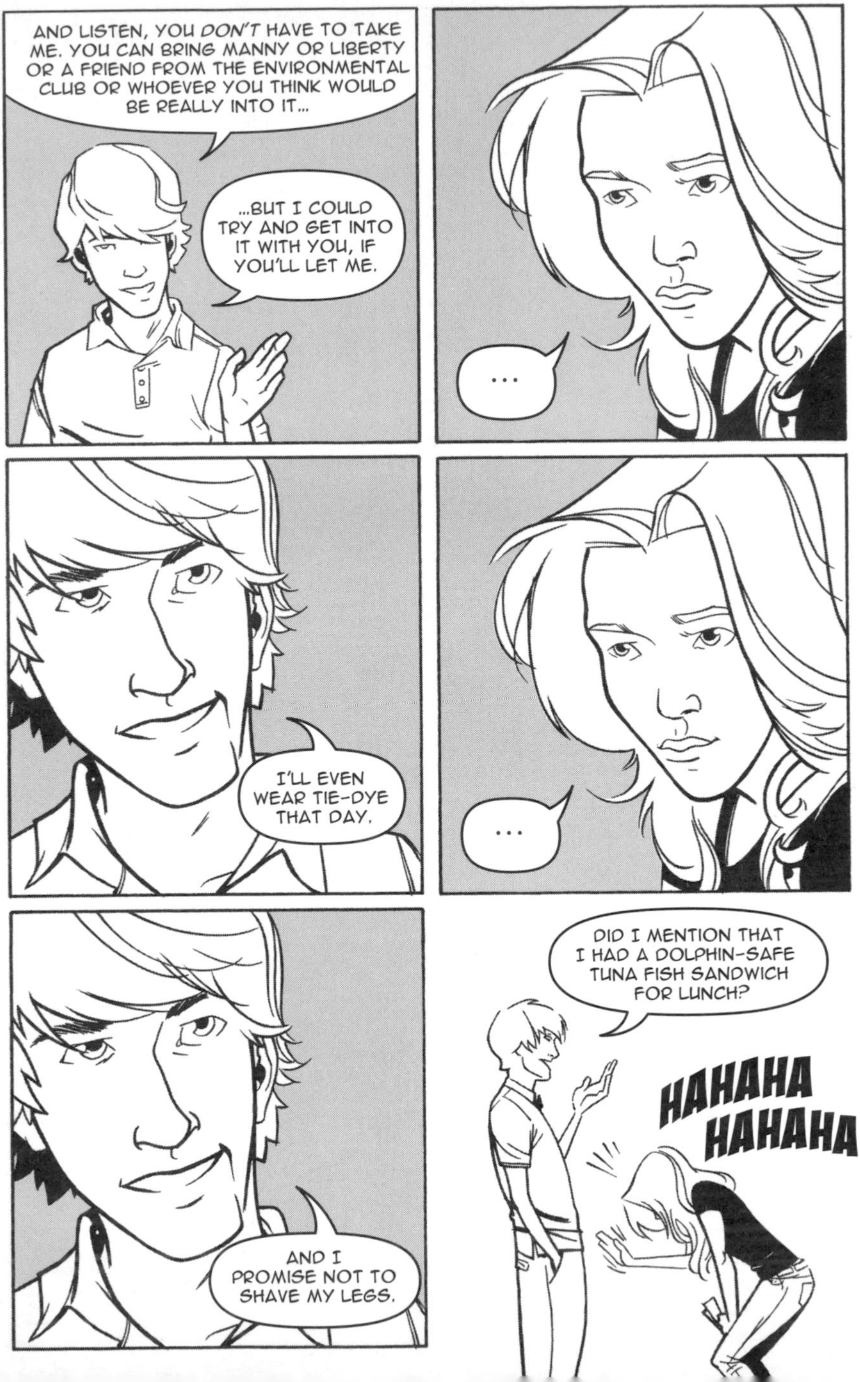
AND LISTEN, YOU *DON'T* HAVE TO TAKE ME. YOU CAN BRING MANNY OR LIBERTY OR A FRIEND FROM THE ENVIRONMENTAL CLUB OR WHOEVER YOU THINK WOULD BE REALLY INTO IT...
...BUT I COULD TRY AND GET INTO IT WITH YOU, IF YOU'LL LET ME.
...
I'LL EVEN WEAR TIE-DYE THAT DAY.
...
AND I PROMISE NOT TO SHAVE MY LEGS.
DID I MENTION THAT I HAD A DOLPHIN-SAFE TUNA FISH SANDWICH FOR LUNCH?
HAHAHA HAHAHA

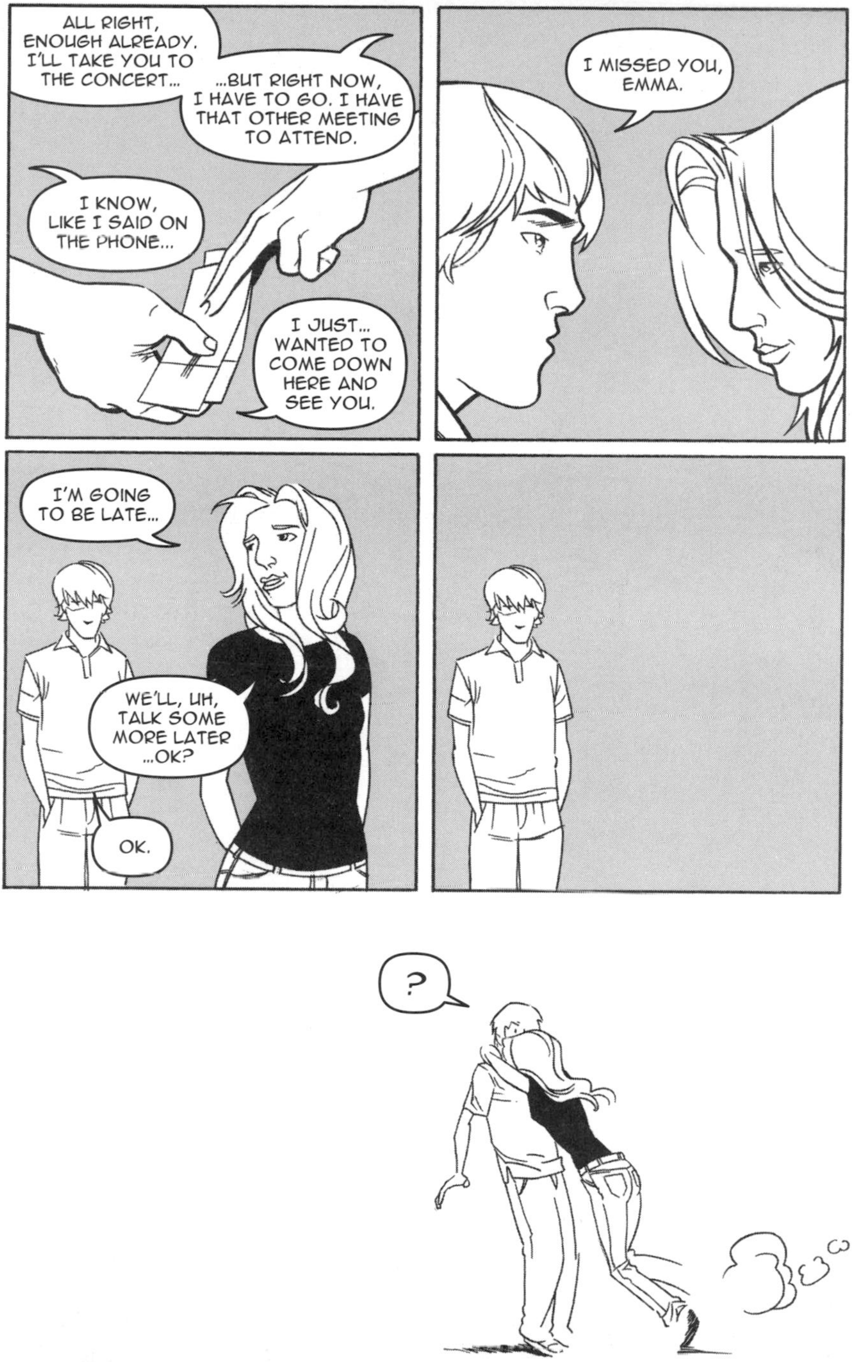
ALL RIGHT, ENOUGH ALREADY. I'LL TAKE YOU TO THE CONCERT...
...BUT RIGHT NOW, I HAVE TO GO. I HAVE THAT OTHER MEETING TO ATTEND.
I KNOW, LIKE I SAID ON THE PHONE...
I JUST... WANTED TO COME DOWN HERE AND SEE YOU.
I MISSED YOU, EMMA.
I'M GOING TO BE LATE...
WE'LL, UH, TALK SOME MORE LATER ...OK?
OK.
?

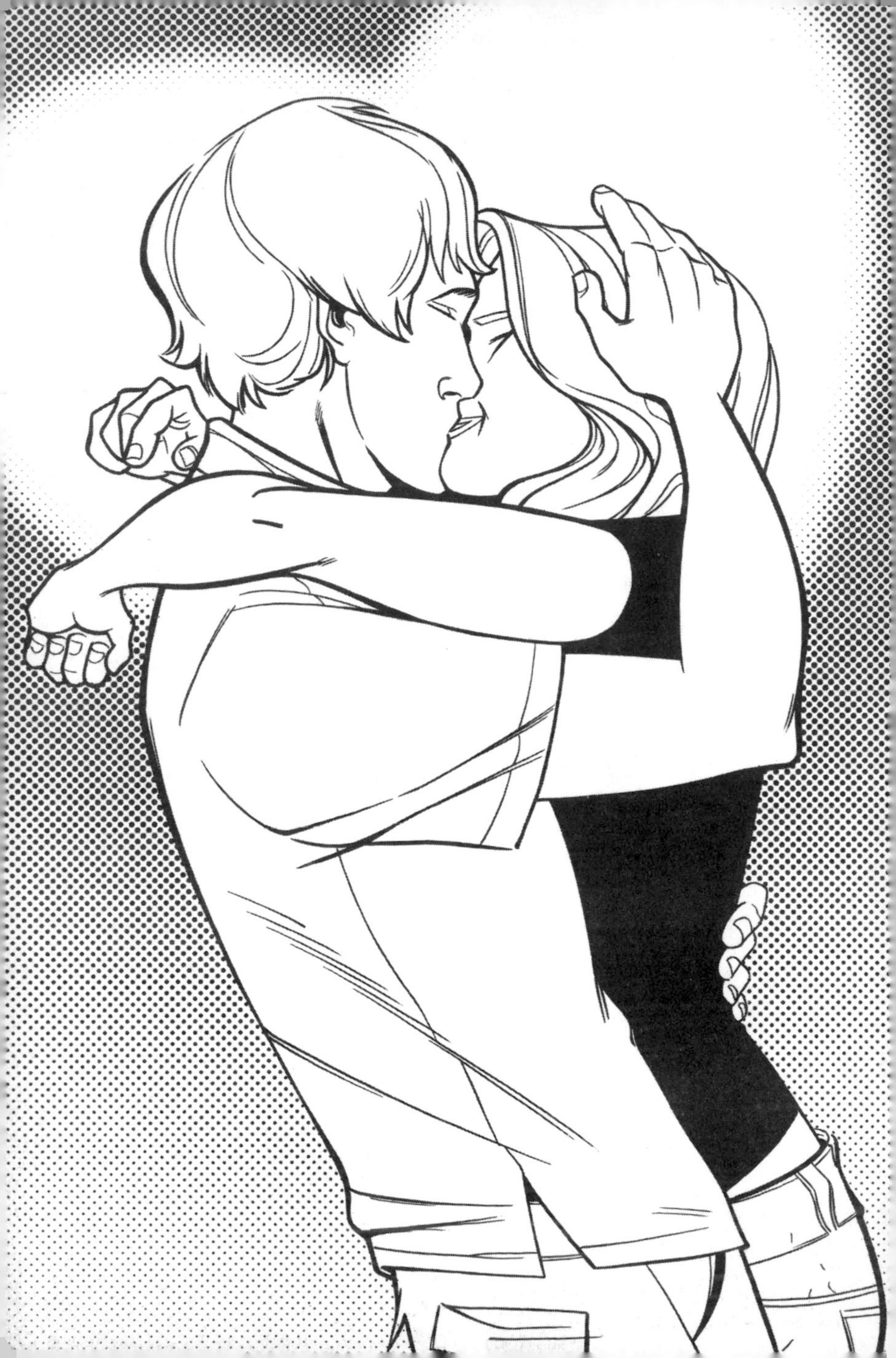

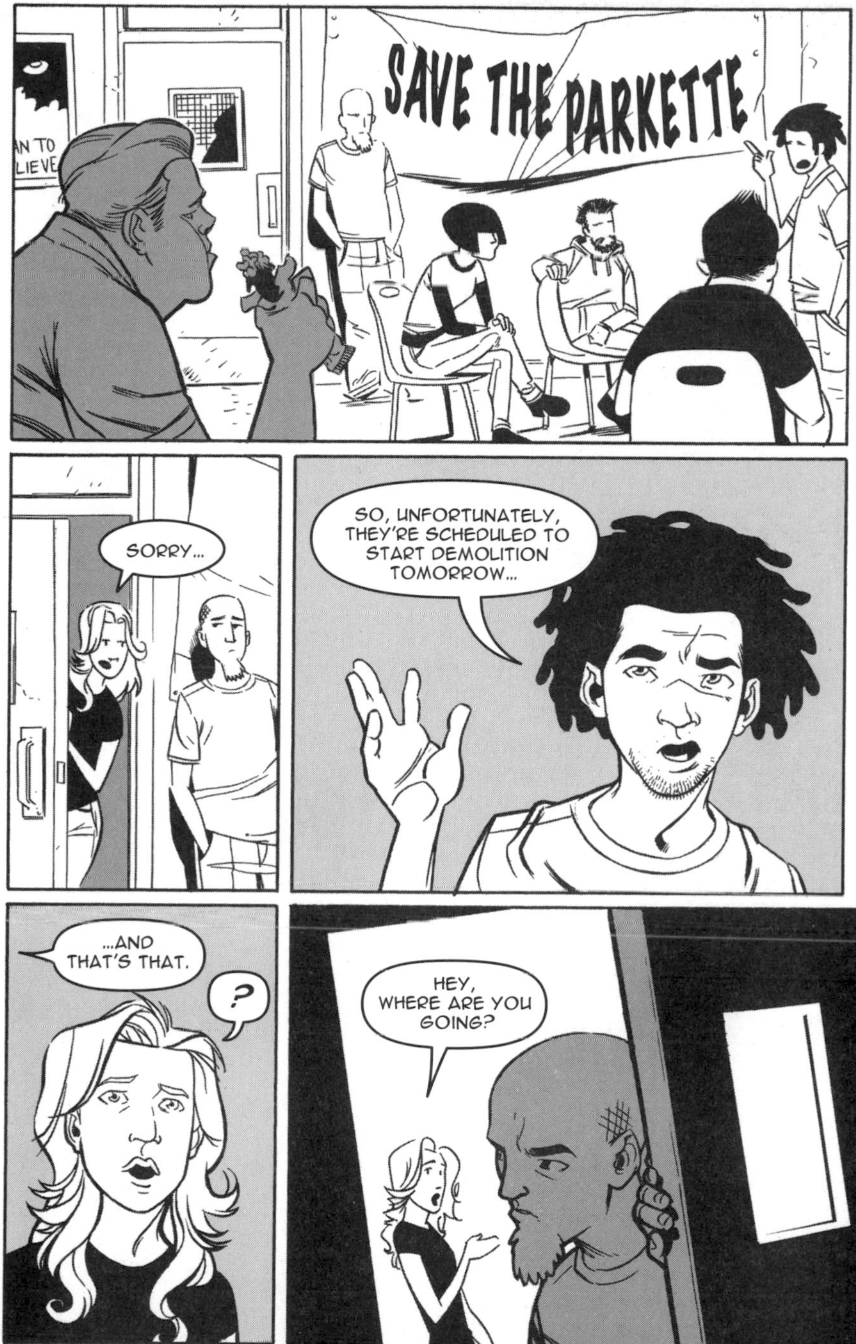
SAVE THE PARKETTE
SORRY...
SO, UNFORTUNATELY, THEY'RE SCHEDULED TO START DEMOLITION TOMORROW...
...AND THAT'S THAT.
?
HEY, WHERE ARE YOU GOING?

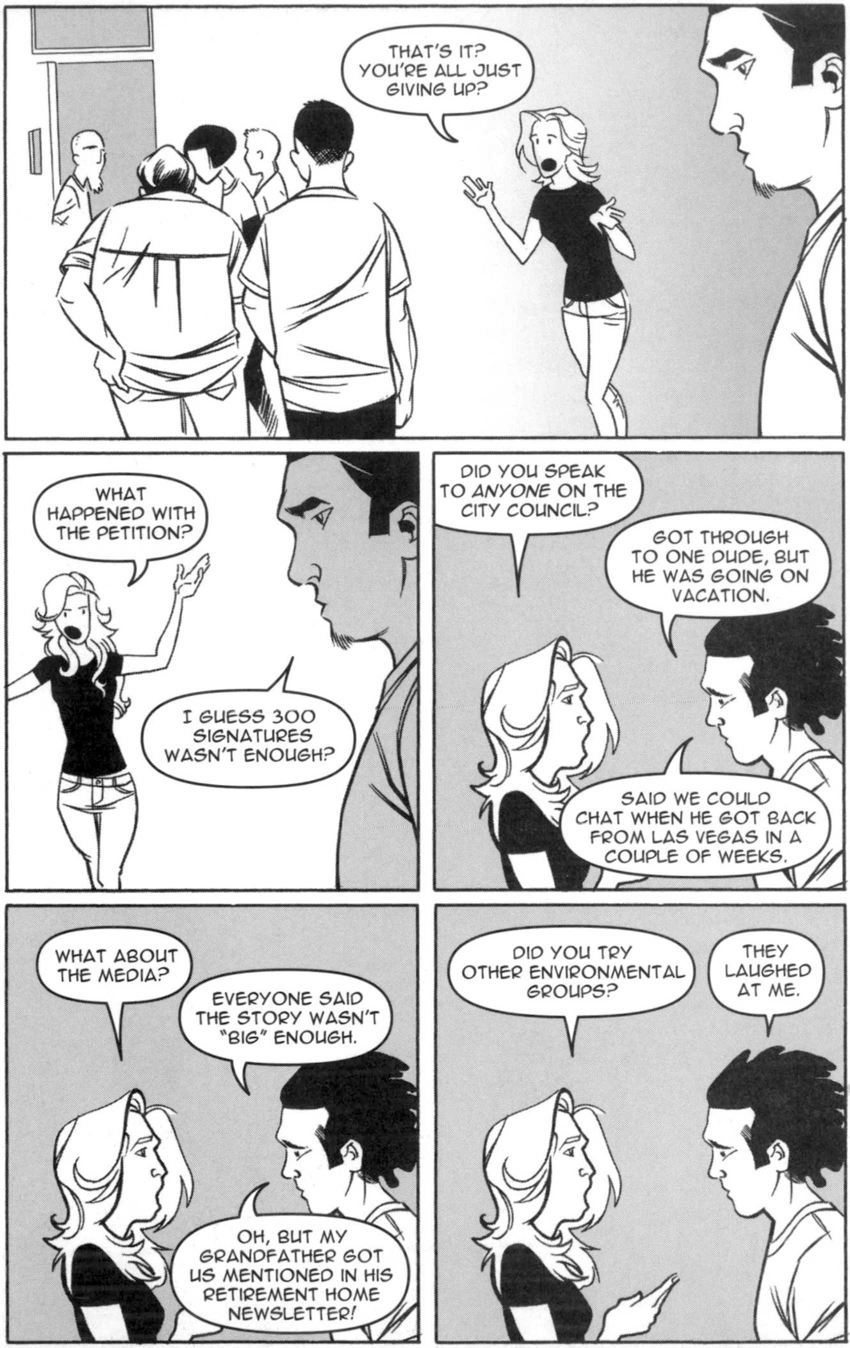
THAT'S IT? YOU'RE ALL JUST GIVING UP?
WHAT HAPPENED WITH THE PETITION?
I GUESS 300 SIGNATURES WASN'T ENOUGH?
DID YOU SPEAK TO *ANYONE* ON THE CITY COUNCIL?
GOT THROUGH TO ONE DUDE, BUT HE WAS GOING ON VACATION.
SAID WE COULD CHAT WHEN HE GOT BACK FROM LAS VEGAS IN A COUPLE OF WEEKS.
WHAT ABOUT THE MEDIA?
EVERYONE SAID THE STORY WASN'T "BIG" ENOUGH.
OH, BUT MY GRANDFATHER GOT US MENTIONED IN HIS RETIREMENT HOME NEWSLETTER!
DID YOU TRY OTHER ENVIRONMENTAL GROUPS?
THEY LAUGHED AT ME.

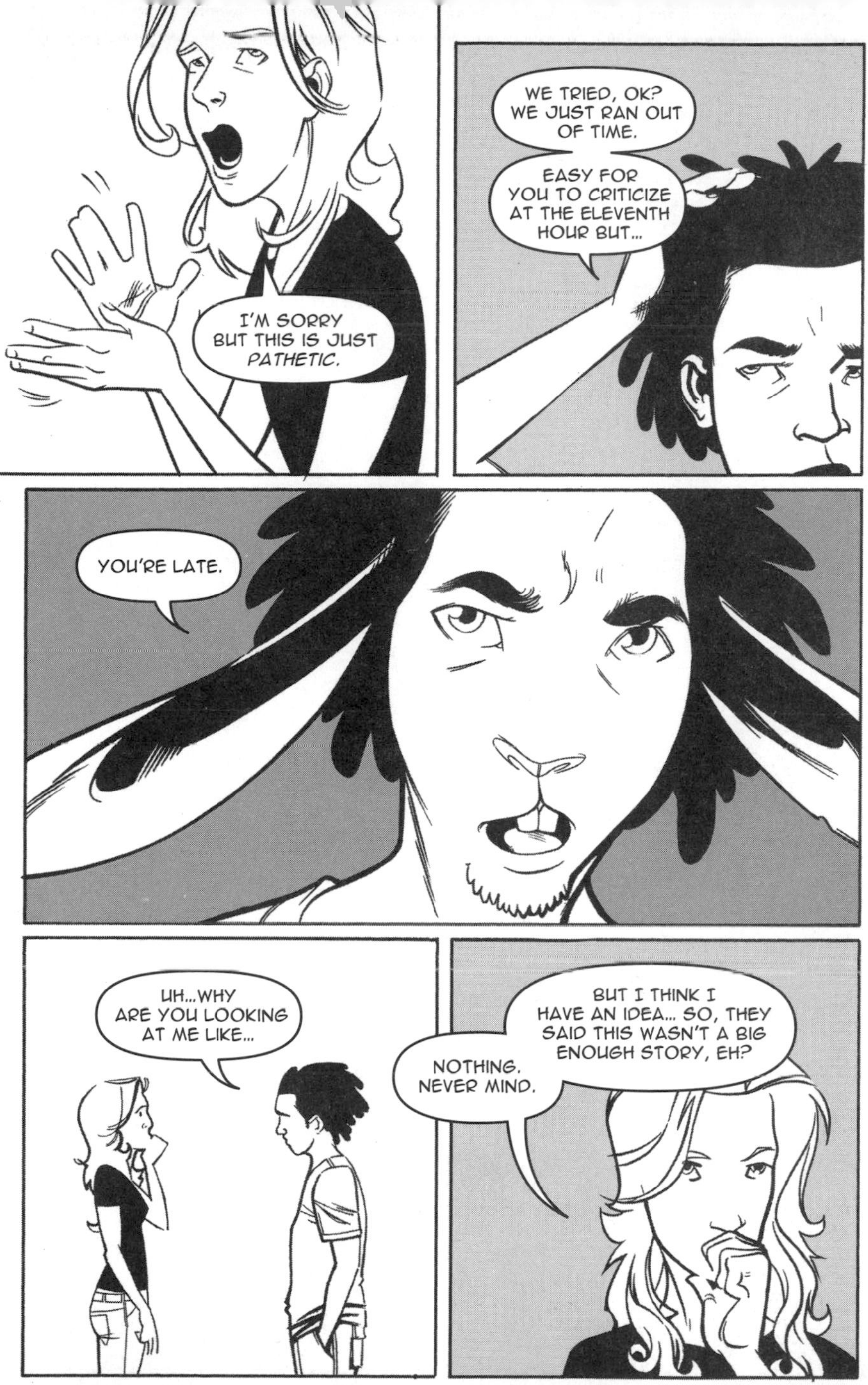
I'M SORRY BUT THIS IS JUST *PATHETIC.*
WE TRIED, OK? WE JUST RAN OUT OF TIME.
EASY FOR YOU TO CRITICIZE AT THE ELEVENTH HOUR BUT...
YOU'RE LATE.
UH...WHY ARE YOU LOOKING AT ME LIKE...
NOTHING. NEVER MIND.
BUT I THINK I HAVE AN IDEA... SO, THEY SAID THIS WASN'T A BIG ENOUGH STORY, EH?

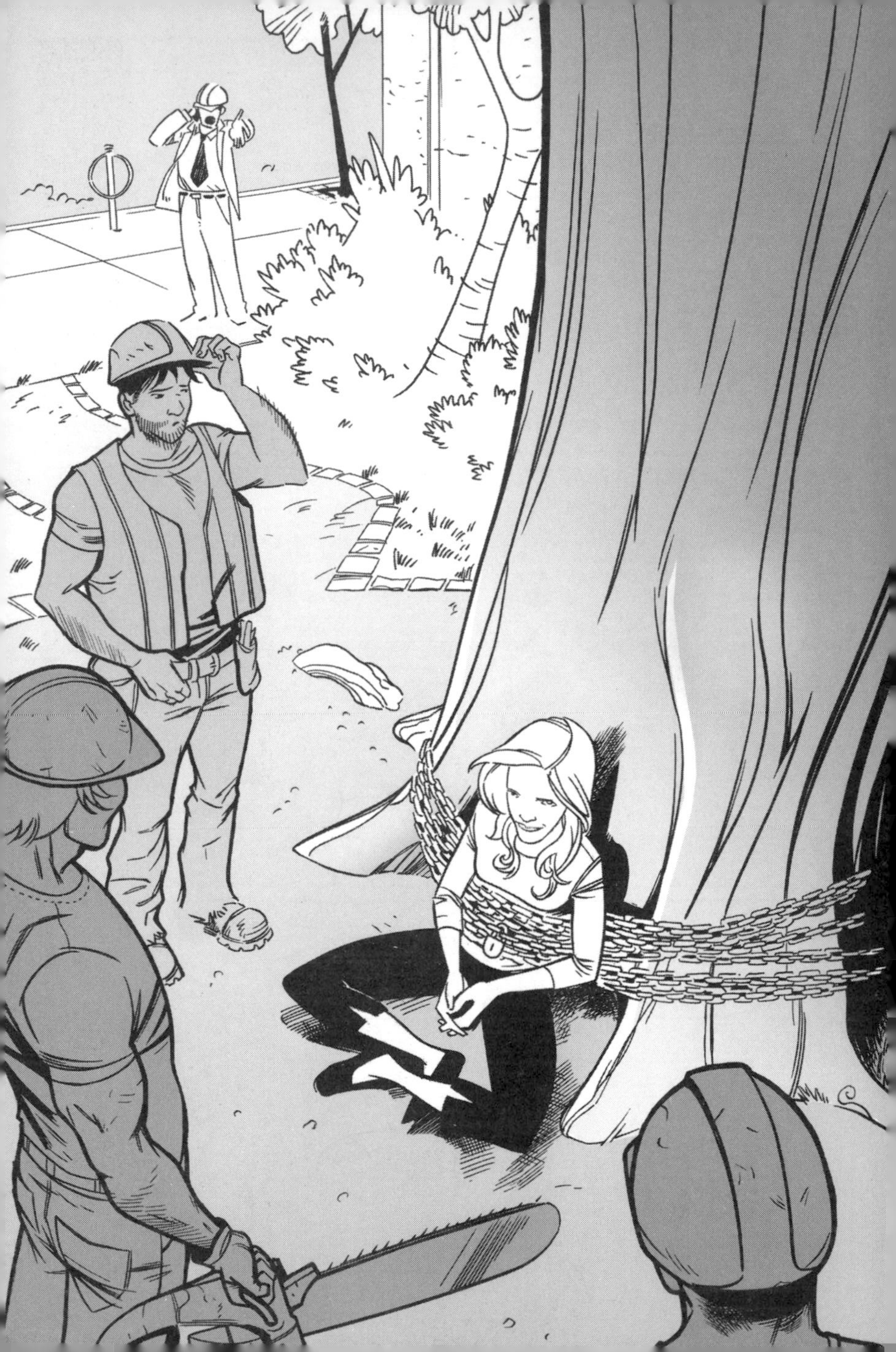

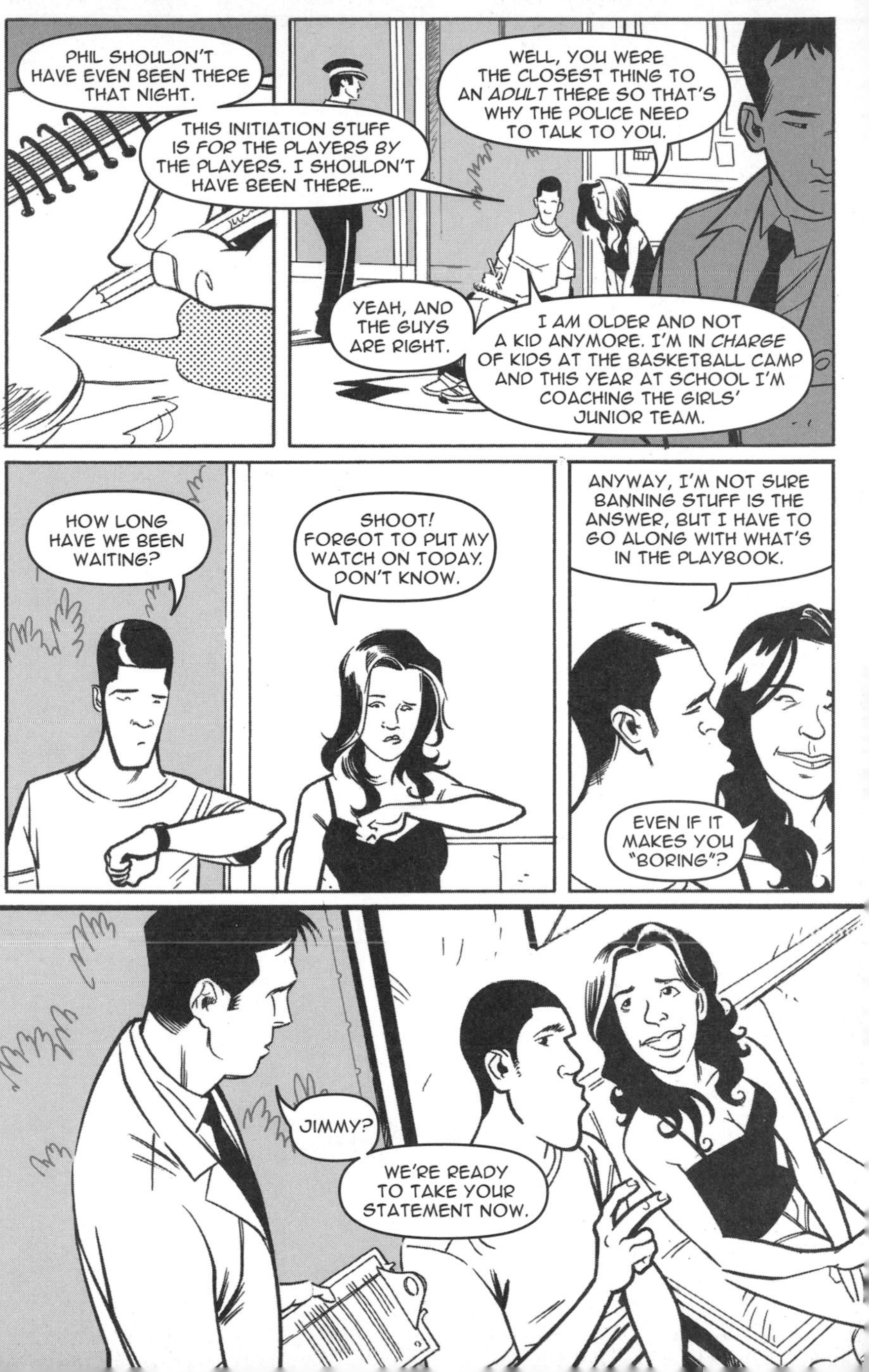
PHIL SHOULDN'T HAVE EVEN BEEN THERE THAT NIGHT.
THIS INITIATION STUFF IS *FOR* THE PLAYERS BY THE PLAYERS. I SHOULDN'T HAVE BEEN THERE...
WELL, YOU WERE THE CLOSEST THING TO AN *ADULT* THERE SO THAT'S WHY THE POLICE NEED TO TALK TO YOU.
YEAH, AND THE GUYS ARE RIGHT.
I *AM* OLDER AND NOT A KID ANYMORE. I'M IN *CHARGE* OF KIDS AT THE BASKETBALL CAMP AND THIS YEAR AT SCHOOL I'M COACHING THE GIRLS' JUNIOR TEAM.
HOW LONG HAVE WE BEEN WAITING?
SHOOT! FORGOT TO PUT MY WATCH ON TODAY. DON'T KNOW.
ANYWAY, I'M NOT SURE BANNING STUFF IS THE ANSWER, BUT I HAVE TO GO ALONG WITH WHAT'S IN THE PLAYBOOK.
EVEN IF IT MAKES YOU "BORING"?
JIMMY?
WE'RE READY TO TAKE YOUR STATEMENT NOW.

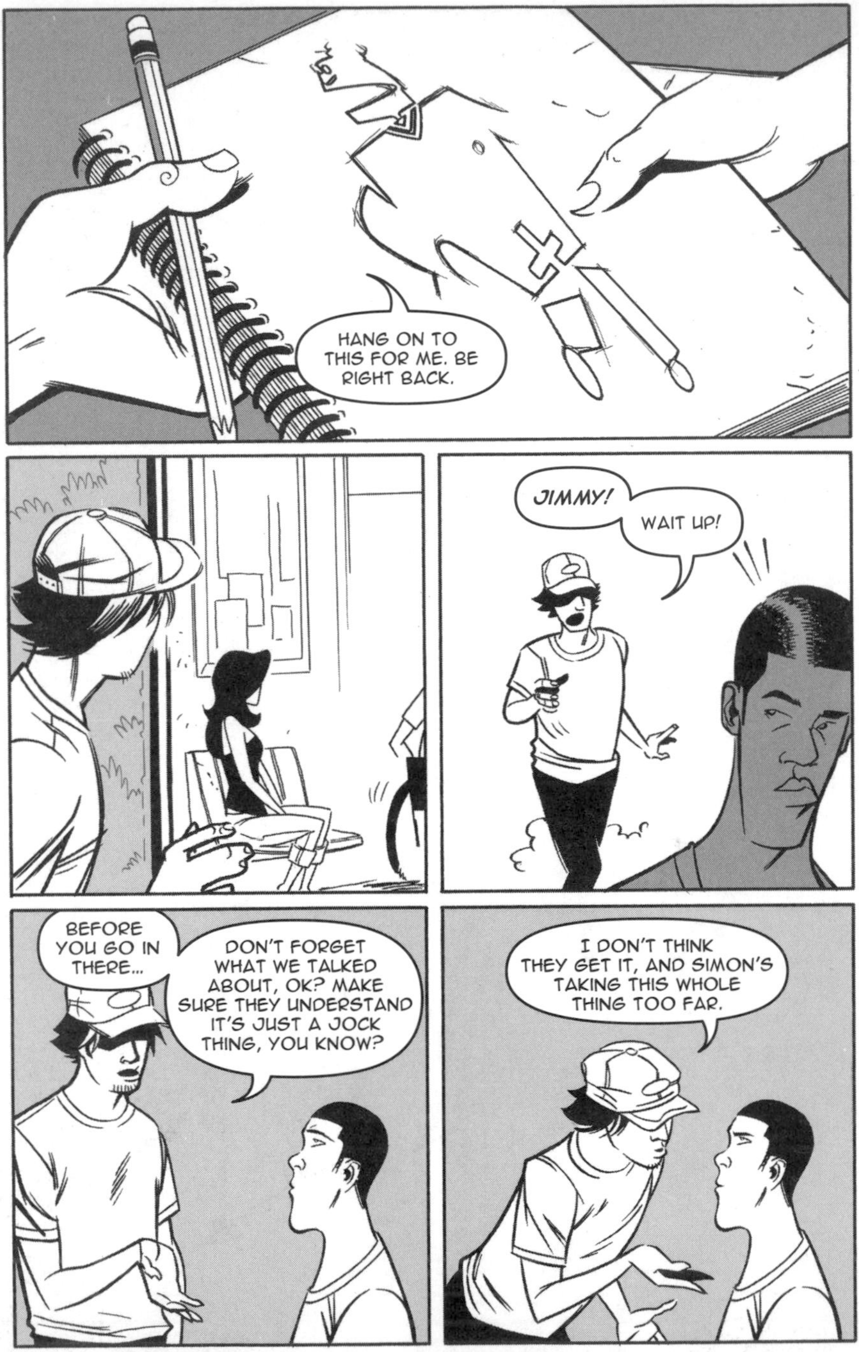
HANG ON TO THIS FOR ME. BE RIGHT BACK.
JIMMY!
WAIT UP!
BEFORE YOU GO IN THERE...
DON'T FORGET WHAT WE TALKED ABOUT, OK? MAKE SURE THEY UNDERSTAND IT'S JUST A JOCK THING, YOU KNOW?
I DON'T THINK THEY GET IT, AND SIMON'S TAKING THIS WHOLE THING TOO FAR.

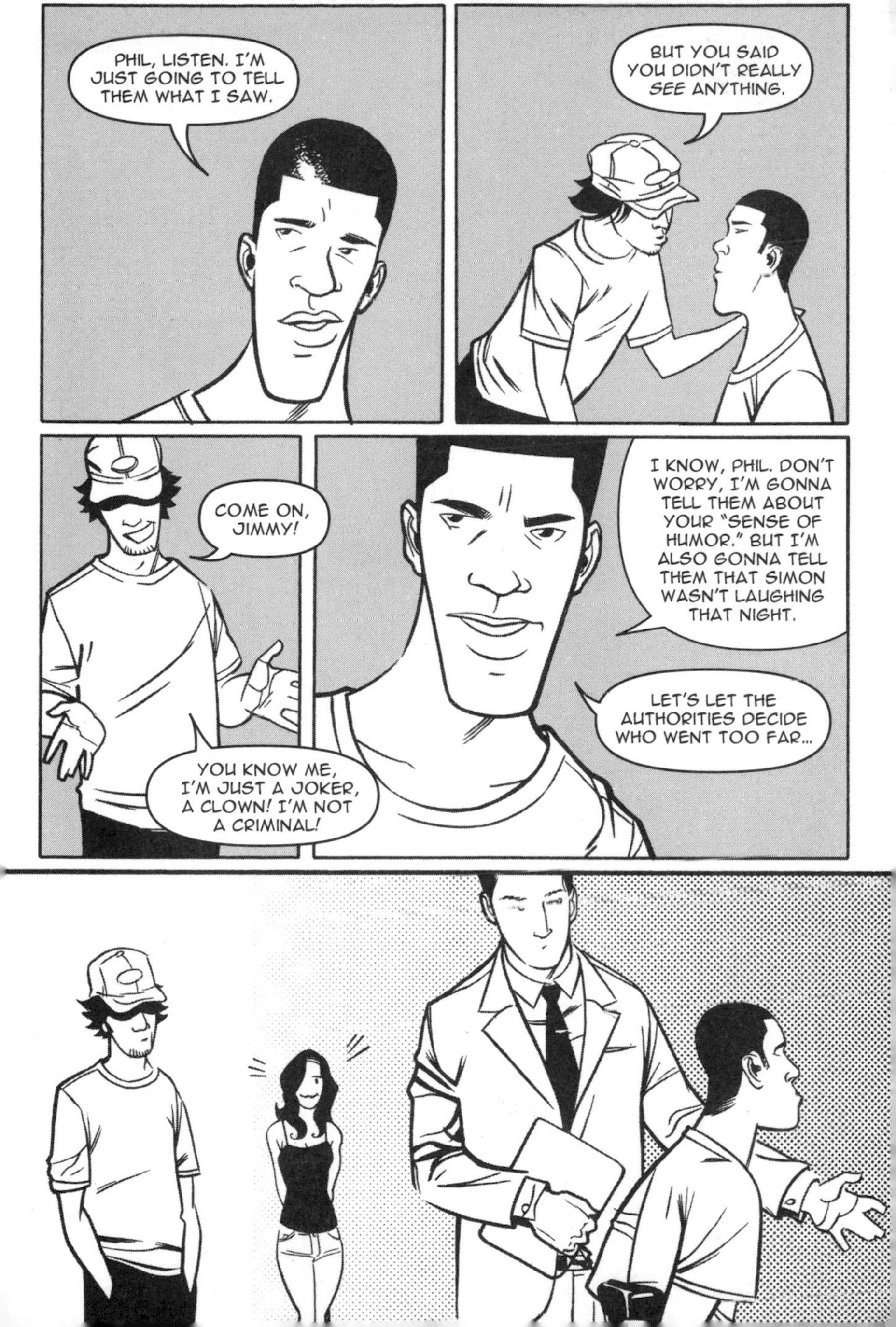
PHIL, LISTEN. I'M JUST GOING TO TELL THEM WHAT I SAW.
BUT YOU SAID YOU DIDN'T REALLY SEE ANYTHING.
COME ON, JIMMY!
YOU KNOW ME, I'M JUST A JOKER, A CLOWN! I'M NOT A CRIMINAL!
I KNOW, PHIL. DON'T WORRY, I'M GONNA TELL THEM ABOUT YOUR "SENSE OF HUMOR." BUT I'M ALSO GONNA TELL THEM THAT SIMON WASN'T LAUGHING THAT NIGHT.
LET'S LET THE AUTHORITIES DECIDE WHO WENT TOO FAR...

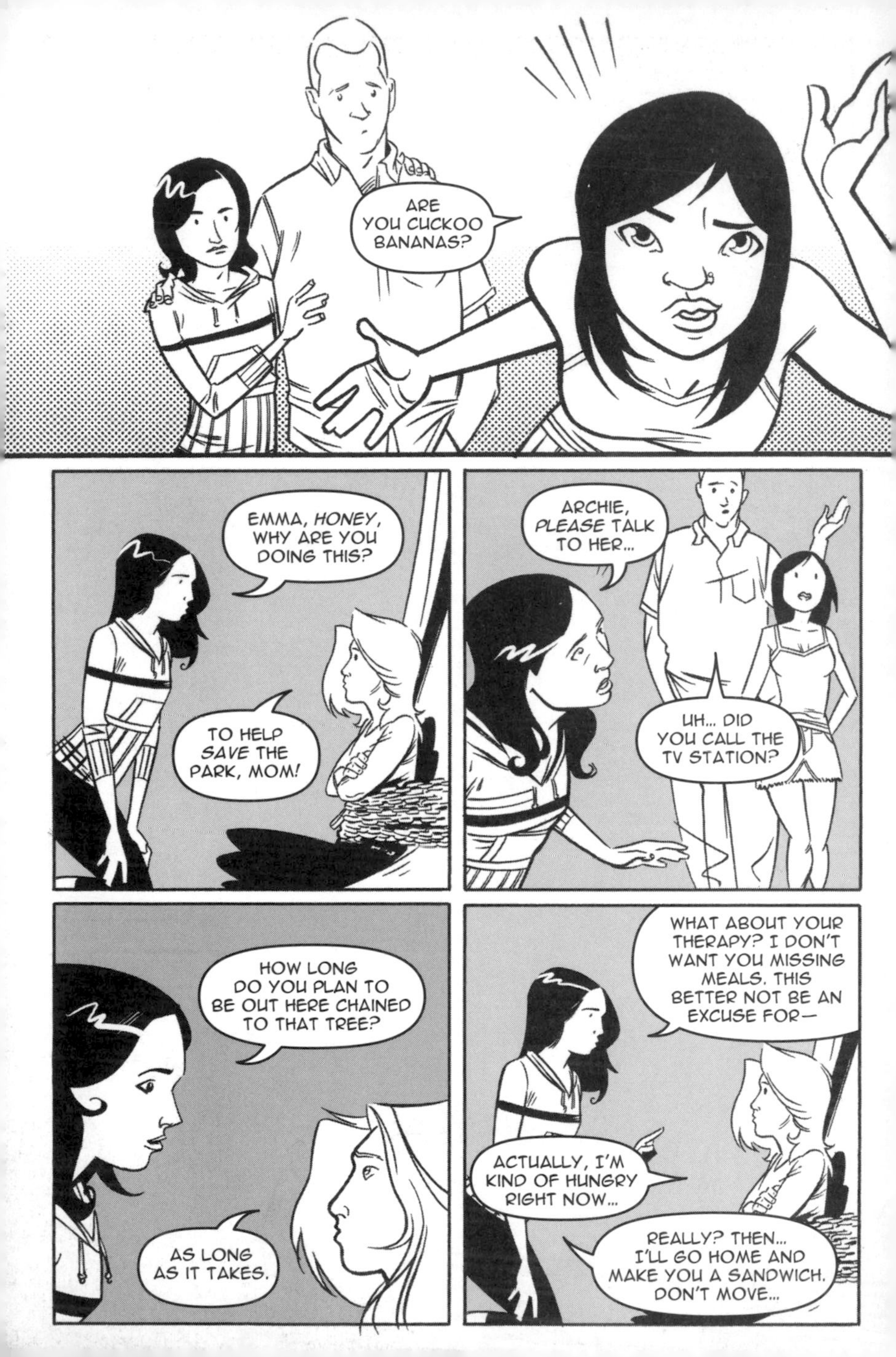
ARE YOU CUCKOO BANANAS?
EMMA, *HONEY*, WHY ARE YOU DOING THIS?
TO HELP *SAVE* THE PARK, MOM!
ARCHIE, *PLEASE* TALK TO HER...
UH... DID YOU CALL THE TV STATION?
HOW LONG DO YOU PLAN TO BE OUT HERE CHAINED TO THAT TREE?
AS LONG AS IT TAKES.
WHAT ABOUT YOUR THERAPY? I DON'T WANT YOU MISSING MEALS. THIS BETTER NOT BE AN EXCUSE FOR—
ACTUALLY, I'M KIND OF HUNGRY RIGHT NOW...
REALLY? THEN... I'LL GO HOME AND MAKE YOU A SANDWICH. DON'T MOVE...

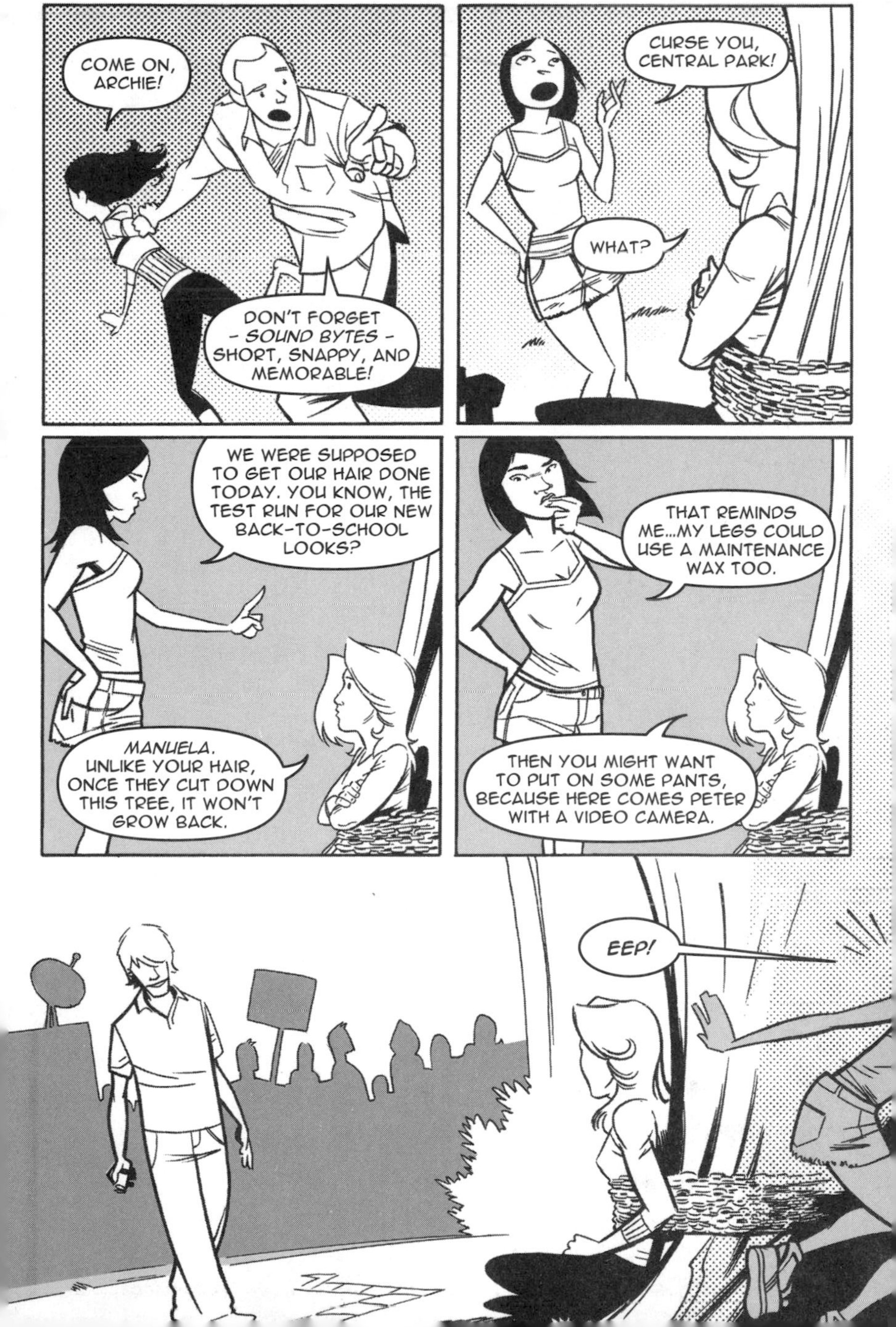
COME ON, ARCHIE!
DON'T FORGET - *SOUND BYTES* - SHORT, SNAPPY, AND MEMORABLE!
CURSE YOU, CENTRAL PARK!
WHAT?
WE WERE SUPPOSED TO GET OUR HAIR DONE TODAY. YOU KNOW, THE TEST RUN FOR OUR NEW BACK-TO-SCHOOL LOOKS?
MANUELA. UNLIKE YOUR HAIR, ONCE THEY CUT DOWN THIS TREE, IT WON'T GROW BACK.
THAT REMINDS ME...MY LEGS COULD USE A MAINTENANCE WAX TOO.
THEN YOU MIGHT WANT TO PUT ON SOME PANTS, BECAUSE HERE COMES PETER WITH A VIDEO CAMERA.
EEP!

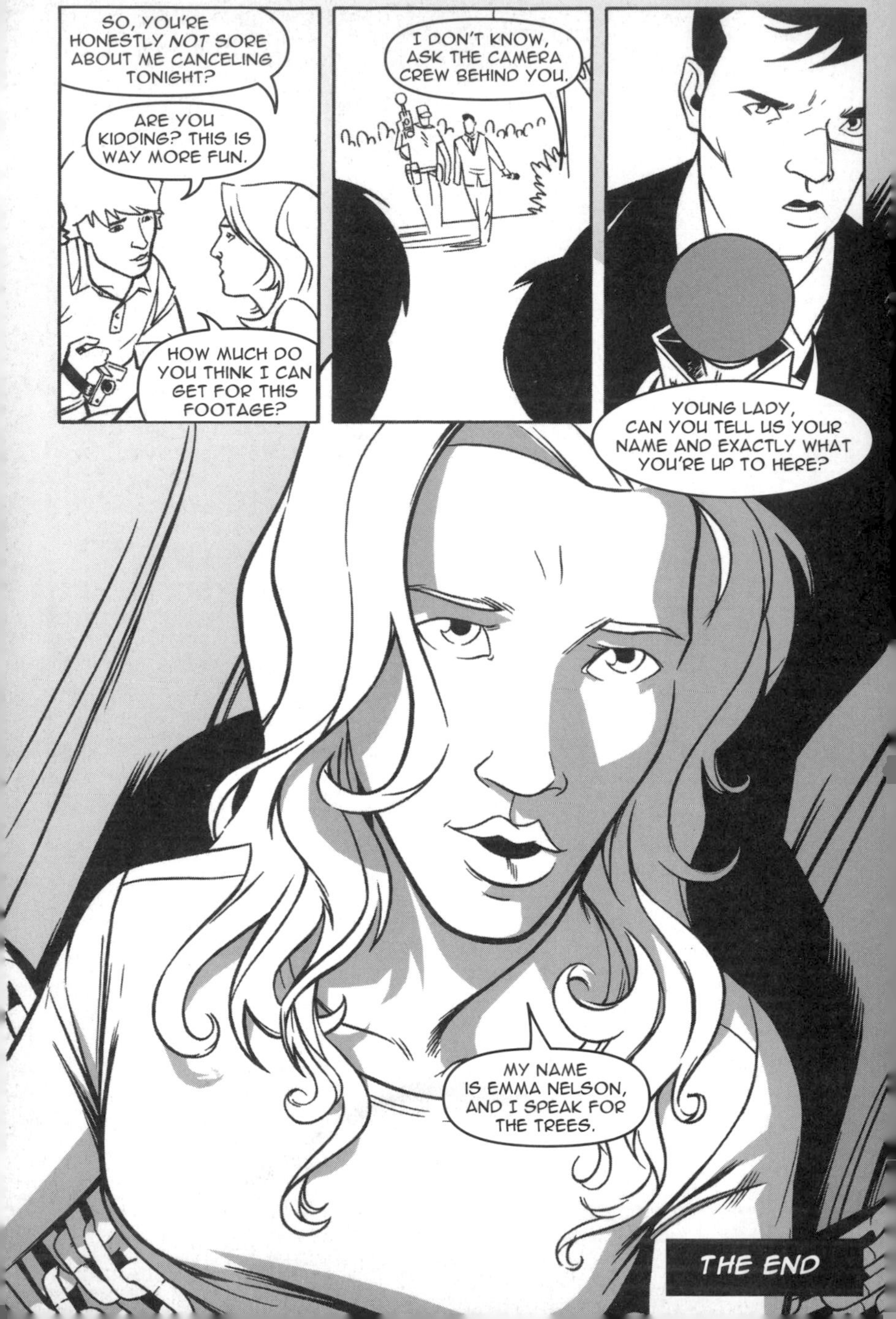
SO, YOU'RE HONESTLY *NOT* SORE ABOUT ME CANCELING TONIGHT?
ARE YOU KIDDING? THIS IS WAY MORE FUN.
HOW MUCH DO YOU THINK I CAN GET FOR THIS FOOTAGE?
I DON'T KNOW, ASK THE CAMERA CREW BEHIND YOU.
YOUNG LADY, CAN YOU TELL US YOUR NAME AND EXACTLY WHAT YOU'RE UP TO HERE?
MY NAME IS EMMA NELSON, AND I SPEAK FOR THE TREES.
THE END

Next time in...

Degrassi
THE NEXT GENERATION

eXTRA CREDIT

Spinner promises God that he will be a good boy and never cheat on Darcy again, if He will bring Darcy back to him. But Spinner finds himself faced with a long, hot summer surrounded by temptation while Darcy is away at Bible camp. Finally, he decides to hit the road to visit her...but he has to rely on the notorious Jay to get him there.

Liberty spends the summer trying to accept her decision to give up her baby for adoption. Her parents begin to suspect she may be planning to run away to Seattle to see the baby. Is that really what's on her mind, or is there someone else she can't get out of her thoughts?

THE CREATORS

J. TORRES is the author of the immensely popular **TEEN TITANS GO** monthly comic book for DC Comics. He also writes the graphic novel series **LOVE AS A FOREIGN LANGUAGE** and contributes to **HI HI PUFFY AMI YUMI**, seen on the Cartoon Network.

RAMÓN PÉREZ is the artist and one of the creators behind the comic **BUTTERNUTSQUASH**. Over the past decade, he has also created interior illustrations and cover artwork for a variety of comic books, magazines, children's books, role-playing games and collectible-card games.

Additional Inking
Nick Craine
Pat Davidson

Toning & Lettering Assistance
Andy Belanger

Cover Art
Ed Northcott